SEE: SUCCUBUS

BOOK 1

TANTRI WIJA

*For Caitlin,
every word.*

Incubus (n.) A seductive male demon that feeds on the vital energy of humans by having sexual intercourse with them in their sleep.
    see: SUCCUBUS.

PART ONE

A STUDY IN SCARLET

PROLOGUE

LADY IN RED

Midtown West, Manhattan
 Tuesday night
 Late September

It was that time of the month, and all he could see was red. The man in the silver coupe slowed down at the intersection despite the green light ahead and eyed the scattered flock of working girls under the overpass. They strutted in circles like pigeons dressed as birds of paradise in short skirts, fishnets, and platform heels, listlessly scanning the traffic for a cash-clutching throbbing knob looking to make the most of a Tuesday night. Their clothes were too tight to be fashionable, but the constricted lumps and curves, bra straps cutting into flesh, loose sequins, and cruelly teased hair were exciting, like the smell of cheap hamburger: meat, ground down to submission, making its case for rapid and easy consumption.

The man in the silver coupe scanned the faces of the girls until he found what he was looking for. She stood under the streetlight as if waiting for him, burning like an ember in a cherry red raincoat over a red dress far too short for the September chill, all that red stroking him to irritation like a matador's cape to a bull. He could tell she was different from the others in exactly the way he needed her to be, and a snarl bubbled up within him, a snarl deeper than a man's. The pupils of his eyes dilated as a familiar pressure began to pulse behind them, and his muscles swelled almost faster than his skin could stretch in accommodation. It became harder to steer as his jacket pulled tight around his arms and his pants pulled tight against his crotch.

He rolled down the window and the girl in red leaned in. His gloved hands gripped the wheel as the price was agreed upon without any haggling, and she climbed into the passenger's side. Then the shiny car pulled off into the night, a silver bullet moving in slow motion through the streets.

Chapter 1

Men In Black

Black underwear. Black bra. Black dress. Black oxfords, tightly laced, with delicate but sturdy two-inch heels. Dez regarded herself mercilessly in the mirror as she got dressed, checking at every phase of the procedure for wrinkles, rips, or smudges. A loose thread on her hem almost escaped her, but she snipped it away with nail scissors from the tiny kit she always kept in her bag, along with tweezers, a hair brush, and clear nail polish for insubordinate ladders in her opaque black tights. Unfettered, her hair fell halfway down her back in silky brown waves, but she pinned it up into prim submission until she looked acceptable.

Unobjectionable.

And no one, she reminded herself as she attacked her dress with a lint brush, could begrudge her basic self-respect. Her black wool sweater dress slid over her lithe curves like a friendly acquaintance, but not so tight as to suggest prurient familiarity. She left no transgressive flashes of skin; the turtleneck collar covered her to her chin, the hem hit just below the knee, and the sleeves extended past her wrists. She kept her toilette simple; the black eyeliner and mascara standard for any woman in the city. Only a swipe of red lipstick was a faint slash of rebellion in an otherwise deferential composition. Dez smiled appreciatively at her reflection for a moment, and then with a tiny, resigned sigh, reached for a tissue and blotted most of it off, leaving only a faint flush that could be ascribed to the autumn chill, if anyone wanted to judge.

Which, of course, they would.

Her new apartment was an undersized corner studio in an otherwise expensive building—the real estate agent had euphemistically described it as "cozy"—but Dez was used to living in small spaces. Her flat in Cambridge had been no larger, and her only furniture comprised an antique roll-top desk tattooed with marks and dings, a vintage leather desk chair that made her feel professorial, and a set of bookshelves that dwarfed the apartment, waiting to be filled by the towers of books stacked in a temporary undulating skyline across the floor. She had arranged them by topic according to her own logic: maritime disasters paired with sea monsters, alchemy flowing into witchcraft, myths about Hindu gods consorting with the lives of Orthodox saints; hundreds of volumes dotted with Post-its sticking out like impudent tongues. She possessed no sofa or dining table, and the bed sat in the center of the room, tightly tucked sheets hidden under more stacks of books. An observant person would have noticed that there was nowhere left for her to sleep.

And though Dez certainly never had guests, she had already begun to decorate, after a fashion, studding the walls with an arcane collection of ankhs, mirrors, pentacles, crosses, and other more obscure talismans, nailing them up in measured rows at painstakingly equal distances. But that was actually the second task she'd completed upon moving in; the first was to line the footprint of the apartment with a white ring of salt, pouring it all around the seam where the walls met the floor, across both windows and along the doorjamb without a single break in the line. It was not a perfect security system, and it would do nothing against the city's more quotidian criminals—she had a door fitted with multiple deadbolts for that—but such measures had proven to be effective against the kinds of intruders Dez was *really* worried about.

With a pleasing sense of routinized martyrdom, she drained her cup of black instant coffee—the only breakfast she ever bothered with—and then cast a final adversarial glance at her image in the mirror. She pulled on her long black overcoat, buttoned it up to her chin, and ventured out of her building for her first-ever commute to her first-ever actual job. She would have preferred to do her work from home as she had in Cambridge, with a thick door between her and the rest of the world, but that was no longer an option, so she trotted dutifully along the Upper West Side's wide sidewalks, heels tapping on the leaf-strewn concrete, dodging other bleary-eyed commuters blinking at the morning sun through the steam rising from the coffee cups in their hands and the subway grates beneath their feet.

She could feel them all as they passed her, sensing their heat, their hurry, their stress or excitement as the air immediately around their bodies mingled with hers, and the glints in their eyes if they happened to look at her. She tried to block them out as she walked by, but it was only her third day in the city; she still felt overwhelmed among the looming monoliths and unforgiving crowds whose ceaseless energy vibrated through her body like whale song. The city itself was like a living thing made of glass and steel, shimmering with an invisible tremor of activity that Dez sensed in every cell of her body, and distracted by that constant din, she worried every moment that some nefarious figure might sidle up behind her and snatch her purse. She kept her head up, intending to project a hopefully reasonable facade of streetwise confidence, but she undermined it periodically by glancing around like a hunted animal.

She approached Central Park, its trees reddening as if irritated by the frost in the air, along the block of Central Park West dominated by the neoclassical stone edifice of the American Museum of Natural History. She paused to gaze at the building, glowing faintly in the morning sun. It was not quite the British Museum, of course, but it was still one of the world's most venerated academic institutions, chock-full of strange specimens and some reportedly spicy dioramas, and she looked forward to eventually exploring it from top to bottom, corner to corner, reading every plaque and poring over every exhibit until she'd fully consumed its myriad delights. *Eventually,* but likely not today, for while the freshly laminated employee ID tucked in her pocket identified her as one "Desdemona Cross, Research Assistant" at that very museum, her real job did not require her to ever physically set foot inside the building.

She hoped that she'd properly memorized the way to the entrance of her actual workplace, as she couldn't very well ask anyone for directions. As directed, she stalked into the museum's underground parking garage, peeking around constantly for hidden attackers as she passed rows of cars and then increasingly vacant parking spaces, until, in the mostly-empty depths of the exhaust-fumed maze, she found a nondescript door tucked behind a set of metal stairs. It was locked, of course, with a keycard reader on the wall next to it so faded it looked as if it couldn't even remember the last time it was used. She waved her ID over it and the door opened with a soft click, admitting her into a lonely stairwell facing a set of metal elevator doors. The arrow on the elevator's sole call button pointed up, and Dez was headed in the other direction, but she pressed it anyway, as she'd been instructed.

The doors opened into a dingy service car with lazy graffiti on the walls and carpet that smelled of feet. She wrinkled her nose and held her breath as she stepped inside and glanced over the buttons on the panel, all of which corresponded to floors above her. Dez ignored them, instead pressing the "Door Open" and the "P" buttons at the same time, as she'd also been told to do. With an creaky jolt, the doors slid shut and the elevator moved somehow downwards despite being ostensibly on the lowest level, which would have been alarming had Dez not expected it. Still, during the unsettlingly long trip down, she nervously rubbed her fingers together inside her black leather gloves, the petroleum jelly she had smeared on her hands before pulling them on that morning squishing comfortingly between the lining and her skin.

Finally the carriage hit ground, and Dez waited for the doors to open.

But they didn't.

Had some last step been left out of the instructions? Should she press another button? She tried not to panic, but her mind, usually razor-sharp, often stuttered under pressure. However, now was not the time for performance anxiety—an incorrect choice could result in real unpleasantness—so she ransacked her mind for lost threads. *Was it a significant number, an alphanumeric code, or some arcane symbolic reference?* The longer she stood in that elevator, the stronger the smell of feet grew, and she wondered if she was being suffocated on purpose.

Then, scanning the indifferently graffitied walls for clues, she noticed that most of the buttons on the panel were oddly clean. In fact, only three were smudged with fingerprints: "P," "Door Open," and the only one she hadn't yet touched, "Door Close."

So she took a deep, pungent breath, pressed "Door Close," and held it. And held it. And after a tense moment of nervously contemplating her own mortality, the doors finally slid open, and she exhaled with relief and stepped through them into her new place of employment, the New York City headquarters of the world's most secret society, referred to only in whispers as "the Order."

———

Sounds were muffled underground, the Order's low murmurs absorbed by walls carved out of old brick and older stone. Dez stepped into the severe entrance foyer, a cylindrical hub that branched out to innumerable hallways that snaked through the underlying bedrock, becoming a subterranean labyrinth that sprawled like a nervous system through the depths of the Upper West Side as it connected covertly with the rest of the city's endless warren of forgotten tunnels. Even with the elevator rigamarole, it seemed unsettlingly easy to enter Order headquarters, but that was by design. It was unwise to sneak in, after all.

Once you were in, they had you.

In the center of the foyer stood a black stone desk, behind which sat a cadaverous man with hands like white spiders that he was using to shuffle desultorily through a folder on his lap. He looked up at Dez as she came in, but did not greet her.

"Good morning," she began, stepping forward with prim politeness, "My name is Desdemona Cross."

"Devices," the man rasped, nodding impatiently and pointing at a box sitting on the front of the desk.

Dez bit down the rest of her attempt at niceties, turned off her phone, and surrendered it as she flicked her eyes back up at him. In a flash, she took in his entire physicality—frail, bored, and vaguely smelling of some wasting disease—and mentally stripped away his black garments, reconstructing for her private observation the likely contours of his pale, withered body. She suppressed a wicked little smile, offering him instead a mildly deferential nod, and then eyed the two burly armed sentinels standing on either side of the elevator door. They, in turn, sized her up as a stranger, and one stepped forward with an RF-indicator wand in one beefy hand. Dez obediently raised her arms to her sides like a crucifixion as he scanned the perimeter of her frame, checking for hidden cameras. He, Dez archly assessed, would make a far more pleasing picture naked, judging by the faint sheen of healthy male sweat she could detect from the crevices of his elbows and armpits, and how tightly his biceps filled the sleeves of his black combat jacket, but she kept her eyes away from his, her face a bland mask, and her thoughts to herself.

The cadaverous concierge then gestured to a freestanding silver font next to him, which looked like a birdbath with a pile of worn religious relics resting on the bottom: stars, crosses, ankhs, Tibetan prayer beads all mingling together under several inches of clear water. Dez approached the font with practiced coolness; every Order member had to take the water test upon entry, every day, every time they came in or out of the facility, without exception. She'd done it numerous times back in London, and had never had a problem.

Yet.

With perfect sangfroid, she tugged off her right glove and plunged her middle and index fingers into the water, submerging them for a full five seconds and then holding them up, still wet, for the guards to see. One guard moved to perfunctorily examine her hand, but stepped back deferentially as another man emerged from one of the hallways. The new arrival was prim little teapot of a person, his birdlike frame swallowed up by a heavy black sweater that draped off his shoulders like a monk's robe. As Dez slid her glove back over her damp fingers, her eyes automatically darted from the liver spots on his head, with its fading ring of white hair, to the orthopedic brogues on his feet, and she smelled a trace of mothballs and virtuous soap in the dusty bouquet emanating from his aging flesh.

"Miss Cross, I presume." The little man's voice was creaky with formality, and he blinked at her through his glasses as if she were too bright for the room.

"You must be Brother Justin." Dez knew him by name only, but he'd corresponded over email about her transfer, and his manner matched his punctilious missives.

So this was the new researcher. Brother Justin knew she was young—twenty-seven years old, according to her file—but thought she was rather prettier than necessary. Her face with its arched brows, high cheekbones, and suspiciously flushed lips subtly flouted the Order's stark aesthetic, and while the modest hemline of her black sweater dress and primly laced heels were academic enough, her severe black overcoat only managed to outline her troublingly curvaceous frame. Despite her demure demeanor, she looked like a girl who was aware that she was beautiful and only reluctantly apologized for it, and though her expression was decorous enough, there was mischief in the way those feline eyes glanced around the room, landing on everything for slightly too long.

However, she'd come highly recommended, so he hoped that underneath all that glossy hair was the bookish Cambridge brain he'd been promised. Desdemona Cross was rumored to be a genius and a polymath, possessing an encyclopedic knowledge of history, folklore, and religion, an ability to wrangle ancient texts in a number of languages (many of them dead), and a particular affinity for the arcane. The Order had precious few people with such qualifications in their ranks, and New York had been lucky to get her. The need to keep its information hidden made the Order wary of academics (who were second only to journalists in their tendency to pretend loyalty while stealing information), and Justin did think it odd that this polished young woman with her smooth British accent and subdued poshness had forgone the sparkling future in some vaunted, honorarium-laden ivory tower that had theoretically been hers for the taking, willfully exchanging it for a dank, airless cavern and the Order's almost perfunctory salary. She hadn't even bothered to finish her doctorate, and among the graduate faculty at Cambridge, she had acquired a reputation as a bit of a time-waster.

But, hopefully, she would not prove so in New York.

"This way please," he nodded, and then she followed him for what felt like forever down hallways illuminated by jaundiced lightbulbs dangling from the ceiling, all powered by black wires slithering across the walls like tar-filled veins, their innumerable doors hiding the Order's innumerable secrets, though from the seams around their edges Dez occasionally smelled air saturated with distress.

"I see you managed the elevator without any trouble. You may use our other entrances if you prefer, but that one is the most…hygienic." He glanced down at her shoes. "Many of the others involve sewer access," he added, "or tunnels with—ahem—vermin."

"It was no trouble at all," she assured him.

"The main campus stretches from here to the other side of the park," Justin explained as they walked, "but everything you'll need will be close by. Do make a note of where the restrooms are."

Dez glanced at the little man sideways. His countenance had the forehead crease of a worrier, and while his eyes were sharp, they were kind. She surmised that he had once been a Benedictine monk, and he still looked like one in his prosaic black pullover with the white lapels of his shirt poking out like a priest's collar; ex-monks, she'd observed, tended to wear sweaters made of the kind of cheap wool that allowed them to retain a sense of martyrdom. He was no longer a monk, of course, as Catholics who joined the Order were excommunicated from the Church if they were discovered, but she noticed his hands twitching inside his sleeves as he pushed a string of rosary beads through his arthritic fingers. She was not sure if still he wanted to be called "Brother," but it was a sensitive subject for some, and as much as it pained her to be imprecise, it cost her nothing to be courteous. After all, this wee mushroom of a man was the administrative head of the Order's New York chapter, and therefore Dez's new boss.

They passed some of her new colleagues in the hallway; some gave a nod of respect to Justin, and most gave Dez a once-over, as the Order had few nice-looking women and most of them hid themselves under boxy clothes. Like Dez and Justin, they were all clad in various shades of black with an occasional accent of white, and Dez gave them each a once-over as well, automatically reading in the contours of their necks and the set of their shoulders what their bare bodies looked like underneath those severe garments. All wore the usual Order mask of grim determination. She also saw in every face a tremor of underlying trauma left over from whatever nightmarish incident brought to them to the Order in the first place.

"The passages down here can be a bit chaotic on busy days," Brother Justin apologized as he and Dez pressed themselves against the wall to sidestep a rolling cart stacked high with frosted packets of frozen blood. "We encourage the retrieval and storage departments to use the side tunnels as much as possible, but everyone is always in such a hurry and...aaah, but here we are." He said that last with the satisfied smile of one about to bestow a gift as they approached a set of ponderous steel double doors, and he invited Dez to follow him into the Archive.

The doors were heavy, requiring real effort to pull them open on their silent rolling casters, but when she stepped inside, the hallway's low ceiling ended and the walls shot dramatically upwards into a vast, Cathedral-like chamber carved out of bedrock and brick, housing innumerable rows of tall metal shelves on which thousands of files in black manila sleeves stood in rigid lines. Silent archivists in black cotton gloves glided through the aisles on precarious rolling ladders, replacing and reordering and making notes to ensure the thousands of records that chamber held were complete and up-to-date.

Dez inhaled the dust, the stone, the glue, and even the ink on the pages with ecstasy, as if she could smell the centuries of secret knowledge, although like all ecstasy it came with agony at the knowledge that it was impossible to read every single file, given the limits of time and space.

But she could try.

"Our system is similar to London's," Justin explained with dewy eyes; he too loved a good filing cabinet. "Files are searchable in the catalog by incident name, location, date, and, of course, phenomenon."

Dez ran her gloved fingers along a row of files with the tenuousness of a first caress. *Possessions / human, possessions / animal, possessions / inanimate objects.* One could drill down into the specific: *Scars / spontaneous, scars / spontaneous / bite-shaped, scars / spontaneous / bite-shaped / neck, scars / spontaneous / bite-shaped / neck / two-pronged.*

"This office serves all five boroughs, northern New Jersey, and a bit of Connecticut," he continued. "Anything further north we pass to the New England branch, and south is Philadelphia's territory. But we're one of two A-level hubs in the United States—the other is Los Angeles—so we have a full set of records here, just like London. And not to disparage Los Angeles, but...well, have you ever been to the Los Angeles Branch?"

"I have not."

"Oh yes, your file said you've never traveled outside of England," Brother Justin murmured absently to himself. "That's surprising. You seem so cosmopolitan. Well, suffice to say, Los Angeles has a very...West Coast attitude about the reduplication of marginalia. Here in New York we believe the Devil really is in the details."

"Everything important is in the marginalia," Dez agreed with a crisply cosmopolitan little nod laced with a tinge of irritation that was utterly lost on Justin.

"I knew you'd understand," he smiled, pleased. "Most people don't appreciate the nuance of a catalogue like this. We have so few academics. I did my graduate work at Harvard Divinity school, but that...well, that was another life...just please remember to mark all your changes in the files...we keep Post-its in the supply cabinet for the purpose...please stick to yellow if you can. The archivists prefer it. Though," he dropped to a whisper, "the color makes no difference. But we all have our little territories to defend." He flashed Dez a knowing smile, and Dez, who had waged similarly mundane battles with many academics and archivists in the past, smiled knowingly back. "Oh, and as you know," he added as if as an afterthought, "files are not to be removed from the premises except by Investigators."

"Oh, but before—in England—they would bring me files," she hemmed. "To college."

"Yes, the arrangement you had there was unusual," he allowed with twisted lips; the London branch was run by mavericks who often pushed the boundaries of the Order's tenets, and while Brother Justin could not argue with their stellar solve rate, he objected to their methods as slapdash. "Here we keep all original materials in-house; it's less of a liability," he explained, not unkindly. "I know this is your first time working *at* headquarters, but I'm sure you'll get used to the routine."

Dez sighed silently as she followed Justin out of the Archive and then into a crooked hallway so slender it looked more like a gash in the brick than an intentional passage. A small, unassuming sign that read "RESEARCH" hung above the entrance. Its rows of doors were mostly ajar, revealing tiny chambers, each inhabited by a black-clad individual seated at a desk, poring over a stack of files. Several sets of eyes flicked up as Dez and Justin walked by, continuing until they reached the end of the hallway and Brother Justin nudged open the very last door.

Inside was a cell-like office, a mouse hole that could be described as either cozy or stifling depending on one's disposition toward suffocation. A clunky, metal army desk took up most of the space, covered in teetering stacks of black files, some so old they were fading to green. Photos, clippings, notes, and bright Post-its were plastered all over the brick walls, with lengths of string attached to push-pins linking everything together. The air was tinged with dust and the smell of old chocolate, and plastic figurines of Dracula and the Wolf-Man stood under a lamp next to a typewriter that had survived both World Wars.

"This is your office, and these are your cases." Justin picked up one of the dustier files. "Most of these have gone cold, as you'll see. Your predecessor—Brother Pascal—shared your interest in edge cases, but he didn't have your academic pedigree. We haven't moved anything," he said, gesturing toward the mess of string on the wall. "Some things may not be pertinent anymore, so feel free to throw out anything you like," he added, glancing at the figurines.

"How did he die?" asked Dez.

"That is...well...currently being determined. But at this rate," he sighed, "his file may very well end up on your desk also."

"Ah," Dez nodded. For Order members, dying by means unknown was an occupational hazard, although Research was supposed to be the safest job in the organization. People rarely died from paper cuts, after all.

"We do appreciate your willingness to join us here," said Justin. "The loss of Pascal has left our research department a bit understaffed."

"Subject to the requirements of the service," Dez smiled smoothly; though actually, Pascal's death had been a lucky coincidence, giving her the very opportunity she needed just when she needed it.

Lucky for her anyway; less so for Brother Pascal.

"Then I'll leave you to it," Justin said, and then closed the door after him, leaving Dez alone in her new little coffin of an office, like some ghoulish night-creature willingly buried alive.

But Dez released the breath she'd been holding with real relief, glad to once again have a closed door between herself and everyone else's pungent feelings. She then perched on the edge of the desk and waited a full two minutes, checking her watch impatiently, to make sure Justin was truly gone before gingerly tugging off her right glove. Her index and middle fingers were reddish and irritated, but the petroleum jelly that coated them had kept most of the font's holy water from penetrating her skin. The burning sensation, though uncomfortable, would fade in an hour, and her fingers would be healed by midday. She wiped the remaining goo off with a handkerchief, blew on her stinging fingers, applied a fresh coat from the tube in her makeup bag, then put the glove back on. It was an unpleasant ritual, but now that she was working at Headquarters she'd have to get used to it. She was accustomed to interacting with the world through a prophylactic; Dez had worn gloves everywhere outside her home since she was a teenager, even in summer, and she pretended an imaginary skin condition and had fake medical records to back up the practice, so no one had ever questioned it.

She perched on the edge of her chair, a relic of brown leather cracked from years of accommodating a heavyset man, and began to arrange the mess of files into stacks. She gingerly brushed old crumbs onto the floor; everything was a bit sticky, and a petrified candy bar peeked out of a drawer. The residue of Brother Pascal's portly, sweaty, celibate self lingered on all the surfaces, the musty smell of his body hovering in the stagnant air. She couldn't say much for his organizational skills; nothing seemed sorted in any meaningful way, and some files were so old the papers had yellowed around the edges. Others were crisp and new, so she started with those, since there was a chance the cases within might still be relevant.

To whit:

• A "Sasquatch" was supposedly camping in the Central Park

Ravine, with reports of footprints, stool samples, and "snorting noises" in the trees,

• a mysterious flame was rumored to be luring people into subway tunnels,

• a group of teenage girls in Queens had seen "Bloody Mary" in their bathroom mirrors,

• ghostly apparitions were causing car crashes on the New Jersey turnpike,

• vats of a Brooklyn microbrew had turned to blood,

• certain statues in the Cloisters were rumored to move around at night, and

• tentacles had been spotted in the East River.

The cases each had different investigators assigned to them: Sherif, Yamamoto, Novak, Hunter. Most Order investigators worked with the same researchers over and over, but cases that could not be resolved because of certain maddening fringe qualities had clearly eddied over to the tiny office at the end of the hall that now belonged to Dez.

But then, back in England, such cases had ended up in her lap anyway.

She glanced up at the map on the wall, the finger-shape of Manhattan was augmented with more maps haphazardly superimposed, cut-outs of faces tacked on top, illegible notations, and Post-it notes in every color except yellow. At least Pascal had been familiar with the city, unlike Dez, who worried every time she stepped onto the subway that she'd end up in New Jersey. *Where were the Cloisters? Was there something about Brooklyn that would cause a vat of liquid to transanguinate? How did one get to Queens?* She barely knew where to buy groceries. She'd solved more than a few puzzling cases back in England, but she'd been working remotely from the University as a consultant, so any failure could be chalked up to a lack of access to the Order's complete archive. Now that she was a full member, any "lack" would be her fault alone. *If she failed, would they send her back?* The Order didn't *fire* people; not in the usual way. Perhaps Pascal had simply been bad at his job and the Order had done whatever they did to people who needed to be replaced. He had left quite a backlog, after all.

A wave of homesickness hit her; leaving Cambridge had been disorienting, as she'd spent her adulthood hidden away behind its solid stone walls, though she'd been a failure as a scholar, fickle in her subject matter and drawn to the bizarre like a magpie after tin foil, unable to finish anything that even looked like a thesis. To the few people at college who asked where she was moving, she'd said that the was going to America to "work on a book," which was such an indeterminate amount of time none of them would wonder at never seeing her again.

———

Tentacles—see: squids, octopuses, natural and otherwise, see also: sea serpents, see also: Kraken, see also: sea monsters, see also: Japanese pornography. Dez stalked down the rows of the archive, her eyes flicking hungrily along spines of the files, reading the ghoulish delights within. *Bullet holes / disappearing. Cryptids / aquatic / lake monsters / North American. Transanguination / alcohol. Entities-misc. / non-corporeal / malicious. Apparitions / reflective / mirrors / religious / Mary-Bloody, Mary-Queen, Mary-Virgin.* She allowed herself to trip along the aisles with real enjoyment, pulling some files for work and some just for recreational perusal, until the stack began to strain the limits of her hands.

However, though Dez was perfectly able to navigate the interior of the well-ordered archive, getting back to her office proved trickier. Her sense of direction was dismal, with a tendency to second-guess herself into circles, and she found herself wandering up and down the halls with her arms full of files like a lost schoolgirl. Brother Justin was right about everyone using all the hallways; while searching for her office, Dez encountered a twitching body on a gurney, a steel cage full of something covered in scales, and a janitor pushing a broom with his one remaining arm, but she felt absurd asking any of the people carrying monsters or machetes or boxes of three-eyed skulls where her damned office was.

Out of desperation, she headed for the first open door she saw, peeking into what proved to be a cavernous, bustling incident room full of competent-looking individuals trading information over stacks of paper and glass computer consoles. The walls shone red with pinned-up photos of dead people with torn faces and eviscerated bellies, and Dez startled at the sight. She should have been used to such images—her files were full of them—but it was still jarring to see the twisted contortions a human body could manage if pain was not a consideration.

"You look lost," someone observed.

He was a sturdy, handsome man; a wide-shouldered, fit forty-something with youthful eyes and tawny hair that looked boyish even peppered with grey. He wore black trousers and a shirt in institutional white, but she spotted tiny red sailboats in his tie, and Dez, with her swipe of lipstick, understood such tiny heresies.

"Oh yes," she hemmed, "I'm a bit turned around. I'm in research and I have...eh...misplaced my office. It's my first day."

"You must be the new Pascal," he mused, looking at her a bit harder, and Dez's blood jumped under his lively hazel gaze. She was close enough to smell his obvious aura of coffee, healthy male physicality, and honest sweat tinged with the kind of maritime-scented soap that men buy for themselves. But Dez's particularly sensitive nose could also sense the tinge of lanolin from his laundry, the aroma of leather from the scuffed brogues on his feet, and the fact that his day had been spent indoors. Nothing suggested a woman's touch in his life: his shirt was clean but needed ironing, the scruff on his jaw was a couple of days past an ideal shaving routine, and he needed a haircut. The image of what he probably looked like underneath those somewhat rumpled clothes popped into her mind as a matter of habit, but she blinked it away, unable to both think about that and listen to what he was saying.

"Did they give you his cases too?" he repeated when she didn't respond.

"Oh, yes. He and I have similar interests. Or...had, I suppose, since he's..." Dez paused circumspectly.

"Dead? Better get used to saying that word if you're gonna work here." He smiled at her indulgently. "Anyway, you took a wrong turn two hallways ago. This is the anthrochimera department."

Anthrochimera: the official Order term for werewolf, or were-dog, or were-puma, or were-anything else, referring to those unfortunate individuals whose minds and bodies expressed animal traits from chains of archaic DNA. *See also: Therianthropist, Navajo skinwalker, Turkic atai, Irish silkie, Norse berserker and North African hyena-man.*

"Are these all werewolf victims?" Dez blinked at the gore-decorated walls. The "wolf" type was the most common and the most violent of the anthrochimeras, so the Order colloquially used the same word for all of them.

"These are all the active cases," he explained. "I think Pascal ended up with most of the cold ones on his desk. Some real puzzlers. Go back down the hall and turn left at the bathroom to get back to your office. But hey, hang out here if you want. We have lots of *this* to go around, if you're bored."

"No, that's alright," Dez swallowed, self-conscious about being thought ghoulish by a man who dealt with carnage all day. "I've had my fill." She headed back to her cubbyhole, where the walls were covered in notes rather than blood, and restrained herself from looking back to see if he was watching her walk away.

CHAPTER 2

CRYING WOLF

The Garment District
Wednesday, noon

The smoking'll kill ya. That's what Louie's wife kept telling him, and it couldn't happen soon enough in his opinion, so he sucked on the Camel and enjoyed the sizzle of almost-well-being as he hoisted two full bags of restaurant trash into the dumpster with a porcine grunt. It was an industrial dumpster full of building slag from the construction site next door to his deli, and Louie wasn't supposed to use it, but he'd been tossing bags in there for weeks and nobody had complained, and with what he was saving on trash fees, maybe he could buy that ballbuster he'd married the cruise she was always fantasizing about.

He peered in to see what else those unionized jerks had tossed out as they cleared old offices. Once Louie had acquired a perfectly good printer. Today it was just lunch trash from Trattoria Norma down the street, judging by the overcooked pasta and tinny red sauce. They never came to *his* place, although his house-made sausages were the best in the...

Odd. Among the congealing spaghetti and drywall chunks, Louie spotted a leg. He stared at the curvaceous limb protruding from the construction crumbs, tracing the line of flesh down a calf to an ankle, culminating in a delicate female foot, the toenails painted a vivid cherry red.

————

Dez had spent the morning chipping away at organizing the tiny office, creating squared-off piles of black folders, uncovering caches of old candy, and making a mental note to bring in a Dustbuster. Pascal had had a tendency to squirrel things into corners and nooks, tucking away hidden piles of old folders he'd covered in incomprehensible notes and then apparently (or intentionally) forgotten about, and Dez suspected the man's real role was to bury the unsolvable in the grey area of the perpetual indeterminate, hiding inconvenient files away until time made them irrelevant and they could be decently reshelved again.

By noon she'd cleared the top of the desk, and settled in to flip through the cold anthrochimera files that the rather nice-looking man in the werewolf department had mentioned. None of the cases were interesting from an arcane point of view; most had gone cold simply because the perpetrators had never been caught. Dez nurtured a secret fascination with werewolves: people hiding in plain sight, pretending to be normal citizens while carrying homicidal time bombs inside themselves. Much of the obvious lore about them was based on fact: people with anthrochimeric DNA suffered a severe allergic reaction to silver and silver alloys, so the Order accordingly stocked silver-enhanced bullets in the armory, and while many were unaffected by the moon, some felt its monthly swell pulling like a magnet on their insides, triggering their worst impulses on a regular schedule that was, Dez knew, part of the reason emergency room traffic picked up when the moon was full. But generally speaking, a werewolf bite did not turn a person into a werewolf; most anthrochimeras were, in fact, born and not made. The genes sometimes skipped a generation, but emerged down the line, so if someone landed on the Order's radar as an anthrochimera, all their relatives were suspect as well. The only anthrochimera she was aware of having met in person was one don at college who she was quite sure was a werewolf. She knew several other people that she *suspected,* but had no idea how many she missed. After all, she'd spoken to that don a dozen times before she happened to see his spectacled facade crack under the frustration of a dead car battery in an empty parking lot, watching as a ripple passed over his features, his shoulders jumped and his eyes bulged. But he'd just as quickly collected himself, pulled out his phone, and called for a boost, and he must have had the condition under control, because the man never had an incident on record, as far as she knew.

By mid-afternoon, Dez had a neat stack of well-annotated anthrochimera cases, with recommendations circled in red. She supposed she should report on her progress to someone, but she didn't know where any of the investigators' offices were, so she could only bring them to Brother Justin. She got slightly lost looking for it, of course, but a helpful man moving a massive specimen jar containing a set of giant, dried-up, disembodied bat-like wings had been kind enough to direct her, and she tapped on his door with a feeling of mild triumph.

"Come in," he called, and she did so. His office was spare as a monk's cell, the desk lined with neat piles of paperwork waiting for his meticulous processing. But Dez paused awkwardly in the doorway when she saw two men in the office with him, one sitting in the office's sole guest chair across the desk, the other standing.

"Oh, I'm sorry—" she began.

"Come in, Miss Cross," Justin repeated. "Gentlemen, this is Desdemona Cross, our newest addition to Research. Miss Cross, this is Father Solomon." Justin nodded at the man in the chair. "Our head Investigator."

Dez nodded at him blandly; Investigators were at the top of the hierarchy, and while Brother Justin was nominally the administrative head of the New York chapter, Father Solomon, as head Investigator, was, no doubt, equally in charge. He was a Black man in his sixties, severe and dignified, his tall, lanky frame draped in a black garment that looked as much like a priest's cassock as it could without actually being one. He seemed cold-blooded and sweatless, and the lines of his smoothly shaved face looked as if its sculptor had cleaved the marble once or twice and decided further contours were unnecessary.

"Welcome to New York, Miss Cross," said Father Solomon, his voice smooth as glass. "We are pleased to have you join us."

"And this is Investigator Alan Hunter," said Justin, nodding at the handsome man from the werewolf office.

"Hello," Dez replied coolly, as if they hadn't met.

"Hey there." Hunter smiled raffishly, and a breaker switch inside her body flipped on.

Most Investigators were either former clergy or former law enforcement; appropriate, since both involved extracting confessions. Hunter was a well-worn shoe of a man with the streets of Chicago in his speech, gun callouses on one hand, and a countenance that rarely registered surprise, and now with Father Solomon to compare him to, Dez made him for an ex-cop, with a hangdog demeanor that was more fetching than otherwise.

"This your first day?" asked Hunter wryly.

"We poached Miss Cross from the London office," Justin explained. "What can I do for you, Miss Cross?"

She handed him five neat black folders with the orange tabs on the sides indicating them as "problem cases." The files had fresh sheets of research notes appended to the back, tabbed with regulation yellow Post-its.

"What are these?" he blinked.

"Some of Pascal's backlog," she replied, realizing too late that she sounded a bit heartless; Dez, on a bad day, would still be called "polite," but even on her best day she never quite managed "charming."

Justin opened the first file and looked through it, while Dez waited awkwardly with her hands folded like a waiter, wishing the other two men would say something instead of scanning her for cracks. With them staring at her, Dez felt uncomfortably like a suspect. Or a sinner.

"*Jorgenson-Brenner...Stuyvesant possession*...we gave up on this months ago," Justin marveled.

"I recognized the pattern. It reminded me of an incident I came across last year...*Hermann/Wittenburg, 1854.* I listed the references in the footnotes. I think it's the same issue."

"Are these all...solved?"

"Researchers do not solve cases," Father Solomon interjected. "Researchers present information. Investigators determine whether a case is solved."

"No, not solved, of course," Dez clarified tightly, soothing herself by imagining the harsh planes of his bare physicality under his shapeless garment, visions of long, bare grasshopper legs and his probably nonexistent rear end flickered, taking the edge off her nerves. "I've just suggested some lines of inquiry."

Justin glanced at the clock on his desk; it was only three p.m., but Desdemona Cross had already cleared five stagnant cases without leaving the building, raising the New York office's solve rate significantly in a single day.

"These cases are all cold," Solomon pointed out, peering at the folders in Justin's hands.

"Yes, that first one dates from three years ago," Dez agreed tartly. "But Japanese *yurei* are tenacious, so the entity at that microbrewery may still be there. If an Investigator wants to have a look."

"This one is yours, Hunter," said Justin, ignoring her somewhat acerbic tone and handing him one of the folders.

Alan Hunter. Dez hadn't been listening when he was introduced, but now she recalled his name from the case file.

"You did this one today?" asked Hunter.

"It wasn't as complicated as..." she hemmed. "Someone misidentified the attacker as a werewolf. It's an easy mistake to make, but..." Dez fumbled for phrasing that would sound less insulting.

"That someone was me."

"Hunter is the head of our anthrochimera department," Solomon explained with a trace of irony.

"That must keep you rather busy," Dez offered lamely.

"Most moonies behave themselves most of the time," said Hunter, twisting his lips. "When they're good, they're very, very good. But when they're bad, it's front page news."

"Not if we can avoid it," Solomon put in.

"But this wasn't a werewolf," Hunter clarified.

"Probably wasn't." Dez glanced at each man in turn, unsure whose argument she was supporting. "The handprints suggested it was, but the bite marks indicate a creature with flat teeth—if you look closely you can see the unusual indentations. I made a list of possibilities. One of them is more likely...I circled it in red."

"How observant of you, Miss Cross," said Solomon with terrifying joviality. "It seems you have a talent for seeing things others miss."

Dez's heart stuttered, but she kept her face blank.

"Miss Cross was an academic before joining us," Justin mused, glancing up through his glasses. "We could use more people who read."

"Marks like that can be confusing," she explained, trying not to sound condescending and failing. "I assume that's why you never caught the killer."

"We had a suspect," admitted Hunter. "But we weren't sure, so we decided that bringing the guy in wasn't worth the missing-person's report." He looked pointedly at Father Solomon.

"As you know, Miss Cross, we have to be judicious in our activities," Solomon sniffed. "And since the suspect didn't do the crime, as Miss Cross pointed out, we were right to be cautious."

"Plus, the guy knew the mayor," Hunter muttered.

"He was a person of social significance," Solomon clarified, annoyed. "I'm sure Miss Cross understands that a highly publicized disappearance is a liability we should only incur when necessary."

That was an understatement; everything the Order did was secret and illegal, so despite their formidable arsenal and ubiquitous presence, they had to pick their battles and not kill every less-than-human individual they liked. Even so, the number of missing persons the Order generated would have classified it as a terrorist organization, had any government officially known about them.

"This one is yours, Father." Justin handed Solomon another file. "I recall you took it over from Miller before declaring it cold."

"*Garbalosa/Bellevue*—did you solve that one too?" Hunter whistled, craning his neck to read the tab.

"I suspect the phenomena—the bleeding walls—were evidence of a sub-corporeal entity," Dez explained, pedantically using the Order jargon for "ghost." "It may even be trapped in the structure of the building itself. An Investigator can check under the foundation for a body. If they like."

"Well, Miss Cross," said Solomon, "If you can sort out all our cases from an armchair, the rest of us can take early retirement. I wonder that London let you go." He then graced them with an icy nod and then stalked out the door.

"Thank you, Miss Cross," said Brother Justin, ignoring the chill left by Solomon's sarcasm. "This is excellent." Then, as if to let her know the conversation was over, he sat complacently back in his chair and opened the top file on the stack before him.

Dez glanced at Hunter, who inclined his head slightly in the direction of the door, so Dez gratefully followed him out.

"Sorry," he sighed. "That wasn't much of a welcome."

"Oh, please don't apologize," Dez coughed, caught off-guard by his collegial candor, rare in the Order. "I'm sorry if I stepped on any toes. I've been told I'm not entirely house trained."

"Maybe slow down a little. You're making everybody else look bad."

Dez paused, wondering if he was serious.

"I'm kidding," he grinned. "The organization always appreciates diligent work on behalf of our most sacred mission, of course." His grey-green eyes crinkled with hidden mirth, and she couldn't help smiling back. "Never apologize for doing a good job, Cross," he chuckled. "Solomon can be territorial. It does no one any favors."

"Excuse me, boss." A meaty, earnest young man poked his head out of the incident room. On his neck was a ragged scar, long-since healed but still pink, the kind of wound made by inexperienced vampires.

"Yeah?" Hunter responded, and Dez sensed he was annoyed at the interruption.

"New one," said the young man. "Midtown, near the Garment District."

"Breather or body?"

"Body. The street team thinks it's ours. A moonie attack, I mean," he clarified, glancing shyly at Dez.

"Reilly, this is Cross. Cross, Reilly. Cross is in research. Reilly does most of the real work in our department," he added with an indulgent grin, and Reilly's face blushed to the color of his scar.

"How often are there new bodies?" Dez asked.

"Oh, of the ones we find...around three or four a month," Hunter mused. "There are probably just as many we don't find. But that's only the deaths. We get around a dozen nonfatals a month too. Sometimes people think someone's trying to rape them, when actually..." he shrugged eloquently. "So we comb through the city's assault reports every day looking for anything funny in the testimony."

"The cops found this one, though," said Reilly.

"Ah shit," Hunter huffed. "When that happens, it's more of a problem. For us. They—" Hunter gestured at the dead people on the walls— "don't care who finds them."

"Andrews says she'll go to the scene."

"Nah, I'll go. It's my turn." He cocked his head at Dez, still gazing through the incident room door, her dark eyes reflecting the gore on the walls. "You ever been to a crime scene?"

"I have not."

"Wanna come along? For research purposes."

"Oh, I...shouldn't. I..." *should behave myself and stay in the stacks.* "I have a pile of files to sort through."

"You sure?" he grinned. "I'd hate to misread more bite marks."

Despite the grimness of the offer, something within Dez twitched—that same itch that led her to collect eyewitness accounts of lake monsters and spend her evenings parsing through books about voodoo. It might, she reasoned, be useful to see how the investigations teams went about their business, if only to figure out why their files were riddled with so many mistakes. Hunter struck Dez as rather intelligent, but that error about the bite marks was careless at best.

"Will we be back by sundown?" she queried.

"Oh, long before that, I think."

"Then I'll get my coat," she told him.

———

The crime scene was on a construction site near the on-ramp to the Lincoln Tunnel, hemmed in by rickety walls of particleboard and chain-link fence. The street was a mess of redirected traffic and orange barriers, the body hidden from view by the scaffolding that patched up the ever-healing wounds in the city's infrastructure, providing enough chaos to hide its nightly sins. During the day, the spot was mobbed with hard hats, but at night it became a temporary dark corner in the middle of a busy Manhattan street. Compared to the peace of an English college town, the endless pulse of shoving, yelling, grasping life teeming amongst the hulking high-rises was overwhelming, and Dez's attention was constantly drawn to faces in the rustling crowd: the ghoulish child begging its mother for a glimpse of the body, a frail old man eager to see someone else he'd outlived, a pair of teenagers clutching each other all the harder for their proximity to death. She closed her eyes and took a deep breath to shut it out. *She lived in a city now, cities were full of people, she had to get used to it.*

Hunter, meanwhile, approached the site like a man confident that nothing would start without him. He took Dez's arm as if they were a couple on a stroll, guiding her into an ideal corner from which to observe. A black trench coat as scuffed as a city sidewalk hung off his wide shoulders, and he had a fetching way of holding his head, tilted quizzically to the side, as if he was about to catch someone in a lie. His arm was firmly muscled, Dez noted, and though he politely released hers, it was clear he didn't mind holding it.

At the crime scene, detectives in suits conferred while a crowd of onlookers clustered around the police tape like flies on a wound, feet battling feet for prime of place on the sidewalk. Dez spotted a few other Order members lurking among the scattered throng. They blended in perfectly in their non-uniform uniforms, but she caught the canniness in their eyes that came with their hidden sense of purpose. New York City's five boroughs boasted an average of five homicides every day, and the Order showed up at each of them, even the shootings, although those tended to be human-on-human crime and therefore not the Order's problem. But of course, those were just the bodies the police *found*; the Order covered up many others. However, this morning the cops had arrived first, and the remnant of the night's horrors was in their hands, for the moment.

"The vic's a woman," Hunter read from a text on his phone. "Probably a professional."

"Professional what?" Dez asked.

Hunter raised an eyebrow at Dez as if she ought to know.

"Keep up, Cross," he nudged her genially. "This isn't *Sesame Street*."

"I don't usually do this sort of thing. I'm an academic."

"Fair enough," he shrugged caddishly. "You *are* wearing the wrong shoes for this." Dez looked down and realized she was standing in a spit-colored puddle that had splattered city filth all over her oxfords and ankles. "It's too bad about Pascal," he added. "But I'm sure you'll fill in the gap."

"Only if I start eating eight meals a day," Dez muttered. "Oh, sorry, I shouldn't have said that out loud."

"That's nicer than what everybody else used to say."

"Still, the man is dead," she chided herself halfheartedly.

"He was the office black hole. He didn't mind; he didn't get anywhere with those files, but he seemed happy to take them off our hands. Now we can do the same to you *and* expect you to solve them."

"Researchers don't solve cases," Dez reminded him sententiously.

Hunter smiled at that as the CSU techs began setting their feet to hoist the body out of the bin.

"Which one of them is..." Dez searched for the correct word— "ours?" It sounded funny in her mouth, like an affectation.

"It's Wheeler there." Hunter pointed with his chin at one of the techs, indistinguishable from the others except for manicured eyebrows and round glasses peeking out under his prophylactic hood. Operatives like Wheeler were called "Regulars": seemingly normal people with real jobs who did the Order's work from within the police, the fire department, city hall, etc., and Wheeler blended in seamlessly because he was a genuine forensic technician. Inch by inch, they lifted the body onto a gurney on the ground, and Dez saw flashes of red dress and red raincoat, all of it coated in brownish-red blood. The girl was ripped to shreds, sprawled like a doll with limbs picturesquely akimbo like a fashion model posing among chic urban decay. But to Dez, the most disturbing thing was not the gore, but the trash that clung to her: bits of drywall, packing peanuts, a filthy candy wrapper matted in her hair.

Dez swallowed, turning green.

"You alright, Cross? This can't be your first dead body."

"They don't generally bring corpses into the library," she muttered, afraid that if she spoke too much she'd vomit. "It's rather different in person."

Dez had seen thousands of photographs of mangled humans, but never a corpse in the flesh. Even among the smells of trash and effluvia, the pungent-sweet scent of death and blood cut through the air. The scent was oddly familiar, and she wondered then how many times she'd been in the vicinity of a dead body without realizing it. A remnant of hectic vibrancy clung to the dead girl, as if the corpse might sit up and start screaming. Dez calmed her roiling stomach by looking at anything besides the body: piles of construction refuse, lost-cat posters and band fliers, and she even noted a nearby sewer grate, a black slit leading to the city's underbelly, and wondered if anything living beneath had witnessed the crime.

And then, in a pile of trash spilling out of the dumpster, something moved.

It caught her eye immediately: a shuffling, jerking motion as if the garbage itself was wriggling. *The rats in this city are bold,* she thought, disgusted, until a pair of unblinking eyes met hers and she realized what she was looking at was no rat. A trash pile the size of a throw pillow was moving by itself, scooting along the pavement with the canny motions of intelligence and an aura of gooey air around it that told her it was invisible to most people. Her wide-eyed glance lingered on it just long enough for the entity to silently acknowledge the connection, but she quickly yanked her eyes away.

"Hey, Cross," Hunter whispered, "if you're gonna puke, just warn me."

———

Above their heads, Adrael stood in a vacant office and watched the crime scene through a cracked window. He looked like a off-duty statue; a tall, burly, sculptural mass of efficient, undulating muscle standing preternaturally still. His face was strikingly beautiful in a way that was more of a threat than a lure, with canny brows and a shadow of stubble on his cleft chin. With his chiseled frame wrapped in grey and his dark hair buzzed short, he had the look of a professional mercenary, but his cherubic mouth seemed to be perpetually edging towards a half-smile, a cupid's-bow ready to spring. He appeared to be anywhere between twenty and forty years old, depending on the light, but his sapphire-blue eyes gleamed with an ancient shrewdness as he observed the theatrics below.

With pickpocket fingers, he silently tugged open a plastic bag of gummy bears and settled his broad shoulder against the wall to count how many Order members he could spot. It wasn't just that they were wearing black—half the population of New York wore black clothes every day—but the subtly clerical touch of white was distinctive, as was their way of holding themselves, upright even when slouching, shrewd even when nonchalant. They looked like crows circling carrion, waiting on the sidelines for the alpha predators to have their fill before they swooped in to pick apart what was left, a little too close to the action, always a few inches past the yellow tape in a spot with the best possible view.

"You bring popcorn to this shit-show?" said a voice behind him, nasal and full of the Bronx.

"Candy," he replied, holding out the bag.

"Nah, boss, I never eat the stuff," Rat shook his head as he came in. "Sugar kills my stomach." He was a wiry little man with a pointy nose in the middle of a peaked face with bushy eyebrows shading eyes as hard and round as birdshot, and a tweed driving cap pushed down over mousy brown hair to roundish, protruding ears. Rat was thirty years old, but reedy and under-grown, easily mistaken for a teenager, and even more easily overlooked, which was usually to his advantage. "Anytime there's a corpse, the Roaches show up," Rat muttered, taking off his backpack and pulling out a camera with a telephoto lens.

"I think even actual cockroaches would object to the association," Adrael remarked, popping another little red bear into his mouth.

"You don't need to be here, Boss, I got this," Rat told him, panning his camera back and forth along the window, snapping pictures as he went. Adrael had delegated to Rat the task of taking photos of suspected Order members at the city's daily crime scenes, and while Rat did not mind Adrael's presence in theory, he hated being micromanaged.

"Don't mind me, I'm just here to amuse myself," Adrael chewed. "This is better than feeding time at the zoo."

"All work and no play, I guess," Rat muttered. Rat was born and bred in the Bronx and had met every flavor of person the five boroughs could produce, but he'd still never run into anyone like Adrael, whose lofty whiff of aristocracy jarred with the frankly sordid things he did for a living. His sense of humor was, Rat thought, rather savage, but everything he said sounded incongruously polite rendered in his velvety voice with its elegant BBC-announcer accent.

"Look at the photos again," Adrael suggested. "Zoom in."

Rat paused to scroll through the snaps he'd already taken, and then raised one bushy eyebrow.

"Oh, hold on..." Rat peered down at the dead girl through the window. "I get it now. How'd you know?"

"I didn't. I heard about the body and had a hunch."

"You think this was our boy?"

"I suppose it could be a coincidence," shrugged Adrael.

"Don't believe in coincidence. Always seems like an excuse for doing something you ain't supposed to be doing."

"Most policemen would agree, but I've found coincidences to be inconveniently..."

Then...*Hello.* As Adrael skimmed the crowd, one face stood out to him. He was familiar with the dour countenances of many of New York's longtime Order members, but had never seen the girl with the dark hair before, a shipshape creature with a delicate face and feline eyes, her body a tantalizing rollercoaster of soft s-curves outlined by a black coat that hugged her like a shadow.

"Lookit the new fish next to Sam Spade in the trench coat." Rat indicated Hunter and Dez, zooming in. "Prettier than their usual buncha nuns. She's got a whole 'sexy librarian' thing. And just wait'll she turns around."

Rat glanced at Adrael for a reaction, but Adrael refused to oblige. He had hired Rat himself six months ago, and while he was pleased with his work—the man was devilishly sneaky—Adrael found his jocular toadying tedious.

The girl was *sort of pretty, though,* Adrael noted. *Maybe...more than sort of.*

"I recognize Trench Coat," Rat continued. "He's out here a lot. Always moonie cases." Rat, as an anthrochimera himself, was attentive to such things, though his offending DNA was rodentine and he considered himself an entirely different species.

"I've seen him before." Adrael assessed Hunter with a professional eye. "He's their chief werewolf hunter."

"Huh. Well, somebody's gotta to clean up after those maniacs, I guess."

Adrael didn't disagree, and he had seen enough bodies ravaged by werewolves to know that this was another case of the same. The body itself did not interest him, and his eyes kept flicking back to the new girl. She *was* too pretty for the Order, he thought; she had a fetching hauteur, out of her element in that gritty corner. Maybe she was new to the organization, unused to the carousel of carnage; she looked away from the body, a bit ill, and...

And then looked at something else. Her eyes went wide with surprise, but she quickly caught herself staring and turned away with a flush on her face that looked, to Adrael, like guilt. From where he was, he couldn't see what she saw, though a wild guess did occur to him.

But no. That was...unlikely.

He waited for her to communicate her discovery to Mr. Trench Coat, via a tug on a sleeve or a whisper, perhaps, but her face remained blank.

Impossible.

Adrael slid his eyes towards Rat, but he was busy snapping photos in another direction and hadn't caught the moment, so Adrael didn't mention it.

"I guess anybody coulda killed that girl," mused Rat. "This city *is* full of psychos. Like those fuckers in black down there. Gives me the willies knowing *they're* walking around."

"Doesn't it just," Adrael murmured.

———

The Order
1 a.m.

Dez was lost in a sea of paper, meandering between musty piles of books and rows of dusty black manila files as if taking the air through Central Park, breathing in the stuffy archival atmosphere to clear her head. *Apotamkin* to *Beelzebub* to *Gryphon* to *Zlatorog*; no matter the horror, the Order had a spot and a method for handling it. Yes, the files were full of carnage, but they smelled comfortingly like old paper instead of blood and flesh, and the monsters within were confined to two dimensions. Down in that cozy catacomb, immersed in an ink-splattered euphoria she shared with only the bookworms and the dust mites, it was easy to forget she was in a new and terrifying city. The view from a book was always the same.

It was late afternoon when they returned from the crime scene, with plenty of time to get home before sundown. Dez had intended to be safely home before sunset, as always, but headquarters was underground and thus had no windows, and Dez, lost in both the perusal of her new piles of reading material and contemplation of what Hunter's solid arm had felt like entwined with hers, had lost track of time. So it was with an unpleasant jolt that she shook her attention from a thickish file of urban goblin sightings, glanced at her watch, and realized it was already one a.m. She could, in theory, have stayed at Headquarters all night; the Order was a twenty-four-hour operation and kept comfort cells to house weary Investigators. But Dez's practically dead files did not warrant an ostentatious work ethic, and appearing to try too hard would endear her to no one. So she packed her bag, collected her phone, went back up the elevator and through the parking garage, and emerged for the first time into New York City after dark.

Fortunately, in the city that never slept, streetlights flooded the sidewalks with artificial day from sundown to sunup, but the world was still a different place after the sun went down. The thousands of pockets of blackness that remained in basement stairwells and behind bushes were populated by night people, visible and otherwise, shadows without bodies flitted in and out of doorways, scaly things crept around corners, and unnaturally clever rats skittered under bushes. Dez pretended not to see them, keeping her eyes determinately forward, clutching the can of pepper spray laced with holy water that she always carried in her pocket. She'd learned how to discern the way light bent around the softer forms of things that were invisible to everyone else, but if they thought *she* couldn't see them, they generally left her alone. She would have preferred to take a cab, of course, but she balked at asking any of the city's notoriously grumpy cab drivers to take her such a short distance, as she'd already been scolded twice for that, and her apartment was only a fifteen-minute trot away if she hurried.

So with grim determination, she decided to walk. A slimy tendril reached out of a sewer grate, but after a momentary lurch of her heart, she collected herself and stepped over it. *If regular people knew what was slithering around them all the time,* she often reflected, *they'd never leave the house at night either.*

But then, as she turned off the brightly lit wide avenue and onto a side street lined in darkened Upper West Side townhouses, she sensed a flare of heat behind her.

She stopped short but didn't dare look around. It disappeared for a moment but then returned, blinking on and off like a striking lighter that sparked but didn't catch. It didn't feel heavy and clammy like a dead thing, didn't smell ripe and musky like an animal, and non-corporeal entities felt like living electricity moving through the air. But whatever this was felt very warm, and very solid.

She made herself turn, but saw nothing behind her. She was alone.

She broke into a run and headed for her building, a faceless Upper West Side slab nestled among rows of the same. Inside her empty vestibule she waited for the elevator, her heart pounding, rode alone up to the fourth floor, unlocked her door with shaking fingers, darted into her apartment, locked all five deadbolts again, and, with her back against the wood, finally allowed herself to breathe.

As her heartbeat slowed, she cast her eyes around the small space, checking the salt line for gaps as she pulled off her shoes. She'd chosen the tiny studio to live in specifically because it had almost no interior walls for anyone or anything to crouch behind, other than the thin drywall that separated the bathroom, which was a necessity. Still, her eyes flicked constantly towards the bathroom door, watching for movement.

Or extra shadows.

Or eyes.

Finally, fairly confident that nothing would attack her at home *that* evening, at any rate, she sank into her desk chair and pulled off her gloves. She used a paper towel to wipe off the clear petroleum jelly that coated the index and middle fingers of her right hand, which made the inside of her glove unpleasantly gummy, but she would have to use it every day now so there was no point minding it. She then minced like a cat through the narrow alleys of books to the bathroom, reemerged in a black cashmere bathrobe, shuffled over to the tiny kitchen, and opened the fridge to retrieve a half-eaten container of yesterday's shrimp pad Thai, which she nibbled at, cold, while standing over the sink. She had been fed by either servants or school kitchens for most of her life, without much enthusiasm in either the feeding or the eating, but when it came time to fend for herself, she'd learned felt that the best part of modern civilization was that a whole world of flavors could be ordered by number, and now, in the culinary cauldron that was New York, her neighborhood take-out options had multiplied exponentially.

Digging around the container for any remaining shrimp, she flipped open her companion for the night: a tattered volume of Algonquin folk-tales. But even its gory illustrations—which looked, to her expert eye, suspiciously lifelike—failed to capture her shattered attention that evening. She felt like a balloon after a party, deflated and inclined to settle on the floor rather than bounce. So she let her chair sink around her like a hug, leaned her head back on the well-grooved leather, and simply listened to the sirens and traffic noise outside. Nighttime in the city was surprisingly loud, but to her surprise, she found that she preferred New York's companionable cacophony to Cambridge's unsettling quiet. It felt less lonely being alone among several million people, somehow.

Less. But still lonely.

Midtown West
   2:30 a.m.

The construction site, which that morning had been a snarl of onlookers, forensic technicians, and tiny yellow evidence cards, had been patched up by yards of police tape, the block settling down from the bloody excitement of the day. All that remained of the NYPD was a pair of bleary cops standing guard over the crime scene, chitchatting and showing each other videos on their phones.

Adrael loitered nearby for a few minutes, watching them with the desultory amusement of a habitual voyeur, but they were oblivious to his presence, even when, to entertain himself, he moved close enough to them to smell their dinners on their breath. They also failed to notice him peeking into the very dumpster where the body had been found, poking gingerly around inside with a discarded length of rebar, but since the individual he sought was not in residence, he left them to their cat videos and meandered one block down the street to a tiny half-alley lined with oversize trash bins. There, his sharp senses probed the air for movement, sounds, smells; any sign that what he wanted was nearby.

Which it was.

So he sidled up to one of the trash bins and leaned his broad back on the wall next to it, for all the world like a sightseer merely taking in the garbage-scented air.

"Rough day?" he observed jauntily to, apparently, no one at all.

"Tell me about it." The response came from within the bin; a sticky voice muffled by layers of debris.

Adrael smiled to himself and pulled a bag of candy from his pocket, crinkling the wrapper suggestively as he dangled it above the garbage. M&Ms, he'd guessed when shopping at the all-night bodega a few minutes ago, did not often end up in the trash.

"Who're you?" the voice asked.

"No one in particular," he replied.

"Those peanut?"

"Peanut butter." Adrael dropped the bag of candy into the bin and peered down into it as the trash shuffled around seemingly of its own accord, creating a vortex into which the package swirled and then disappeared. Adrael waited a moment for a "thank you" that never came, and then observed, "This neighborhood's rather going to pot, isn't it?"

"You said it." Inside the bin, the garbage itself began to rise up like a vile wave, swelling until a portion of it crested over the lip of the bin and coagulated into a backpack-sized blob of refuse and sticky effluvia, topped by a pair of black eyes on gooey stalks that stretched out to peer at Adrael as a stranger. "So, you new to the neighborhood watch, or what?" the creature asked.

"No, I'm just nosy," Adrael beamed unrepentantly. "And horrified by the degeneration of society in general."

"Tell me about it. I was at the bottom of the bin having a snooze last night," the entity told him, "and woke up to some kerfuffle."

"Kerfuffle?"

"Y'know. Fighting. Fucking. Whatever you people do. You all look alike; just a buncha arms and legs and hair."

"But you didn't see what happened?

"Nunna my business," the entity sniffed. "Bums been goin' behind that dumpster to do each other up the butt and sniff their spoons or whatnot since they tore up that building. Whaddo I wanna see that kinda thing for? Went on for, I dunno, few minutes. And then I felt somethin' get tossed on top a' the dumpster. I peeked out and saw a guy walk away, from the back. I guess he kinda looked like...well...like you, I s'pose." The trash demon—which did, apparently, have eyelids—squinted at Adrael suspiciously. "Coulda *been* you for all I know."

"Anything's possible," Adrael allowed.

"Yeah, well. Turned out to be, you know. A dead girl." The entity snuffled. "Last thing I needed."

The creature then extruded tendrils from somewhere within the depths of its mass, prehensile limbs that it used to rip open the bag of M&Ms, popping the bright balls of chocolate into a mouth that opened up like a sticky wound. "Oh hey," it muttered. "These ain't bad."

"I have peanut in my other pocket," Adrael told it.

"Uh huh." The trash demon eyed him again, doubly suspicious. "What's it to you?"

"I knew her," Adrael lied. "Childhood friend."

"Oh, sorry," the creature mumbled. "I didn't know it was a dead girl last night. I just went back to sleep. Figured I'd have a look later, trash just gets better with time. Sorry, insensitive. Then this morning I got busy and forgot, 'til that meathead from the deli started screaming. He leaves me a lotta pork parts. Dead girl and dead pig smell mostly the same, the pig just wears less perfume. Sorry. Insensitive. Anyway, then it was a goddamn nightmare, all those people around. I had to hang out all afternoon and make sure those NYPD jerks didn't take any of my valuables. I got a pile a' gristle from that deli I've been curing for weeks, and that's just the kinda thing they'd think was 'evidence.' And *then* those creeps in black showed up." The creature, like many nonhuman individuals, apparently had a superstitious horror of mentioning the Order by name, as if it might summon them on the spot.

"No one in the Order can see you," Adrael assured it.

"Yeah? Don't be so sure. I'd swear one of them looked right at me."

"Oh?" Adrael's face remained stoic, except for a less-than-disinterested blink.

"Her and me, we made eye contact. Saw it in her face, she *saw* me. She looked away pretty quick, but..." The entity shook what passed for its head, aghast.

"I wouldn't go around saying that," Adrael warned it mildly. "Sounds a bit paranoid."

"I'm tellin' you, those people are terrorists. They'll grab you right off the street and no one'll ever see you again. I've even seen 'em do it to other humans." The entity shuddered. "Cannibals, that's what they are. And that was my new favorite spot. Three different restaurants sneak their trash in there right now. Now I can't go back there for days. After the cops get bored, the Ord—those jerks might come back to 'cleanse' the place, spraying that stuff everywhere, that...thoughtwater. I fall asleep there, I might wake up dissolved."

"They are truly uncivilized," Adrael agreed.

"So," hemmed the trash demon, "you gonna eat those peanut ones?"

"Help yourself." Adrael dropped the second bag of candy in after the first.

"Thanks. I've smelled the empty bags a hundred times, but people don't toss the candy. Not around here. Maybe it's different uptown. I stick to my area and don't go north of Grand Central. I don't like to ask for trouble."

"I can appreciate that."

"But I owe you for these," said the trash demon, burrowing back into his nest. "Need any restaurant recommendations down here, you come see old Glub. I can tell you that deli's terrific, judging by their trash."

Interlude

Desdemona

Twenty-six years ago

The little girl sat in her crib in a bunny-print nightgown and peered through the bars at the spindly shape moving behind her closet door. It had peeked out at her every night for weeks, veiny fingers probing and flashing ragged teeth. Too frightened to sleep, she hoped with a child's logic that if she kept her eyes on it, it wouldn't come out.

On the first few nights, she screamed until her German nanny, Ute, rushed in to comfort her. But then the people in black came and waved their book and their crosses and their beads over her head, and tried to splash her with the horrible water. A drop splashed on her hand once, and it burned her, but Dez bit down her pain and Ute wiped the water off when no one was looking.

So she gave up crying, because she didn't want those people in black to come back. Young as she was, she already understood that she was no safer with them than with that thing in the closet anyway.

CHAPTER 3

IN THE COMPANY OF WOLVES

The Second Circle Nightclub
Thursday morning

Lucius Dark stood in his lofted office and stared down at the dance floor of his empty nightclub through mirrored glass walls. No matter how much money he threw at his palatial pleasure house, the glittering décor of New York's hottest hotspot always looked slightly seedy with the house lights on, revealed as the dressed-up feeding trough it was, complete with the mosaic of stains and smudges of its unhinged nightly revelry.

And as it was daytime, the evening's dancers and drinkers were replaced by stout-necked criminals, the cadre of thugs, mercenaries, and knee-breakers that protected Lucius's business interests—werewolves and vampires, mostly. They spent their off-hours guarding the property while playing video games, napping, adjusting their Fantasy Football leagues, and comparing firearms with the ponderousness of mortgage brokers. Necessary as they were, Lucius more or less hated them all, so he shifted focus to his own reflection in the glass, which showed a golden-haired Adonis with a face like an angel and eyes the color of honey. He alternately looked like a teenager, a young man, or a man in his prime, depending on his mood; eternally youthful, the glint of his true age showing only in his expression. His gold man-jewelry and half-unbuttoned shirt held a whiff of Eurotrash, but the cheerful American accent he preferred to use these days sounded like California. Technically Lucius was born in Italy, but that was before "Italy" was even a concept, so he didn't consider it relevant to his image.

Momentarily lost in admiration of his own face, he startled as his eye caught the reflection of Adrael standing behind him. It always unnerved him that Adrael could move in and out of rooms without being noticed, but still Lucius couldn't help a spike of habitual lust at the thought of lying on his back like a woman and pulling Adrael's heavy frame on top of him before flipping the man over and violating him while holding his head under a pillow.

But that was not an option, so, as usual, Lucius kept it to himself.

"I don't suppose Mr. Luppi came in to pay his tab," Lucius said instead, draping his body over his white leather captain's chair like Jesus in the *Pietà*.

"Not yet," Adrael replied.

"Should I hold my breath?"

"Don't let me stop you." Adrael leaned on the wall, folded his brawny arms, and tried not to touch anything. He was not by any stretch squeamish, but he always felt sticky in Lucius's office, a palace of cream suede and gold filigree bedecked with several centuries of paintings depicting naked people rutting with satyrs. The art was priceless and authentic, much of it bought or "acquired" from under the noses of jealous curators at the Met, the Getty, and the Louvre, but it all looked tawdry hanging above Lucius's snow-white polar bear rug. And if there was a surface big enough for a dinner plate in that office, Lucius had definitely fucked someone on it. "Would you like to cut your losses?" Adrael then queried with professional neutrality, like a waiter asking if Lucius was ready for the check.

"I can't let him get away with stiffing me. Everyone else will get ideas. What if I give him another week?"

"He either can't or won't get you what you want, if he hasn't by now."

"If Vito's not getting his needs met here, he must be going elsewhere," Lucius groused.

"I checked *elsewhere*. Even the low-rent spots in Queens. They haven't seen him."

"Would they tell you if they had?"

"I didn't say I asked. I said I checked."

"So where's he been for the last two weeks? At home wanking off?"

"If that did the trick, he wouldn't have a five-hundred-thousand-dollar tab with us," Adrael pointed out.

The office door opened and Rat sidled in with the nervous obsequiousness he manifested around Lucius, hovering near the sofa without sitting down. Lucius sighed with barely disguised distaste; Adrael had insisted on hiring the man, and much like the more muscular members of the club's staff—"Adrael's Boys," as he called them—he counted Rat as just another bitter pill Adrael made him swallow for his own good.

"Do *you* have anything useful to add?" Lucius asked him.

"The mayor's a no-go," Rat dutifully reported. "As far as anyone can tell, he's in bed every night by nine-thirty with his wife and a book."

"How depressing."

"Well, but—" Rat continued with a smug smile, "The *deputy* mayor has a shoebox full of goodies in the back closet that he hides from *his* wife. The maid found it while 'cleaning.' " He wiggled his eyebrows suggestively, two hairy caterpillars jumping for joy.

Adrael mustered a smile of mild encouragement. Rat's usefulness outweighed how tacky he was, so Adrael tried not to demoralize him. He'd hired Rat away from a private detective agency, correctly judging the little sycophant to be perfectly suited to the job of digging his pointy nose into other people's dirty laundry, and the fact that Lucius disliked him so much was, to Adrael, just a bonus.

"Then tell whatshisname—Goldberg—if he brings in the deputy mayor, he can have a discount," said Lucius. "A *tiny* discount." Arvo Goldberg was an investment banker and a city councilman, and his insatiable desire for exotic anal adventures with barely legal Asians of any gender made him a regular Second Circle customer. While there were cheaper places in the city, Lucius offered an environment safe from police, prying eyes, oblivious spouses, and potential blackmailers. The fact that Lucius fell in to that last category was an uncomfortable reality that his customers almost managed to forget, and Lucius—who counted tact among his few real virtues—found that maintaining a light touch encouraged them to do so. "But Goldberg's developing expensive taste," Lucius added. "We don't want to let his bill get too high. Speaking of which..."

"Nobody's seen Vito Luppi all week," coughed Rat. "Or his cousins. But the cops found a dead hooker downtown yesterday, so maybe he's getting take-out now."

"Found?"

"The body was left in a trash bin," Adrael clarified. "What was left of it."

"Was she wearing..."

"She was."

"Then find Vito quickly, please, before that also becomes our problem."

"If you're displeased with my work, feel free to fire me," Adrael replied silkily, flashing Lucius a subversive smile that made him feel like a lamb being soothed for the knife. It was far too easy for Lucius to forget that the two of them weren't actually friends. After all, Adrael was a blue blood, sort of; he even sounded like one, although the Queen's English he spoke now was still tinged with the inflections of some long-dead Teutonic dialect from the barbaric mud pile that Lucius still thought of as "*Brittania*." But while Lucius's origins were far grimier,

Adrael still obeyed every command Lucius gave him, and Lucius never got tired of it.

Rat watched them bicker in fascinated silence. He did not quite understand their relationship. Lucius vacillated between bossing Adrael around and letting Adrael subtly bully him, so Rat assumed they must be a couple, or that there was at least some steamy quid pro quo situation between them. Rat saw Adrael leave the club with women often enough to know that he chased tail like any other red-blooded man, but Lucius would fuck pretty much anything—man, woman, or in-between—and Rat found it hard to believe that he would be able to keep his sticky fingers out of someone who looked like Adrael. He certainly ordered the man around like he owned him, and although Adrael and Lucius did not seem to like each other, that was true of many couples, in Rat's limited experience of romance.

Downstairs, a shocking *bang* rang out as a gun went off, and something heavy and made of glass smashed to the floor.

"Deal with them, too," Lucius scowled. "That sounded expensive."

Adrael nodded once, like a prince to a liege lord—a gesture he'd maintained through the centuries, but which had become more sarcastic than otherwise—and stalked downstairs with Rat on his heels. He was not inclined to mention the strange new Order girl to Lucius; surely he could sort her out himself.

———

The Order
Thursday afternoon

"The dead girl's a Jane Doe," said Hunter, pinning the photos of the body onto the wall in the werewolf room. "So at least no one'll make too much of a stink about her." He stood back to regard his work, tilting his head like an artist, and then looked at Dez apologetically. "Pardon me, Cross. We get a little jaded around here."

"Well, this isn't *Sesame Street*, as you said," Dez allowed, poring over the photos. In two dimensions the body seemed less real, so Dez was able to look with a colder eye. The girl was unmistakably a prostitute, in her torn red bodycon dress and chipped nails, one plastic gold hoop dangling from her remaining ear, her body wrapped in a cheap red raincoat painted redder with her blood. Ordinary women out on the town were sometimes hard to distinguish from working girls in clubbing clothes, but the dress was a little too tight, and the one remaining shoe was a six-inch red vinyl platform—hard shoes to dance in.

"We think she was killed last night, at midnight or before," said Hunter. "Too bad our dogs didn't find her before the cops—I think the sausage smells from that deli confused them."

"It was a slow news day, though," Reilly pointed out, glancing at the photos with twisted lips. "And this kill is pretty gruesome, even for a moonie attack. Like...really gruesome. Kinda artistic, even—"

"Reilly—" Hunter coughed.

"Anyway the papers are making a meal out of it," Reilly concluded sheepishly.

"Page one?"

"Page three, metro."

"Then don't worry about it. They'll be over it tomorrow. That's the thing about prostitute murders. A guy's gotta kill a whole bunch of them to get any attention." A shadow crossed his face that Dez read as contempt. But for whom, she didn't know.

The dead girl had been pretty, her pouty lips and almond eyes suggesting a mixture of Black and Asian. Candy-bar wrappers, drywall chips, and flattened soda cups comprised her final bedding, her curled hair entwined among the wormlike strands of a discarded spaghetti lunch. What was left of her body was mangled, her jaw broken and twisted, one arm torn completely away. Everything below her navel was a mess of pastramied flesh and crusted blood, and her nipples had been chewed off, as if she'd been savaged by something between an overeager lover and a wolverine. It could plausibly have been a human attacker; plenty of serial killers savage enough for that existed in the annals of crime. But the strength it would take to rip her apart that way, and the nature of the bite marks, suggested a werewolf.

"Reilly's right, this was particularly...vigorous," Hunter frowned. "It's...I dunno, theatrical. Nobody gets too upset about a dead hooker, but when it's this photogenic, people get kinda interested, if you get me. And all that extra attention makes everybody over at One Police Plaza jumpy, that slows us down getting access to the body...et cetera."

"How often do you catch these killers?" Dez asked.

"More often than you'd think. Most moonies' first attack is someone they know, and we try not to let them get to a second one. But if they do get away with it, and keep doing it, they get good at it, and then they're harder to nab. And when the vic's a working girl, the perp could've been a tourist, or anyone. That's why prozzie murders rarely get solved. By us *or* the cops. But..." he dropped his voice to a mutter, speaking only to Dez, "she was still a person. And now she's dead, and I get stuck on the idea that somebody should give a shit."

"Incoming." Reilly handed a printout to Hunter with a list of the evidence that the detectives had so far compiled, surreptitiously collected by an Order operative within the police. "The NYPD canvassed the area where the girl worked," said Reilly, "and a couple of the other working ladies down there swore she got into a silver two-door late-model sports car—one was a hundred-percent sure it was a Porsche—sometime before eleven p.m. They don't know the girl's name but they noticed the Porsche. Driver was supposedly a male, dark hair, Caucasian, young."

"A silver sports car, huh." Hunter and Reilly both chuckled.

"Why is that funny?" Dez asked.

"It's a werewolf joke," Hunter explained.

" '*You want the silver bullet that kills you to be the one you drive,*' " Reilly intoned. "Is what they say."

"I didn't know werewolves had their own humor."

"Just the one joke. And they all think they made it up." Hunter sighed again, this time with the weariness of a long-time defender of justice faced with a world that remained largely unrepentant. "But it's a sign we're on the right track. We can check the database for the car. Get names on the board."

"May I do that?" Dez offered, surprising herself.

"Why?" Hunter raised an eyebrow. "It's not the Loch Ness Monster. We can get one of the regular research monkeys to run this down for us."

"I'd like to do it." After all, she'd gone to that alley and ogled the body, and she felt she owed it to the girl with spaghetti in her hair to do her bit, even if it was just compiling a list. "Although....I've mostly worked with cold files and cases that involve manuscripts. I've never used our live database. I'll be trained on it tomorrow."

Hunter raised his other eyebrow.

"Just how long have you been in the Order?"

"Depends what you mean," Dez told him, suppressing a blush of embarrassment. " Officially...this week. This is my first real posting."

Hunter peered at her as if seeing her for the first time.

"Helluva good start, so far."

"Thank you." This time she did blush.

"Well, come on, I'll show you the database. You'll like it. It's indecent. Even for us."

———

The Upper West Side

The Order girl wasn't home. Adrael hopped twenty feet in the air to grab the bottom of the fire escape and monkey-climbed up to her fourth-floor window. He popped open the latch with a pocket-sized pry bar and then stepped into the apartment, knocking salt to the floor as he did. He'd forgotten about the salt, although he'd noticed it the night before when he'd followed her home.

He wasn't surprised that an Order member would pick a room facing a windowless brick wall over a narrow alley. She had obviously just moved in, her boxes neatly flattened against the wall, waiting for trash day. But her apartment looked more like a museum basement than a living space, its dense collections of items organized and knolled into submission. Despite his contempt for anything related to the Order, Adrael couldn't help marveling at the walls studded with artifacts. He scanned the voluminous collection of books, wondering at the strange logic of the meticulously stacked piles. She had a little bit of everything, from science to Scientology, dragons to Darwin, and more books about fairy tales than he'd ever seen in one place. He picked up a dog-eared copy of the *Arabian Nights*. Flipping open the cover, he saw a name written on the fly-leaf: *Desdemona Cross.*

Desdemona. What a name for an Order member. If that *was* her real name. He checked the books below it to find that she'd marked every volume the same way. He rifled through the rest of her things delicately but unrepentantly, reading the intimate traces of her like tea leaves: torn pieces of paper sticking out of books where she'd encountered some gruesome tidbit, a cup with an inch of cold black coffee in the bottom and the reddish print of her soft lips on the rim. Her pantry was bare except for a packet of English tea biscuits and a tin of instant coffee, and he saw no cookware except a kettle and a single mug. He opened the refrigerator and felt a twinge of pity at the contents; it was empty except for a container of aging Thai food, sitting in the very center of the middle shelf like a museum display, complete with used plastic fork.

She did enjoy some creature comforts; a soft black cardigan was folded over the back of her chair, and Adrael recognized cashmere when he felt it. The contents of her closet were also entirely black, and classically conservative; turtleneck sweaters, cigarette pants, tailored black pencil skirts all long enough to touch the knee. In a drawer he discovered a cache of high-end black silk underthings, but they were too tasteful to be adventurous; underwear meant to be enjoyed by the wearer but not necessarily seen. He checked the bathroom: high-end shampoo, nude nail polish, black eyeliner, and a couple of lipsticks in shades of muted red.

As Adrael closed the door to her empty medicine cabinet, he saw his own face looking back at him in the mirror, and an unfamiliar sensation of discomfort shivered through him. Trespassing was part of his regular routine and a necessary part of his job, and came as naturally to him as breathing. But it occurred to him that if this Desdemona Cross woman were to find him in her home, touching all of her personal objects and turning over her laundry, he might slightly mind what she thought of him for doing it, and that was a sentiment of which he'd forgotten he was capable.

She'd certainly be alarmed to know that he'd perched on her window ledge the night before and watched her as she came home, took off her coat, and sat down in her desk chair. Then, he recalled, she'd wiped something off her fingers, and he saw then that the paper towel was still in the grocery bag she was using as a trash can. He fished it out and found it smeared with a clear, sticky, odorless goo. His thoughts veered from scientific to prurient before an explanation occurred to him. He pulled open her desk drawers one by one with the meticulous touch of an experienced burglar, careful not to disarrange the precisely placed contents, probing around the wood itself until he found the trick latch that popped out a hidden compartment containing several pocket-size tubes of petroleum jelly.

———

Record-keeping, in the Order, was largely analog. All files were hand-written or typed with old-fashioned typewriters onto water-soluble paper and watermarked, like currency, to prevent photocopying, which made research a time-consuming affair. But keeping such materials in hard copy only made sense; any snoop would have trouble physically entering their underground vault, much less getting out again, and the Order understood that if a few of those precious black files did leak out, nobody in their right mind would believe what they were reading.

But they still needed to make use of police records, government files, and financial data, and attach information to the names of perpetrators, so they tracked two distinct categories of information—"natural" and "supernatural"— maintaining a wall of secrecy between the two. "Natural" information was their fanatically compiled data about the lives, birthdays, jobs, families, Social Security numbers, taxes, cars, addresses, and even bank accounts of the city's nonhuman individuals—whatever could not be gleaned from public records and police files would be scrubbed off the internet by their hackers. All that collected information was shielded from the internet behind layers of encryption, accessible only within Order headquarters from a sterile chamber fitted with rows of computers, next to which old-fashioned notepads and pens were placed for the researchers' convenience. This was known, in the Order, as "the database."

"Log in and do a search by car type and color," Hunter told Dez. "You'll see what I mean about the silver-bullet thing." He leaned on the desk next to her and she caught a trace of his musky aftershave.

"I'm sorry, the car type was..." she coughed, distracted.

"Look up two-door coupes. For color, search silver, grey, and gunmetal."

The query resulted in a dishearteningly long list; the triumph of gallows humor, Dez supposed.

"We need to narrow this down," Hunter chuckled. "Make that a Porsche. Late model, so stick to the last five years." The computer offered a list of fifteen males residing within a hundred miles of Manhattan. "And now control for hair color and race, brown or black hair, Caucasian, and throw Latino and Middle Eastern in there too, witnesses can't tell the difference."

"That's only eight people," Dez blinked. "In all of New York?"

"Plus northern New Jersey and Connecticut."

"But that's a pool of millions of people."

"Well, Moonies only make up about half a percent of the total population of this city. Half of those are women, and we're not looking at them. Also eliminate the Black ones, the blond ones, the Asians. We only want the guys between, oh, eighteen and fifty years old, to be generous; they said it was a young guy, but moonies don't always age like us. And this city's expensive, so if the guy can afford to even park a new sports car here he's in a smaller club of about five-percent of citizens in general. Five-percent of half a percent of those millions of people, narrowed down by all that other stuff...and you get a really small list. And of that group, some buy Ferraris, Beemers, Audis...but we're only looking at the Porsche owners. The only reason we have eight guys at all is because so many of those unoriginal playboys buy the exact same car."

The list comprised a wide range of types: a professional athlete (a group well-represented among were-people), an investment banker, a real-estate broker. Dez scanned the addresses, occupations, and financial minutiae with the practiced eye of an scholar used to parsing old documents. *Professional chef with multiple bankruptcies, tech executive paying too much alimony...*

"Almost none of these people have files," Dez noted.

Because the computerized database contained only the "natural information"— defined as data generated by regular people in the course of living their lives—nowhere did it state that a person happened to be a werewolf, or list any details about their crimes. This was by design; if that database were to fall into the hands of anyone outside the Order, it would simply appear to be evidence of some large-scale identity theft. The more "sensitive" information was kept on paper only, and each entry in the database included a shorthand code to let researchers know where in the archives the relevant files could be found. But since the majority of New York's were-people never actually hurt anyone, most of their names were coded "P.O.," or "Pre-Offender," meaning they did not yet warrant their own case files.

"Looks like the moonies on our list are just citizens," said Hunter.

"Might be that the only thing our perp's ever done wrong in his life before this is take too many tax deductions. Moonies are like that. After a whole life of keeping it together, they just snap. That's why we keep track of all this shit. In case."

"*This* person definitely has his own file, though." Dez zeroed in on one name. "Male, Italian-American, Capricorn...no debt, no job history, and his profession is listed as 'organized crime.' " Dez looked at Hunter quizzically. "The rest of it just says "*see file.*"

"Yeah, Reilly does most of the data entry for us, and he gets pretty swamped, so when the subjects do have files, he sometimes..." Hunter waved his hand lazily, "makes us look it up ourselves."

"And it says *you* have it."

"What's the name?" Hunter quirked a brow.

"*Vittorio Antonio Luppi.*"

"Vito Luppi. Aha." Hunter looked perturbed.

"Well?" Dez nudged.

"He *would* have a Porsche," Hunter muttered. "And...huh...look at that, his home address is in here, that's surprising. It's probably old, though."

"It says it was updated a month ago."

"Wow," Hunter whistled. "Reilly must be putting in the extra hours. But forget it, Cross. That one's not what it looks like."

"Oh?" Dez paused with her fingers on the keys and slid her eyes archly at Hunter.

"Alright, if you're gonna eyebrow me like that, I'll show you why," he chuckled. "Follow me."

Hunter's office was just down the hall from his incident room, and looked like an extension of himself: a bit disheveled, a bit dusty, but undeniably professional, with precarious towers of files testifying to his heavy caseload. He pulled down a bricklike folder from the shelf and handed it to Dez. It was an old one, its black card stock faded to grey, with a worn spine threatening to tear from the strain. The tab read "*A/C: Luppi-NYC-current.*"

"This is all one man's file?" Dez marveled.

"Not exactly," said Hunter, flipping it open for her as she needed both hands to hold it. He turned over fat chunks of pages until he hit a section of the file labeled *VITTORIO ANTONIO LUPPI.* "Here he is, in all his glory."

Werewolves ranged widely in attractiveness from grotesque to sublime, but Vittorio (Vito) Antonio Luppi, aged twenty-five, was a notable specimen of the latter, with dark wavy hair and a pretty face sporting heavy brows, a day of Brillo scruff on his movie-star chin, and the languid eyes of a cupid in an Italian painting. In the picture, snapped outside the back door of a nightclub, his sturdy frame was draped in slick evening clothes, his arm wrapped around a pretty girl in a cocktail dress.

"Is that him?"

"I know, the kid looks like a movie star," Hunter yawned. "Every nice girl likes a bad boy, I get it."

"He's certainly wearing the costume." Dez flipped through several more photos, in many of which Vito sported a flashy black-leather moto jacket that had perhaps been "rescued" off the back of some Italian designer's truck.

"Don't get me wrong, he *is* pretty bad," Hunter clarified. "He's just more Michael Corleone than Jack the Ripper."

"Meaning what?"

"To understand Vito, you need to understand the family."

The Luppi, as the file explained in detail, were an old-school Italian Mafia clan sprawling the five boroughs and into New Jersey. The men were all swarthy, with dramatic brows and thick beards they shaved twice a day, and while the older ones were swollen with age and wine, the younger ones were handsome, though none compared to Vito.

"Are they *all* werewolves?" Dez marveled.

"Most of them," Hunter nodded. "And the thing is, Cross, I'd love to bring in Vito Luppi. I'd like to bring in his whole family. So would the cops. And the Feds. And the damn ATF."

"Then why don't they do it?"

"Well, most of these guys have a few arrest records to their names—you'll see that noted there, there, and *there*—but cops have to worry about little things like evidence and due process. And the Luppi are too careful to get tripped up by details like that. They're professionals."

"So why don't *we* deal with them?" The Order was not a legal entity (quite the opposite, in fact) and thus did not have to worry about evidence or due process or even anything as fluffy as "human rights." Merely being "extranatural" was itself a crime to them, and she would have thought that an entire clan of werewolves was something that the Order would not tolerate.

"They've got relatives all over the city," Hunter told her with the sigh of a man moving a mountain with a wheelbarrow. "If we get into it with them, it'll turn into a citywide spectacle. As Solomon keeps reminding me."

In ignorantia, salutis. In ignorance, salvation. The Order's mantra was stamped into Dez's mind just as it was branded into the iron plaque at the front door. Because while the Order threw a long shadow over the lives of those they surveilled, in truth, they were not numerous or powerful enough to go after everyone they wanted. Their primary mandate, above monster-hunting or justice or saving lives, was secrecy. They made it their mission to make sure that the world's humans knew nothing of the hidden *demimonde* that hunted them in the dark, reasoning that no one could encounter such horrors and live a normal life afterwards. It destroyed people's concept of safety, their faith in institutions, even their belief in science, and through the ages the result of such knowledge had always been chaos. So in the Order it was secrecy over everything, even human lives, since dead bodies were easier to erase than people's memories.

"I suppose the Luppi don't break nearly as many laws as we do," Dez remarked tartly.

"That's true, Cross. And that attitude took a little getting used to for me, I can tell you. It's hard to stop being a cop just because you don't have a badge anymore."

"So you *don't* think Vito Luppi killed that girl? Or are you saying that if he did, you can't do anything about it?"

Hunter flipped to a photo of an imposing middle-aged man with a grey streak in his black hair and a stare like a gargoyle.

"Who's that?"

"Massimo Luppi, head of the family. Vito's father." In the photo, snapped outside a restaurant, Massimo Luppi was lording over a group of other scowling Italian men gathered around a platter of smoked meats. He was tall and bulldoggish, with the planes of a handsome face showing through the jowls of age. "Nothing in that family happens without Massimo's say-so," said Hunter. "Vito specializes in stealing expensive shit out of other people's warehouses, and we've got him pinned for a whole list of business-related murders, always with guns. But that guy doesn't do anything without a family work order. And I don't see daddy telling him to cut up a hooker in a dark alley. To Massimo, that would probably be more of a distraction than otherwise."

"So you're saying the Luppi are above that sort of thing."

"I'm sure that's how *they* would put it," he replied wryly, taking the file back from her. As their hands touched, he noticed hers were encased in black leather gloves. "Are you cold, Cross?" he asked.

Her pulse jumped, but the familiar lie slid into place like a train onto a track.

"I have a health condition. Skin allergies. I avoid touching anything moldy or dusty."

"Good thing you work in the archives, then."

"All jobs have their difficulties," she shrugged.

"I guess the gloves save you from the paper cuts."

"That is a peril, in my field."

"Mm-hmmm," Hunter murmured, looking distinctly amused. "Well, I'll check out the other guys on this list." He waved the paper she'd given him like a flag of surrender. "I have my night cut out for me.

But *you* just got into town, you should go to a show. All work and no play, as they say."

"I don't really go out," she shrugged.

"Man, you picked the wrong city to be a homebody. You don't want to become one of those shriveled little raisins that pass for women down here. Go on, live a little. I hear the new *Into the Woods* revival is pretty hot right now."

"I'll consider it," she smiled.

"Trust me, these dead people aren't going anywhere. And the ones that do are somebody else's department."

CHAPTER 4

DARK ALLEYS

Thursday evening

Dez hurried home as the last traces of dusk gave way to the night sky, her fear beginning to fade in the relentless glare of artificial light. Unlike the shadowy lanes of Cambridge, the constant streams of people in a city the size of New York drove the night's darker inhabitants into the crevices, and walking around after sundown was bearable even with eerie faces peering at her from every shadowy corner, since she had large planes of clear sidewalk to stride through.

So, thusly emboldened, when she passed the subway station outside the museum, she dithered, taking a moment to stare at an MTA chart on a pillar. The city seemed increasingly vast the longer she lived there, but after working on the live database she recognized some of the neighborhoods and streets. Slowly, like an illiterate worrying at a restaurant menu, she followed the colored lines and arrows along their paths across the city. *So that's how one got to Brooklyn...and there was Queens...How long did it take to get from the Museum to the Cloisters? Was it realistic for something to crawl out of the East River and make its way to, say, her neighborhood?* And she had no idea how long it took to get anywhere if one factored in waiting for trains.

Then, academically, she started looking for another address, one she'd memorized from the database earlier that day. She was feeling less imperiled every minute; there were ordinary people around her, and they mostly made it home in one piece every night, so there was no reason that Dez should give into her habitual fear and slink home when she could potentially answer her burning question with a short trip downtown.

One train and a few blocks later, she reached Crosby Street just north of Little Italy, in front of the building that the Order database said contained Vito Luppi's apartment. The block was a quiet one, and most of its ground floor businesses were closed for the night, so she was more or less alone. *She was only there to look.* Hunter was surely right about Vito Luppi; he understood this city and its resident moonies far better than she ever could. Everything she knew about the Mafia came from television, and anyway, Vito Luppi hardly looked like a guy who needed to resort to prostitutes for company. She just wanted to see if his silver Porsche was parked near his apartment, and a peek in the car window might tell her if a girl been recently murdered inside. If not, she could, in good conscience, leave the matter alone. But if it was torn up and splattered with blood, she'd let Hunter know, since he, at least, did not seem to mind being told when he was wrong.

And then there it was: a silver Porsche, parked baldly on the street as if it had no reason to hide. She approached it circumspectly, trying to see into the windows without looking as if she was about to smash one, but the glass was tinted black. It definitely was Vito's car, though; she remembered the license plate. At first Dez was elated, but realized belatedly that if Vito *had* murdered a girl in his car, he'd probably have dumped it at some mob-owned chop shop, and not left it sitting out in the street to be ogled by anyone.

A group of drunkish tourists tumbled loudly into the sidewalk from a sushi bar on the corner, and began shambling in her direction, so she stepped into the alley beside Vito's building to avoid being noticed as a lurker. She decided to wait a few minutes for him to either emerge or arrive; the car was parked, so he might well be home, but that was no guarantee in a city where no one needed to drive.

The tourists disappeared down the street, taking their noise with them. In the relative quiet, the alley echoed with a listless drip of creamy fetid runoff, its walls splattered with the illegible spray-painted pissings of a frustrated artist claiming a space he could own no other way. A shuffling sound in the trash behind her made her jump, recalling the entity she'd spotted at that crime scene, but squinting into the dark, she saw nothing unnatural. *It must have been rats.* The scritching of their claws digging into garbage, the distant whoosh of city traffic, and the hum of streetlights were all standard New York night noise, each sound tickling over her skin with its own frequency; harmless, but still unsettling. In that grimy solitude, Dez's familiar fear began to creep over her afresh. *What a ninny she was being,* chasing a possible killer when she herself was a magnet for anything hungry. She took a deep breath to calm her nerves, inhaling cold asphalt and sewer breath and the ghosts of empanadas past emanating from the garbage, and then looked up past the tops of the building to the sky where a milky waxing moon peeked out at her from behind a cloud. At least *that* was still where it belonged, even if *she* was not. She'd spent most of her life behind walls, first in a series of cloistered private schools and then at colleges where dense medieval stone shielded her from what her old colleagues dismissively referred to as "the real world." But that alley's sticky, obscene walls felt less like a sanctuary, and more like...

A trap.

A flash of heat sparked behind her, there and then gone, like a shadow made of light flitting across the back of her mind. *It was back.* She spun around—nothing, nothing, nothing. She was alone. Except...

"Hello."

A man was now leaning against the wall across the alley in a spot that she could have sworn was empty just a moment ago. Immediately she was struck by a visceral impression of the physical power coiled up in his taut, elegantly muscled frame, like a human switchblade ready to spring out and cut someone to the bone. His wide shoulders rested lightly against the graffitied wall, his face half-hidden by the shadow of the fire escape ladder above him, his burly arms folded with languid nonchalance, as if he'd been standing there for hours.

How had she missed such a large man in such a tiny alley? She sensed the proximity of his mass as if he generated his own gravity, and tracked the lines of his shoulders down to his robust forearms and long, elegant fingers. There was something uncanny about the way he moved, breathed, and vibrated in space, so she could tell he wasn't human, but he was too hot-blooded to be a vampire, radiating like a bonfire in the chilly night, and she realized that the sensation of something sparking behind her like flint the day before must have been *him.*

Was this Vito Luppi? He did look a bit like a werewolf, predatory and relaxed like he owned the place, but when he stepped forward into the line of light, she didn't recognize him. This man was even more handsome than Vito, his sculptural, almost angelic face framed by short dark hair punctuated by a caddish widow's peak, with something between a scowl and a smile on his incongruously pretty mouth. And while Vito's file said he had brown eyes, the eyes boring into her now were startlingly blue.

"It's dangerous to wander around this city alone," he purred. "A girl was killed in a dark corner like this just the other day." *Was he threatening her?* He was definitely the type who threatened, though his voice was deep and heavy as a firm caress and his silken English accent soothing. Her first instinct was to run, but she stopped herself; if you ran from predators, they just ran after you. He was a powerful animal, and he could do anything he liked to her before she'd have time to scream. Her holy water/mace spray sat in her pocket, but it seemed impotent now.

"I did hear about that," she managed. *White male, dark hair, five-o-*

clock shadow, notably attractive. She wondered if he owned a silver Porsche as well.

"Yes, I saw you and your friends at that crime scene yesterday, like crows waiting for your turn to pick at the body."

You and your friends. Dez's heart sank; he clearly knew who she worked for, and, ominously, he clearly didn't care.

"Which friends do you mean?"

"I don't know their names. They do like to lurk where they aren't invited, but they never bother to introduce themselves." He spoke genteelly, and the polite expression on his face held a wistful tinge, as if he were about to be sorry about something. And although he looked freshly showered, Dez suspected he had a trace of someone else's blood under his fingernails.

A frenzied rustling from the trash startled her and she whipped around, staring hard at the pile of debris.

"He's not here," Adrael assured her.

"Who—who do you mean?" Dez sounded disingenuous even to herself.

"His name is Glub. And yes, I believe he's single."

"I...don't...." Dez tried to say, but there was too much to address all at once, and her ability to prevaricate on the fly had evaporated in the flush of heat now coursing through her body.

"I know you saw him," he prodded, an ominous hint of impatience rippling through his velvet voice. "*He* knows you saw him."

"How—"

"He told me so," Adrael informed her. "And I saw you see him, and then I saw you look away. And since the average human can't see him, if *you* can, I'd think that would be terribly useful in your line of work. So it's odd that your colleagues don't know you can do it."

"Who...says they don't know?" she scoffed weakly, with the last crumbs of her courage.

"*I* just did. Do listen, please, I hate to shout. It wakes the roaches."

He had a playful manner, this handsome monster, both courteous and mocking, and he stared at Dez as if she were a specimen under a glass bell. He took a step towards her, moving close enough to grab her by the arm, or hair, or anything else he liked, and a wall of subliminal scent flooded her brain. Food smelled like food, blood like blood, perfume like perfume; but however potent and evocative those smells were, they were a mere shade of the scent rolling off him in waves, as if he had been suppressing it and was just then letting it loose. *Was this how werewolves smelled?* No, there was an animal muskiness to werewolves. *This* was something else. This was the scent that all other scents dreamed of being—spicy and oily and heady and distinctly male—and she inhaled deeply as her lungs instinctively tried to bathe themselves in it.

Adrael tried to catch the streetlight in her brown eyes, but they shifted away, making him want to grab her by the face and hold her still. She smelled warm, as if her blood was spiked with cinnamon, with an unusual note in her personal perfume that he couldn't place, and he was functionally imperceptible when he wanted to be, but she had detected him trailing her from the subway the night before, which no human should have been able to do.

But it was impossible. The Order did not allow individuals with even a hint of something "off." Such a taint was not only a disqualification, to them, but a capital crime. People with a tinge of the faerie in their bloodline—what Adrael's long-dead nursemaid called being "touched" —often manifested odd characteristics like scales or wings or strangely colored eyes, but she showed no sign of that, unless she was hiding a tail someplace. She was definitely not-quite-human though, and trying to pass, and, somehow, succeeding.

"I think there's a lot *they* don't know about you. Like this, which I found in your desk." He reached into his pocket and pulled out a tube of petroleum jelly, uncapped it, and smeared a bit on one finger, coating the skin. "Is this how you do it?" He tapped his thumb against his sticky finger, glancing pointedly down at her leather gloves.

Run. Fight. Lie. Lie faster. But Dez's brain, addled by his heady presence, failed to form the life-saving falsehoods she relied on.

"I think you've got me confused with—" she began, but halfheartedly, and her voice failed as she noted a trace of impatience flicker across his face.

"Humans don't need to protect their skin from thoughtwater," he reminded her, as if she didn't know.

"Holy water," she sighed, correcting him with a pedantic sniff.

He flashed a triumphant half-smile, as if rewarding her for her candor, which she immediately resented.

"Call it what you like," he smirked. "Do they test the whole hand, or will a finger do?"

"I do two fingers, to be safe," she confessed, her voice hollow.

"This is really all it takes to pass?" He wiped his finger on his sleeve distastefully. "That's disappointing."

Actually, it had taken a lifetime of carefully woven lies, all rendered moot by this man who now had her at his mercy. To have the truth laid bare seemed pathetic—amateurish, even—a pointless thing to be annoyed about now that her end was rushing toward her like a spiked wall.

"But," he insisted, pretending to be oblivious to her silent distress, "to join the Order in the first place, you'd still have gotten the bath." He was referring to the "first bath," the full-immersion baptism in holy water undergone by every new Order member to prevent anyone who wasn't human from infiltrating the ranks.

"You know rather a lot about the Order," she muttered sourly.

"I know a lot about everything," he assured her with a cocky tilt of his chin, though to Dez it sounded more like a confession than a boast. "I would like to know, though, what they would do to you if they found out."

"I'm sure you can imagine," she swallowed.

Adrael thoughtfully played with the tube in his fingers. He had been prepared to detest this woman the way he detested all things connected with the Order, but the idea of her lovely body dissolved in a bathtub did not please him as much as he would have thought. He'd come there expecting to have to break her neck, but his mind was already churning with alternatives. He had spent the better part of a long life collecting useful contacts, but an Order member would be a first for him. And while dealing with the Order rarely had an upside, rarely also was the idea wrapped in such an exquisitely wrapped package.

Dez blinked at him expectantly, quite aware that she was waiting for her sentence to be pronounced.

"So shall I call you Desdemona," he finally said, "or is there something shorter?"

Her eyes widened in dismay.

"How did you..." She trailed off, too upset to finish her sentence.

"If you're so concerned about anonymity, you shouldn't write your name in all your books," he pointed out.

Unbelievable. He must have been in her private space, touching all her things and prying into her life, and she felt utterly violated.

"How long have you been stalking me?" she demanded, her face flushing with rage.

"I'm not stalking you."

"You followed me here."

"No, I didn't. I'm quite surprised to see you here." This, in fact, was true; a hefty bribe to the right underworld contact had finally procured him the address of Vito's Manhattan crash pad, and Adrael had been watching the place since sundown. "I was about to ask what *you* were doing here," he added, although he had a guess; it was possible that more than one individual on the Order's target list lived in that building, but Adrael, despite sometimes suggesting the contrary, was not a big believer in coincidence.

"I'm—just—" she began, but then:

Click.

The front door of the building creaked open and they both froze to watch a man wearing a hoodie under a familiar black-leather moto jacket stride out of the building. The sweatshirt's hood encased his head, but as he passed under a streetlight, Dez saw big eyes, a scruffy jaw, and rakishly combed waves of black hair, and recognized him immediately from the photos in the file. *That,* indeed, was Vito Luppi.

Dez and Adrael glanced at each other with a mutual flash of conspiracy.

"Follow me," he said then, in a tone that managed to be both an order and a request.

Dez hesitated. It was the worst idea in an already long night of bad ideas—and Dez always bridled against orders—but Vito Luppi was right in front of her, climbing into his car, and every cell in her body needed to know what he was about to do. So, ignoring the voice in her brain insisting that she stop, she followed the man in grey as he disappeared around the building wall.

As soon as Dez saw the sleek navy blue Bentley sedan, she knew a vehicle so simultaneously understated and outlandish—and parked halfway on the curb—had to belong to him. He unlocked the car and opened the passenger's side door for her with disarming courtesy. Dez climbed warily in, he shut the door for her, and seconds later, much faster than Dez expected, he was sitting beside her in the driver's side.

Dez shrank down in the buttery tan leather passenger seat and scanned the glittering dashboard. The interior was oddly clean, as if it was either brand-new or had been recently detailed, though several trashy thriller novels had been discarded like fast-food wrappers across the backseat.

"I suppose this has an ejector seat," she sniffed.

He flashed a surprised sideways smile, his slightly prominent eye teeth making him look like a sly fox.

"You've seen too many Bond movies," he chuckled.

"*I've* seen too many Bond movies?"

Down the street, the Porsche turned on, headlights flaring and tail lights blinking to red.

"Seatbelt," Adrael reminded her pleasantly, as he maneuvered the Bentley off the sidewalk.

———

The city rolled by like a loopy carnival ride as the Bentley turned up and down blocks, staying one car behind the Porsche, following it towards the river. Dez watched her new acquaintance's profile move in and out of shadow as they passed under streetlights, the dashboard casting a golden glow across his features. She ran her eyes over him the way a car enthusiast would have scanned the premium machine he drove, tracing the muscles of his forearms, the length of his fingers, and the symphonic composition of his ear, sideburn, and jaw. His clothes were of varying shades of concrete grey, and were entirely utilitarian except for the expensive watch on his wrist, and while he looked well-groomed enough for the city, the shadow of scruff on his chin looked like several days natural outgrowth rather than manicuring. And to Dez's finely honed sensibilities, the structure of his hands told her how he used them to grip a waist or a gun, the curve of his neck let her know how he answered the phone when it was a woman he wanted on the other line, and by the way he adjusted the clutch, she knew how he touched himself in the shower. The vision of all that lethal physicality unclothed sparked in her mind unbidden and scorched it, like staring at the sun with naked eyes, and she shoved it desperately away.

What was he? Not a werewolf, not a vampire, so...a fairy? *Fairy - see also: nymph, faun, Slavic hudra, Japanese tennin, Irish sidhe,* or simply the *"fallen,"* as the Order called individuals that defied categorization. *See also: Demon.* Such eccentric creatures had once been put to death as changelings. But he didn't look eccentric. He looked like a demigod, imposingly tall but not so tall it made him unwieldy, big but not so bulky it would slow him down, and was so handsome it hurt to look at him. Like a leopard, nature had designed him for killing, but made him more beautiful than he needed to be for the purpose.

She questioned her sanity at getting in his car; while he wasn't the type to rip up a hooker in the street, she smelled violence on him like cologne. But surely he wouldn't wish to stain his Bentley's upholstery. If he wanted to kill her, he already knew where she lived.

"What's your interest in Vito Luppi?" he asked her after a moment.

"He's…a suspect," she hedged.

"What's he suspected of doing?" Adrael pressed, and Dez heard another tinge of impatience in his velvet voice that sounded like a snarl in tall grass.

"Killing someone," Dez replied vaguely.

Adrael smirked at that. He detested the Order and the way they kept tabs on people, but it had taken him a lot of money and trouble to discover where Vito hung his hat, and for her it had likely been as simple as looking it up in a file, which could prove useful. And the most useful things were often the most distasteful, in his long experience.

"Well, whoever it was, he probably did it," he assured her.

The silver Porsche turned a corner and pulled up to a curb under the Manhattan Bridge, and a gaggle of working girls pushed off the wall to investigate the newcomer. Vito rolled his window down and nodded at one girl standing a bit apart from the others: a kittenish, bleach blonde naif with skin like a porcelain doll, wearing red plaid short-shorts and a tight red sweater.

He was doing it again. Dez was disappointed in Vito; what a waste of good genes. She glanced over at her new acquaintance in the driver's seat, who was doubtless another example of the same. Dez wondered if he too preferred his women by the hour—he had picked up Dez in an alley, after all. Although, to be fair, she'd climbed into his car with as much alacrity as that prostitute had climbed into Vito's.

Adrael piloted the Bentley behind the Porsche as both cars crossed the Manhattan Bridge into Brooklyn. Vito pulled into a rust-veined alley between two warehouses by the river, so Adrael turned the Bentley's lights off and slipped it into a dark adjacent nook that afforded them an unimpeded view.

He then turned off the engine, and they sat in the dark. And waited.

"So," Adrael eventually asked, "how well can you see right now?"

"Well, they're right in front of us, but—"

"In the dark, I mean. How well can you see compared to the average human being?"

"As I have no idea how well an average human being can see," Dez replied cagily, "and I obviously have no idea what else there is out there that I *can't* see ... I have no objective basis of comparison."

"Fair enough." He seemed to find her amusing, which Dez resented.

"Well, next time you see—or don't see—our little friend, you'll find him rather chatty if you bribe him," he informed her. "And no one knows more about a neighborhood than the local garbage entity."

"Bribe him with what?" She could only imagine what a vile entity like that craved.

"He seems to like chocolate."

"Aha. So then did it—he—tell you who put that dead girl into the trash bin?"

"He isn't sure," Adrael replied. "But he told me he definitely saw *you*, so it was still a worthwhile conversation." He shook his head at her. "So you've been seeing these strange individuals your whole life and you never stopped to say hello?"

"No. I've never talked to one of...you...before either. Not on purpose."

"One of *me*?"

"An Unnatural," she clarified crisply. "One of the Fallen."

"You people," Adrael scoffed, "and your wretched jargon."

In truth, Dez was years into her childhood before she realized that regular humans, like her nanny or her mother, couldn't see the things she did, and certainly couldn't see in the dark like she could. It was quite black in that car without the light from the dashboard, but her eyes adjusted, picking up meager auras of starlight that painted the world in undulating planes of grey. Her other senses tracked the movement of air particles around the lines and ripples of the car—and of the man beside her—her brain rendering it all into an image that was as sharp, in a way, as what her eyes saw in daylight. She was sure that his eyes could do the same, but he did not seem to be looking at anything in particular, gazing idly through the windshield as if waiting for a carhop to bring him a milkshake.

Ahead of them, Vito's car, which had been jiggling as if the two people inside were negotiating their clothes off, then began to shake more violently than even the most eager hip-thrusting could generate.

"That was quick," Adrael mused. "But I suppose he is paying by the hour."

"But...he's going to kill her. Just like he killed the girl at that building site."

So that was her interest in Vito Luppi. Adrael sighed internally; the Order was, it seemed, sharper than was convenient. *Or this girl herself was.* Adrael wondered then if she was operating on a personal hunch of some kind; she had an air of guilty trespass about her that an agent on an approved mission would never manifest.

"Probably," Adrael agreed.

"And...are you just going to sit here and watch him do it?" Dez gaped at him, aghast.

"Those windows are tinted, so we're not quite *watching*. I know that's frustrating. There are a couple of novels in the backseat, if you're already bored."

"Then why did you—we—even come here?" Dez gasped. "Are you just following him around to amuse yourself?"

"I'm not some nocturnal avenger in a cape," Adrael chuckled. "Vito and I have business, but dealing with him when his blood is up is more trouble than it's worth, so I'm happy to wait my turn."

Dez realized it was foolish to expect gallantry from a man who had thus far displayed no other virtues whatsoever. But then the Porsche begin to shake even more vehemently, and a woman's hand slapped against the interior window glass with a dull *thunk*.

"You have to stop this," Dez insisted.

"I don't *have* to do anything. I have nowhere else to be and there's candy in the glovebox. I can afford to be patient. And anyway, you people are everywhere and you still let innocent humans get killed all the time, as long as they're just being killed by other humans. Or as long as nobody finds out about it."

Dez's brain throbbed as images of the dead girl came back in a rush, stretched-out red lycra cutting into sliced flesh, guts shredded like taco filling, left to bleed out in a pile of garbage. She could not sit there and watch it happen again. But of course, her new friend was right: Order members did just that every night. The organization viewed all human-on-human crime as outside their purview, and ignored it, but Dez had never had to practice such strategic heartlessness before and found it difficult to stomach.

She turned to look at the man in grey again, but he was glancing down at his phone now, texting someone.

Yawning.

Oh, for God's sake. Before Dez had time to think better of it, she darted out of the car, scrambled across the alley to the Porsche, almost stumbling in her desperate haste when her heel caught a crack in the concrete, and tugged open the Porsche's passenger side door.

"Get out!" Dez hissed. "Run!"

The blond girl tumbled out of the car topless, yanking her red shorts back up. Dez hastily surveyed her for damage, but she seemed unbruised. And seeing her up close, Dez realized that she had, perhaps, made a bad mistake. The girl *looked* young, with soft cheeks, rosebud lips, a delicate jaw and eyes ringed in black, her pretty face a mask of childlike vulnerability. But beneath that was something twitching and shifting before Dez's eyes, like an unctuous shimmer hovering just above her skin. *This was no girl.* The glint of a hungry predator shone from the girl's mascaraed eyes, and Dez smelled the potent pheromones she emanated like a cloud.

She was a succubus.

"Nightcrawler" was the vulgar word that the Order used for such creatures, demons who fed on people's very life force by stirring them into a sexual frenzy. The Order classified them as energy vampires, *see:* hungry ghosts and *huli jin.*

"What the fuck are you doin'?" the girl caterwauled, shoving Dez away. "Is this your man, or what?"

Then the Porche's driver-side door opened and Vito Luppi climbed out. He looked halfway like a man, but his face was swelling as his muscles expanded under his skin. His shirt lay open under his jacket, revealing a cartoonishly muscular chest covered with black curly hair, and his unzipped pants pulsed with an urgent erection. Canine musk radiated down his elongating limbs, fingernails extending into talons as he panted clouds of angry breath into the nippy air. His guttural snarl rumbled through Dez's body, and her muscles betrayed her, seizing into the agonized rictus of prey as he lunged—

—and was stopped mid-leap by a hand grasping his throat.

The man in grey dangled Vito several inches off the ground, pressing a gun against his chest.

"Hello, Vito." Adrael smiled, his blue eyes hard as marbles. "You're a hard man to reach these days."

Bang. What sounded like a ball dropping onto sheet metal was, Dez realized belatedly, a gunshot. *Did the man in grey just shoot Vito?* No, Vito's chest was intact, and the man in grey was staring down the alley in surprise. Someone was shooting at *them.* Two figures stood at the end of the alley, with two silver cars—a SUV and a Miata—blocking them all in together.

Adrael dropped Vito on the pavement like a rag doll, aimed at their attackers, and fired. One figure fell backwards with an agonized howl. Adrael aimed and fired again, but the second man ducked behind a dumpster.

"Come on, stupid," the prostitute urged, tugging Dez behind the Porsche as shots rang out like fireworks. She had a doll's face but a grown-up woman's voice, her kiss-smeared red lipstick ringing her mouth like a shadow of blood. "Goddamn gangsters. I shoulda known that trick was all mobbed up. Not a banger—old school mob, like in the movies." The girl then turned to look at Dez, sussing her up. "You guys cops?" she asked dubiously.

Dez had never seen a nightcrawler prostitute up close before—or any prostitute for that matter—but she knew there had to be plenty of succubi among the city's population of working girls. From a distance the girl looked unremarkably human, but up close the difference was obvious, an invisible halo that Dez sensed rather than saw. And she could smell her, the acrid, honey-sweet miasma she produced making Dez's eyes water.

But then the scent of the succubus was abruptly overwhelmed by a cloud of animal musk. Dez looked up to see Vito Luppi crouched over them, silhouetted with the moon behind him. His transformation was further along, his leather jacket stretching to contain his swelling body. His pupils dilated, filling his eyes like a dog's, and his beard thickened moment to moment, hair follicles forcing themselves through his skin with angry beads of blood that slid back into his pores.

Dez's trembling hand found its way into her pocket, closing spasmodically around her pepper spray. Willing her muscles to act, she pulled the little canister out, aimed it at his nose, and pressed the button. The spray hissed and Vito howled, the droplets hissing further as they burned his flesh, and then Dez felt an angry sting on her own forehead as the vapor drifted back towards herself. She jolted away from it, smacking her head against the car.

Adrael whirled around at the sound of Vito's cry. *Where was the Order girl?* He saw Vito, in pain, clutching at his head. *Had he been shot?*

Bang.

Another shot rang out from behind the dumpster, and a shock of red-hot pain exploded in Adrael's thigh. Vito dove for his car, clawing into the driver's seat, and Dez and the succubus staggered to their feet and ran in opposite directions. Half-blinded by the thoughtwater and mace, Vito jammed his keys in the ignition and tore out of the alley, scraping the wall and gouging the Porsche's door.

Bang bang. Dez startled, but those were not gunshots; they were the doors of the SUV at the end of the alley slamming shut as the attackers climbed in and peeled away after the Porsche, abandoning the Miata. Sirens screamed in the distance—someone had called the police. Dez felt herself being pulled backwards into the Bentley's passenger side, and she yanked the door shut herself as Adrael backed the car into the street, leaving the bewildered prostitute standing in a puddle in thigh-high socks, her bare nipples rock-hard in the frigid autumn air.

———

The Bentley shoved into a lane, ignoring the angry honks. Flashing sirens loomed up behind them, but Adrael pulled to the right and the string of police cars sped by. The Porsche and the SUV were long gone.

"Who were they?" Dez gasped.

"The NYPD, I imagine."

"No, the men in the alley!"

"Oh, those were probably Vito's cousins."

Dez's hand felt oddly wet, so she looked at her black glove and found it sticky and damp.

"You're bleeding," said Dez. One leg of Adrael's pants was indeed shiny and slick; his blood looked dark against his grey clothes but gleamed bright red where it smeared the car's tan leather interior.

"I noticed."

"Quite a lot. If you have a towel or something, I can—"

"I'll sort it later," he replied, unconcerned.

So he bled. But practically everything with a body bled; it was really a question of whether bleeding was a problem for him or not. He did not seem bothered, and Dez had to take his word for it, since not-quite-humans did not usually go to hospitals, and anyway, he looked like the type to fix himself up with duct tape.

Dazed, she sat back and tried to put the last few minutes together.

"That girl wasn't human," she murmured.

"Yes, I wasn't sure you could tell."

"I didn't realize at first. That's why I..." she let the rest die in her mouth.

"Cared?" he finished for her with a grim smirk. "I did consider mentioning it."

"I'm sure it was more fun not to."

"I didn't think you'd get out of the car, you daft cow. If that's how you operate you won't last long in the Order."

"So Vito knew she was a..." Dez couldn't bring herself to say the word—it sounded like a slur.

"Nightcrawler? Yes. That's rather his thing. I gather." Dez thought there was an edge to his voice; maybe it was the gunshot wound. "Either one of them could have killed the other, but that's not how it usually goes in these scenarios."

"How does it go?"

"How does what go?"

"*That*, between werewolves and..." She trailed off.

"Do you mean sex?"

"Yes. That."

"How long have you been in the Order?" He cocked his brow quizzically.

"This is not my area of expertise," Dez reddened.

They hit a stoplight and he took a long look at her, his tongue tucked into his cheek.

"Then what is your 'area of expertise'?"

"I'm more of a..." She couldn't think of anything she was plausibly suited for other than the truth. "I'm in the research department."

"That's what you were doing outside Vito's apartment? Research?" His beautiful lips curled into a coy smile.

"If you examine the definition of 'research,' I think you'll find it exactly describes what I was doing," she sniffed.

He seemed to find that funny, because he laughed a little, drawing a nervous hiccup of a laugh out of her too.

"It's like this," he said, as the light turned green and they continued down the street. "Werewolves don't usually get to do...*that,* as you say... *as werewolves.*"

"You mean...sex."

Adrael smiled sideways at her again.

"I think most of them don't even want to," he continued. "Transforming can be painful for some of them, and I think your average moonie citizen tries to avoid it. But some like it. Some really like it. But even if the human girlfriends or husbands know what they are, they still can't do...that...*as werewolves,* because they'd tear their partners to pieces." He glanced at her. "You did know that much?"

"I'm generally aware," she coughed. "But with sex demons, things are different?"

"Very different," he nodded, and Dez heard that edge again, more pronounced this time. "A nightcrawler doesn't just have sex with a werewolf. She plugs into his mind and puts him into a kind of trance. A really effective nightcrawler can practically control him. The poor bugger thinks he's doing things he's not actually doing, but it's things he'd *like* to be doing. So everybody gets what they want. The werewolf gets to lose control, and that loss of control is what a sex demon feeds on. Win-win."

"So there's no...ripping and tearing?"

"A skilled nightcrawler can make him *believe* he's doing the ripping and tearing. Like a..."

"Like a waking dream."

"I was going to say 'like a nightmare,' but call it what you like."

No wonder that succubus girl was so mad, Dez realized, *she'd interrupted her feeding.*

"You seem to know Vito well," Dez observed.

"I take an interest in people who owe me money."

"So you don't think he murdered the girl they found in the trash bin?"

"He wouldn't be my first choice," Adrael shrugged.

"I thought you said he was a killer."

"He's a professional killer. That's not the same thing."

"Oh no?"

"I think once you get paid to do something, you rather balk at doing it for free," he said. "Your average prostitute would probably agree."

So maybe Hunter was right about Vito Luppi; it was *his* area of expertise. It was beginning to seem unlikely to Dez that Vito would have picked up a human at all if he preferred his sex supernatural. Perhaps some other stalwart were-citizen was not aware that soliciting the services of a succubus was a good way to deal with his darker urges.

"How much do you know about the Luppi family?" Adrael spoke placidly, but Dez sensed the hunger of a man tugging on a fishing line.

"I skimmed the file," she hedged. "I know they're all werewolves."

"Everyone knows that."

"Well, it's not my case, strictly speaking."

"Still, it must bother you that the family operates with such impunity," he mocked. "I'm appalled that you people do nothing about it."

"We can't just—" But her words caught in her throat. The practical limit of the Order's power was one of its most closely guarded secrets. They threw a long shadow over the lives of those they surveilled, but in truth, they were not numerous or powerful enough to go after everyone they wanted, so it was essential that its targets *believed* the Order could do anything at any time. Confessing to this man that they allowed a family like the Luppi to exist because they did not want to write a check they could not cash was dangerous.

But Dez suspected he already knew all that, and was just trying to see if she'd admit it.

Instead, she stared out the window at the oily ripple of river, in which the reflection of the chubby half-moon floated sideways like a boat that had capsized. It was a moody scene, gothic and grim; the ideal romantic study for brooding young ladies who dressed all in black. But to Desdemona it looked ominous, the vast swath of dark water reflecting the cold lights of a city that was a stranger to her. Concrete buildings, glass windows, construction scaffolding, and shopfronts flickered by like a zoetrope, a thousand advertisements flashing from every corner at the streams of people loitering in front of bars and restaurants and reeling drunkenly across gum-speckled streets. Gyro dives were wedged up next to cell-phone shops next to exotic-pet stores next to corporate coffee shops; thousands of compartments, each its own isolated pod, a zoo of animals dangerously protective of their territory. Anything could move into New York, rent a few hundred square feet, and exist unmolested as long as it liked.

To Dez, that thought was both terrifying and comforting.

"Do you think Vito will go back to his flat?" she asked.

"He's not that stupid."

"So where will he go?"

"Pardon me if I don't share my thoughts on that," Adrael smiled. "It will be inconvenient if you people find Mr. Luppi before he and I can transact our business."

Adrael maneuvered the car to the curb, and Dez realized they had arrived at her building. He then pulled the tube of petroleum jelly out of his pocket and held it out to her on his broad palm. "I'd start locking my desk drawers if I were you," he added.

Dez plucked the little plastic offering out of his hand, waiting for an "and" with some terrible request after it. Now that he knew her secret, he had could make her do anything he liked.

But he just flashed her another polite smile and unlocked the car.

"You'll forgive me if I don't get out and open your door. Bloodstains on the sidewalk might raise questions in this part of town."

Dez climbed out of the car, quietly shut the car door, and walked to her building in a daze. As she reached the building, she looked back—

the Bentley was still there. The windows were so heavily tinted that she couldn't see him, so she could only assume he was watching her as she slipped inside.

The empty lobby was peaceful, civilized, serene; surreal, after the night Dez had just experienced. She stepped calmly into the elevator, then to her apartment door, undid all the locks, stepped inside, and did the locks back up again. Only then did she collapse, sinking to the floor as her legs went to jelly.

Stupid stupid stupid. She should not have gone to Vito's home, or gotten into that man's car, or gotten *out* of that man's car in that alley... the chain of decisions that led to her getting attacked by a werewolf for the first time seemed unnervingly foolish now.

But whatever peril she'd faced from the Luppi cousins was nothing compared to what she was in for now that the man in grey knew the truth about her.

Dez was often able to forget that she wasn't completely human, but the awareness of it lingered in the recesses of her mind like something shoved into the back corner of a closet. She'd gotten used to all the tiny lies and adjustments that one made to give the impression of normalcy. Everyone lived with shame; figuring out how to store it was just part of becoming an adult. People were always checking lipstick in the mirror, tugging support garments back into place, blackening the grey in their hair with dye. Dez's own secret had seemed no more dire than that.

But in truth, particularly given her situation, her lie was a death sentence if it were ever discovered.

And now *he* knew everything, and she had no idea what that meant for her.

As the adrenaline in her body subsided, she shivered and her skin began to ache. It was how she'd heard people describe the flu, which she'd never experienced, but which was, she knew, exacerbated by the same things: stress, overwork. *And fear.*

She cast baleful looks around her new apartment, the bed not yet slept in, her books not even on the shelves. Maybe it was safer to leave town. *But where would she go?* Explaining to the Order why she needed a transfer less than a week after moving to New York was impossible. And no one, having joined the Order fully as she had done three months prior, could just quit. They could sometimes retire from age or infirmity, but otherwise, one was in service for life.

Maybe she could fake her own death. Or even *not* fake it. A familiar heavy curtain of anxiety dropped from the rafters of her mind where she'd stowed it for the move to New York, hoping it would stay tucked away forever. The direst of ideas flooded in like uninvited family members, finding their usual seats in the darkest corners of the theater of her soul. But all the complications came back to her too: what if the available methods would not suffice, and she'd have to live with some terrible mistake? Suicide, for those who were not sure of the limits of their mortality, was an even more frightening proposition than dying.

Dez opened her clenched fist and saw the Vaseline tube in her palm, the plastic warm and pliant from her gloved hand. It seemed asinine that such a little tube could be the sole barrier between herself and life-threatening exposure. She wondered if that man would have picked her out as different without witnessing her behavior with the entity in that dumpster; if there was anything else incriminating that he could see, or sense, or smell about her. She would meet him again, of course, and next time he would have some terrible request. The thought was chilling, but beneath that rumbled a tremor of transgressive heat that suggested she might be more upset if she *didn't* see him again.

But that was a ludicrous sentiment, and Dez banished it. One did not place one's tongue on an electrical socket, if one wanted to live.

She smelled something tangy in the air, and realized that it was *her*, drenched in sweat that reeked of fear. She needed to shower, preferably in scorching hot water. As she stood up, she left a wet red handprint on the floor—her left glove was soaked in that strange man's blood. And what was *he?* Images flashed unbidden to her mind: the line of his neck to his shoulder to his arm as he drove, the solid mass of his thigh as it bled out on the upholstery, the set of his jaw when he was vexed. But beautiful though he was, the man in grey was definitely some sort of criminal, and one that did business with other criminals.

Although, to be fair, Dez was technically a criminal herself, and now she had the bloody glove to prove it.

PART TWO

DATE WITH THE NIGHT

It would begin with circles under the eyes, evidence of a sleepless night. Friends would express concern, and offer sleeping pills or melatonin. *It was just a bad dream,* the victim would protest, promising to go to bed early. And he would then keep that promise, secretly hoping to have the "bad dream" again.

If he was lucky, he'd wake up refreshed—and disappointed—the next day. If he was unlucky, the coming days would find him wearier each morning until he collapsed or went mad from sheer fatigue. He might tell friends about someone he'd been seeing, someone intoxicating and near-otherworldly, but none of his friends would ever meet them. He might also confess that this devastating individual was only interested in sex, showing up at night and disappearing by the time he woke up. No traces of them were left—no panties, no fluids, no stray hairs, and if the man was really lucky, his lover might one day disappear for good. The man, broken-hearted, would recover, and eventually persuade himself it was a recurring dream. Later, he might catch a glimpse of his lover on the street, or in the reflection of a store window, but if the poor man caught up with his beloved, fervently clutching at a sleeve for recognition, he would be only rewarded with the glassy-eyed stare of one stranger to another, and would have to let go and watch them disappear into the crowd forever.

If he was lucky.

C H A P T E R 5

———

O V E R T H E M O O N

The Meatpacking District
Friday morning

Adrael sat in his windowsill in his underwear as the sunrise winked at him from between the skyscrapers. Using a diamond-tipped scalpel, he sliced open the half-healed gashes on his leg and, with a pair of tweezers, extricated the bits of cloth that had sealed into his wounds overnight from yesterday's torn pants. His flesh sometimes began to knit back together before he could undress, and he was constantly having to cut things out of himself: cloth, bullets, teeth.

Et cetera.

Adrael was not an obsessor: things came and went and passed through him like sand through splayed fingers. He could walk out of the space he barely bothered to refer to as "home" at any time and never go back without suffering more than a twinge of annoyance at having to replace all of his weapons. But though he didn't need to sleep every night, he'd intended to try, if only to stop thinking about that stupid Order woman for a while. Sleep refused him however, so he spent the remainder of the night beating up his lead-filled heavy bag and doing thousands of pull-ups. The endless reps synched his thoughts with his heartbeat, like rosary beads that built biceps, and such mindless training had gotten him through centuries of long nights.

There was no reason he should still be thinking about her. He'd already decided not to try to fuck her—the inevitable hurt feelings on her part would just cause complications, rendering her useless for his purposes. Yes, she was beautiful, but Adrael could fish equally lovely women out of the nightclub any day of the week, and any one of them would be less abrasive. He did find her appearance unusually pleasing, though he had no theoretical preference for dark hair vs. blond or dark eyes vs. light, and appreciated a whole spectrum of breast sizes with equal enthusiasm. But all night he'd been twitching like a coltish adolescent at the thought of the elegant limbs and plush curves he could imagine under all that black wool. There was something fetching in the quizzical way she held her head, and an archness to her somewhat thorny manner that made him want to catch her eye across the room, which surprised him. It was disorienting to meet a person he didn't feel like he'd already met a million times before, behind a million different faces.

But in his situation, it was dangerous to get attached to things. Or people.

Especially people.

Ironically, the Order would not have regarded her as a *person* at all. Adrael suspected she was *mostly* human—she looked and smelled the part—but to them, any trace of the extrahuman would have negated her from the start. Maybe she was a spy, an infiltrator from another shadowy organization like the Masons, or the Illuminati, or even the Catholic Church; placed there to destabilize the Order from within. But Adrael had had many dealings with the Order in its various incarnations, and thought it unlikely that someone with so little street sense would be able to maintain that big a lie under such pressure unless she was real Order and she meant it. All those books, all those talismans, and all that salt could only belong to a woman who distrusted the night. *Why* she worked for them Adrael didn't know; it had to be either idiocy or masochism. But as he dug into his own flesh with the tweezers, ignoring the searing pain as always, he reflected that he was hardly qualified to criticize her for either of those things.

———

Brooklyn

Massimo Luppi sat in his leather armchair, the chair no one else would dare sit in, and poured his whiskey from a crystal decanter with his name etched onto it in the five-bedroom house he had paid cash for, and wondered how he had lost control.

His black hair with its streak of silver was mussed from sleep interrupted by a ringing phone. What came through it, via the shrieking voice of his sister Ella, was that her son, his nephew Teo, had been deposited on her front porch that morning with a gaping bullet wound in his side that was festering him into a coma. *No, she had no idea how he got there—somebody rang the doorbell and drove off, leaving him. No, he wasn't conscious. No, she had no idea where Giulio and Vito were, though the three young men were usually inseparable.*

Massimo then called Vito's number, and had to listen to the phone ring and shift over to voicemail over and over again. Calling an unanswered phone is a special kind of hell, and even with his lack of imagination Massimo could concoct a million scenarios leading to Teo out cold on the porch and his son not answering his phone. He leaned into a headache, gazing impotently down at his own phone without any idea who to call next.

He looked inanely around his office—or rather his *study*, as his wife insisted on calling it, to justify how much the fucking carpet had cost. Not that Massimo didn't understand the expenditure; he was head of the family, he needed to keep up appearances, though he gave zero shits about carpets as long as there was no evidence on them. But he wondered if someone was beginning to think he'd gone soft, with his study and his whiskey and his decanter and his silk pajamas and his thousand-dollar rug. In that family, there was always someone ready to take your chair if you so much as got up to piss. And while he had many beefs all over town, that was the cost of doing business, in his business. Nobody would be stupid enough to shoot his nephew without warning. He'd told Ella not to call anyone else in the family about this; not until he discovered what was going on, and whose fault it was.

He wondered if his son was dead.

The headache mounted and he rubbed his temples as a familiar sensation erupted all over his body: the prickling of pores that accompanied his raised blood pressure, the hairs growing under his flesh forcing themselves outward as if arming him for battle.

"Mona," he called, "honey, can you make me a cup of tea, please?"

———

The Second Circle

Adrael and Rat walked into Lucius's office to find him sipping his morning coffee-and-cognac and poring over the grain of a 17th-century painted altarpiece leaning against the wall. In the center panel, a curvaceous Virgin Mary was being informed that she was about to be roundly pregnant with the son of God, hearing the good news from a nude, muscular angel whose rosy mouth hovered suggestively close to her blushing ear.

"Admit it. It's lovely," Lucius purred. The piece had just arrived from Palermo, where it had been sitting in a dusty church getting dustier with each passing century, and Lucius always loved a piece all the more if he'd rescued it from the Catholics.

"Beautiful," Adrael agreed, without bothering to look at it.

"Oh, pardon me, we didn't *all* grow up in a world where an axe splattered with the blood of our enemies was considered art."

"Speaking of which, I found Vito," Adrael informed him.

"And?" Lucius's gold eyes lit up.

"It's complicated." Adrael then perched on the back of the couch and relayed to Lucius what occurred the night before, though he fudged a few details and left out the Order girl entirely. "But the good news is that Vito's gone back to his old habits, so hopefully there won't be any more bodies left in trash bins," Adrael concluded.

"That's...something." Lucius looked slightly relieved, though still sour. "What's the bad news?"

"I shot one of the cousins. I forget their names. I didn't realize they were following him."

"Teo and Giulio Luppi," Rat piped up.

"You *didn't realize* they were there?" Lucius coughed. "You missed something? *You?*"

"It does happen occasionally," grimaced Adrael. "And it might be a problem that I shot him. Although I may have frightened Vito enough to make him pay you. I have LeMarcus and Trey watching their apartment in case they go back there, but they probably won't."

"They'll come back for their belongings eventually," Lucius put in.

"It's just their crash pad," Rat shook his head tartly. "They're Italians; I guarantee you they still live at home."

"We broke in and had a rootle around, but there's not much in there besides guns, cash, dirty sheets and a giant television," Adrael shrugged. "They're professional criminals *and* moonies. They know better than to leave laptops and receipts lying about."

"I hate Sardinians," Lucius groused. "They're just a bunch of sheep-licking land pirates. But I suppose the world has always been run by criminals."

"That's lucky for us," Adrael reminded him, nodding at the altarpiece that Lucius had purchased from an art dealer who looted graves on the side.

"Well, time is of the essence, boys," Lucius huffed. "Vito Luppi can't hold himself together forever. We need to find him before he melts down, or God forbid, confesses everything to his father."

"He would truly have to be desperate to do that." Adrael couldn't even contemplate having such a conversation with his own father; centuries later the thought still made him shudder.

"Or *they* might nab him," Rat added ominously.

Lucius's face darkened again, and Adrael bit his lip and stared at the ceiling. All three of them knew who "they" meant, but even Rat usually knew better than to mention the Order in Lucius's presence.

But, "Let's hope it doesn't come to that," was all Lucius said.

———

The Upper West Side

Dez had spent the night curled up on her bed with only the sharp corners of her books sliding into her back for company, flipping through a volume of German fairytales in which magical men who harassed helpless girls always got their comeuppance. When morning came, she rolled to her feet and pulled a fresh turtleneck over her head, weary in a way that could not be cured by sleep. She padded into the kitchen and stared into the old container of pad Thai as if reading tea leaves, but the coils of stiffening noodles had nothing to say about her future.

She smoothed her hair, finished getting dressed, coated her fingers in petroleum jelly, tugged on a clean pair of black gloves, stepped into her oxfords, and dragged her feet all the way to work, arriving at the museum before the streets were awake. The city was stiff as a corpse, the air clammy, the light grimly blue. Even the trees, blushing in the brisk fall air, looked like pale watercolors of themselves in the wan light. But where the rising sun hit them, they glowed. *He glowed, too.* That man's image must have seared itself into the interior of her eyelids, because she saw him whenever she closed her eyes. The arc of his eyebrow echoing the curve of his wide shoulder sloping down to a coiled bicep sent shocks down her legs and curled her toes. She'd never seen anything like his composition of sinew, stubble, and supple skin, his every motion smooth and molten as mercury.

And probably just as toxic.

As the sun came up, Dez went down, descending in the elevator to the chthonic labyrinth where her fellow saviors of humanity burrowed beneath the earth like worms. She dipped her fingers in the font in the entrance foyer, sure that the guards would notice the thin veneer of jelly that day, and sure they'd realize that she could see and smell and sense their presence better than any regular human. She caught them glancing at each other, and her heart fluttered with alarm, but then one of them let his eyes drift from her feet to to her waist and she realized she was just being ogled. In the hallways, she nodded to her colleagues and they nodded back, oblivious to her duplicity. Still, the panic rose, and by the time she got to her office and shut the door, she was sweating under her sweater. She built a wall of dusty files on her desk to hide behind, and buried herself in a haven of minutiae and marginalia.

She plowed away at her work for hours, the work soothing her shattered nerves. This is where she belonged. It had been temporary insanity that led her to stalk Vito Luppi at his home. She'd never been able to tolerate an unanswered question—leading to many rapped knuckles as a child—but she'd previously been sensible enough to limit her sleuthing to an armchair. There were thousands of killers in that city, and many of them could be found among that half-percent of the population with latent animal DNA. There was no rational reason to think that the first werewolf she came across in New York was the next Jack the Ripper. That was the type of error naive schoolgirls made, and if she was going to survive in the city she had to stop being one of those, immediately.

When she looked up from her work, it was afternoon. She hadn't eaten that day, but she wasn't hungry. She felt peaky, irritable, and fussy like an unchanged baby, uncomfortably aware of her clothes, the silk and cashmere brushing against her skin like sandpaper. So she headed home, moving self-consciously through the corridors as if they were an intestine and she a foreign irritant to be ejected.

"Going home already, Cross?" Hunter's handsome face smiled at her from his open office door, and a spike of heat shot through her veins.

"I had a long night."

"Did you have a date?"

"Not exactly."

"I don't know what this city's coming to if *you* don't have a date. But I hope you had fun, whatever it was."

Hunter's warm body under his rumpled shirt and the wry expression on his face were so reassuring that, for one wild moment, Dez fantasized about burying her head in his arms, confessing everything to him, and letting him whisk her away, like the pirate on the cover of a bodice ripper. Instead, she flashed a plastic smile and shrugged.

"We looked at everyone on that list you came up with," he informed her. "A lotta alibis, some of them pretty good, some of them iffy."

"You talked to all of them?"

"Talked to some, checked out the others."

"Even Vito Luppi?"

"I went by his place myself, just to oblige you."

"You did?" she swallowed, her mouth going dry.

"Yeah, but he wasn't home."

Did Hunter see her there with...? But Hunter seemed unperturbed. He must have arrived after they'd driven away. Still, mingled with the relief, Dez tasted the bitter tang of guilt at the back of her tongue.

"But that list is a pretty sketchy starting point for a case like this," he continued. "That girl could have gotten into anybody's car *after* she finished with the driver of the Porsche, which itself is only a theoretical car that a couple of our less-than-reliable citizens of the night *said* they saw."

"That's true." And after the revelations of the night before, Dez wasn't inclined to press the issue. What Vito Luppi wanted, that poor dead girl couldn't give him anyway, so the killer was probably some other anonymous monster that she was even more ill-equipped to deal with.

"I won't fault you for your enthusiasm," Hunter grinned. "You'll get over it."

"Hey, boss..." Reilly stuck his head out of the werewolf-room doorway.

"Is our guy done with the body yet?" Hunter asked. The Order's members embedded with the medical examiner's office made an effort to steal problematic corpses, but sometimes too much police scrutiny made it impossible, so they had to deal with them *in situ*.

"No..."

"Is it the new guy?" Hunter shook his head, annoyed. "These recruits need better train—"

"Sir, it's not that he didn't try to process her. It's something else. He said you have to go see it. He sounded rattled."

Hunter turned to Dez.

"Up for another field trip, Cross? If I end up with a file full of weird shit, it'll just end up on your desk."

"I really shouldn't," Dez replied, the way people decline cake before they take a slice anyway.

———

The morgue smelled of human waste, chilled flesh, and bleach, capped off with a whiff of microwaved breakfast burrito. Dez avoided brushing against the frigid metal tubes containing the bodies, because if any of them were vibrating with the residue of some dead person's bad feelings, she didn't want to share them. The medical examiner himself was upset.

He was a stolid, mid-career professional, lab-coated and bespectacled and balding, and he'd happily eat lunch next to a brain in a pan. But what he'd seen that morning unnerved him, and he hid it badly.

He pulled a refrigerated drawer out for Hunter and Dez, revealing the corpse of the dead girl from the alley—or what was left of it.

"What the hell is happening here?" he quavered.

He'd opened that drawer an hour ago to do his duty by the body, or more precisely, the Order's duty: the bodies of werewolf-murder victims, if they couldn't be absconded with, had to be carefully doctored to cover up evidence of their unusual cause of death. The medical examiners on the payroll would first take photos for the Order, and then "adjust" the damage to make it look like an ordinary murder by cutting away the bite and claw marks.

But on this body, there was not much left to adjust. Something had gone awry. The girl had been dead for less than two days and spent most of that time in a morgue freezer, so she should have been firm. The body on the slab was already falling apart, crumbling into a cheesy mass as if bathed in a corrosive agent that ate away the substance of her flesh, dissolving it into a quivering matrix of cells. It could have been the effect of some bizarre venom, an unknown toxin, or even stomach bile from some cryptid digesting her from the outside in. But Dez had a horrible inkling of what they were really looking at, though she'd never seen such a thing in person before.

"She's not human," Hunter informed the medical examiner, crinkling his nose at the honeycombing flesh. "That's the problem."

"Oh, God...should I have known that?" This medical examiner had joined the Order only a few months ago, after the body of a weeks-dead Haitian girl climbed off a gurney and attacked him with a scalpel. He survived the encounter, but his sanity almost did not. A colleague who was already in the Order assured him that the event truly had occurred, thus saving his mind, and then, from a sense of mission to protect others from the same experience, he joined the Order himself. But that day's unnerving job was proving just a bit much for a man who up until recently had been a lifelong skeptic.

"You'll get the hang of it," Hunter assured him. "Eventually you see everything once."

"But...but then, what is she?"

"I'd say she's—she *was*—a succubus," Dez said.

"I'd say you're right," Hunter agreed. "And this is a little unusual, even for us." The Order rarely found dead sex demons; such creatures were insidious masters of camouflage, almost impossible to spot in the general populace. If they died, wherever and whenever that occurred, their strange bodies rarely lasted long enough to examine. The invisible substance that held their cells together—the Order ironically called it *ichor*—rapidly evaporated into the air, leaving oil and carbon and something like wet sand that eventually dissolved into the ground. Dead, the girl had looked convincingly human at first, but in reality, her body was so ephemeral it had to borrow life from other people to hold itself together, and could not do so for long. This girl's flesh acidified as it rapidly broke down, eating away her clothes and bones, her blood evaporating to a peeling brown film. Even her hair and nails were dissolving, leaving flakes of bright red polish among the shells of the brittle, branch-like claws that used to be her hands.

So that's what they look like dead. Dez stared at the body on the slab with an uncomfortable prickle in her spine. She'd saved the life of one of these creatures the night before, believing her to be a human woman, and then felt a lurch of dismay when she found out otherwise. *This* body had looked human at first too, and Dez had been sickened by what had been done to her. Knowing now what this girl really was, Dez wondered if she would have bothered to save her, given the chance.

"So she's not even a...a person?" the medical examiner stammered.

"Officially, the Order would say no, she wasn't," Hunter shrugged, "though she might've disagreed."

"Do you think the killer knew what she was?" Dez asked.

"I think any moonie would have been able to tell. They pick these girls on purpose."

"Do they really?" Dez blinked as if she'd never heard such filth in her life.

"They really do," he assured her with a mischievous smile. "And your moonie has more vitality for the nightcrawler to—um—consume —than a human man, so it's a mutually beneficial arrangement. Too bad they can't just stick to fucking each other. It's a win-win for both parties."

"Well, not for this one," Dez pointed out.

"I've only seen two dead nightcrawlers in my life," said Hunter. "One was shot through the head—by us—and the other had a broken neck, not by us. So they die pretty easily, compared to vampires or moonies, but I think they usually have pretty good defenses for this kind of thing. Hell, maybe her John just didn't want to pay her. Back when I was a detective I saw people kill each other for stupider reasons. Anyway," he concluded, "now we have to take her with us."

"What? I can't just lose this body!" the medical examiner objected. "The case was on the front page! There's an active investigation! They're expecting a goddamned autopsy! I'm supposed to be taking DNA samples!"

"She doesn't have DNA, so either way, we'll have to swap the bodies," Hunter pointed out. "There must be somebody in one of these drawers who's a close fit. You'll have to recreate the damage on another corpse and switch the paperwork. Then you make sure *you* do the autopsy and *you* sign off on it. No one'll ask any questions after that, trust me."

"Recreate the damage? But I was told to *remove* all traces of the... werewolf attack..." he objected. The outré vocabulary of his new profession still sounded like a foreign language in his mouth.

"We still gotta approximate what was done," Hunter pointed out patiently. "Like, they'll notice if your corpse suddenly has all her organs again."

The medical examiner nodded nervously, sat down at his computer, and scrolled through his list of morgue residents for a body that would fit the bill; a body no one would miss, hopefully, although sometimes a grieving relative came looking later. But the New York City medical examiner's office was known for being careless (only partially due to the Order's frequent interference) which made it easier to get away with such things.

"How about her?" He tugged open another drawer to reveal the body of young, recently dead human woman with the same hair and body type as the dead succubus. "Another Jane Doe. Overdose."

"Perfect," Hunter nodded grimly.

This replacement dead girl was less pretty, with years of hard-living homelessness showing in her wrecked teeth and haggard cheeks, but at the end of the process about to ensue, most of her face would be gone anyway. The medical examiner looked from one dead girl to the other, his face blanching. The Order had trained him to adulterate bodies, but replicating werewolf violence was, for a first-timer, a daunting prospect.

"I'll call in the artists," said Hunter, sending a text to summon specialists from the Order's forensics team, professionals who spent as much time fabricating evidence as they did recovering it. "You might want to go home, Cross," he said with an apologetic smile. "This'll get a little gooey."

———

Dez managed to catch a taxi and headed home, gratefully inhaling the the stale cigarettes-and-armpits smell emanating from the driver to flush out the scent of antiseptic death that clung to the inside of her nose.

So the dead girl was a succubus too. Still, Vito couldn't be the only werewolf with a silver car who liked succubi prostitutes. The Porsche might just have been a red herring, as Hunter said. A whole rogue's gallery of other possible suspects—known killers—was hanging on the back wall of the anthrochimera room...

But something distinctive about the girl she'd met in the alley reminded Dez of the dead girl in the morgue. They didn't look much alike, but she couldn't shake the feeling that they were connected by more than their unusual nature, though the why of it eluded her. She couldn't share her suspicion with Hunter, though, because she couldn't tell him what she'd witnessed the night before with that awful man in grey; there was no way to spin an acceptable version of that story. And thanks to Dez, the second nightcrawler girl didn't die, so there was no second murder and no reason for Hunter to reconsider Vito as a suspect. As far as the Order knew, the girl dissolving in the morgue was just a lone unfortunate in a sea of similar—but unconnected—unfortunates.

But if the first girl's killer *was* Vito, that made it twice in three days he'd picked up working girls, which suggested a powerful compulsion. Even if he was spooked by the bloody theatrics of the previous night, the moon was waxing above their heads, so Dez bet he'd be at it again soon enough, with no reason for the Order to give him a second look unless he kept hunting in the same car. But given how he'd damaged it in that alley, that was unlikely. No, he was off the hook unless he left his driver's license wedged in the next dead girl's mouth.

With that cheering thought, Dez bolted into her apartment and did up all the locks. She let her bag drop to the floor and sighed as she kicked off her shoes and hung up her coat on the rack by the door, settling in for the night.

Only when she looked up did she see the flowers.

An explosion of twisting greenery sat on her desk, sinuous leaves artfully arranged in a gleaming crystal vase. The arrangement had no visible blossoms, just alien-like round pods rising from sturdy stalks, tight little balls of sepals giving a hint of their contents at the tips where the petals had already begun to tease apart, revealing tiny kisses of coral.

The man in grey—and he was, once again, wearing grey—was sitting in her desk chair now too, leaning back with his thick arms crossed in a manner unique to those who are waiting patiently but don't think they should have to. The setting sun flooded the apartment with dying amber light, making his skin and the hair on his arms glow russet gold.

Extreme physical attractiveness has a disruptive power, like extreme ugliness, or extreme size, turning the subject into a distracting freak. It elicits as much rage as desire, inspiring the urge to destroy it if it cannot be possessed. Like a loaded weapon, it derails thoughts by constantly drawing the eye, and one feels unsettled in its presence, as if a person that disproportionately desirable might be a portal through which the uncanny could creep into the everyday world. So Dez might be forgiven for being at a loss as to how to react to the man in her apartment, when her every animal mechanism switched on in his presence. She realized grimly that there was no keeping him out if he wanted to come in; the salt border, effective on non-corporeal entities, would not keep someone as solid as him out. Her door locks were securely still fastened when she came in, and while it was not unbelievable that he might break in and then lock them again, she suspected he preferred to cut the Gordian knot in such matters, and had simply come in through her locked fourth-story window. She was not surprised that he was there—given the leverage he had over her, it was inevitable that he'd try to use it—but she'd had no inkling he was in the room until she saw him. Dez had read theories about how such a trick was achieved, perhaps by dampening pheromones or emanating some subsonic vibration that tricked the ears into tricking the nose into tricking the eyes into believing that nothing was there.

"You could have rung first." She forced disdain into her voice, but instinctively noticed how his wide shoulders stretched the cloth of his shirt, his lethally trim waist arching like a ski slope to his meaty thighs.

"I could have." He turned to the books lying open on her desk, which he'd been flipping through. "Is this what you do all day? Track down Bigfoot?"

"My area of research extends to the fringes of our concerns," she coughed.

"Does that include UFOs?"

"And whatever tentacled thing is living in the East River, if you have any thoughts on that," she huffed, crossing her arms in annoyance.

"Oh, stay out of the East River," he advised her. "In general." He smiled then, and maybe it was a trick of the afternoon light, but the mask he perpetually wore seemed to slip and his face became oddly expressive, as if he were thinking a thousand things besides what came out of his mouth.

Dez kept her eyes on him as she slid suspiciously over to the flowers. No one had ever brought her flowers before, but she knew better than to be flattered by gifts from an extortionist.

"You have some unusual hobbies," he observed, glancing at the talismans on her walls. "Or you take your work home with you."

"It seems to come home with me anyway," she retorted, using caginess to fend off the vibration in her body.

"I just wanted something pretty to look at while I was here," Adrael said, nodding at the flowers. "You're not much of a decorator."

In truth, Adrael had selected the flowers with neurotic care; roses were too purposeful, gardenias not purposeful enough, tulips were inane, lilies were moribund. But these were peonies, the floral equivalent of brushing your hand across a woman's back at a cocktail party. And these peonies, yet unbloomed and wrapped so tight in their greenish-brown coats they might as well have been fists, reminded him particularly of her.

She plucked the address card out of the greenery. *"For Desdemona Cross"* was all it said in bold, slanted handwriting.

She glanced up and caught him with that keen look again, as if he were waiting to see how she liked them.

"It's just 'Dez,' " she sniffed, refusing to be pleased. "I've never cared for 'Desdemona.' "

"It is a bit theatrical for a fake name," he opined, leaning back languidly in her chair.

"What makes you think it's fake?"

"Oh please, you people all use fake names."

"We have enough people using aliases as it is," she conceded, peppery. "Those of us that *can* use our real names do so."

"So are you saying this driver's license is genuine?"

Dez blinked and found the chair in front of her suddenly vacant, and she turned to see him standing right behind her, holding her purse and peering at her New York State ID. She hadn't seen him get up, much less move across the room or pick up her bag.

"It's... not a driver's license," she gaped. "I never learned to drive."

"Don't get out much?"

"I live in Manhattan."

"You've lived in Manhattan for less than a week."

"England has trains." His preternatural mobility was jarring, and she backed away from him, pressing herself against the wall like a piece of extraneous furniture.

"And how is Cambridge these days?" he asked offhandedly, hanging her bag neatly back on the coat rack. "I haven't been there in years."

Dez was, at first, floored by his apparently omniscience in regards to her life, but quickly realized that he must have read the shipping labels on the flattened moving boxes stacked up against her back wall. She would have blacked out any identifying information with a marker before throwing them out, of course, but had not yet done so. It was obvious that she no longer had an expectation of privacy from *him* even in her own apartment.

"It's much the same as always," she ground out. "That's rather the point of Cambridge. But that depends what you mean by 'years.'"

He was aware that she was fishing, and didn't bite. Instead, he meandered around the ordered piles in the room, picking things up, peering at them, and placing them back down precisely where he'd found them; the mark of a practiced cat burglar. He dwarfed the already tiny apartment with his tall, commanding frame, both intrusive and courteous at the same time.

"Could you please not move everything?" she huffed as he picked up a worn paperback with *Hidden Mysteries of Atlantis* on the spine. He raised an eyebrow at her and flipped through it perfunctorily before deliberately putting it down in the wrong spot. "Do you think this is adorable?" she frowned.

Adrael paused and considered the question, and recalled, through the fog of years of forgetting to care how people felt, that perhaps intruding on someone's innermost sanctum was not terribly charming.

In response, he picked the book back up and put it back in the correct place, and nodded a curt apology.

"How's your leg?" she asked then. He was stalked around as smoothly as a tiger sniffing a deer, so there couldn't be much wrong with it anymore.

"It's fine. The trousers didn't make it."

"I'm sure you just pulled another pair of the same off the pile this morning."

True enough. Bloodstains could be removed from dark fabric, but nothing could be done about all the bullet holes, burns, and tears his clothes were subjected to any given week, so when Adrael found a garment that suited his purposes, he sometimes bought fifty at a time.

"Saves laundry. What's your excuse?"

"Why are you here?" she prodded, uncomfortably aware that her face was flushing as he circled towards her, his fingertips grazing the spines of her books as if feeling for weaknesses. The most flattering answer was the least likely. He did not strike her as vain, but he was definitely unburdened by false modesty and knew he didn't need to bring flowers to get a woman's attention.

"I'm here to apologize for last night," he shrugged. "I shouldn't have brought you with me to that mess."

"You didn't *make* me go," she reminded him diplomatically.

"Didn't I?" he asked, maddeningly. "Well, I didn't warn you that you might be shot at. That was wrong of me and I'm sorry." He sounded sincere—or rather, he sounded as if he knew he should sound sincere. He ended his maddening circumambulation and leaned forward onto the desk that was now the sole barrier between them, and Dez couldn't help noticing the rippling of his biceps as his arms flexed to hold his weight. It was, she imagined, just the way they'd look on either side of her head if she were lying down with him looming above her. His scent swirled through the air like a ribbon of heady perfume, radiating from the body heat in his armpits and elbows and the tunnel of air between his shirt and his chest. She stood with her fists balled awkwardly under her crossed arms; her palms had started to tingle, and if allowed to run free, she feared they'd rub themselves against his chest like a pair of cats. But a man who could manipulate people's senses could also make himself seem harmless, even appealing, to his quarry— sex demons and some vampires could do the same—and there was no reason to think that anything Dez was feeling was authentic.

"I thought you and I could transact a little business."

There it was. The inevitable ugliness.

"Like what?"

"It pains me to say it, but I haven't been able to find Vito Luppi since last night, and that's becoming an expensive problem. So I would be obliged if you would use the resources that are uniquely at your disposal to assist me."

Dez was not surprised that this was the nature of their transaction, but she still resented it.

"Obliged," she repeated tartly.

"Awfully," he averred.

"Well, unfortunately, I can't help you," Dez replied, perversely happy to disappoint him. "That address was all we had for him."

"Oh come now," he clucked, an ominous tinge of displeasure creeping into his voice. "You people keep files on everyone you find who doesn't fit your stringent definition of human—"

"Everyone who *isn't human*," Dez amended.

Adrael raised an eyebrow, waiting for her to acknowledge her hypocrisy, but she didn't.

"If Vito's in distress, he'll run right back to his family," he continued. "It's that sort of family. And I'm sure you have all *their* addresses, since you people are so thorough. Really, any information on the Luppi family in general would be—" here he paused, and it seemed to Dez it was for effect— "helpful. "

Helpful. Whenever Dez's mother wanted her to do something unpleasant, she used that word. But what this man was asking was impossible.

"I...I can't do that."

"I imagine that it will require some expenses on your part," he coughed delicately, "for which I'm happy to compensate you."

"Are you trying to bribe me?"

"I'm offering to make it worth your while."

"I'm not interested in your money." Dez twisted her lips with infinite scorn, as if the idea cheapened him even more than it did her.

"Nobody gets rich working for the Order," he chuckled, with a knowing tilt of the head that made Dez feel sordid.

"We don't care about money," she informed him.

"Cashmere sweaters don't grow on trees."

"I manage." Dez found the conversation distasteful; she had been raised to understand that it was in poor taste to discuss finances. Her mother was well-off, either from family inheritance or some other reason, and like all other matters in her mother's life, Dez never questioned it. Money was rarely relevant to Dez anyway; her upbringing had been confined to the all-inclusive system of boarding schools, she'd been raised wearing uniforms and more or less still did the same, she had no real life outside of work, and the Order paid her adequately for what she needed, which mostly just ran to rent, books, take-out, and the occasional morsel of black luxury wool.

"But no, I'm not trying to bribe you," he amended, leaning over the desk to peer into her face. "I hardly need to bribe you when I can blackmail you."

His expression remained placid despite the vibration rumbling through his body, growing in force by the minute. *What was this?* In all his long years, Adrael couldn't remember feeling this twitchy about a woman. He wanted to ascribe it to his hostility toward the black-clad hypocrites she worked for, but his intimate acquaintance with hostility in all its forms wouldn't allow it. This was uncomfortably different, and he found himself inching closer to her without exactly meaning to. "And it's not quite blackmail either, since you haven't *refused*," he continued. "And even you have to admit, we're not working at cross-purposes. Even if I were to—hypothetically—*kill* him, I'd be doing the Order a favor. 'Let them murder each other,' isn't that what you people say?"

"It's true, we wouldn't care if you killed him," Dez admitted. "And despite what you say, I think he *would* have killed that nightcrawler in his car if we hadn't stopped him."

"Why's that?"

"Because we discovered today that the dead girl we found was *also* a succubus."

He stared at her with one eyebrow cocked like an accent mark over his laser-blue eyes, and Dez wondered if that was because he thought she was an imbecile, or because there was something to the idea.

"Did the body start..."

"Yes."

"You've never seen that before?"

"In person...no," she confessed quietly, but they were standing so close together he could have heard her even if she'd whispered. "And you said that if a succubus is good at what she does, she can take on a were-wolf as a lover with no problem," Dez continued, blushing as the word 'lover' escaped her mouth. "But what if she's *not* good at what she does?"

"Oh, then she shouldn't take on werewolves at all, or they'll be scraping her off the street."

"Or scooping her out of the trash," Dez swallowed.

He blinked at her and cocked his head skeptically.

"Since when do you people care about dead nightcrawlers?"

"We care about dead bodies when the police find them and the newspapers start writing headlines about 'a new Jack the Ripper' and they fall apart in the morgue like the one I saw today. It's a lot of faff to keep that kind of thing quiet."

"Well, if the Order thinks he did it, why don't you catch him? I hardly need to fight with you over Vito Luppi. If you people want him, I'll leave you to it."

"I thought he owed you money."

"The money itself is meaningless," he shrugged. "It's the principle. If you people make him suffer, that saves me the bother."

"Well...the Order doesn't think he did it, strictly speaking," she hemmed. "*I* do. My superiors, like you, believe that Vito Luppi is too much of a gentleman criminal to tear up prostitutes."

"And you can't tell them why you believe otherwise, because you can't explain what you got up to last night with me?" That sounded more suggestive than Adrael intended, and with surprise he realized his heart was *racing*. Even when that bullet had blown a hole in his thigh his pulse had barely risen, so it was odd to feel his body winding itself up to full alertness for no reason other than this troublesome woman's presence.

"That is the quandary," she nodded.

"So you want me to sort him for you."

"As you said, I think our agendas are aligned in that regard."

Adrael had to smile at that. He'd gone there expecting to have to figuratively twist her arm, but she was playing him right back. He wouldn't have thought the prissy little bookworm had it in her.

"And you do care about dead nightcrawlers, for some reason," he added.

Care was a strong word, Dez thought; those girls were predators—the Order considered them to be even less valid as "people" than werewolves—but Dez still felt viscerally sick at the idea of them getting shredded to pieces and thrown in the trash.

"I...suppose I do."

"That's just because you don't know any," he retorted coldly. Still, it was obvious to both of them that a deal had been struck. This man obviously possessed no conscience and understood the value of a knife plunged silently into someone's ribs in the dark, which was entirely to Dez's purpose, and if he could hold his nose and deal with someone in Order, she could do likewise. "So you'll give me what I need to find Vito?" Adrael concluded.

"I'll give you what we have," Dez replied, feeling sick at her betrayal. *But in for a penny...* "But it might take me a few days to get it."

"I'll be back in a week."

"And if I don't have it, you'll break my kneecaps?"

"Just one kneecap," he assured her. "I find that people are more helpful if they have something left to lose."

Helpful. There was that word again. Dez eyed him, unsure if he was joking, willing to bet that he wasn't.

"Fine."

"And after that, leave him to me," he added scoldishly. "No more skulking around at night in dark alleys. It's not exactly a job for the—ahem—research department. You're no use to me in pieces."

"If they find out what I'm doing, there won't be any pieces left anyway," she muttered tartly.

He blinked at her, his lips twisted pensively.

"Look, you seem intelligent, Desdemona," he said then. "Being intelligent seems to be your personal brand, really. So surely you know that every day you show up to work you take your very life in your little jelly-smeared hands."

"Life is full of risk," she deflected, trying not to look into his eyes and failing.

"And even though you dress like a Catholic schoolgirl, you don't strike me as a 'believer.' All this paraphernalia aside." He rolled his eyes at her walls of talismans.

"I don't have to *believe* anything. I only deal with things I have evidence for." Though Dez had grown up surrounded by high church

Anglicanism, she had nothing but distaste for religion, including the one she subscribed to simply by showing up to work every day. But on a practical level, the Order's religion was, at least, one of science, of objective truth and hard reality, and all questions regarding its more esoteric aspects were thankfully above her pay grade.

"You're a member of a death cult," he prodded.

"It's not—"

" *'If it doesn't die, it's not alive,'* " he taunted her contemptuously. "Isn't that what you people say?"

"There are more terrible things in the world than the Order," she snapped. "And the Order goes after those things. Things that hurt people, even kill people. And worse."

"And you're afraid of those things."

"Of course I am. Have you seen what's out there?"

He blinked at her as if she'd said something naive.

"I *am* what's out there." He said it matter-of-factly, without a hint of reassuring boastfulness, and a flash of jet-black fire crossed his face. "And I'd be willing to believe you're as big a coward as you claim if you hadn't jumped out of my car to save a prostitute from a werewolf," he added. "Bloody hell, that sounds even more idiotic when I say it out loud."

They stood frozen like two snakes waiting for the chance to strike. There was only a barrier of fragile wood between them now, something Adrael could smash into splinters if he wanted. His brain told him to break whatever spell had them bound there, but he couldn't force his body to act, knowing he could have her pressed against that wall in half a second, and his lips pressed on hers half a second after that. He could almost feel the contours of her sleek limbs in his hands, and his jaw clenched as he impulsively raked her body with his eyes like a common Lothario.

Dez should have found him repellant. He was obviously immoral, intrusive, manipulative, and, according to his own admission, plausibly some kind of supervillain. But the way his eyes scanned her with raw male compulsion made her heart throb and her thighs clench, even more so when he didn't touch her, though she could feel his body vibrating with the desire to do just that.

"Well, we ruined Vito's evening last night," Dez swallowed. "So perhaps he'll try to find another date tonight. Where does one go to find prostitutes in this city?"

"Chelsea. Battery Park. Nolita." Adrael feigned breeziness as he made himself step back out of the vertiginous snare of her proximity. "Wherever you find a steady supply of tourists and a bodega that serves French fries."

"French fries?"

"Prostitutes love French fries," he said. "This is a fact."

"You know a lot about prostitutes."

"I work nights and I drive around a lot."

"So you're either a drug dealer or a chauffeur."

"Sharp," he grinned. "You'll be an Investigator in no time."

"Who says I want to be an Investigator?"

"There is only one other career you could be practicing in an alley at midnight, and frankly, you don't have the wardrobe for it."

Dez scowled cattishly at him.

"I do love French fries though."

"Then I should have brought those instead of flowers," he retorted. He continued to back away from her, but his body was humming in a new, unsettling way, so he made himself climb back onto the window ledge, clumsily knocking more salt onto the floor as he did so.

"You could use the door," she pointed out.

"I could."

"And if we're going to..."—Dez started to say "*do business*," but the phrase disgusted her—"If we're going to help each other," she amended, "I should know your name."

"Yes," he agreed. "You should." Then, with the strangely hectic look of a man escaping a jail cell, he hopped out the window, and was gone.

Dez sank absentmindedly down into the chair he'd just vacated, but found herself enveloped in a cloud of his dizzying warmth and scent, so she stood up like a shot, frustrated at her own weakness. Her face was flushed but her body was ice-cold, so she marched over to the window, slammed it shut, and locked it. But she still shivered, as if her body, deprived of the heat source it craved, refused to generate heat for itself in protest. And those stupid flowers kept catching her eye, threatening to burst like little bombs. She wanted to throw them out, but that command her body would not obey. So she sat down on the edge of her bed and turned her back to them, hoping that by the time she turned around they'd be wilted.

Chapter 6

Red Tape

Saturday

Massimo Giacomo "Mr. October" Luppi......See file.
  Giulio Giovanni "Little Gucci" Luppi......See file.
  Teodoro Lanzo "The Tube" Vitale......See file.
Over and over, and over, *"See file."* For every Luppi family member in the database, the address field contained the same maddening redirection. The Order gave researchers and Investigators clandestine access to government databases as well, so Dez had already checked the FBI and NYPD databases from her laptop at home and found extortion, bank robbery, credit card fraud, shipping container theft, and even art theft connected to the Luppi. But the slippery bastards had managed to avoid tipping off the authorities to any of their residential addresses. Dez thought members of the Mafia were generally easier to find than this, with homes and businesses and strip clubs that the cops would occasionally raid. But the Luppi were *not* human, and thus had additional reasons to be cagey about where they lived.

So the only way for her to get the information she needed was to look at the Order's physical file, which was in Hunter's office. Each file had a backup stored in the deep archives; only high-level administrators like Brother Justin had access to those. Another city's Order office would have at least a partial copy of the Luppi file, but the case was active so Hunter would be alerted if Dez requested it. There was nothing for it; Dez would have to sneak into his office and copy what she could by hand.

She slunk back to her office, tired and agitated. The air grated against her skin, as if the dust motes were particles of glass. She tried to turn her mind to her other cases: *the "Bloody Mary" incident in Queens was a hoax, the "Sasquatch" in the ramble was something carnivorous and possibly invisible*...but her mind kept returning to the girl they'd left in the alley. She was, of course, as much a predator as Vito, but her skinny arms and pink nipples stiffening in the cold night air made Dez feel sorry for her as she flipped listlessly through the leather-bound volume on her desk, landing on a 17th-century woodcut of a woman lying on top of a naked man, her long braided hair wrapped around his throat like a noose, his face expressing agonized bliss. The caption read *"Attack of the Succubus."*

It was perhaps a shame Dez had interfered that night—the girl might have killed Vito herself and saved everyone a lot of trouble. But then, the man in grey had wanted to acquire Vito in one piece, which contributed to the fiasco. If he wanted someone dead, Dez reflected, he'd likely handle it more efficiently. It was remarkable that his leg healed so fast; a werewolf would take days to scab over a gaping gunshot wound, and while an average vampire body repaired itself faster than that, he was no vampire. Meanwhile, Vito was probably already curb-crawling in some new car, and it was only a matter of time until he found what he was looking for, as the moon swelled inexorably toward full.

Hunter's office was on her way out, she considered, as she packed her bags and left for the day, *so she had one more chance to...*but no, when she approached his door, she found him standing in the doorway talking to a woman-shaped creature wearing a shapeless black garment that did her backside no favors. Dez tried to walk by without comment, but Hunter stopped her.

"Hold on Cross, you got a minute? This is Beatrix Kragin. Kragin, Desdemona Cross. Our newest researcher."

"Welcome," the woman said, lips pursed like a coin slot. She peered at Dez from behind her unflattering glasses, the two of them like a pair of cats sniffing each other in an alley. She was a boney creature with a pointy chin whose uncared-for skin made her look older than her thirty-five years, sandy hair pulled severely back and twisted into an unforgiving bun. It was not a beautiful face, but with a little eyeliner and a few hair products, Dez thought, she could be a nice-looking woman. She was dressed like a house draped in mourning, but Dez traced the contours of the body hidden among the awkward folds, and allowed there was probably some potential under there, despite an endomorphic frame and unimpressive breasts.

"Cross has stepped in for Pascal, and inherited all his cases," Hunter explained. "Kragin's our sex demon expert."

"Don't call me Kragin, please, this isn't a fraternity," she chided him. "It's just 'Beatrix.' And the word is 'somniophage.' "

Somniophage, i.e. "dream-eater." In the Order, extranatural entities were mostly classified by what they fed on, since that was, to them, the most pertinent feature. Dez usually found the pedantic terminology comforting, a wall of sanitizing academia against the howling night, but from Beatrix it sounded unpleasantly institutional.

Hunter chuckled, and by the flush in Beatrix's cheeks, Dez suspected the schoolmarmish disapproval was a sham. Her sensitive nose discerned a ripe, repressed femininity under those virtuous garments, the warmish aura of which was being wafted in Hunter's direction.

"I asked Beatrix to look at the corpse when it came in to make sure I was right about what it was," said Hunter. "There wasn't much left by then, though."

"There was enough, and you were," Beatrix informed him with a smile like a proud tutor.

"Beatrix basically *is* the somniophage division," Hunter explained, his tone of fond mockery layered with frank professional admiration. "She's the only Investigator dedicated to them full-time."

"We only need one person?" Dez queried.

"Well, somniophages are so elusive it's impossible to really track them," shrugged Hunter. "And most people who are attacked by somniophages never even know it."

"But if you're volunteering, I'd love the assistance," Beatrix smiled acidly. "There's far more in the records about them than people think, I assure you."

A healthy young man might expire in his apartment of a heart attack one night after a nightclub, and cocaine would be listed his cause of death. A young woman would suddenly develop cancer and waste away. Loved ones would send thoughts and prayers, but only God—or asbestos in the walls—would be available to blame. The Order could only follow breadcrumbs left by shameful penitents confessing to their priests, police reports of hysterical citizens claiming to have been attacked in their bedrooms by invisible assailants, or the occasional "virgin" birth of unnatural offspring. By the time they even heard about a sex demon case, the perpetrator was usually long gone.

"It's there, hidden between the lines," Beatrix averred.

"If you squint," Hunter smiled.

"At the moment, most of what we do is just keep tabs on the victims," sighed Beatrix. "And I am barely adequate to that task, though I *am* also a victimologist."

It was, Dez thought, ironic that this tightly wound woman was the authority on supernatural ravishment in the city of New York, but it did make sense that she was a victimologist. Order victimologists performed the precarious art of interrogating the terrified, dredging the facts from their spasmodic memories to determine the true nature of the incident that had traumatized them. Most people who were assaulted by something otherworldly had no real idea what had done the assaulting, conflating their attackers with ghosts and demons and anything else they may have seen on television that week. It took a particular type of personality to sit with damaged people and unwind fiction-like fact from actual fiction. Conflating the issue further, the common terms "incubus" and "succubus" were frequently slapped on anything that crept up in the night or killed with beauty, including ghosts, mermaids, ordinary human rapists, and, of course, vampires. But true sex demons did not suck blood; their method of feeding was more elegant, and unlike vampirism, could not be acquired.

"Cross here was wondering how often sex demons get hot and heavy with moonies." Hunter asked the question with all the seriousness of a seasoned detective, but Dez noted a mirthful glint in his eye.

"Somniophages, please, Alan," Beatrix chided him fondly. "And we think it happens fairly often. It seems to be a mutually beneficial relationship for everyone involved. If only they'd stick to each other."

"Why don't they?" Dez tried not to sound too interested.

"I think even werewolves don't like feeling used," Hunter smirked.

"And how often are somniophages the victims of anthrochimeras?" Dez asked punctiliously; if Beatrix wanted to play the jargon game, Dez would humor her.

"Victims?" Beatrix scoffed. "I don't know if I'd put it that way…if somniophages ever become 'collateral damage' of this mutually beneficial predation, we don't find them, but their bodies dissolve so quickly I suppose we just can't know. In my five years here, most of the dead ones I've seen, we killed ourselves."

Dez sensed the tang of vendetta underneath Beatrix's contempt, and conjectured that it was a somniophage that had brought her to the Order in the first place. Order members did not necessarily work on the same phenomena that they had experienced—for some it was too upsetting—but others found a calling in their past trauma. That also explained Beatrix's aversion to the term "sex demons"; she looked as if she'd rather melt into the floor than admit she'd ever had a naughty fantasy.

"You know, I estimate there could be as many as one per thousand people in the five boroughs," Beatrix continued. "That's a dense population by any standard, but...well, this isn't exactly a God-fearing city is it?"

"And they all hang out on the same street corners," added Hunter.

"Actually no, Alan, they don't," Beatrix corrected him with an indulgent smile. "Somniophages are territorial. They avoid each other. You may find one on any given street corner, but not two. And we keep our eyes on the city's population of working girls, but it's hard to tell the Unnaturals from the humans until after they've attacked someone. Unfortunately we can't bring them in on pure suspicion unless we're sure there won't be consequences."

"Pity," said Dez. She had no doubt that Beatrix would have loved to send Order agents to the streets to spray every prostitute in town with thoughtwater, but they'd just get sprayed back with the mace those girls kept tucked in their bras.

"We have to deal with the same parameters," Hunter pointed out. "That's why we can't bring in Vito Luppi like Cross here wanted us to do a couple days ago."

"Luppi? Oh, you mean those Mafioso moonies?"

"One of them showed up on a list based on the description of the car we got from a witness," said Hunter. "But...you know."

Beatrix shook her head and dropped her voice.

"There's *caution*, and there's...well... *letting them get away with it.*"

"In my old job we'd put Vito Luppi away in a second," whispered Hunter. "The guy commits larceny like most people get haircuts. But Solomon would rather have me chasing down taxpaying citizens for being a little too hairy." He spoke breezily enough, but Dez heard frustration in his voice. "And the thing is, the Luppi do behave themselves. Yeah, they're violent, and they get into a little bit of everything: nightclubs, smuggling, gambling, plus they have typical Mafia-family power struggles, which means the usual routine of bodies buried in the woods. But the key is, they don't do it *as moonies*. Controlling their condition is a thing with them, they're proud of it. They even drink this tea—it's supposed to be a secret family recipe, but I think it's mostly marijuana —and I guess it helps keep the urges down. And you know the tune around here: as long as they kill people with guns instead of their teeth, they're on the back burner."

"But even if they don't rave around like lycanthropic lunatics, what they *are* still gives them an advantage," hissed Beatrix. "They're faster, they're stronger, and they can get shot more times without dying. That means those they rob and shoot and kill are victims of their Unnatural advantage. That should be reason enough for us deal with them decisively, whatever the fallout. That advantage offends our entire purpose here." Hunter inclined his head in agreement, and Dez wondered if Beatrix's vehemence on the subject had been amplified a tad in order to elicit his approval.

Glancing past Hunter's fluffy head, she saw the Luppi file on the shelf, taunting her with its proximity. But Beatrix and Hunter clearly had no plans to leave that doorway.

"I have to go, but it was nice to meet you," Dez said to Beatrix with a disingenuous smile.

"Likewise. And if anything bizarre crosses my desk, I may come see you," Beatrix promised.

CHAPTER 7

INFERNO

Two Bridges, Manhattan
   Saturday night

The underside of the Manhattan Bridge was captive to endless construction, a grimy snarl of corrugated metal and orange netting along which Dez minced with her chin buried in the collar of her coat, her shoes increasingly splattered with riparian sludge. The air was a miasma of gasoline and salt and urban residue, coating everything like a bad taste on a tongue. It was a badly lit spot, and even the homeless people bedding down under nearby tarps did not notice her as she quietly passed.

But other things were also hanging out under the bridge, things that only people like Dez could see. Myriad eyes gleamed out of the odorous darkness like subterranean stars, their owners snuffling invisibly among the debris or clinging with spindly legs to the concrete above, waiting for prey, just like everyone else out there that night. A row of long-lashed entrepreneurs lined the construction fencing, leaning out at the passing traffic like sea anemones tracking fish. This was not a glamorous place to be a streetwalker, but it was efficient—customers could pull up next to the merchandise and a deal would be struck with no parked cars to get in the way.

Dez meant to go home, but once again had not done so, instead making her way back to the spot where she'd watched Vito pick up that second girl. The girls out there all looked perfectly human that night, shivering in the frost-nipped air, scowling out of habit, laughing out of nerves. But, as Beatrix said, sex demons were territorial, and Dez suspected that, like any predator, the girl in the red shorts would be hard-pressed to give up her hunting ground once she'd claimed it, even if it meant risking running into Vito Luppi again.

So when Dez saw the distinctive blonde a few yards away sitting on a concrete traffic barrier, she was not surprised. The girl sat apart from the others, scanning the cars for the type of date she wanted, looking bored as she sucked on a vape pen.

Yes, this girl was a succubus. Dez sensed the invisible haze around the contours of the girl's body, both magnetic and repellant. She edged closer, sidling along the edge of the concrete barriers, until the girl noticed her.

"Oh...shit." The girl stood abruptly and backed away.

"Wait, wait," said Dez, "I'm not here to—"

"No, no, you just fuck right off. I don't wanna get involved in no gangster shit," the girl protested. "I don't even know that dude's name, so whatever you wanted with him, it's got nothin' to do with me."

"I'm not here to...to *fight* you," Dez assured her, although the idea that anyone would consider her a threat seemed ridiculous.

"What do you want then?" the girl hissed. "I'm trying to do business here."

What did she want? Dez was unsure how to justify her presence there, even to herself.

"I just want to know about your...'client'...from the other night," fumbled Dez. "The moonie. You met him here, yes?"

"He picked me up here."

The girl glared at her skeptically, giving away nothing, but Dez had come too far not to wade in a little deeper.

"And did he know what you...are? When he picked you?"

"What I *am*?" The girl's face went briefly blank, a picture of confused denial. But then, as she stared hard at Dez, she relaxed into a cynical smirk, like one criminal recognizing another. "Yeah. Course. That's what he was out here lookin' for."

Dez could not quite decode her knowing look, so she tried to ignore it, hoping she'd imagined it.

"And you knew what *he* was when you got in the car?" she pressed.

"Oh yeah. He was already all furry." The girl laughed at that, a bubbly giggle that forgot to be street-hardened and came off disarmingly girlish. "Did your friend with the gun catch up with him yet?"

"Not yet," hedged Dez, trying to make that sound like intentional strategy rather than failure. "That's why I'm here. You saved my life the other night."

"It wasn't personal," the succubus said awkwardly, embarrassed to be thanked for something. "You just didn't look like you knew what the fuck you were doing."

"Yes, well," Dez coughed. "I'm just here to warn you to be careful."

"To warn *me*." The girl raised her eyebrows, the e-cig drooping from her mouth. "About what?"

"That moonie might come looking for you again."

"Oh shit, I hope he does. He had a wad on him. Two, actually." She snickered like a kitten saying dirty words.

"But he almost killed you."

"Man, it was all fine until you guys pissed him off. Moonies are alright if you don't freak 'em out. He just wanted a little release. I coulda handled him." She blew a ring of pineapple-scented smoke into the air. Just talking to her felt like trespass; she was so audaciously nonchalant, as if those minuscule red shorts were just a standard work uniform. Up close, the potent aura around the girl grated against Dez's skin, but there was a quality to her—maybe her unrepentant bravado—that Dez still found difficult to really dislike.

"A girl was killed on Tuesday night," Dez informed her. "She was also one of...you."

The girl paused mid-vape, her eyes wide.

"I didn't hear that. I don't really do news."

"That bit wasn't on the news," Dez retorted drily.

"How'd you know she wasn't human?"

"I'm...in a position to know." Dez left it at that, and the girl, with the street sense of someone who realizes it's better to know less rather than more sometimes, didn't press it.

"You sure *that* moonie did it?" she asked instead. "He didn't seem like a weirdo, and I know from weirdos. He got all puffed up—" she made her fingers into claws and hunched her shoulders— "but they all do that."

"I'm reasonably sure," said Dez, sounding rather the opposite.

"Maybe she didn't have the skills to handle him," the girl shrugged heartlessly. "Not everybody can. I specialize." She dropped her voice, and continued, "I even used to work at the Second Circle. But I quit. I got sick of answering to a pimp, and that's the biggest pimp in town."

"What's the Second Circle?"

"The nightclub," the girl blinked at Dez as if she were an utter idiot. "In the Meatpacking." Dez shook her head, lost. "Not your scene, huh?" the girl snickered. "Well, it ain't a secret. You can Google it." She scanned Dez from lace-up shoes to high collar, narrowing her eyes. "You know, you pass really well. At first I thought you were human. But now I see it."

"See what?" Dez swallowed.

"Whatever. None of my business."

"Anyway..." Dez backed away, unnerved. "Watch out for yourself."

"*You* watch out for *you*," the girl smirked. "It wasn't *me* they were shooting at in that alley."

Dez wondered absurdly if there was something she could do for that wretched creature—give her money, or perhaps a bus ticket somewhere. But, she reminded herself, that girl wasn't like the others on the block, standing on a corner with her tits half out because she had no better options. That little blonde was there to hunt, just like the spiders suspended on microfilaments from the underside of the bridge, and her willowy limbs and girlish lashes were merely part of the trap. So Dez nodded her goodbye and turned to leave.

"Oh, what was the name of that club again?" asked Dez.

"The Second Circle. Why, you gonna go?"

"Just curious."

"Be careful if you do," the girl warned her. "I'm safer out here than you'll ever be in there."

———

The Meatpacking District
Still Saturday night

New York is not an easy city to impress. It has seen everything a million times and done it all better, and no matter what novelty is presented, it is already over it. Paris may be more sophisticated, London more urbane, and New Orleans more debauched, but no city can beat New York when it comes to being cool.

Still, in a city where almost nothing is new or avant-garde enough to raise even one carefully tweezed eyebrow, the Second Circle nightclub managed, on any given night, to raise both.

The club announced itself with a tiny steel square branded with a minimalist "2" in the center of a pair of concentric circles. The oblique hieroglyph hung on the wall next to a heavy metal door cut into the bottom floor of a seven-story industrial building that looked like a disused warehouse. It could be felt, heard, and even smelled from the outside, as music pulsed through the ground, and a whiff of air impregnated with glitter and sweat puffed out whenever the door was opened, heavy with the pungent scent of the human mating dance. The Meat-packing District was full of such clubs in buildings camouflaged by nondescript shabbiness, waiting for their clientele with the streetwise nonchalance of drug dealers, their existence marked only by lines of twitchy, impatient party animals snaking down the sidewalks. The Second Circle's line curved around the block, a barbed wire rope keeping the crowd in single file. Every once in a while, someone would bump the wire and get zapped lightly with electricity, but nobody left the queue.

There. She'd seen it. She could go home. The driving curiosity that had brought Dez there was dissolving under the scornful glances of the street's pouting revelers. She could imagine for herself what went on inside, and could think of no reason not to turn around and leave.

Until she saw the silver Porsche.

It was parked on the street, right in the open outside the club, as if it had nothing to hide and had not been party to a recent murder. *Was that Vito's car?* There was no smashed door. She circled around to the back to check the tags. *Not Vito's plate. But he was a gangster, maybe he'd gotten the body fixed and swapped out the...* Then she glanced across the street, and saw another silver Porsche. And further down, a silver Ferrari. And in the adjacent pay lot, two more silver sports cars of differing models. In fact, now that she looked, the whole block was peppered with silver sports cars. Perhaps, Dez realized, the Second Circle was the very place that the one percent of moonies who bought expensive cars went on a Saturday night. And car or not, one of those moonies could very well be Vito Luppi.

The line at the Second Circle looked much like the crowd outside any other club—the men with their blazer collars popped up, the women with cleavage pushed up to their necks and artfully unwashed hair. Dez stepped meekly into to the back of the queue, and for the next half hour she scooted inch by inch toward the door, surrounded by a mist of aftershave, body spray, and pheromones. Everyone there would claim they'd come there to dance, to blow off steam, or to party with friends. But with their goods fanned out for display like charcuterie in a meat case, soft mounds pushed up for emphasis and cologne lacing their sweaty crevices, it was obvious why they were really there. A few people looked Dez over with mild curiosity, but she kept her eyes down and they quickly lost interest in the one woman there showing no skin, although a few eyed her like she might be there to arrest someone for drugs. Dez squirmed; it seemed worse somehow that she was covered from head to toe in black, as if her ostentatious modesty suggested she had something more than usually perverted to hide.

As she neared the front of the line she noticed that the bouncer was randomly refusing people entry according to no criteria Dez could divine. Surely, dressed as she was, Dez wouldn't make the cut, so she considered leaving, but either she would have had to step over the barbed wire (unappealing, possibly painful) or push her way through the line behind her (likely to result in confrontation). So she sighed and resigned herself to the brief—but inevitable—embarrassment of rejection. But when she reached the front of the line, the bouncer cast his eyes over her only briefly and then held out his hand.

"I.D.," he said. She presented it, he glanced perfunctorily in the direction of the printed birthday, and produced a rubber stamp, tapping it on a pad of blacklight ink.

"Hand."

She tugged one black glove off and presented her bare hand to him. *Tsssssss.* The stamp burned like acid, searing the club's "2" symbol into her skin.

"Ow!" She yanked her hand away as the bouncer noted the burn and accordingly added her to one of the two counters on his belt. Dez then realized that the ink on the stamp was made with thoughtwater, to keep track of the humans vs. the not-so-humans, and he had one counter for each. Her heart sank at what she'd so stupidly given away, but no one was paying attention to her, wanting her only to step out of the way so they could move ahead. The bouncer waved her in without asking her for a cover charge, so with a flutter of trepidation, Dez stepped through the red velvet curtains into the Second Circle.

The curtains opened to a raised platform overlooking a vast dance floor full of bodies grinding to throbbing music, surrounded by platforms on which people were performing suspiciously authentic-looking sex acts. A packed-to-capacity crowd undulated through its lounges and grown-up play areas, and red velvet drapes wound around gold-flecked columns carved with giant orgasmic faces. A dramatic bar anchored the back of the room, its two-story wall of gleaming bottles glittering like cave crystals, and everywhere were flashing lights, flashing tits, flashing teeth, and flashing credit cards as things, acts, and people were bought and paid for. In the strobing orange light, the room appeared to be on fire, like a nightclub in Hell.

Blowing on the back of her burning hand, Dez approached the coat check booth, where a young woman with skin like milk took her coat with the ostentatious care of a nurse cradling a newborn. Dez had considered keeping her gloves on, but that felt so outlandish given where she was that she slipped them off and shoved them into the coat pocket. The woman's fingers were heavy as lead as they brushed Dez's shoulder, ice-cold even through the wool of her sweater dress, and Dez shivered as she realized she'd just handed her things to a vampire.

"Phone," the woman requested politely.

Dez hesitated—that seemed so unwise, but everyone around her was handing over devices to be slipped into locked cubbyhole lockers behind the coat check, receiving a numbered key on a red ribbon in exchange. The show of security didn't reassure Dez much—there was no reason the staff couldn't access those cubbies from the other side of the wall— but she reasoned that the system was unlikely to work for long if customers routinely got robbed. Dez was nobody important, there was no reason that anyone would be interested in what was on *her* phone, so trusting the safety of her inconsequence, she handed it over and took the numbered key. Another bouncer with a distinctly wolfish grin waved a metal detector and then an RF detector at her to make sure she was entirely free of recording devices; the Second Circle, much like the Order, apparently treasured its privacy. Then, with her locker key dangling from its red velvet ribbon around her wrist, Dez stepped down from the entrance platform to the dance floor below.

The Second Circle was not obviously a sex club. It had no swings, no black-leather harnesses or gimps on leashes (not on the main floor, anyway). But Dez watched a man half-falling out of his suit grope a chubby Asian woman covered in gold body paint, her squishy curves making him gnash his teeth, while nearby a gorgeous androgene sat among a pile of giggling Japanese businessmen sliding their hands in and out of whatever flesh they could reach. There was a quality to real, animal sex that couldn't be replaced with the Broadway version—a fervent jiggle to the thigh, a gritted jaw, the uneven rhythmic thrust of someone trying to hit their magic spot with someone else's, and Dez suspected that more actual copulating went on at the Second Circle than at any other establishment ostensibly meant for the purpose. She pushed further into the club, dodging through fashionable urbanites swirling complicated cocktails and laughing too loud with traces of colored powder on their noses. The club's scents, sights, and sounds plucked at her like a thousand soft fingers, and an ache surged through her system as the smell of a thousand mingled pheromones hit her brain like a drug. The bass pounded through the floor and into the air, the walls bouncing it back at her ears like surf hitting a beach, naked flesh flashing from every corner. All the surfaces and furniture were suggestive, offering soft things where you wanted soft things and hard things where you wanted hard things. Shafts and nipple-like knobs were everywhere, designed to plug into the most primal part of the human limbic system and activate the urge to rut. Curly smoke drifted through the air, adulterated with something that made everyone want to touch everybody else.

Looking around, she then realized that while the majority of patrons were human, none of the employees were. There were neckbiters behind the bar, werewolves at the door, and everywhere, *everywhere*, incubi and succubi. She had no trouble spotting them, and was obviously getting better at picking out Unnaturals by sight, though any Order infiltrators —there had to be a few—would have been able to identify many of the moonies and neckbiters. But no human would have had any real idea to what degree they were surrounded by a swarming cloud of sex demons. Many were attractive, but some were fat, or alarmingly skinny; others flat-out bizarre-looking: something for everyone. Dez could never have imagined so many sex demons in one place, leaning on the railings, draped on the sofas, go-go dancing on platforms. She'd come across references in her reading to sex demons working together in ersatz clans or brothels, and perhaps, like zoo animals, they were so well-fed at the Second Circle that they'd learned to tolerate one other. After all, they worked there purely to fire the engines of the clientele so they could consume the amorous energy they released, which they had to do anyway, to survive.

And at the Second Circle, they also got paid for it.

There was also plenty of non-human clientele, many of them high rollers and even some recognizable faces: a pro athlete, a city politician, someone who looked like Middle Eastern royalty. Many were moonies— doubtless the owners of the flashy silver cars outside—and some were already losing their self-control. Dez noticed it first in their faces, as their features twitched in feral ecstasy. She scanned the VIP areas for Vito's striking features, but the club's deep shadows and incessantly flashing lights made it difficult to see anyone clearly.

A raucous cheer rose up from the crowd and a thousand faces tilted upwards as an elevated platform covered in fluffy white cushions descended from the ceiling in a swirling nimbus of dry ice vapor. Atop it slithered a writhing ball of naked people, their tongues, fingers and lips finding each other's counterparts in manic joy, and in the center of all that flesh sat a golden god. He smiled beatifically at his guests as they strained to rub against his body, draped in a cream-colored silk shirt that fell open over his exposed chest and matching silk trousers that would have been effeminate were it not for the generous, turgid cock outlined by the shiny fabric. Maybe it was the club lighting, but he looked like he was radiating light from his blond hair to the soles of his exquisite bare feet, like a priest of the libido presiding over a baptism-by-bodily-fluids. Dez recognized an apex predator when she saw one; that divine man was the very embodiment of human lust, his very skin soaking up the air around him as it became drenched with the pheromones from the howling crowd below. His gleaming eyes looked down to strafe the dance floor and, in their passage across the throng, landed on Dez.

And paused.

Their eyes locked and the rest of the club seemed to disappear, the pounding of the bass becoming a full-body symphony playing only for her, the air seizing up as if the room itself was gasping. His eyes were as gold as ancient coins, his steady gaze asking questions and answering them simultaneously, exploding her shell of anonymity as if her inner-most secrets had been laid bare and presented for his consumption. She had no idea how long she stood there, but she eventually became aware of a buzzing in her head, like a distant car alarm that one eventually real-izes is one's own vehicle. Something in his beguiling eyes struck a false note in the music in her head, and it jolted her out of her stupor.

Her feet unlocked beneath her, and she turned and ducked into the crowd, heading blindly for the shelter of one of the lounges where figures climbed over each other on plush velvet furniture that looked like mounds of flesh. Tripping over someone's feet, she fell into a man's lap; an attractive man, as it turned out, meaty and mature in his late forties, his hair a sculpted wave. He smelled like expensive aftershave and even more expensive gin, his breath itself a potent cocktail.

"Hi there," the man purred, gripping her arms as she slid awkwardly across his lap, her chest sliding under his chin. The urgency of his need hit her like the scent of blood to a shark, and her jaw clenched as their skin seemed to fuse, growing increasingly warm, almost painfully so. Her brain told her to pull away, but her fingers rebelled, tightening their grip on his thighs instead. Then without consciously meaning to, she slipped her hand inside his shirt, exploring his collarbone with tenuous fingers, and he moaned in her ear as her other hand slid into the pomaded waves of his hair.

"Excuse me, sweetie." Long-nailed fingers grabbed Dez's arm, yanking her to her feet with alarming strength. It was a woman—no, not a woman, a succubus—with a big Cleopatra nose, coarse black hair, and a sensual overbite lined in perfect maroon lipstick. At first glance she struck Dez as ugly, but she radiated sex like rancid perfume. A surge of instinctual rage welled up inside Dez and an unwise comment bubbled up in her throat, but before it erupted, another hand grabbed her other arm: a rougher one this time.

"Come on, honey," said a bruiser of a bouncer in a black leather suit jacket and gold neck chains, whose clammy skin betrayed him as another vampire. His grip was like stone, and Dez didn't resist as he dragged her away—not towards the exit, but to the back of the club and up a set of metal stairs, at the top of which was a closed door plated in gleaming gold.

"Where are you taking me?" she objected as he pulled her up the steps.

"Mr. Dark wants to meet you," he informed her.

———

The bouncer pushed Dez through the gold door and shoved it shut behind her. As the latch clicked shut, the pulsing beat of the club abruptly disappeared, leaving her in fuzzy silence. She found herself in a luxurious chamber bedecked with white fur and gold filigree that looked somewhat like an office, kitted out for surveillance with a long white desk lined in white computer monitors all facing away from her. A wall of one-way glass overlooked the dance club, and from up there, the colored lights sparkling around the gyrating crowd looked like holographic fireflies. The floor thrummed under her feet, but the glass blocked the music, and the sticky, silent air was threaded instead with sweet strains of piano: Satie, *Gnossienne No. 1,* soothing and melancholy.

She took a hesitant step forward between the two ancient marble satyrs that flanked the door, and her heels sank into the pillowy white carpet. Priceless art was everywhere, some of it mounted, other pieces leaning on the walls and floor as if reclining, millions of dollars in *objets* tumbled into one place like an overbooked party. Copulating figures writhed on canvases that had the unmistakable patina of age, broken marble torsos twisted in frozen ecstasy, and a life-size bronze Indian *yakshi* danced silently in place with one leg perpetually raised to display the folds of her intricately carved vagina.

A vast painting dominated the back wall behind the computer monitors—a work in the style of the medieval fabulist Hieronymus Bosch. It was a masterpiece of grotesquerie; the nine levels of Hell expressed in a series of concentric rings, in the center of which was the devil himself rutting with a bevy of chimerical snake-people wearing then-stylish, now-comical hats.

And Dez, drawn into the vortex of the composition, recognized the face of the painted demon in the middle as that of the golden-haired man from the nightclub platform.

"I don't suppose you've read Dante," purred a liquid voice behind her.

She turned around and saw that very man now leaning on one of the two marble satyrs, posing like a third statue himself. He was so beautiful he looked almost imaginary, unsettlingly ageless, with the face of a young angel and the smile of an ancient jackal. His features bordered on delicate, his mouth like a lush flower, but with a man's jaw and strong brow framed by a mane of wavy blond locks. A gleaming snifter of cognac dangled tenuously from his fingertips.

"A bit, at school," she lied, unsure if she should admit how many times she'd read Dante; he was, after all, an Order apostate, and his work figured prominently into their worldview.

"You do look like a girl with an expensive education." His every word dripped in her ears like honey falling on warm skin. "Sometimes I think the name of my club is lost on every one of those sticky plebs that walks through the door," he sighed. "Would you like a drink?" Dez managed to shake her head no. "Give a wink if you change your mind," he said as he took a sip from his own glass and regarded her with gleaming amber eyes.

Dez wondered what universe she'd stepped into to be once again confronted with another disturbingly attractive man, the second in as many days. In his sylphlike, ethereal way, he was even more beautiful than that creature in grey, and Dez could not pull her eyes from him, though the sensation was less like admiration and more as if he were a loaded gun pointed at her head.

"Won't you sit down?" He gestured at his white, fur-draped sofa.

Dez considered it, but worried that it wouldn't let her get up again.

"The furniture may be a little gauche, but it's not carnivorous," he remarked, and she startled. *Could he read her mind?* She tried not to form any more thoughts, and failed.

"This is your first time in my establishment, I think," he said then.

"Yes," Dez swallowed.

"What's your name?"

"Des...irée." *Alright, she'd managed half a lie. Good enough.*

"Sure it is. Are you new in town, *Desirée?*"

He said her name like he didn't buy it, but was willing to play along.

"I just moved here."

"From where?"

"England." Dez felt unhinged, as if air in that room contained a truth drug, but whatever was affecting her was coming directly from him. She squirmed under his probing gaze, unsure if he was going to kill her or seduce her or eat her. He moved like a flickering candle, his yellow-gold hair reflecting the light, all sharply peaked features and lean, sculpted limbs, and he smelled spicy and gingery, like sticking her nose into a rose made of the most appealing human flesh.

"Well, what do you think of my collection, Desirée?"

Dez looked around again and noticed there was a theme to the art in that room: In every corner, satyrs clutched unwilling maidens and winged demons loomed over nude victims with amorous intent, all rendered in marble or canvas by every artist she could name. She spotted a Botticelli depicting a minotaur clutching a young Grecian virgin, next to which some lissome Waterhouse water nymphs seduced a dazed man into their drowned bed.

"You don't see many old masters in nightclubs."

"Old masters," he grinned. "So you took art history at school, too." He smiled knowingly, and Dez felt she was utterly transparent to him. He gestured at a canvas hanging on the wall above the bar depicting a plush naked woman wrestling coyly with a giant white waterbird, her blond hair entwined intimately in the webbing of its feet. "You'll know this story then."

"*Leda and the Swan.*" Dez's education had been a thorough one, her young mind fully saturated in art, literature, and the classics, so she knew every story in that room by heart, and did not need to be told what the theme of the collection was. *Salomé, Sleeping Beauty, the ladies who bothered the Buddha*...supernatural ravishment was this man's obsession, and the whole history of demonic rape in art was accumulated on his walls, doubtless at enormous cost. *Sinuous sirens, draped dryads, coquettish Japanese fox-spirits*—the collection was comprehensive and international in scope, and Dez could only guess what that nipple-filled Giotto on the wall was worth on the black market. "I'm not sure about this Europa and the bull painting, though," she couldn't help pointing out, pedantic to a fault. "In that story the bull was...well... just a bull."

"Maybe," he allowed, "but that's fun too, in its own way."

Dez, squirming under his gaze, turned to find something, anything, to look at on an opposite wall and found herself facing a row of paintings strikingly different from all the others. They were hung vaguely chronologically, Byzantine ikons giving way to medieval panels; Renaissance canvases followed by neoclassical compositions; ultimately finishing up with modern canvases, each of them depicting the same theme: the jarringly Christian image of the Virgin Mary being anointed by an angel. To Dez, the sedate religious pieces seemed rather out of place among that celebration of sin.

"Then why these?"

"Ah, well, these are special." He sidled up behind her. "You like them?"

"Not especially," Dez coughed; then, realizing that sounded rather rude, she amended: "They're very different."

"Are they? Look again. I know what the usual interpretation of the theme is, of course, but what if that 'angel' is doing something other than tapping poor Mary with his finger, hmm? Look at him climbing in her window like some heavenly Romeo. Imagine if the painter *hadn't* given him a halo and wings." His face momentarily looked like a cruel carnival mask before snapping back to beatific. "Consider: how *else* does a virgin become pregnant?"

How indeed. Dez largely disdained purely religious art, but now she saw those pious images with new eyes. It was subtle, but it was there, in the hungry expressions on the faces of the angels, and the way the Virgin Mary's cheek arched upwards to "hear the good news." And, ironically, the Order agreed with this bizarrely beautiful blond man on the point of virgin births. Such phenomena smacked of supernatural "interference," which the Order did not tolerate in any form, including that of Jesus.

The Order had, after all, killed him twice.

"What an exotic face you've got." Dark assessed her then as if she were a painting he might buy. "You have such delicate bones, but that generous peach of an ass you're carrying behind you is a nice surprise. There's something vaguely Eastern in the eyes too, makes you look a bit, oh, Russian, maybe... you see that over there; a little color leftover from those gloriously rapey Mongols."

"My mother is half-Japanese," Dez blurted out, blushing at the bald description of her body parts and wondering why she was telling him the truth. His voice seemed to reach into her head and pull out answers.

"What fun. Ethnic ambiguity is *so* useful. Anybody can believe almost anything they like about you. Is your mother...human?"

The question hit Dez like a slap—not only did he see she was different, but she was *so* other-than-human...

"Yes," Dez confessed.

"Totally human?"

"Yes." Dez was defensive on that point, as if he was trying to catch her in a lie.

"So your father..."

"I don't know who my father is."

"Well, of course not."

"I don't..." she began, but there were so many things she "didn't" about that situation that she left the thought unfinished.

"Well, it worked out beautifully," he beamed. "I love cocktails." And then, without warning, Dark abruptly slid his hand into Dez's, entwining their fingers and pulling her hand up to his face to peer at the angry "2" burned into her skin. She felt a tickle as his skin leeched at hers, exchanging energy for a softly electric vibration that, had she been fully human, would have been orgasmic. But Dez sensed a coldness too; the hollow black hole of his need nipping at the part of her that was mortal with the ravenous hunger of dark matter. She was enthralled, like a deer about to be eaten, terrified but yearning for the sweet release of death.

He looked her in the eyes then, an unreadable expression on his face.

"I don't wish to be ungracious, Desirée," Dark purred. "You're lovely, and normally I'd say you're perfectly welcome to drink at the bar." He dropped her hand and crossed the room away from her, as if finished with her. "But in an establishment like this one, we just can't allow freelancers."

"Freelancers?"

"We've established that you're not stupid, so it's too late to play that card," he said, refilling his drink. "I realize that it seems unfair, since every moonie and neckbiter in town comes in here whenever they like. But given our business model, the only succubi I want to see in my club are the ones on staff. Do you understand?"

Yes. She understood. She didn't want to, but she did. Because despite all her efforts, despite a lifetime of careful control, what she was, what she *really* was, was clearly obvious to this man and his gleaming gold eyes.

See: Nightcrawler; sex demon; somniophage.

Succubus.

"Earth to Desirée," she heard him say then, and she wondered how long she'd been standing there, staring with unseeing eyes at a Pre-Raphaelite painting of a dreamy-eyed woman in flimsy medieval garb dragging a dazed-looking knight off his horse.

"I'm not a..." But the objection died with nothing to feed it.

"I have to say, you do pass remarkably well for human. Even I wasn't sure when I first saw you downstairs, and it wasn't until you walked through that door and I got a look up-close..." he circled around her. "You were...born?" He asked it with a grimace, as if the idea was nauseating.

"I...I think so," Dez stammered, although she was unsure of even that. She had always assumed so, but...

"Do you eat food?" he pressed, interrupting her stream of panicked thoughts. "Not for fun, but because you *have* to?"

"Yes..." She got hungry at regular intervals, though not always daily, and it had never occurred to her to try starving herself to see if she would die. But at times something inside her asserted itself, and in that state, food couldn't fulfill her needs, and a raging appetite for alternate sustenance took over.

"God, you even *smell* human. You would have fooled ninety-nine-percent of the jokers down there if you were careful. Lilith only figured it out when she saw what you were doing to that man in the lounge."

"Lilith?"

See: Lilith, the "Queen of Hell" in Abrahamic folklore. The ultimate temptress, Adam's original wife, fallen long before hapless Eve and her unfortunate fruit-picking expedition. *See: the myths of Babylon, the "Night Hag," and the "Lamia."*

See also: Succubus.

"I know, it's such a cliché." He rolled his eyes. "I told the Girls downstairs that only one of them could call herself 'Lilith' at work, otherwise they'd all do it and confuse the clients. Our Lilith is a bit territorial, but it's her job to make sure there are no poachers on my dance floor."

"I wasn't..." she stammered. "I tripped."

He stared at her, considering. Dez didn't know *what* he was considering, but she saw conflict flashing across his exquisite face.

"You know, this kind of thing—" he drew a circle with his glass in the air at her— "*your* kind of thing—could go over really well here. That authentically "human" feeling is...I mean, even I can't..." he shook his head philosophically, as if he'd long ago accepted his own limitations with grace. "Some people would pay for that," he concluded.

"Are you...offering me a job?" Dez gaped in dismay, as if the very suggestion sullied her beyond repair.

"We handle all the billing and you're paid a fair percentage of your rate. But trust me, that rate will be about a hundred times what you can get on your own, so you'll find the math works in your favor. All cash, no taxes."

"But I'm not a..." she tried again to deny it, but the words wouldn't come out. "I'm not a professional," she managed instead.

"No one is until they get paid, darling." He smiled brightly at her and it hit Dez like a burst of sunshine: dazzling and a little too hot. "Sleep on it. If you sleep. Which I doubt. But if you do come back..." he scanned his eyes over her outfit. "We like the sausage out of its casing here, so maybe lose the clerical look, unless you want to specialize in nun fetishists. Which, trust me, you do not." He plucked a business card out of a gold stand on the desk and handed it to her: it was a simple black card, heavy stock with a texture unsettlingly like human skin, and blank except for the club's "2" logo embossed on the front, barely readable and tastefully obscure. "Bring that if you change your mind," he told her. "But until then, my dear, I'm afraid I'll have to tell you to get lost."

Dez wondered if that meant she was allowed to leave. She took an experimental step towards the door, and when he didn't stop her, she took another, and another, out the door and down the stairs and through the club, barely remembering to retrieve her items at the coat check, and then she found herself back outside in the street, gulping in the cold, garbage-scented air.

She stood on the sidewalk outside the club's front door, the world so much more alive than it had been a half-hour ago. A drunken laugh hit her ears like a thunderclap, a heady cloud of stench wafting up from a sewer grate choked her, and the traffic headlights whooshing by looked like comets barely missing her in their race across the city. Her body could still feel the bass notes of the club thudding through the ground, shuddering up her body from the soles of her feet, rattling what was left of her self-possession. She should not have gone in there. The scent of sex had shredded her willpower to pieces, and the thing inside her that she considered her worst enemy was now clawing at the seams to get out.

A passing cabbie spotted her and, miraculously, made her for a fare, pulling up right beside her. Dez stared at the yellow taxi for a dazed moment before snapping to reality enough to clutch at the door and fling herself inside.

"Where you headed?" the cabdriver asked.

He was a youngish man, Iranian judging by the name on his taxi ID, and not unattractive, though this cologne-drenched, manicured type of man was not usually for her. But repelled as she was by the cloud of Drakkar Noir that filled the car, when she looked at him, rather than a man, she saw a man-shaped mass of pulsing heat. Her mind generated a map of erogenous zones laid over his skin like a subway map, rushing from his ears down his neck and emerging out the cuffs of his shirt to his wrists and palms. Even the cloying cologne was laced with the tang of his skin, a scent that hit her lungs like nicotine to a smoker, flooding her with terrible exhilaration.

She briefly considered getting out of the cab, but it was a long way home and in that state she could not fathom navigating all those people on the subway. So she mumbled her address, sat as far back in her seat as she could, and rolled down her window to let the chilly air flow over her face. The smells of street and steel and sewer almost washed away the scent of the driver, but not quite, and Dez sat on her hands to quell the jitter shuddering beneath her skin as the part of her she constantly worked to repress fought to assert itself. She should never have looked at it—if you don't look at something, you can plausibly ignore it, she'd known that since childhood—but now that she had, it refused to be dismissed. She tasted her own blood on the inside of her lip where she'd bitten it out of tension, the pain mingling with the buzzing agony of her flesh healing over with unnatural speed. At a stoplight, she glanced forward and caught the eyes of the driver staring at her in the rearview mirror. She managed to pull her own eyes back to the buildings whooshing by until, with a lurch, the cab pulled up to her block and she tugged on the door handle to jump out. But it was locked.

"Um...hey...what's your name?" The driver turned around in his seat to look at Dez directly. It was a forward thing to say, but he spoke hesitantly, as if compelled, with the wide-eyed expression of prey rather than predator. And something he saw in Dez's eyes made him quietly turn back around and unlock the doors for her. She jumped out and trotted toward her building without looking back, forgetting to pay him. Before she even reached her door he'd backed into the street, almost hitting another car in his haste, and Dez realized that both of them had had a narrow escape. She rushed into her building and up the elevator, and when she was safe behind her locked door, she sank to the floor, and burst into hot, angry tears.

———

The Second Circle
  2 a.m.

The club's books were stuffed to the gills, and Lucius's secondary books were even fuller; Mr. Goldberg had brought in the deputy mayor, and after a free sample the zesty politician had opened an account of his own. But it had been a stressful week, and Lucius was peckish, so he left the city fathers downstairs in the capable hands of the staff and, having spotted a pair of ecstasy-addled coeds on the dance floor pretending to be lesbians, he invited them and a bottle of century-old cognac upstairs for a snack.

If the Sistine Chapel ran a brothel, it would have looked like Lucius's penthouse apartment. Perched on the top floor of the building that housed his pleasure palace, everything was creamy velvet, suede, and gold, and the art was even more over-the-top than the stuff he kept downstairs in the office.

"That's pretty," the blonde said as she rolled over her friend to get a better look at a bedside painting of nymphs locking ivory thighs around a centaur. The brunette was already asleep; she was the languid, smokey type; sensuous, but low on energy, an appetizer at best. But the blonde was enthusiastically horny, and Lucius could have fed off her tenacious desire for days.

"It's Italian," Lucius yawned. *And four-hundred years old,* he added silently, lying back on his satin sheets and resting his head on the brunette's lush double Ds. He smiled up at the mirror above his bed, admiring the way the lighting framed his flawless naked body. *Who really needed art,* he mused, *when you had mirrors?* But his mind drifted back to the girl he'd met that night who probably did appreciate art, and whose name was definitely *not* Desirée. He'd met plenty of hybrids over the course of his long life; the couplings of humans with sex demons often resulted in offspring, though of those that survived gestation, many were born insane, or died quickly thereafter. The more demon there was to them, the less human they were, and when someone looked as human as that girl did, the nonhuman part was generally so diluted that the effects barely registered. A certain hectic energy, perhaps, or a potent come-hither gaze was usually all that was left, but she had none of those things either, and if one wasn't looking pointedly at her, she blended into the crowd like any mortal. She'd gotten past the boys at the door, who were supposed to shut out other sex demons, but he could hardly blame them since he had almost missed her too. Indeed, when he'd spotted her on the dance floor, he had no idea what he was looking at, and had only been sure when he touched her and tasted a delicious human vitality followed by the hungry draw of a sex demon tugging fruitlessly at him for something he didn't have. The pull was so strong that, had he not known better, he would have sworn she was as much a sex demon as he was. If her mother was fully human, her father must have been fully otherwise to have such a strong effect. But if so, she should not have been able to pass for human, not to someone like himself. True cambions—human/sex demon mixtures— were rare, their origins still a mystery to Lucius himself, since sex demons were generally sterile, but those he'd met before had been far more obvious.

He couldn't make up his mind if he wanted to see her again or not, but he supposed that if hiding what she was was so important to her, she would hardly have the cheek to set foot in the club now that she'd been exposed. It was a shame, though; that authenticity couldn't be faked. Not only would she smell human to the clients, but she'd feel human. Lucius idly stroked the female thigh that was nearest to him and wondered how much more money that was worth, per hour.

The elevator doors dinged open and revealed Adrael, freshly returned from wherever he'd been that night doing Lucius's dirty business; finding Vito was a priority, of course, but there were always other matters that needed tending via Adrael's satin-soft, razor-sharp touch. Adrael was as coolly composed as usual, but Lucius smelled adrenaline on him, the scent of it seeping into his clothes from the crevices in his body, with a tinge of iron from someone else's blood in the creases of his knuckles.

The blonde's eyes grew round with hope as she saw Adrael, wondering if he was going to join them, but Lucius patted her back down to the bed.

"Did you take care of it?" Lucius asked Adrael.

"I did."

"Wonderful." Lucius nestled his head back on the brunette's soft breasts, glad he now had one less business rival to worry about, at the very least.

Adrael placed a small black-lacquer box on a side table next to Lucius's blond head, containing the bloody little token that Lucius had requested. It wasn't meant as proof—Adrael could always be trusted to perform, or be truthful about having failed. But Lucius, an avid collector, did like the occasional memento, even if it was just a fleshy chunk of some medium-time gangster with whom he'd condescended to fight over something as squalid as professional territory.

"Busy night?" Adrael asked.

"Our new friend with the city showed up," Lucius told him. "He seems enthusiastic."

Lucius didn't mention the cambion girl; not with a human audience, even if they were just a pair of stupid, drug-addled fluffers. Not that Adrael would care; as little as he regarded sex demons, even if that girl ended up working there, he'd never even bother to learn her name.

"Wonderful. Goodnight, then." Adrael stepped back into the elevator, heading home to take a shower to wash off the residue of fear-sweat smeared on him from the unfortunate individual he'd dealt with that night on Lucius's behalf. It had been an ugly—if routine—little act of violence, but was a welcome distraction from his racing mind. He'd spent most of the evening lurking in a walk-in closet, waiting for the man to come home, and thus had ample time alone in the dark to chew over the fact that, according to Dez, the dead hooker from that dumpster was also a nightcrawler. That added an interesting wrinkle to the problem at hand, but Adrael could hardly tell Lucius about it without explaining how he'd found out. Lucius tended to be excitable when it came to the Order, so Adrael saw no upside to informing him that he was on speaking terms with one of their members. His golden head might explode.

Speaking terms, indeed. When that Order girl wasn't directly in Adrael's consciousness, she hovered like trace perfume at the edges of his brain, coloring every thought with her presence, and he'd been grateful for the opportunity to do something that night to replace the scent that lingered in his brain with the iron reek of someone else's blood; a smell that he didn't necessarily *like*, but that made him feel centered, which was as close as Adrael ever got to feeling at home.

INTERLUDE

SUCCUBUS

Desdemona had been an ordinary-looking baby. Yes, she sometimes cried hysterically for hours, a problem ascribed to colic or teething, but only when she became old enough to point at things did her unusual nature become obvious. She would gesture vehemently at nothing, or have babbling conversations with no one in baby language, waiting for a silent response and then answering the empty air.

And subsequent developments proved that no matter how innocently she drank milk or ate baby food, Desdemona wasn't totally human.

The trouble started at boarding school. St. Agatha's was an all-girls institution with chaperones and high walls, its students circling like goldfish waiting for cats to come pick them out one by one. That only made the boys at St. Dominic's down the road more creative, but the virtue of the girls of St. Agatha's was strictly guarded; head counts were taken throughout the night, and no one was out after curfew. Reading material was monitored for content, swearing was banned, and any talk of sex was done in hushed tones behind closed doors. Dez, who rarely participated in those adolescent debriefings, acquired a reputation as a prude, and the other girls made a game of trying to shock her.

But anything those girls did during stolen afternoons in village corners was child's play compared to what Dez did in her sleep to boys she didn't even know.

As a child, she had never once been sick; not a cough, not a cold, not a stomach-ache. But puberty crept up on her like a mugger in the night, beginning with the vivid dreams starring boys that Dez had only met once or twice, peeking over the school walls or in the village shops. Those dreams at first involved nothing more than long stares and hand-holding, but she woke up sweaty and shaking, wondering if she were going mad. When she was thirteen, she started looking pale one day, so the nuns sent her to bed with a hot-water bottle and an Advil, explaining that it was her first 'time of the month.' Dez obediently took to her bed, but soon discovered that her body didn't work like the other girls'. She learned to fake it though, complaining monthly of water retention, moodiness, and cramps she didn't have, even throwing away unused menstrual pads to keep up appearances. No doctor ever saw anything unusual about her, and so no one told her what was happening to her, or what she was, and she was afraid to ask. She thought of herself as human, just human with caveats; special problems, maybe, or a condition.

Meanwhile, her own unique cycles continued, in secret. She began to go without sleep for weeks at a time, and because the girls at St. Agatha's had private bedrooms, teenage Dez could keep herself awake at night by reading with a pen light under the covers. But if she went too long without sleep, she would grow cold and tired and, for the first time in her life, unwell. Despite herself, she would then nod off and slip into another upsetting dream featuring the boys from down the road who she wasn't supposed to speak to. Dez was shy, but she sometimes caught some of them staring past the other girls' wholesomely braided heads and tinkling laughs in her direction, as if they recognized her for the little deadly demon that she was.

Maybe they dreamed about her too.

Then, the year Desdemona turned fifteen, one of them spoke to her.

His name was Asher, and he was beautiful, only sixteen, but built like a man and emanating fresh testosterone from every suntanned pore. Dez, not yet aware of how attractive she was becoming, was confused by his interest in her. Over several weekends he sought her out among the bookshelves of the village bookshop to ask about her day, and the furtive bliss of their adolescent fumbling was a revelation for a girl who had gone most of her life without being touched by anyone.

It was wonderful, until Asher got sick. First he failed to show up at the bookstore, and then she heard that he'd come down with some vague ailment that sent him to bed with waxy skin and fatigue; then that he was in a coma, then that he was dying. She had no idea how much of it was true, but she stopped going to the bookstore, and out of worry, didn't sleep a wink. A week later, she heard that Asher's condition had improved, and two weeks later he was playing rugby like it never happened.

He never spoke to her again, turning away whenever their eyes met in the street. He couldn't have known what really happened, but his animal instincts told him to stay away. And as much as it broke her heart, she realized it was for the best.

Another week, and she might have killed him.

CHAPTER 8

———

RED IN THE FACE

Sunday

Black underwear. Black bra. Black tights. Black dress. Dez stared dully at herself in the mirror as she'd been doing all night, until the bluish light of morning began to fill in the hollows under her eyes. She was still wearing her clothes from the day before, the dress now wrinkled, speckled with glitter, and reeking of other people's hormones, the tights marred by a long rent from ankle to inner thigh. Her manicured image had fallen away to reveal the snarling creature within, and she looked quite slatternly, really, with her eyeliner smudged into the corners of her eyes and the remnants of lipstick staining a mouth pursed shut with tension. But it was a fitting look for her, on the whole. Given what she was.

Dez had first come across the word "succubus" as a child, in a book of folktales, and at the time it held no more significance for her than "boggart" or "basilisk" or "troll"; just another of the night's many horrors to be memorized and catalogued in case of an encounter. The accompanying images and drawings, generally of long-haired women perched upon the chests of gasping men supine in their beds, had been somewhat titillating, but at the time Dez had no clear idea of how such a creature, lacking fangs and claws, might deprive someone of life, so the concept held low priority in her hierarchy of personal nightmares. It was only later when the fullness of womanhood began creeping up at her back, with its particular suite of special issues apparently reserved only for her, that the word began to take on a shadowy significance in the shameful back closet of her mind. She'd tried to avoid it, skipping over it when encountered in a paragraph, mentally eliding such creatures with vampires or sirens to deny the uncomfortable resemblance their particular list of recorded traits had to phenomena she was beginning to experience with ever-increasing regularity.

And while for years the idea hovered dimly in the distance like an approaching nightmare from the future, an inevitable sentence for a crime she hadn't yet committed but couldn't avoid, the real power of denial, she now realized, was its ability to feel like personal growth. She'd quietly absorbed the truth of her nature without accepting the label, as if a person could be exactly like a thing and have the characteristics of a thing, and still somehow choose not to be the thing itself; as if her very nature was a flaw she could eradicate with good behavior.

But Dark saw right through her, as did that Lilith woman, and even that slutty girl-creature under the bridge.

Because it takes one to know one.

If only she hadn't gone into that nightclub. Long-repressed urges, emboldened by the club's booming bass and lack of leash, nipped at her like a hungry shadow-self, eager to escape the austere cage she'd built around it. *Yet Dark called her "lovely."* What a perversion of beauty that was, from the world's foremost pervert. But through his honey-colored eyes, Dez caught a glimpse of what it would be like to simply be who she was, without shame, without lies. The idea had never occurred to her before.

Still, she reminded herself, people like her needed to lie. If she wasn't *in* the Order she'd have to worry *about* the Order, and she had to admit that, in terms of ubiquity at least, they were by far the most terrifying of all the many entities that stalked the night. There was nowhere to go that they were not, and Dez did not have the wiles and resources that someone like Dark could call upon to disappear.

And she had no fangs or claws.

If only.

No matter how much she longed to wallow in shame, she knew she couldn't hide in that apartment forever. The ticking of her quaintly analog bedside clock tapped on her sensitive ears like a SWAT team pounding on a door, urging immediate attention. She simply did not have time to feel as terrible as she liked, because if she didn't go to work eventually, her colleagues would come looking for her. She'd already gone through all this math a few days ago, after meeting that horrible man in grey, and circumstances hadn't changed. If she was a monster, she'd been a monster every other day of her life, and no one had yet noticed. All people saw was the conservative wardrobe, the standoffish attitude, and the stacks of books in her arms. If her persona was a costume, it was a good enough one that even she had believed it. She just had to pull herself together, put on fresh clothes, and bloody well get on with it.

She threw out the dress, the underwear, the bra, and the torn tights with vehemence, shoving them into a paper bag destined for the building's trash incinerator, and then stood in a blisteringly hot shower and scrubbed her body raw with chamomile soap, her skin steaming and red. It was only when she stepped out of the bathroom that she noticed the peonies on her counter had begun to bloom, the petals pushing out of their straitjackets, erupting as vivid coral fluff and emitting a sweet, troublingly gamey scent. They seemed to mock her as she donned her human costume and prepared for her job hunting down others just like herself from the comfort of a windowless cell where, hopefully, she could remain walled up like an anchorite until anyone who might have been paying a bit too much attention to her moved on to other things.

Dez did not *need* to find out anything more about Mr. Dark and his dangerous nightclub. It would be smarter to forget she'd ever gone there, but the man reckoned time in centuries instead of years, and that was not something she could leave unexplored. However, after a morning of determined searching, she concluded that "Mr. Dark" did not seem to exist outside the nightclub at all. "Dark" was itself a commonish name, which made things more difficult; she did find a few peripheral mentions of someone *possibly* named "Dark" in connection with various criminal activities, but the Order's details were sketchy since those crimes were just about money.

But that was a real Bosch in his office. And Hieronymus Bosch was Dez's favorite painter—a medieval genius-cum-maniac whose sprawling canvases were peopled with grotesque figures romping through Heaven, Hell, and landscapes in-between—and Dez had spent hours as a child gazing at details from his works. She saw equally strange things every day, sticking their faces out of hedgerows or peering at her from inside trash cans, so to young Dez, Bosch was a kindred spirit. To teenaged Dez, he was a reassurance that she wasn't insane. To adult Dez, he was a reminder that it was important to express the truth about the invisible world in a way that allowed for plausible deniability.

So she recognized his work when she saw it. And if Dark was *in* a Bosch painting, he had to be at least five hundred years old.

Inconveniently, New York did not have a copy of the Order's file on Hieronymus Bosch. Many older records had not been copied to the regional hub offices, and given the filing department's backlog, the task was unlikely to ever be completed; the archivists informed her that the original file was in Amsterdam, with copies in London, Berlin, and Shanghai. Dez requested a rushed copy from Amsterdam, which would have to be copied by hand and translated into English, as Dez's knowledge of medieval Dutch was sketchy. The London office's copy would already be in English, but Dez did not want to involve London. It was unlikely that anyone there would have time to get curious about her requests for obscure files, but Dez could not live with even the possibility niggling the back of her mind.

For the fifth time that day, she peeked down aisle S-9 in the archive. There was always someone there looking up another "S" file and taking forever about it, but this time she found it empty. So with a pang of guilt, she headed towards the shelf where the file for the "Second Circle" could be found. Dez privately disagreed with whoever thought it should be listed under "S" instead of the number "2," but she was relieved to find the file there on the shelf, and thus not currently central to any active cases.

She expected the club to be an established landmark, maybe from the 1960s, or even the Roaring '20s. But according to the city paperwork, that former meatpacking plant had been purchased, renovated, and converted into a club only three years ago, opening its doors on Valentine's Day with a bacchanal so unbridled the archdiocese of New York declared the place a public menace. The owner was listed as "Second Circle, LLC," with a note added in the margin stating simply "*proprietor = Dark (m.).*" Everything looked to be on the up-and-up, legally speaking; they even had a proper liquor license. The Order knew it was a sex club, a brothel, and a hotbed of nightcrawler activity, but they had to leave the place alone. An establishment like that was too big to burn down or blow up without blowback, and supposedly even the police were paid to take special care of it, so the Order could not afford to start trouble. And since the club produced no suspicious dead bodies, the Order deemed it rational to tread lightly and bide their time.

"Do you ever take a day off, Cross?"

Dez slapped the file shut and saw Hunter smiling at her from the end of the row.

"Do you?" she shot back. That sounded more harsh than she intended, but Hunter didn't seem to mind as he sauntered down the aisle, and as he approached, her body lit up like a Christmas tree.

"Let me guess...Sasquatch." He tilted his head to read the label and then smiled as if he'd caught her looking at naughty pictures. "Uh-oh… watch out for those cover charges, Cross. The Meatpacking District'll clean you out."

"It came up in one of my cases. I'd never heard of it."

"Not really my scene," he said, lowering his voice to the murmur that people use in libraries. "Black latex doesn't suit me."

Dez reflected that Mr. Dark would object to that crass description of his carefully crafted nightclub concept, but heroically restrained herself from correcting him.

"We don't even surveil it?" she queried instead.

"Anybody we send in there gets kicked out pretty quick. Solomon doesn't like us going at all anymore in case they keep pictures of us."

That thought had not occurred to Dez, and it made her ill.

"So, I should pick another place to host my birthday party," she quipped, trying to sound nonchalant.

"Heh, you're ok, Cross. Even if you do wear the wrong shoes."

She glanced at her oxfords.

"This is the ideal footwear for my profession," she averred, and as she looked down she realized their toes were almost touching. "Is there… any progress on the dead girl?" she asked, groping for the least sexy topic she could think of.

"The case grows colder by the day," he sighed. "Destined for the back burner, not that anyone cares. But in my old job the attitude wouldn't have been too different."

"You used to be with the police?"

"I was a homicide detective for ten years in Chicago. Then one night —my night off—I was at a bar and went into the alley behind it to have a smoke, and there was this guy hanging out who asked me for a light. He didn't look unusual, just a guy, so I gave him a light. Next thing I know, I'm on the ground and he's on top of me with his claws digging into my chest."

He reached up and unbuttoned the top three buttons of his shirt, moved his tie aside, and showed Dez a crisscross mess of scars across his broad chest and breastbone.

"I pulled my service piece and I shot him. I think I winged him, but I never found out 'cause they never caught him. I got my ass to the hospital and told them what happened. And wouldn't you know," he smiled ruefully, "they locked *me* up."

That was not an unusual Order story. Victims of supernatural attacks were often rescued by the Order from the churn of the mental-health system. If they were deemed valuable, they were inducted into the Order before their sanity, regarded as madness, truly became so. Hunter's honesty cost him his badge and earned him a damning mental-health diagnosis, but the Order rescued and then transferred him to New York City for a fresh start as a new kind of cop, and he repaid the service by pledging them the rest of his natural life.

"So, I showed you mine..."

"I'm sorry?" she swallowed.

"What's your story? Why are you down here instead of up there with all the other pretty people?"

"I don't have a story." *Not one she could tell, anyway.*

"We all have a story. No one joins the Order for fun. Most people here have an embarrassing file in a psych ward someplace."

Dez stared at the map of old pain carved across that plane of his chest with its healthy grove of soft blond hair. Her treacherous eyes met his, which were fixed on her with a smoky gaze that left no room for alternate interpretation. If he leaned forward he could kiss her, and if she moved towards him he would do so. And that would be a disaster, because she'd shove him up against the shelves, press her mouth onto his, and slide her tongue—

"Miss Cross?" A snappy whisper from the end of the row stopped them both cold, and they turned to see one of the archivists peering down the shelves. "Is that you, Miss Cross?"

"It is," Dez coughed.

"Father Solomon would like to speak to you," said the archivist.

"You're to go find him in his office." She then flashed Hunter a look of prim disapproval as he melted back into the stacks, his eyes meeting Dez's like a pair of accomplices.

———

Father Solomon sat behind his desk, a vast slab of oak that had been through a fire, charred on one side as if it had been dipped briefly in Hell. The acrid odor of carbon lingered over it, and Dez, sitting across the desk, brushed the smooth surface of the blackened wood with a gloved fingertip, feeling hardened cells compacted together with the pressure of centuries. The office was clean, even clinical, Solomon's work carefully tucked away in the monolithic metal filing cabinets behind him.

Only a single black file sat on the desk under his elegantly folded hands. *DESDEMONA CROSS*, it read on the tab; her personnel file.

"I hope your move has gone smoothly, Miss Cross."

"So far," she replied, squirming under the scrutiny of his expressionless eyes. "I get turned around in the subways."

"I'm sure you'll figure out the city in no time. Smart as you are." His manner was gracious, but every word was sharp as a razor, and she imagined him feeding, lizard-like, on frozen mice. He was undeniably patrician, undisturbed by the weight of his authority. The head rising out of his cassock resembled a bust of some ancient autocrat placed on a pedestal, the kind of man for whom thousands of lives and deaths were mere accounting problems.

Breathe. Even humans can smell fear. A thousand terrible scenarios flashed through Dez's mind as she waited for him to explain himself. The Order's spies were everywhere, and perhaps someone saw her go to that nightclub, saw her standing outside Vito's apartment, or even saw that stupid man climbing in her window. But those were not crimes that warranted a "strong talking-to."

If she were in real trouble, they wouldn't bother to warn her.

"How are you adjusting to your new role with us?" he finally asked, after allowing her ample time to squirm.

"Research is research," Dez blinked, the picture of innocence.

"I understand you served as an outside consultant before you fully joined us. That is an unusual arrangement."

He paused, waiting for her to explain herself, in the usual way of school headmasters and professional interrogators.

"My area of study made it pertinent."

"Still, there aren't many bona fide experts in our ranks," Solomon told her. "Brother Pascal—your predecessor—only possessed the knowledge of the amateur enthusiast. I'm sure you're already miles ahead of him. May I ask, why did you choose to come to New York? Surely London could have used someone of your caliber."

"London has some of the finest Order researchers in the world," Dez replied coolly. "Here, as you mentioned, I don't diminish as much by comparison." It was a poisonous response to a poisonous question, but he couldn't claim there was anything impolite about it. "I'd heard such good things about this division," Dez continued in an attempt to soften her tone, "so I jumped at the chance to be transferred here. I'm grateful for the opportunity."

"And I imagine that being Izumi Cross's daughter gave you a head start."

The sound of Dez's mother's name hit her like cold water. At least now she understood what this "chat" was about. Izumi Cross was in the Umbra, an obscure division of the Order tasked with hidden agendas of which even upper members like Father Solomon had no knowledge. Perhaps he believed Dez to be an Umbra spy, planted there to surveil someone or something under his purview; maybe even himself. Her first thought was to decry the insinuation, but she kept silent. He wouldn't become her ally just because she declared herself harmless. And even if he believed her, men like him did not repay obsequiousness with respect.

"My mother's influence did help me develop a broad frame of reference, yes," Dez replied frostily.

"I gather you're working with Hunter on his latest *anthrochimera* case?"

"If I can be of use."

"Hunter was formerly a detective, and occasionally those people come with the residue of unhelpful attitudes," he said. "Each of us has our own garden of bad habits, but everyone here is deeply devoted to the cause. The true cause. We prioritize the organization's mandate for secrecy above all else, whatever emotional reactions we may sometimes display."

Dez raised her brows at that; it seemed that Father Solomon was not oblivious to the way some of his underlings talked in private. And in a way, it was touching to see him be protective of Hunter, who he didn't even seem to particularly like, and Dez didn't appreciate being viewed as a sinister interloper, but that came with being Izumi Cross's daughter. Overbearing even in her absence, the intimidating specter of her mother hovered over everything she did.

"May I ask, how many people here know who my mother is?" she asked.

"Only Brother Justin and myself."

"Perhaps that's for the best. It tends to make people uncomfortable."

"I heartily agree." Solomon then slid her file into his desk drawer without ever bothering to open it, which Dez took as her cue to leave. Still, vibrating as she was with nerves, she decided to venture one more daring question to which she simply had to know the answer.

"Have you ever met my mother?"

"Once," Solomon said, and Dez thought she caught the briefest shiver of discomfort in his voice at the memory. She considered a number of appropriate responses, but opted, in the end, to nod politely and leave. *The less she said in general,* she thought, *the longer she would live.*

Dez made her way to the coffee room nearest her office, aromatic with an acrid, ever-percolating brew that was as alert and severe as those who drank it. The room was empty, but someone had recently started a fresh pot and would soon be back to collect it. Dez sank into a chair and stared at the dripping brew with longing; a few more minutes and there might be enough there to revive her for the rest of the day, or at least warm the relentless chill that was taking over her weary body.

"Oh, Desdemona, you look *tired.*" Beatrix Kragin came in with an empty mug in her hand and sat down next to Dez, peering into her face with an approximation of solicitous concern. Dez waited as if for a verdict; of anyone in the office, Beatrix was the most likely to be able to identify an ailing succubus. To Dez, she reeked of rancid hormones, her body rebelliously pumping them out despite her resistance to doing anything with them, but perhaps that simmering repression kept her attuned to the unique frequency of sex demons, and she'd sense some twitch or tell that Dez was unaware of.

"Those dark circles might be from dairy," said Beatrix. "I used to get them, but they're gone since I went vegan. That's not *why* I went vegan —that was because I can't stand the thought of eating anything with a soul—but it was a wonderful side effect."

"I haven't been sleeping," Dez replied. *Which was, technically, true.*

"Hunter tells me you're interested in the Second Circle," she said, as if Dez had been asking about organic produce.

Damn you, Hunter. Doubtless he was trying to be helpful, but she made a note to be careful what she said around him, as she had no idea how often Beatrix waylaid him in the hallways for breathy chats, and Hunter might bring up Dez's name purely out of mischief.

"It was mentioned in an old case file," Dez lied. "I was curious about it so I had a root around."

"That place isn't that old," Beatrix pointed out.

"My file was only from a year...or two years ago. But cold. Quite cold. I wanted to get some context. It's not important." Dez made another note to get her facts straight before she spoke to Beatrix again. But Dez herself knew very little about sex demons; she'd avoided the topic her whole life, her subconscious mind refusing to let her learn too much lest she discover something she couldn't continue to ignore. Now she needed to know everything, and if that meant talking to Beatrix, so be it.

"Well, that club isn't the only place like that in the city," Beatrix informed her. "There are others, but the Second Circle is the most... notable. It's not just that some of the employees are Unnaturals in there...we think they *all* are. Can you imagine?" Beatrix's eyes flashed as she warmed to her subject. "I have no idea how so many somniophages work together in one place, but it must be one big watering hole for all the predators. I've seen videos of lions and cheetahs hanging around a wadi together, picking off the gazelles. Perhaps it's like that, except we're the gazelles."

"That must bother you," Dez ventured. "It's so...flagrant."

"Oh, it does, but they seem to have some sort of—well—system," Beatrix grudgingly allowed. "The people who go into that club come out not particularly worse for wear, so the Unnaturals who work there must be incentivized to control themselves. And there's no indication that the human clientele know that it's anything other than an ordinary nightclub."

"So, the staff somehow avoid killing their victims?" Dez queried, her pulse quickening. "How?"

"Restraint, I suppose," Beatrix scoffed, as if the very idea was ridiculous. "Personally, I think that no one comes out unscathed from a somniophage encounter. It's impossible to tell what damage it does further down the road, but that doesn't stop people from smoking, does it? And frankly, people who do go into the Second Circle are literally asking for it. If they went to an ordinary brothel they'd come out with venereal disease instead, so as long as they don't know the nature of what's *really* happening in there, that aligns acceptably with our mandate. Those aren't the victims I'm primarily concerned with. I'm more interested in saving the poor innocent souls who get attacked in their bedrooms at night. If only *those* somniophages were so well-regulated. "

"The file says someone named "Dark" owns the place, but nothing else about him." Dez was playing with fire, but she needed to find out what extra tidbits Beatrix might be aware of that weren't written down.

"Dark...Dark...maybe. That sounds like a fake name to me. 'Dark,' hmph. So dramatic. Solomon thinks the owner is a wealthy sanguinophage. I've even heard a rumor that the place is owned by an *incubus*, but that's ridiculous. Sex demons are like animals; they can't think past their own urges long enough to run a business. I wouldn't put too much stock in some supposed "owner." Whoever he is, I'm sure he's just there to turn the lights off in the morning and be the fall guy if we—or even the police—decide to take more of an interest. Places like that are all run by shadowy Mafia syndicates. It could be the Luppi for all we know. I'd love to burn the whole building down, but one thing at a time. They'll get theirs eventually."

"Thank you," said Dez. "That's very helpful."

"Of course," Beatrix beamed at Dez like a police flashlight as she got up to pour a coffee, topping it off with a splash from a carton of oat milk that she waggled suggestively in Dez's direction. "We girls have to stick together. It's such a boy's club down here."

CHAPTER 9

DARK CORNERS

Chinatown
Wednesday
Midnight

Vito Luppi's phone buzzed relentlessly in his pocket, ringing over and over as it had been doing all night. But he couldn't answer it, no matter how much he wanted to know if Teo had woken up. He couldn't turn it off, either; that felt too much like rebellion, so he ignored it as he and his cousin Giulio sat on their beds, or what passed for beds in the flophouse Chinatown hotel in which they were hiding. They couldn't go back to their apartment, which Massimo owned and was probably being watched by Dark's guys. And their credit cards were under Massimo's name, so they had to find someplace that took cash.

"Teo'll be fine," Giulio assured him, looking up from the inane videos he'd been watching to stop ruminating over whose fault this all was. Vito had caused the main issue with his lack of self-control, but it was Giulio who had followed Vito over the bridge that night, and then Teo must have spotted Giulio leaving and followed *him* in his Miata.

And it was Teo who encouraged Vito to keep going to that bougie nightclub in the first place, convinced it would solve Vito's "little problem." The "little problem" itself Vito could hardly be blamed for. That was down to God, and for Giulio, blaming God was always the default starting point.

"I said, Teo'll be fine," Giulio repeated, when Vito didn't respond. Vito was fidgeting, tugging at his collar, his chiseled face flushed.

"Yeah," Vito managed. "You're right."

Vito and Giulio had tried to dig the bullet out of Teo themselves as they'd done before, but they couldn't find it, and Teo passed out from the pain. Afraid their apartment was being watched, they dropped Teo on his mother's porch to get medical attention and fled to that cheap hotel. When Teo regained consciousness he would have to rat them out, but once Giulio and Vito got an accurate measure of Massimo's wrath, they'd determine how to make amends. It would be alright in the end; Giulio, Teo, and Vito were the scions of the Luppi clan, the young bucks, the soldiers, and they were needed back in the fold. But they'd have to do penance first, and it would come off better for them if, when they met with Massimo, Vito wasn't such a strung-out wreck.

"We need to eat," Giulio declared. "You look like my sister when she was trying to fit into that wedding dress." Vito managed a wan smile at the memory of his cousin Talia, ashen and panting, trying to squeeze into a gown she'd optimistically ordered two sizes too small.

"Ok," Vito agreed unenthusiastically.

"Anything in particular?" Giulio asked.

"No Chinese," Vito smirked, looking almost like his old self.

"Ok. I'll hit up the place on Mott with the good bánh mìs."

"Ok," Vito nodded gratefully as Giulio left.

Then, alone in the room, Vito did some math.

Realistically, it would only take Giulio twenty minutes to run down to the sandwich shop and back, but Vito was operating on a junkie's logic; to him, that was plenty of time to get downstairs, climb into the stolen green SUV they were now driving, zip down to that spot under the bridge, do his business, and return. Giulio would never know he was gone. He'd behaved himself for days, hiding in that squalid hotel room with the curtains closed so he wouldn't see the moon relentlessly swelling every night. But he felt it in the twitching of his skin and the hectic fury in his bones as the month marched on. Giulio and Teo were largely unaffected by the lunar cycle, but Vito had pulled the short straw in the family gene pool in that regard, and got testy whenever there was more moon than not in the sky. And tonight it was full, bursting at the seams like he was, a feeling that Giulio just couldn't understand.

So, slipping on his leather jacket, Vito headed out for something to take the edge off the night.

———

The Order
Thursday morning

Three days. Three days of pacing the halls, watching Hunter's door, and getting nowhere. Moonie activity increased during the two weeks when the moon was fat, and Hunter's work ethic was fierce and so were his assistants, who she unfailingly found bustling around the hallway whenever Dez thought Hunter had perhaps gone to the bathroom. And it did not escape Hunter that Dez had been passing his office more than she needed to. He caught her eye as she walked by, smiling at her in a knowing way that made Dez's heart skip. Bowing his head over a map of werewolf victims like a bloodhound primed for the scent, sometimes one bronze lock would escape the waves of his hair and tumble over his forehead. As she stalked him, preparing to invade his space like a spy, his smile and lingering glance made Dez feel worse; there was no one that she would have less liked to betray.

Meanwhile, Dez did not feel well, and was running out of ways to hide it. She could muscle through the weariness with cup after cup of black coffee, and try to ignore the ache in her muscles and coldness in her core, but the blue circles under her eyes would soon be noticed. Her fingers stung more than usual from the holy-water test at the door that morning, and they wouldn't heal for hours. If they took too long, she couldn't come in at all the next day. And unlike a normal woman, Dez couldn't take care of the problem alone; touching herself left her feeling worse, as the part of her that wasn't human fed desperately on the part of her that was.

So it was most unfortunate when, on the way back to her office with an armload of files, she ran into Hunter striding down the hall; luckily he was in too much of a hurry to notice her blush.

"There you are," he said. "If you have a minute, come to the morgue with me."

"The morgue?"

"Not the city morgue. Our morgue. We found another one."

The Order's in-house morgue was a cold chamber embedded deep in the city's concrete, one wall rumbling intermittently from a nearby subway line. A rack of ominous medical instruments sat at the ready, scalpels and bone saws lying next to iron crosses and stone talismans. The Order's autopsy tables even came fitted with restraints, in case (as happened frequently) the bodies lying on them were still a bit lively. But the body on the slab that day was unlikely to get up again: the young woman in question was shredded to bits, her insides gouged out like a ripe fruit, with a man-sized, animal-toothed bite mark across her neck. A Night Watchman with a cadaver dog had found the body that morning; the Order tried to sniff out tell-tale bodies before the police discovered them. This girl exhibited all the signs of a werewolf-ravaging, so Order operatives posing as construction workers absconded with the body before the real crew showed up for work, bringing her down to headquarters via the warren of hidden tunnels and passages that Swiss-cheesed through the undercity.

Dez and Hunter found Father Solomon and Beatrix already standing by the body, eyeing it with a distaste that had less to do with the gore and more with the nature of the dead girl, as Beatrix turned the bloody bits over with the dispassionate interest of a museum curator.

"The victim is another confirmed extranatural entity," said Doctor Boiko, the birdlike Ukrainian woman who presided over the Order's in-house mortuary facility. A glass vial marked only with the Order's circular symbol stood on a pedestal, set apart from the rest of the more prosaic medical equipment. Dr. Boiko picked up the vial with care and plopped a generous drop of the precious substance—potent thought-water—on the back of the girl's thigh, where it hissed and ate away at her skin like acid. "Definitively an Unnatural," she intoned. "Assessment suggests a somniophage."

The girl's face was partially intact, and with a lurch, Dez then recognized her as the cheeky vaping succubus she'd spoken to under the bridge. Her shirt was gone, but her hips were wrapped in the same red booty shorts she'd been wearing before, now slashed raggedly open by a claw.

"We found her in another construction dumpster, in the Two Bridges area," said Hunter. "That's between the Manhattan Bridge and Chinatown," he added for Dez's benefit.

"Whoever this man is, he's doing our work for us," observed Beatrix. "It's a shame he doesn't know how to clean up after himself. But at least that means we have no real victims."

That attitude, Dez knew, was standard Order dogma, and it was ridiculous to get sentimental over a dead demon; cute as she was, the girl was a predator, and whoever killed her may have been justified in doing so. But this creature with a penchant for e-cigarettes and dirty jokes had saved Dez's life that night in that alley, and it was sickening now to stare down at the rubbery mask of death that had replaced her snarky smile.

"It is hard to be sure whether somniophages are of morphodynamic type once dead," Dr. Boiko added, referring to the question of whether the dead "girl" was always a girl or if she switched genders at-will. "But I think this one is always a female."

"Does it matter in this case?" asked Solomon.

"I have no idea," Beatrix shrugged. "Are we sure the killer was a man?"

"We're not sure of anything," Hunter admitted.

"I do not need to point out that these bodies are alarming," Solomon frowned at them all in turn. "We were lucky to find this one before the police did."

"Yes, God forbid some lunkhead cop sees one of these bodies dissolving. No offense, Alan," said Beatrix.

"I happily answer to 'lunkhead'," Hunter replied drily. "But cops don't tell things like this to the press. That gets your badge taken away."

"Do we have a suspect?" asked Solomon.

"We have a shortlist," said Hunter, glancing sideways at Dez. Solomon held out his hand, and Hunter handed him the file, adding, "what I'd like to do is bring in everybody on it for a chat."

"Is everyone on the list a citizen?" asked Solomon.

Hunter nodded, and Dez saw Beatrix throw him a sympathetic look from across the corpse. *Citizen,* to the Order, meant a person with a family and a house and a job; someone who, if they went missing, would be missed.

"It would be easier if it was a homeless scumbag," Hunter allowed. "But the first girl was seen getting into a silver Porsche. That's the only tip we have to go on, and that cuts out the hobos and the drifters."

"We cannot pick up eight citizens based on that, satisfying as that would be," Solomon objected. "Monitor them, but check the 'homeless scumbags' as well. Just because someone saw that girl getting into a car at some point doesn't mean that was the last thing she did that night. And if we find any more of these—" he gestured at the body like it was leftover food— "we must find them before the NYPD. We do not want any more headlines with the word 'Ripper' in them."

Hunter, a seasoned detective, had already done his due diligence with the street people, but said nothing more. Solomon perused the list in the file with a scowl as he reached the name at the bottom.

"Vito Luppi?"

"He's got a silver Porsche. Cross looked up the car in the database, and his name popped up."

"Alan..." Solomon's weary sigh had the flavor of an old argument, "for God's sake, leave those Italians alone. I don't have time for this discussion again. I know the Luppi bother you as a matter of principle —they bother us *all* as a matter of principle—but you cannot make this issue their fault by wishing." He handed the file back to Hunter with exaggerated formality. "This kind of thing is unlikely to involve them. If there's anything those people know how to do, it's hide bodies."

"I know, I know, I crossed him off already."

And with that, Vito Luppi got yet another pass from the Order. Dez's eyes offered the mute apology to the dead girl that she could not say out loud. Even in that somber moment, she still had the tactlessness to wonder what Hunter's lips would taste like, but, she reflected sadly, the girl on the table would have sympathized with that. Dez didn't need to ask what would be done with her remains; what was left of her by the end of the week would be poured into a hermetically sealed box that would ultimately hold nothing but dust and traces of her professional artifice: torn shorts, half a push-up bra, a plastic earring, and a pair of cheap, uncomfortable shoes. *There but for the grace of...*but no, that was a ridiculous way to think. There was an ocean of difference between Dez's life and this poor creature's. Dez could not even conceive of a situation where she would be out on the street wearing spandex and whistling at cars.

———

Thursday evening

Jack the Ripper. It was impossible to look at the mangled bodies of two dead prostitutes and not think about the man who put the fear of men into the hearts of the women of London's notorious Whitechapel slum in the year 1888. However, according to most of the Ripper historians whose credentials Dez respected, "Jack the Ripper" never truly existed. *Someone* murdered a number prostitutes in Whitechapel that year, but the concept of "Jack" and all his trappings was the creation of a notoriously venal press eager to drum up newspaper sales, and the infamous "From Hell" letters that gave "Jack" his famous identity were written by a reporter and then fed to the police to further the depressingly profitable drama. Most of those historians believed there was more than one killer, and that the singular "Jack" was no more than a composite, a golem of Victorian sexual anxiety. But as no one was never officially identified or caught by the police, the world simply let Jack live on in their imaginations as the bogeyman that many secretly thought those wayward women deserved.

And, as everyone kept reminding Dez, prostitutes were killed all the time. The idea hardly needed a poster boy.

She curled up in her bathrobe in her apartment, sipping cup after cup of brackish black coffee and scrolling listlessly through Jack the Ripper articles on her laptop. But her brain kept visualizing flesh against flesh, wet against wet, soft against hard. Her eyes might be looking at some horrific woodcut, but her brain saw a bitable earlobe, a straining bicep gripping a thigh, beaded sweat in the hollow of a collarbone. Next time she was alone with an appealing man she might snap. If it was Hunter, she would merely be dead, but she dreaded what could happen when that monster in grey showed up.

She needed to deal with it.

But Dez had no idea how to handle the situation under her new circumstances. Liaisons in school were easy; a cloistered environment where the population consisted of a self-selected group of candidates answered all important questions in advance. A college student was probably not a criminal, probably single, with no children and no baggage— reasonable sex partners vetted by the institution. Dez had maintained a rotating carousel of crushes; young men that she'd meet once or twice, sleep with, and then never spoke to again according to the soulless logic of modern hookup culture. She'd spot an attractive specimen at the cafeteria or in the library, run into them at a party, and fall into bed without any faff. It was like living in a grocery store. Most of the men she slept with made it so easy—sometimes all she did was make eye contact and they were instantly smitten, as if she'd blown an invisible dog whistle.

The men she saw repeatedly, however, did not fare well; one contracted pneumonia, another mono, there was a nervous breakdown or two, and one young man she'd been particularly fond of left school when he started hearing voices. The one-night stands were the lucky ones, melting away after their night of passion like snowflakes in the sun. Perhaps they woke up feeling more tired than the night before, like a drained battery, prone to illness and infection, with the vague animal sense of having escaped with their lives. It didn't matter; on the endless conveyer belt of a college, there was always another dish rolling out of the kitchen. But in the anonymous urban jungle, people were not what they appeared to be, and everyone was a possibly dangerous stranger. Those two dead girls had been perfectly adapted to handling the situation and they had still met sticky ends at the hands of someone apparently even better adapted. Dez hardly stood a chance.

However, living in a city meant learning more than just the subway lines; it also meant learning how to hunt.

So at sundown, Dez left the Order and took a walk. She pushed through traffic and jaywalked through stoplights, afraid that if she stopped moving she would collapse. The world glistened in shimmering relief, the air brushed against her skin like velvet rubbed the wrong way, and the red *DON'T WALK* sign blared too brightly to look at. She charged ahead, letting the stream of people flow around her, oblivious to her presence. That was one benefit to living in a city: no matter what was going on with her, none of those people knew or cared anything about it.

Her feet brought her to a strip of trendy cocktail lounges and bars full of professionals spending their salaries on drinks with swizzle sticks.

She looked through the windows at people flashing teeth and tits and credit cards at each other over swishing martinis, considering which one might be a likely feeding ground.

Then—*boom.* A cloud of sweat, cologne, deodorant, and hair gel blew into her face as a group of laughing young men strode past her on the sidewalk, imbuing the air with musky perfume. One man turned his head as he passed her, his eyes taking her in with a single flick of his long lashes. He was a heartbreaker, some mother's joy, with a pile of red curls falling over his forehead, Irish-green eyes, a jaw like an anvil, kitten-sweet features, and a beefy athletic frame wrapped like a gift in a tight t-shirt. He turned away to follow his friends, and she watched the group head into a bar—a lounge called the Philistine—and, almost automatically, she followed them in.

The Philistine was a leather-and-lychee watering hole, thematically Asian down to the kimchi-laced small plates and edible orchids. The crowd was stylish, stockinged legs folded like origami, beards manicured like bonsai. Dez perched near the bar, blood pounding in her ears, trying to shut out the soup of desire, hostility, and anxiousness that emanated from the patrons of the city's meat markets and watering holes. The loud laughs and carefully arched wrists and tiny tugs on stockings flickered all around her, and she fought to keep her focus on the man she'd come to hunt.

Irish-Green and his friends packed into a booth, his attention on his drink, on his friends' phones, and on his own reflection in the mirrored wall. This manner of hunting required that the prey comply, so Dez had to let herself be chased if she was to catch her quarry. She made herself look over at him until one of his friends caught her eye, and then they all laughed knowingly together.

Dez blushed with agony. The way that man winked at his friends made her feel less like a predator and more like a tart. She was probably the most dangerous person in that room, but she felt like the most desperate. But no one in that bar knew her name, so there was no reason to worry about her reputation, and she could not afford to be precious about her dignity.

"Can I get you something?" the peppery bartender asked, more a command than a request.

"Scotch, neat," Dez sniffed. "Make it a double."

"Any particular kind?"

Dez pointed at a bottle of single-malt Lagavalin, her preferred libation, brackish with peat and smoke. He slid the drink over to her and she downed it like medicine.

Irish-Green was looking at her again, with the smug expression of a man who didn't have to work too hard for his prize. It made her feel vile, but it was to her purpose, so she forced a smile as he slipped out of the booth and headed across the floor toward her, running his hand self-consciously through his red hair as he leaned on the bar like a kid against a fence.

"Hey," was his opening line, yelled over the heartbeat of electro-swing jazz.

"Hello," Dez replied, her voice smokey.

"What?"

"Hello!" she yelled, losing the smoke in favor of volume.

"Cool!" he yelled in reply, having not heard her at all. "You want a drink?"

"Why not?" she said, intending to be coy.

"Suit yourself," he replied, an answer that only made sense if he'd heard her say "no."

They then stood at the bar together in awkward silence, looking in opposite directions, neither quite sure what to do next. A Second Circle employee would have simply walked up to him, brushed a hand against the back of his neck, and invited him to follow her, mesmerized, to a corner. But Dez's inhibitions were turned up to eleven, so she ordered another double whiskey and stared down at his forearms as they rested on the bar. He was a well-built animal with strong tendons and wrists, his skin dappled with freckles and dusted with gold-red hair. Dez loved a good forearm, and a jolt of hunger spiked through her. She tugged off her gloves and brushed his arm with her finger, feeling a spark as skin hit skin and his emerald eyes met hers.

"Hey," he said, "I need to piss. Wanna come?"

It was not the most appealing invitation she'd ever heard, but they couldn't all be poets. Dez let him grab her hand and her skin nipped at his as they crossed the room towards the glowing restroom signs. They passed his friends, who grinned and gave him a thumbs up; one of them was doubled over with hysterics. Dez blushed harder but ignored them and followed him towards the narrow corridor.

There was, of course, a bathroom line. They stood awkwardly, not looking at each other, their hands their only point of contact, pretending to be strangers waiting to relieve themselves (which was, in a way, true). His human vigor flowed into her skin where he touched her, filling her with a rush of warmth. It was like eating out of a dumpster: unappealing but vitally nourishing, if she could only keep it down.

Finally it was their turn, and Irish-Green pulled Dez in with him and slammed the door. It was a typical club bathroom, tiny and cold, the floor flecked with bits of toilet paper, crass graffiti scrawled on the walls. He hoisted her onto the porcelain lip of the sink, which was unpleasantly wet, pushed her sweater up over her bra, and pressed his mouth onto hers. He was drunk already—she tasted vodka and Red Bull on his tongue. He fumbled at her with sticky fingers, pinching roughly at her nipples, shoving her skirt over her hips and fumblingly grinding his hard cock—or rather, his zipper—against the sink instead of her body. She pushed back at him to keep him from ramming the small of her back into the faucet, but his need pulsed through her in the forceful thrust of his kisses and the tingle of his skin, and she answered him with corresponding frenzy. It passed for passion even if, in reality, she was just his vending machine snack and he was hers.

Then, abruptly, the bathroom door clicked open to reveal an angry metrosexual clutching his crotch out of bladder-related desperation. Irish-Green had forgotten to lock the door.

"Oh, come on, assholes," the man objected, and Dez hastily slid off the sink and out the door, leaving Irish-Green behind to deal with the bouncers. She rushed out into the night, sucking the cool, exhaust-and-shawarma-tinged air into her lungs.

This was ridiculous. Dez seethed at how badly she'd mangled it, and was tired of wrestling with herself. She couldn't exorcise that thing inside her, but she could beat it into submission. And the best place to do that was back at Order headquarters, surrounded by the apparatuses of control to which she reliably responded.

————

The Order
Still Thursday night
11 p.m.

It was Dez's first time in headquarters at night. The Order operated on a 24-hour schedule, but the atmosphere became more charged after the sun went down. Daytime was for the research department, the finance team, the lab techs, even the cleaning crew—all the busy bees that kept the vast machinery of the Order humming.

But the Order's quarry was most active at night, so that was when the hunters came out. Hard, unfamiliar faces passed Dez in the halls, their eyes sliding towards her with more probing curiosity than she got from the colleagues she met during the day. Still, the invisible weight of the city above her, the smell of old paper, and the soft whirring of the climate control system calmed her, though she caught a whiff of Irish-Green's cologne on her clothes.

She dared a peek inside the door of the werewolf room. Most of the faces were unfamiliar—the night shift—intently watching the bank of phones and computers. Night was when werewolf sightings came in, usually via frantic 911 calls eavesdropped on by the Order switchboard, and the team was ready to jump on anything fresh.

Reilly sat the corner taking his work ethic from Hunter, sleepily watching a dot move around on a GPS monitor attached to some unsuspecting werewolf's car. Despite herself, Dez took a quick, instinctive moment to scan Reilly's meaty body like a butcher assessing a cow. She meant to duck away before Reilly saw her, but he looked up as she moved.

"You're here late," he observed. "If you're looking for the boss, he's out on a pickup."

Hunter was not at the office.

"I just had a question about a file."

"Hunter won't be back 'till sunrise. Maybe I can—"

"That's alright," Dez interrupted him placidly. "It can wait."

"Long day?" he asked, eyebrows raised; his tactful way of pointing out that she looked tired.

"Very," she replied.

Dez looked down the hall at Hunter's closed office door. *He was gone. It was now or never.* This was her chance. Admittedly, perhaps Father Solomon and Hunter and that succubus girl under the bridge were all correct: Vito was not necessarily a serial killer just because he was a professional hitman. Women were for sale all over the city, and whores died every day. There was a whole list of other werewolves with silver cars who maybe didn't know that murder was something one was supposed to get paid for. But that succubus's carelessness bothered her; there was no reason Vito wouldn't have gone to find her a second time, and she would have eagerly gotten in his car again.

And if it was Vito, the only person willing to deal with him might stop being so polite if Dez failed to deliver what he'd requested. So under the circumstances, Dez felt justified in the terrible thing she was about to do.

Offices in the Order were rarely fitted with locks because, in theory, Order members hid nothing from one other. There were no security cameras anywhere either, because the last thing the Order wanted was a record of what they did, so if no one saw her, she was safe. With a furtive eye-slide toward the incident room, she laid one finger on the handle of Hunter's office door, pushed down until it clicked open, and slipped inside.

And then closed the door behind her.

One closes a door for so many reasons—to hide a murder, to masturbate, to cry. To read a file one isn't supposed to read. Dez tugged the hefty Luppi file off the shelf with leather-gloved fingers, careful to make no creases or nicks. And with a sickening feeling of betrayal, she flipped the file open and began to read.

———

Dez was surprised by how much information the Order's Luppi file contained about the current state of the clan, and how intimate it all was. Every living Luppi relative had a mini-dossier, with aliases, police records, and notes about family tiffs and favorite restaurants. The family was an old one, their lineage traceable back to ancient Rome, or at least as far back as records existed. They began as a clan of feral Sardinian bandits, carving out their territory by using their Unnatural gifts to pillage other people's livestock and terrorize the locals. Many Luppi still lived on Sardinia, but some had moved to New York in the early 1900s to continue the family business of plundering at knifepoint. The Order's file even contained a yellowing photograph taken at a customs office showing a pair of scowling, bearded men, a wife that belonged to one or both of them, and a litter of Luppi children.

The American branch had multiplied dramatically from Manhattan to New Jersey, all tied to the family business. This meant restaurant murders, drive-by shootings, and heists as well as gentler pursuits like credit-card fraud and racketeering. At one time they'd owned several buildings in Little Italy, and Dez didn't see anything suggesting they weren't still collecting the rent on those properties. They also entertained a proclivity for high-end art theft, beginning when one of their 17th-century progenitors stole a boat, sailed over to Naples, and looted a nobleman's villa just to prove he could. Perhaps his descendants kept up the practice out of tradition, despite having no pretensions to high culture.

But while the Luppi of old were the bogeymen of a Sardinian peasant's nightmares, these days the family's incidences of moonie activity were surprisingly low. Yes, they were violent, but as Hunter pointed out, there was nothing eerie about gang wars and parking-lot battles. Bullets signaled no unnatural mysteries, so the Order watched but did not interfere. Losing control of themselves was now a source of shame to the Luppi, attracting unwanted attention and interfering with the business of making money. These days, even werewolves kept their eyes on the bottom line. There wasn't a word about Vito's affinity for succubi in his file, just a list of mostly unproven charges against him for felonies done at the behest of his father. By gangster standards, he was a model son. But Dez was coming to appreciate the consequences of suppressing one's urges. She smelled traces of Hunter in the air and on the furniture, and it made her insides roil. Repression, she reflected, was an impetus to rebellion in and of itself. You could only bottle up lightning for so long.

Dez then noticed that some pages had the letter "C" written in red in the margins. Scanning down a list of living family members, she saw a single name circled in what looked like the same red pen. *That* individual's dossier was stapled to the back of that page, and she realized what that meant: the Order had an informant, one Mr. Carmine Luppi, currently living at 2828 Avenue J, in Brooklyn.

An informant. No wonder the file was so detailed.

The Order considered its nonhuman informants both profane and, in a way, sacred. Because their position was so precarious, and their input so important, the Order protected them tenaciously. Carmine was the *least* violent member of the Luppi family, and in the photo he just looked like a sad middle-aged man with a bowling ball gut and a droopy face.

Dez could only guess how the man in grey regarded such people, but other Unnaturals usually viewed them as betraying their own kind. Putting Carmine in his crosshairs would be poor repayment for services rendered. Besides, she wanted to keep the man in gray as far as possible from anyone who might mention him to the Order, which Carmine certainly *would* do, if he survived the conversation.

She flipped the file closed *without* adding Carmine's name to her list. There was one other way to find out what he knew, and under present circumstances, it seemed, unbelievably, to be the safest course of action, all in all.

PART THREE

MOONSTRUCK

CHAPTER 10

IN BOCCA AL LUPO

Brooklyn
Friday morning

2828 Avenue J was a rundown brick house with a gabled roof, just like every other house on a series of fading blocks of old suburban lots sporting half-mowed lawns, sun-bleached carport awnings, and children's play sets from a dozen years ago. A rusty 1980s Porsche coupe sat in the driveway of 2828, the paint once silver but since faded to ash-grey.

Dez rang the doorbell, heard shuffling behind the door, and it eventually opened to reveal Carmine Luppi.

Carmine was sixty-two according to his file; just slightly elder to his brother Massimo, but he looked far older. His face bore the strong Luppi features but was puffy from day drinking; slack skin and a sloppy waist suggested he spent his days in front of the TV, and his grey hair was slicked back in a stiff wave that had been dashing when he was young.

He scowled at Dez and pointed upwards at the "No Soliciting" sign tacked to the right of the door.

"Carmine Luppi?" Dez managed to spit out his name, but nothing else. Luckily for her, Carmine then noticed the black clothes and distinct lack of pamphlets, and Dez noted a suppressed twitch of irritation in his slack face.

"Ah," he said. "Then I guess you better come in."

The house was scattered with dusty filing boxes, faded furniture, and pilling floral pillow cases, and the air smelled like old cigarettes and microwaved pasta. The carpet had a path worn down the center from Carmine's habitual movements, from the front door to the La-Z-Boy to the bathroom to the bedroom. There was no evidence that he ever set foot in the dining room except to pile merchandise on the table; Carmine filled his days with online commerce, and his computer was open to a website for dealers of collectible coins.

Nothing about him screamed "werewolf," but Dez smelled a ribbon of gaminess in the swirl of Brill-cream, pain ointment, and old man that comprised his personal aroma, tinged with the same animal musk that she'd smelled on Vito in the alley—the family signature. It blended with the odor of wilting masculinity in a way that both attracted and repelled her, like rotten meat to a starving man, her mind fervently rejecting what her hungry body might mistake for food.

The night before, she had gone home with her list of Luppi addresses ready to deliver to the man in grey, but the man in grey didn't appear, so she'd had all night to churn over the superstitious notion that if Carmine Luppi was the one family member left off the list, he'd be the one who knew where Vito was. But unlike the other Luppi, Carmine was used to giving his information to the Order, so Dez could ask him herself.

This had seemed like a perfectly viable idea in her mind at 3 a.m., when an imaginary Carmine answered her questions with an alacrity only possible in fantasy. In real life, of course, Carmine was only used to talking to Hunter, so Dez was somewhat prepared for an unpredictable reaction from him, but in the cold light of day, she wondered if she was substituting one compulsion for another. Still, she couldn't live with the idea that the solution to her puzzle might be one borough away, left unquestioned purely out of a combination of cowardice and principle. And at least she looked the part; a light rain was dropping like petulant tears, so Dez had swapped her heels for a pair of black knee-high water-proofed leather boots that she hoped looked intimidatingly Gestapo-like; boots with flat heels in case she needed to run away.

"You people ever make appointments?" Carmine grumbled, mixing a morning vodka-and-Gatorade in a sport water bottle.

"It's not procedure," she replied, trying to sound as much like her mother as possible.

"Where's the other guy who usually comes to harass me?"

"I'm his assistant." Hunter was bound to find out that she'd been there, so she planned to tell him, eventually.

When he asked.

"His assistant, huh." Carmine took her in from boots to boobs with an old Italian man's lack of delicacy. "You want a drink? He usually has one of these—" he held up the drink and shook it like a baby bottle— "but you look like more of a cranberry juice girl."

"Not while I'm working," she hemmed.

"*He* never lets that stop him." His rheumy eyes glittered with a sharp canniness, as if he was trying to sniff her. "So," he prodded, "whattayou need from me?" Carmine kept one eye on his auction; she was not threatening enough to warrant his full attention.

Dez was not practiced at interrogating, but she'd been raised by a professional and had frequently been on the receiving end of such questioning for much of her life, so she knew that if she let him ask the questions, he would be in charge of the interview. And the longer she let him do that, the longer he'd have to figure out she was a fraud. *Or worse, that she was, in a fundamental way, very much like him.*

"Why do you think I'm here?" she asked. *Why do you think we're having this conversation?* It was exactly the sort of damning question she herself had grown up confronting, and she always cracked under the pressure.

Carmine shuffled aimlessly around his kitchen a bit, occasionally glancing back at her with a sly smirk, tidying nothing in particular and moving things around on the counters, and Dez vibrated under the awkwardness of their mutual silence, wondering what on earth she would do if he refused to answer. But she kept her eyes on him and her lips determinedly shut, feeling her face harden into a mask she could begin to recognize, even from the inside, as her mother's.

"You're here about Vito, yeah?" he finally grumbled, and Dez felt a spike of victory surge through her. She almost nodded, but stopped herself—an effective interrogator, she'd learned long ago, did not answer any but the most essential questions, and certainly ignored rhetorical ones. She kept her face a blank mask, and, to her joy, Carmine eventually finished his own thought.

"Jesus H. Christ, you people," he groused. "If you know everything already, it's a waste of time to ask me. Yeah, Vito's been getting around. I hear he's doing a little side business with some nightclub. And his daddy's got no idea, if you can believe it. It's that pump joint in the Meatpacking. The Third Base."

"You mean...the Second Circle?" Dez couldn't help venturing.

"See, you already know." Carmine, who suspected the Order rather enjoyed its cloak-and-dagger hugger-muggery, rolled his eyes at the pretense of it all. "But frankly, this seems kinda shady, even for Vito. I heard he's into 'em for somethin' like five-hundred large. And those nightclub thugs are trouble; they're into all kinds of shit that could, you know, cross over into our thing. That mighta been what got my other nephew Teo shot the other day. He's not doing so hot, but I bet you already know that too."

The more he talked, the more he seemed to want to talk. Dez sensed he was pleased to be listened to by someone, even if it was just a low-ranking Order member. As the oldest Luppi brother, he theoretically should have been the head of the family, but a single incident when he was twenty had demoted him in the family ranks from scion to pariah. His trespass had been unfortunately public; a fight in the street had triggered a transformation from man to wolf-man, resulting in a Weekly World News article and a few panicked police reports that the Order had, for their usual reasons, covered up. But the family was upset enough to banish him to the suburbs of Brooklyn, and it was that incident that put Carmine on the Order's radar in the first place. Comparing him to Massimo now, it was obvious to Dez that Carmine didn't have the gravitas his younger brother possessed, and surly as he was, she couldn't help feeling sorry for him.

"If my brother finds out what Vito's got himself into, he'll shit a brick," Carmine concluded. "Not that I'd ever tell him. I'm too old for that soap opera."

"But how do you know about it if Massimo doesn't?" Dez asked, forgetting for a moment to be oblique.

"I hear things," Carmine shrugged, satisfied that he had managed to finally tell her something new.

"Have you heard where Vito is now?"

"No. Seems like no one's got any idea. If he's smart he'll run off to Timbuktu before my brother finds out what he's been up to." He squirted spiked Gatorade into his mouth sideways. "Surprised you already know he's missing. He's only been gone a few days."

"We know everything," Dez told him frostily.

"Then I guess you wasted a trip to Brooklyn," he retorted.

"Thank you, Mr. Luppi," she replied, taking that as her cue to leave. "You've been very helpful."

"I live to please," he sighed officiously tipping his water bottle to Dez as she walked past the coins and the doilies and the dusty furniture and out to the driveway where the rusting silver car sat like a joke that had long ago lost its punch.

––––––––

The Lucky
  Bushwick, Brooklyn
  Friday afternoon

The Lucky wasn't a gay bar. It was just a seedy quasi-Irish bar that happened to be frequented by men who happened to prefer the company of other men. The Budweiser ads on the walls and the $4 Michelob specials repelled more stylish clientele, so the regulars of the Lucky were free to get on with the subdued business of being both homosexual and not particularly gay.

The Lucky was also Rat's fifteenth such bar of the day. He'd been crawling from establishment to establishment, following sketchy leads and hunches until he found Giulio Luppi tucked away in a booth talking about cars and holding hands under the table with a husky construction worker of the ginger persuasion.

"Oh, it's you," said Giulio. Rat and Giulio had met months ago at a Soho nightclub during what Giulio had believed, at the time, to be a random how-do-you-do in the bar line. A little shop talk led to Rat offering Giulio and his cousins a free VIP evening at the Second Circle, an offer that Giulio had taken as a friendly gesture. He knew better now, so was not pleased to see Rat's peaked face again. "How'd you find me?" he snarled.

"I have my ways," Rat shrugged. "We all gotta eat." He glanced pointedly at the ginger.

"Is this guy a problem?" the ginger asked Giulio protectively, but Giulio just sighed.

"Gimme a few minutes. Work thing."

The ginger slid reluctantly out of the booth, throwing Rat a hostile glance as he headed off to the pool tables.

"You here to collect?" Giulio asked Rat.

"I'm just here to drink. Found this place on Yelp. Nice. Different. Good potato skins." He sat on a bar stool adjacent to Giulio's booth and ordered his fifteenth club soda of the afternoon. In theory, having found Giulio, Rat should have texted Adrael his location so he could come deal with Giulio himself in his usual violent fashion. But Rat was not entirely sold on Adrael's way of doing things. In Rat's opinion, bullets and muscle had made a bad situation worse in that alley the other night, and Rat thought he might get a better result with persuasion. So he left his phone in his pocket and sipped his drink instead.

"I should kill you right here." A slight slur in Giulio's speech suggesting he was already a few whiskey-and-sodas into his day.

"That won't punish the people I work for," Rat pointed out. "They don't give a shit about me."

"If you want me to tell you where Vito is, fuck you. I got one cousin already fighting for his life 'cause a'you assholes." As Giulio spoke, tears welled up in his bloodshot eyes.

"I had nothin' to do with that. I'm just here to talk."

"This is *your* fault," Giulio growled, and Rat noted a tremor under Giulio's skin and reflexive swelling around his eye sockets. "You shouldn't have let Vito run up his bill. My cousin wasn't thinking with his brain no more, but I'm pretty sure you guys were counting on that."

"It don't matter whose fault it is," Rat replied calmly. "You and me are the only two people in this situation who haven't lost our minds. Vito ain't doin' *you* any favors hiding out like this."

Rat hoped that Giulio was tired of covering for his more attractive cousin. For the Luppi, who were old-school Italian Catholics, Giulio's sexual orientation was almost as problematic as anything Vito was doing; an unfairness that must also have rankled, deep down. Giulio had not even enjoyed the Second Circle—the "bougie shitbag atmosphere" did not appeal to his sensibilities—and had spent most nights drinking at the back bar alone while his cousin Vito was upstairs.

But Giulio was still not tired enough of the situation to bite.

"If you want me to sell out my family, you shoulda sent that other guy, the big one," he sneered. "Break some a' my fuckin' fingers."

"We don't care about your family," Rat told him sourly. "We don't even really care about finding Vito. Just tell me what my boss wants to know and this whole mess is over."

"You know, I'd like to, just to never have to see your pointy face again," Giulio spat. "But I got no idea where to find what your *fanook* boss wants, and I sure as shit can't ask my uncle. He's got warehouses all over the city, and I have no idea what's in any of 'em. He keeps all that business close."

"He told Vito."

"Yeah, well, Vito's gonna to be capo one day. So."

"And Vito didn't tell you?"

"No. And I didn't ask." Giulio glared at Rat with the defiant pride of the unambiguously loyal soldier, and Rat realized that pushing on his nonexistent ambition would get him nowhere, so he tried another lever.

"Look, this can't go on forever," Rat offered reasonably. "I got no idea where you got Vito stashed, but unless you got him duct-taped in a basement, he's eventually gonna lose what control he's got and end up on the Order's to-do list. And then nobody'll be happy."

"We don't worry about the Order," Giulio informed him with a boastful grin. "They leave us alone."

"Yeah, sure," Rat snorted.

"We're *in* with them." Giulio lowered his voice in the way people always did when discussing the Order. "The family's got someone inside all sewed up."

"Bullshit." The Order were considered to be incorruptible, at least as far as their own principles went, and Rat, in a life of listening at keyholes, had never heard anyone make that claim.

"I guess even the Roaches like money," Giulio shrugged knowingly. He caught an impatient glance from the ginger at the pool table, and rubbed his temples. "Look, I can't help you," he repeated. "I got no idea how to get your boss what he wants, whatever the fuck that is, exactly. You know, Vito didn't even tell me that. *You* wanna fill me in?"

Rat, in fact, was not completely sure either; he'd been given a vague mandate but Adrael kept the details of the issue to himself, as he so often did. But he hardly wanted to give that away, so he sipped his drink in silence.

"Thought so," Giulio huffed. "So it's outta my hands, and your hands. But I bet we're still all gonna pay for it."

"Even Vito?"

"I'm sure wherever he is, he's suffering too," Giulio grumbled as he stood up and signaled at the ginger that it was time to leave. "Hope so. The stupid fuck."

"I hope your loyalty gets you somewhere," Rat shot back.

"Does yours?" Giulio asked, and Rat didn't have a ready answer for that either.

———

Friday afternoon

Dez returned to her office riding a high of having successfully performed an interrogation, the novel excitement of which rumbled through her bones the entire trip from Brooklyn back to the Upper West Side. Her little office seemed even tinier when she returned to it, the dust less comforting and more stifling. But she was pleased to see a fresh stack of cases on her desk that all had Beatrix's name on the tabs; apparently the musty little woman had more faith in Dez's ability to crack her more difficult puzzles than she'd had in Pascal's, and Dez had to appreciate that she seemed to want to solve her tricky cases rather than merely shelve them and move on.

The cases on Dez's desk all had outré qualities—a baffling incident of *glossolalia;* a man manifesting spontaneous scarification in the shape of Africa; an attack by a "pile of animate hair"—but at their core they were all fundamentally sex demon cases. Dez could taste it in the victim testimony, full of shameful euphemisms and roundabout descriptions of what they'd experienced, which would ultimately be the manifestation of their deepest fantasies. The shame of those fantasies was part of the reason such cases were so under-reported; sometimes people just didn't want to want what they wanted.

Dez had to sympathize; her encounter with Irish-Green had taken the desperate edge off, but what energy she'd gained had channeled itself into repairing her body, leaving her fundamental itch still unscratched. Her fingers had already healed from that morning's holy water dip, but the beast inside was far from sated. She should have been reading *anything* but sex demon cases, but there she sat, lapping up the details like a cat attacking a bowl of cream. Between the lines of stammering confessions she read the victims' frenzied spasms in the dark, felt cold sheets clutched at night as a warm intruder slid between lonely thighs, and tasted the salty pressure of invisible lips stealing their breath in exchange for an empty orgasm. It was all so pained, so agonizing, and even in black and white, it made her blood rush through her veins.

Then—

Tap. Tap tap. The door nudged open and revealed the last person in the world Dez wanted to see: Hunter, standing in the doorway like a steak dangling in front of a starving man.

"Hello," she swallowed.

"Long night?" he asked.

"I could say the same for you." Hunter looked a bit tired and disheveled, but still handsome, emanating healthy adrenaline like cologne.

"I was out saving the city from the powers of darkness. What's your excuse?"

"I couldn't sleep. I know I look terrible."

"Impossible," he grinned. "You have lunch yet?"

Say yes, she told herself.

"No," she replied.

"Something tells me you've never had a hotdog."

"I have not," she confessed. Hotdogs were the food of carnivals, of backyard barbecues, and weekends on the wharf, none of which had ever been part of her existence. "I've had sausage rolls," she offered.

"Not the same. Come on."

No thank you, she should have said. *I'm busy. I'm full. I have two broken legs. Anything but—*"

"Alright."

The rain had stopped and the afternoon sparkled like a leftover fragment of summer. They strolled along the park, coats draped over their arms, the museum looming across the street like a neoclassical temple, and approached a hotdog vendor on the corner, its yellow-and-blue-striped umbrella sticking up like an cartoon flower.

"You like onions?" Hunter asked her.

"I like everything."

"Two with everything," he said to the vendor. "Pretty please and thank you."

Dez felt out of place there, like a stiff, clerical shadow ascended from the depths. But Hunter looked completely at home, juggling his trench coat on one arm as he took possession of the two hotdogs in their foil paper wrappers.

"Here." He handed one to Dez and she took it in both hands, overflowing with ketchup, mustard, and relish as bright as traffic lights. "No other hotdog is like the hotdog you get from a cart on the street," Hunter chewed, "though I gotta say, the ones here are nothing compared to a Chicago dog. You're lucky you don't know what you're missing."

They sat down on a bench just inside the boundary of Central Park, the front of the museum peeking through the yellowing leaves that surrounded them like a stage curtain.

"So," said Hunter, "you never told me how you got here."

"To New York?"

"To the job. We've all got a story."

"I was born into it," she said, and it sounded like a guilty admission. "My mother is in the Order."

"You're a legacy?"

"Yes."

"Ah," he nodded, as if that explained whatever questions about her he'd been harboring. "So you never even had a chance to be normal."

"I suppose not." Dez had very little experience talking about herself —indeed, she avoided doing so as much as possible—but Hunter's breezy affability pulled it out of her before she could think better of it. "But being a legacy feels like I haven't earned it," she added, crumpling the ketchup-smeared foil in her hand.

"Hey, I got forty years of normal before my life got torched," Hunter countered. "You were screwed from the start, if you don't mind me saying so. If whatever happened to your mother to make *her* join *hadn't* happened, imagine what your life might be like. You might be married with kids, or have a boyfriend and a car in the 'burbs."

"Did you have a girlfriend and a car?"

"I had a car. And a few girlfriends, I guess. Nobody serious...that job made it hard. Then I found a job that made it even harder." He licked the last of the mustard off his fingers thoughtfully. "It's a special kind of hell knowing the truth and not being able to talk about it. I think we all bury ourselves down there with the other moles just to feel sane. I guess that's why the mission is so important. Nobody should have to have their life ruined because of something that shouldn't even exist."

Something that shouldn't even exist. Like Dez herself, really. She wondered where Irish-Green was at that moment; if he was sick, or even dead. There was no way to know, since she hadn't gotten his name, and she had a clearer mental picture of the hotdog she'd just eaten than of his face.

"At least it helped me kick the smokes," Hunter added. "I quit cold turkey after that. So you never had a bad moment with some creature in the dark? Didn't see something unspeakable in the Tube?" he teased.

Dez shook her head, another lie.

"Well, I'm glad," he said. "You're never the same afterwards."

They sat on the bench with the warm sun dappling their laps, their thighs not quite touching, and Dez considered whether to tell him she'd gone to see Carmine. She *wanted* to tell him, but that conversation had to be managed carefully, and just then she was in no fit state to lie like a professional.

"What does your mother do in the Order?" he asked then.

Dez hesitated; she knew she should not talk about it, but Hunter's breezy tone was so warm and she felt terrible for how many times she'd already betrayed his trust. She decided she owed him one secret, and this was one that she could own up to without reprisal.

"My mother's name is Izumi Cross," muttered Dez.

"Okay..." Hunter nodded quizzically. "Should I know..."

"You won't know her name if she's not your problem."

"What does that mean?"

"It means..." Dez sighed quietly, drawing a circle in the dirt with her toe, "that she's a Shadow."

"She's in the Umbra?" His face flashed dismay, the usual reaction, and he stared at her as if seeing her for the first time.

Fair enough; he might have been less disgusted if she told him she was a succubus, she thought, rubbing a drop of ketchup off her glove. The Umbra pursued their secretive mandates with the fervor and heartlessness of bloodhounds, and if anything was more terrifying to an Order member than the memory of his own trauma, it was the idea that he might be crossing the Umbra in some way. Their authority came directly from above, as if granted by God, and even Father Solomon was subject to their oversight.

"Who else knows?" he asked.

"Solomon. Justin. Me. And now, you."

"That's all?"

"I don't like to talk about it."

"No, I get it, it'd just make people squirmy."

"Yes, it makes me squirmy as well," she admitted, glad to be truthful about that, at least.

"But it's important, what they do," he said.

"I know," Dez sighed. "Essential to the mission. Vital for the cause."

"Doesn't make you many friends though."

Dez managed a dark chuckle at that.

"Do you have many friends?"

"Me? I'm practically the block captain down there. Mr. Popularity."

"Kragin seems to like you," Dez observed archly.

"*It's Beatrix, please,*" he grinned sheepishly. "So...your mother's a professional nightmare...what does your dad do?"

"I have no idea," Dez said. "I don't know who he is." She waited for the usual apologetic awkwardness, but Hunter was unfazed.

"Well, he must have been pretty. If you don't mind me saying so." Hunter smiled and Dez blushed from her toes to the roots of her hair. "Sorry, sorry," he chuckled, rubbing the back of his neck ruefully. "I—" But Hunter was genuinely at a loss for words, so instead he placed his hand on the bench right next to hers, his bare pinkie pressed lightly against the side of her gloved one. Dez kept her hand perfectly still, letting herself pretend that she was just what he thought she was, a girl with one unpleasant secret and nothing else much wrong with her.

In front of them, a group of pigeons did battle over a pile of something crunchy on the ground, wings flapping with a whirring sound like files falling off a shelf.

"We should get back," she said.

"Yeah, those cases won't look themselves up," he agreed, but he took longer than necessary to pull his hand away. It was a tiny tremor of a gesture, and almost no one witnessed it: only Dez, Hunter, and a third person, a man dressed in grey who had purely by accident chosen that day of the week to clear his head by tossing kettle corn to pigeons from his favorite tree, which afforded a view of his favorite museum in the city. But Dez and Hunter didn't see him, so they left the park and walked back to the Museum, believing that no one else was aware of what they'd had for lunch.

It was a long trip back down the elevator, their moment on the bench weighing between them like an overfilled balloon, ready to burst at the slightest provocation.

"Thank you for the hotdog," said Dez, avoiding his eyes.

"Anytime," said Hunter, and it sounded like he meant it.

"Oh, Alan, I've been looking for you." Beatrix popped her head into the hall from behind a door, her tone suspiciously gay considering how narrow her eyes were.

"Went out for food," Hunter replied, leaving out any incriminating pronouns like "we."

"I have a few questions, can I borrow you for a minute?" She said it to him, but she was looking at Dez with a flash in her eyes that Dez did not care for.

"Afternoon," said Dez stiffly, and walked away feeling Beatrix's eyes boring into her back. *If she let it go too long,* she wondered, *would that thing under her skin begin to manifest in a way that Beatrix would be able to see?* She didn't want to find that out the hard way, so she had to take care of herself that evening, before that man in grey showed up in her apartment. In her current state, there was no telling what carnage his annoyingly sexy presence would cause. But she didn't have time to figure out the intricacies of the modern dating scene. What she needed was take-out.

And the easiest way for her to get it was to go where they would literally pay her to take it.

CHAPTER 11

FUMBLING IN THE DARK

The Second Circle
Friday night

Lucius was not giving Mr. Maitlin particularly good service.

To be fair, he was trying. Mr. Maitlin was the chairman of the city planning commission, the kind of man who could waive away building regulations, so Lucius sat on his white sofa, a picture of glistening golden cool, and listened to Mr. Maitlin grow increasingly truthful while describing his fantasies.

What Mr. Maitlin wanted was to violate his housekeeper. He showed Lucius the photos he'd taken of the woman with his phone, blurry snaps of her walking down a hallway with a bottle of Windex in her rubber-gloved hands. She was not an attractive woman, this housekeeper, a potato-shaped Nicaraguan lady well into her sixties, while Mr. Maitlin was a fit, good-looking, happily married silver fox, a prominent city leader admired by every woman he met, many of whom he could have fucked for free. But what he was confessing in Lucius's office was not about desire, or about boredom, or even about sex. Mr. Maitlin's housekeeper was a devout Catholic, endlessly crossing herself and averting her eyes from the modernist nude paintings that decorated his home, and he had developed a virulent contempt for her sanctimoniousness, which manifested as fantasies of penetrating her with household objects.

"The thing is," he said, stammering as his natural inhibitions melted in the pheromone-scented air, "I want her to enjoy it, and hate that she enjoys it. To the point where she cries about it later in the bathroom from shame."

"Of course," Lucius purred.

"And I want to watch her do it to herself," he continued, the contents of his pants standing at full attention. "And I want her to cry while she does that too…"

Fine, fine, all fine. Elderly housekeeper rape fantasies were boringly prevalent among people who didn't do their own cleaning. Lucius tried to look fascinated but was distracted, not because he wasn't relishing the waves of aggression-flavored lust, but because his mind was stuck on other things.

Like Vito Luppi. Vito's loyalty to his family—or to his father—was proving stronger than Lucius had calculated, but it was still unsettling that Adrael had not sorted the problem. In the three years he'd worked for Lucius, Adrael had rarely failed at anything.

"Sorry, could you repeat that?" Lucius said to Mr. Maitlin, realizing he had briefly stopped listening. He was genuinely sorry—there was almost nothing he held more sacred than people's sexual fantasies.

"With the dog," Mr. Maitlin repeated, flushing. "Our dog. Dexter."

"Oh, naturally," Lucius nodded. "No problem."

"He's a Weimaraner," Mr. Maitlin added, helpfully.

"Wonderful." Mr. Maitlin was eagerly taking to the idea—as Lucius framed it—of "replicating" his fantasies, but what he would experience at the Second Circle would be more than the facsimile he was paying for. The employee who serviced him would be selected because she already looked plausibly *like* his housekeeper (chubby-cheeked Fauna was becoming a specialist in that arena), and after a few minutes with her, Mr. Maitlin's lizard brain would believe that she and his unfortunate housekeeper were one and the same person. And far from satisfying him, the experience would be so addictive that he'd keep coming back, his frequency limited only by his bank account and his physical health, since Lucius did not want to damage his repeat customers, so he meted their fun out like medicine, which just inflamed them all the more.

Win-win.

Of course, Mr. Maitlin would never have thought to do any of that himself; he had stepped into Lucius's office with the intent of ordering a threesome with a couple of models and maybe—*maybe*—a prostate toy; an experience a guy could brag about to his buddies without shame. But Lucius's hypnotic influence wheedled out the truth, not by asking what made Mr. Maitlin aroused, but rather what made him *angry*. That, Lucius knew, was a more reliable indicator of what truly got people off.

Beep. Lucius's phone told him that someone downstairs wanted his attention, so he smoothly let Mr. Maitlin know that everything he requested was no problem at all, Weimaraner included (for a slight upcharge). Then, as Mr. Maitlin walked out of the office, fervently adjusting his pants, Lucius glanced through the glass to see who had summoned him.

———

This was stupid. She should not be here. The booming bass shook the club and Dez's brain along with it. She had skipped the queue outside and handed Dark's business card directly to one of the bouncers, and then once again left her coat and phone at the coat check before following him into the crowd. If she did everything right, she'd end up working as a supernatural prostitute in a high-end brothel run by criminals—an iffy outcome. If she did anything wrong...well, that math had too many variables to consider, but the answer would be zero Desdemonas.

Still, if she wanted to stay alive she had to make concessions to her biological urges, and she could think of no other expedient way. Reality did not succumb to morality at the end of the day, no matter how fervently she clenched her fists. Plus, Vito was involved with this very nightclub, so perhaps she could also suss out his whereabouts with a little judicious probing.

Win-win. Since she was already there.

She was wearing less clothing than usual, a wispy black silk cocktail dress that covered what it had to while making clear what was underneath; a dress she'd purchased for a date and had only worn once, for an hour. She hadn't forgotten about what Hunter said about surveillance cameras, but with her eyelids coated in smokey black shadow, her hair cascading over her shoulders, and her lips stained blood red, she looked nothing like herself.

"Desirée, I'm so glad you decided to join us." Dark floated down the office stairs, a radiant sun god of silky skin and tousled hair, and assessed his new hire. She still came off so incredibly human, and if she hadn't pointed herself out, Lucius might have missed her in the crowd again. Adrael's keen eyes might have noticed her, but he was driving to Albany that night to remind a state senator of promises on which the man had failed to deliver. Maybe it was better that he was gone. Adrael detested the duplicity of sex demons, and the fact that this girl came off so human would make him squidgy, so he'd doubtless advise Lucius to have her removed. But Adrael was prone to hennishness, and if Lucius always listened to him, he'd have no fun at all.

"You made me an offer I couldn't resist," she said, almost convincingly.

"That is my specialty," he reminded her. "And I like this new look better than that wool tube sock you had on last time."

"I'm sorry, I'd never been to a sex club before," she retorted.

"This is *not* a 'sex club.' I've been to every sex club in town, with their silly vinyl outfits and idiotic rules." He meandered through the crowd as he spoke, touching people lightly with the tips of his fingers like they were items hanging in his closet. "Nobody comes out satisfied but everybody feels like they did something wrong."

"You don't have *any* rules here?"

"Oh, of course we do. For instance, we have strict guidelines about how far guests can go on the main floor. Anything heavier than petting requires a trip upstairs."

"What's upstairs?" Dez cast her eyes up at the web of silk drapery, shadowy catwalks, and flickering lights above her head.

"We own this entire building," he informed her. "There are several floors of private rooms above your head. Most of the Girls live up there. You can move in too, there's plenty of space."

"Like an old-fashioned brothel?"

"Yes, it's a much better situation. Humans *think* they want to watch other people rutting, but even the hardcore voyeurs get bored when everything's out in the open. Watching two stockbrokers fisting each other in a cage is initially shocking, but after a half hour, even that becomes passé for them. That's why people who watch too much porn eventually turn to videos of Japanese teenagers fondling fish just to feel the tang of novelty." Lucius sighed as if the collective sexual psyche of humanity disappointed him. "The one thing that *never* gets old is denial."

"So you tell them they can't do it downstairs…"

"And by the time they hit the elevator, they're halfway gone."

"Or dead," she murmured, almost to herself.

"Oh please, the staff knows when to stop. We haven't had to dump a body in the Hudson in weeks."

Dez tried not to let the Order member in her shine through, but Lucius saw a flicker of dismay on her face.

"I'm just kidding, darling," he assured her, as if it were the most boring thing in the world to say. "Rule number one is that we don't kill the guests. Dead customers are not repeat customers."

Lucius, watching her carefully, also noted a tremor of longing underneath her standoffish veneer. She really wasn't a professional; in fact, she had no idea what she was doing *at all*. That hectic look on her face was that of an alcoholic facing a full bar. *Because,* Lucius realized, *she wasn't faking being human. She was trying to be human.* He marveled at her utter madness. She would not make a good employee at first, he realized, but that ability to pass was not something that could be taught to any of the others. If she could be trained, she'd be worth her weight in gold.

And Lucius did so love gold.

A woman approached them from the bar—it was Lilith, the succubus who'd objected to Dez's presence the other night. She glared at Dez with distaste.

"The Deputy Mayor is here," she said to Lucius. "Should I start an account for him?"

"He's comped for now." Then, in a lower voice that Dez barely heard over the music, Lucius added, "We may let him pay in-kind. Tell him I'll be right with him."

She nodded obediently, shot Dez a final glance that grated like sandpaper against her skin, and sashayed away, round hips swinging.

"I don't like her either, but she gets the job done," Lucius shrugged. "She's the cat that herds the other cats, otherwise it would be pandemonium down here. But we can find you a nicer tour guide." He snapped his fingers at a lithe little creature that looked like she belonged in grade school: a sweet-faced girl with a long swath of strawberry blonde hair pulled wholesomely over one shoulder, a broad, babylike forehead, and eyes that looked ready to erupt into tears.

"This is Cherry," said Dark as the girl approached. "Say hello, Cherry."

"Hello, Cherry," Cherry replied with a sickeningly girlish smile. But it was an old woman's joke, and Dez inferred that little Cherry had been preying on the city's pedophiles for longer than Dez had been alive.

"Desirée is new," Lucius told her. "Show her the ropes. And the restraints."

He smiled silkily and headed away towards Lilith, who was standing with a youngish man in a suit gulping whiskey-and-soda like a thirsty goldfish. That, Dez realized, must be the deputy mayor of the city of New York, and, as Lucius draped one sculpted arm over his shoulder, he looked as nervous as she felt.

Whether Cherry was bored with her evening or was being paid extra for her time, she proved a willing tour guide. She led Dez around the club's labyrinthine floor plan and through the various themed rooms, VIP lounges, and adult play areas. There was job lingo to learn: by convention, the club's sex workers were referred to as "the Girls" regardless of gender, the bouncers were referred to as "the Boys" (which made sense since all of them were male), and the customers were called "guests" or "patrons" with exaggerated courtesy. Cherry showed her the dungeon in the basement with its black leather walls and concrete floor, the softer lounges on the upper mezzanine where guests tickled each other with feathers and vibrators, and the steamy cavern of heated pools surrounded by obscene frescoes like an ancient Roman bath. On one roped-off VIP platform, a party of A-list celebrity chefs were lapping chocolate off a naked girl seated on a lazy Susan, and she giggled as someone thrust their fingers up between her legs, pulled them out and sucked on the residue.

"That's extra, I suppose," Dez observed.

"Everything goes on the bill. But don't worry, the house handles all that bullshit." Cherry spoke with the worldly ennui of an elderly prostitute, but her voice was high and full of girlish italics—the ideal bait for her preferred prey. Sex demons were often drawn to the flavors of arousal that birthed them: the fervent groping of the shameful Christian, the defiant self-loathing of the zoophile, the fervid adrenaline of those who craved getting caught. Cherry had crystallized out of somebody's Lolita-inspired fever dreams, and the sweaty trespass of the pedophile was her favorite flavor.

All around them the sex demons thronged. Most, like Dez and Dark and Cherry, were definitively one gender, but others were neither, or both at once. Some switched genders, shifting like optical illusions, adjusting their flavors to the desires of the taster. Dez watched a glassy-eyed businessman drool into the mouth of a pixie-haired redhead, her delicate hands rubbing his cock through his pants, and Dez wondered what he was seeing as the Girl hot-wired his brain, putting him into a quasi-dream state in which she became everything he wanted.

Everyone on the dance floor was sticky with sprayed champagne, lint sticking to their skin and the aura of alcohol and other people's saliva on their tongues. It was repellent, but Dez wanted to rub against all of it like a cat in heat. She followed Cherry enviously as the little vixen moved through the crowd, stroking people on their arms or necks, taking little sips of them that made them sigh. It felt unnatural—even nauseating—to Dez to do the same, but the more she did it the easier it became, and the boundary between herself and the nightclub itself began to dissolve.

This was not lost on Cherry, who watched Dez with an amused smirk.

"You getting a little drunk on it all?" she chided Dez playfully. "Don't worry about it; the first time I came here, and that was two years ago, I went bananas. You have to pace yourself or you'll lose control, and that's no good." She glanced at the bouncers standing nearby with their giant arms crossed.

"Do you like working here?" Dez queried.

"You kidding? This place is paradise. It's way easier than walking some corner, and doing that high-end escort 'girlfriend experience' crap takes up time I could be getting my fix *and* getting paid for it. The only bad part is having to be around all these other bitches." She beamed at Dez, mostly without malice. "That scratchy feeling never goes away, know what I mean? Though I don't mind you so much. Maybe it's 'cause you come off so..." She eyed Dez up and down then, her gaze prickling like needles across Dez's skin. "You're, like, partly human?"

Dez nodded, knowing there was no hiding it.

"Maybe that's why," Cherry repeated, unsettled. Cherry's proximity set Dez's teeth on edge as well, but she still found her beguiling; she supposed that was the flesh-and-blood part of her that a creature like Cherry was made to beguile.

"There's lots of rules here though: no fighting, no moonlighting, no seeing clients off the books or outside the property," Cherry continued. "Management gets *pissed*. And no talking outside about anything that happens with the clients. Seriously, you pull that shit, they'll hunt you down." She said it lightly, but a shadow passed across her childlike face. "By the way, that's a nice dress, but anything you wear in here's gonna get stained, so pull something outta the club closet next time. Don't worry, it all gets cleaned, this place is class. And keep track of special requests, 'cause everything's gotta go on the bill. That's a pain, but we get a percentage. Once upon a time I didn't get the point of money, but when you don't have to worry about where your next meal's coming from, nice clothes and shit start to have their appeal. I kinda get the designer shoe thing now."

It was indeed a convenient arrangement; these creatures were safe in that cushy pleasure palace from both the tough competition in the streets and the shadowy threat of the Order. There was no real downside other than having to remain civil with one other, like feral dogs gnawing on the same carcass. But it was a big carcass, with more than enough to go around, and the clientele paid for it all, walking themselves into the feeding pen like willing cattle.

"But the number one rule is: don't overdo it," Cherry warned her. "You send one guest to the emergency room, that's it. You're axed."

"Does that happen often?"

"It happens. It sucks to have to stop right when you're ready to..." she sighed. "But this is a pretty good gig. I've been here two years, and most of the Girls who left got shitcanned for damaging the clientele."

Interesting. That put the girl under the bridge in a new light, if it was true.

They watched a Girl with a wiggle like an eel climb onto the lap of a VIP-section werewolf, some rock star with Versace sunglasses perched in his pouffy hair. Nobody seemed bothered by the expression jittering across his face as he began to turn, like a squid flashing its colors.

"Is that alright?" Dez marveled.

"Orchid knows her way around the moonies. When he starts to get frisky she'll take him upstairs so the normos don't see. But I wouldn't try that my first day," Cherry warned. "It takes practice to handle a moonie. If you give it to them and pull away too fast they get mad. Take too much, they also get mad. You have to have control over them, or it's a goddamn mess."

"How do you get control?"

"Same way you get to Carnegie Hall, honey: practice, practice, practice," Cherry snickered; another vintage joke. "You should try it one day. It can be great; you don't have to worry you're gonna hurt 'em."

What would actual release feel like? Dez eyed the more attractive werewolves in the VIP room with a closer eye; discerning them from humans on sight was becoming easier for her.

"And there's some real money in it if you got the stomach for the rough stuff," Cherry added quietly. "Like these Godfather types who come in here. I call 'em the 'Linguinis' 'cause they're all mobbed up."

The Luppi. It had to be. Dez leaned forward and lowered her voice.

"Are they here now?"

"I dunno, maybe," Cherry craned her neck around. "I don't think I've seen 'em this week. Two of 'em usually hang out downstairs—one's a puppy who likes playing with titties in the pools and the other one's a grumpy fuck who sits at the back bar alone. But I know a couple of the Girls racked up real hazard pay for dealing with the hot one, the main Linguini."

"What does 'hazard pay' mean?"

"The Girls maybe get paid extra to let him shred them a little. That's a thing with moonies sometimes, they'll break some bones, spill some blood...but this guy..." She raised her eyebrows eloquently. "It takes some real skills to let a guy like that off the leash for bit before you hit the brakes."

"Has anybody died?"

"Nah. The boss only gives him Girls that can handle him. I'm not up for getting all torn up, but the money's good, if you're into that stuff. There's always somebody willing to fork over to get some flesh between their teeth. That whole *human* thing you got might be a selling point. I guess."

She said it with disdain, but Dez detected a whiff of envy. Young nightcrawlers were like smoke, ephemeral and often just one meal away from dissolving into thin air. Older ones like Cherry and Lilith, and Dark himself, were more solid, but acquiring such substance took time. Having a physical body that felt pain and could get broken was a liability, but it was the very substance of existence, and thus much to be desired. Dez had been born with flesh and blood, but she still felt the threatening black hole of existential emptiness looming before her when her body began to eat itself to stay alive.

A group of giggling revelers tumbled towards them out of the crowd, a bachelor party for a celebrity groom breaking all his vows in advance, collecting hangers-on in their infectious enthusiasm. And as they passed they scooped Dez and Cherry along in their glitter-speckled joy, and Dez found herself engulfed in a flurry of groping hands, the Girls in charge steering the crowd expertly toward the elevators.

"Time to head upstairs," said Cherry as a man's hairy hands plucked at her underdeveloped breasts, her pink mouth grinning with a predator's joy at the taste of fresh meat. Someone else's hands slid along Dez's lower back, the contact sizzling against her skin, and as the distinction between their bodies melted away, the march to the elevator began to feel like floating.

———

The elevator rose to the third floor and the group spilled out into a hallway lined with red velvet wallpaper, red velvet carpets, and rows of closed doors, like a lavish hotel. From underneath every door wafted the ripe emanations of body parts being worked into a frenzy. Dez peeked inside one cracked door and caught a glimpse of an older man in a leather swing on the receiving end of something that involved a bucket, while in another room, a naked woman had a pink strap-on dildo rising out of her lap, a water gun in her hand, and a glass aquarium teeming with live mice on a cart beside her.

But Dez barely registered any of it as she moved with the throng towards a room at the end of the hall in a whirl of velvet and skin, drunk on the glorious rush of feeding. In that room of pillowy velvet and leather, she lost track of whose body she was touching, and for the first time in her life she felt...free. Guilt was a distant shadow in the back of her mind as the ecstatic revelers roiled like a nest of snakes, anonymous hands sliding luxuriously across her skin. Cherry rode the lap of a sweaty man who smelled like a video-game console, her little hands clutching his wobbly chest with spasmodic vigor. Her body language was that of an inexperienced girl in the throes of her first arousal, but her face had transformed, the black pupils expanding so wide they almost made the whites disappear, and her pink lips, though parted like those of a living sex doll, quivered with the tensile energy of a cheetah gripping the throat of a thrashing gazelle. And then Dez looked up at the mirrored ceiling, and saw, peeking out from the writhing throng, the very same look on her own face. But more faces began to flash through her mind, faces of people she didn't recognize performing acts that weren't happening, and she realized she was tapping into the fantasies of the people around her.

And then, unbidden, images of people she *did* know flashed before her mind's eye.

Of men, specifically. Of Hunter. And Dark.

And the man in grey.

Dez shot up as if a bucket of ice water had been tossed over her. She struggled to her feet; hands reflexively clutched at her, but nobody noticed her leave. The walk down the long hallway was agony as the demonic part of her body screamed for her to go back into that room, but through a fog of arousal, she understood she had almost lost control in the worst possible place to do so, so she summoned the elevator and made herself step inside. She hadn't noticed before that the car was padded with white leather; an effect meant to be kinky, but to Dez it looked like a cell in a mental institution.

Before she could press any buttons, the elevator lurched downwards to the building's second level, the doors slid open, and Dark stepped in, followed by the deputy mayor, his boyish face flushed, a turgid erection threatening the seams around his zipper. Dark had one languid arm still draped around his shoulders, and he flashed Dez a conspiratorial wink as he pressed the button for the fourth floor. She rode up with them until the elevator slid open again to reveal a hallway lined in coral-toned velvet, stretching out before them like an opulent vaginal canal. Dark pulled the Deputy Mayor into it to find out what the rest of the evening would bring, leaving Dez behind.

The doors closed on her again, but the car remained suspended, momentarily unbidden by anyone. And as she blinked blankly at the pearlized elevator buttons with their printed black numbers, trying to make herself remember where she'd been meaning to go, she realized there was something off about the numbers on the panel. Specifically, that they only went up to the sixth floor.

And Dez was sure that the Second Circle's building, seen from the outside, was seven stories tall.

The disparity bothered her, as all puzzles did, and it shook her out of her daze. She contemplated the issue, trying to account for basement levels or mezzanine levels, but though she could imagine a thousand contortive ways to explain it, she knew instinctively that buttons one through six simply went to floors one through six, because no one was meant to simply find their way up to floor seven.

But, she recalled, that was not her first time in a trick elevator. After a moment of hesitation at the very notion of such trespass, she allowed herself to—experimentally—press the "Door Close" button once. Nothing happened. Then, less timidly, she tried floors 1 and 2 together, then 2 and 3 and on in every combination, but the elevator didn't budge. Dez's compulsive curiosity was fully piqued now, and she knew she'd never stop thinking about it if she left without finding out what—or who—was hidden on that seventh floor, so she leaned in examine the buttons more closely.

The numbers themselves were all well-used, though "Door Close" was barely touched. But the red "ALARM" button had a lot of smudging on its surface, and like the number buttons (and practically every other surface in that nightclub) it had traces of glitter stuck to it.

Dez doubted that that shiny, new, barely three-year-old elevator got jammed very often, and the combination of hunger and curiosity hot-wired her better instincts and made her reach impulsively for the red button.

But then she stopped.

Too easy.

Instead, she pressed the alarm button and the "2" button simultaneously—of all the available numbers, that one seemed the most likely. And after a breathless second, the elevator obligingly slid upwards. It passed floor 5, then floor 6, and continued on until, with the gentlest of clicks, it hit the top.

The doors then parted with a gleaming "ding," revealing another set of metal doors, even heavier ones this time, with a numeric keypad next to them.

Never mind. Dez hardly knew enough about Dark to guess his code, and she suspected that even one incorrect entry would trigger some brutal security system. She reached out her index finger to send herself back to the main floor, but then took one more look at the keypad, examining the surface of the numbered buttons themselves, running her finger lightly over the surface of the keys. Out of the twelve, eight were completely clean and did not appear to have been touched recently, if at all. But four of them were slightly sticky, and even more tellingly, had a fine film of glitter stuck on the surface as well: the "0," "1," "2," and "4."

Now all that remained was the combination. A mind like Dark's would have centuries of obscure references to choose from, of course, so it could be a year, a cipher, a reference…Dante's work was itself rife with numerological puzzles…but after racking her brain for a long moment for likely combinations of meaningful digits, all the while waiting for someone to summon the elevator below her and render the whole question moot, a possibility occurred to her that was so asinine she could hardly credit it. *Could it be?* But of course it could. Because of all the dates Dark might have had bouncing around in his mind, the one most important to him could very well be the birthday of the thing he seemed to love most: that nightclub itself.

0214. Valentine's Day.

Her finger tapped the four numbers, and with a polite electronic beep, the security system disarmed and the doors slid open, admitting Dez into the seventh story.

Which was, apparently, Lucius's inner sanctum. The whole floor was one vast penthouse,

If the Louvre had spent the night at an orgy in a brothel and vomited up the result, it would have been that decadent melange of antique furniture, white fur, and gilt paint, like a cake covered in gold frosting half-digested in champagne, the air saturated with fragrant, vaporous clouds of lust seeping through the HVAC from the club downstairs. Priceless art lined the floor and walls, lit by twinkling chandeliers and banks of crystalline mirrors, the rooms full of paintings and sculptures of ecstatic figures being ravished by animals, gods, and satyrs. Everywhere, eager male hands rendered in oil paint or marble grabbed the waists and wrists of struggling nymphs, girls with flowing tresses batted their eyes at descending angels, youths with rosy lips acceded to the pleas of wet-haired mermaids, and bare nipples rendered by long-dead geniuses winked from every corner. But as Dez scanned the pieces, realizing how many centuries of art it represented, she recognized the same face smiling out of many of the canvases, over and over. She saw it on a laughing marble Pan mounting a nymph, in a Botticelli *Amor* clutching at a *Psyche,* even peeking out from under the wide-brimmed hat of a Vermeer roué leering at milkmaid in the usual soft window light. And every painting and sculpture that *didn't* contain that face was clustered around the ones that *did,* art appreciating art.

It was him, the Second Circle's enigmatic owner.

Mr. Dark.

A faint buzz in Dez's brain reminded her that she should leave before anyone else came up, but she was no longer listening to such feeble alarms, not when she might find a final painting in the depths of that chamber that was, perhaps, doing Dark's aging for him.

She tiptoed from chamber to chamber on soft white carpet, passing baroque chaise longues, Persian rugs, and Georgian tea-tables. She peeked into a vast walk-in closet full of silk and velvet designer clothes, a toy pantry full of dildos, butt-plugs, and other more obscure historical sexual geegaws, and even glanced inside a fridge stocked with the kinds of snacks people nibbled on during orgies—Prosecco and grapes and chocolate. The place was a bit of a mess, with clothing tossed carelessly over the arms of chairs and wineglasses with the congealing residue of some vintage Chianti in the bottom leaving rings on the side tables— clearly Dark enjoyed himself up there, probably with guests.

Whether they left via the elevator or some hidden corpse chute was still anybody's guess.

Finally, she reached the back of the penthouse and stepped into the rearmost room, an unassuming, comparatively boring chamber that contained only a Victorian roll-top desk and a couple of armchairs. On the back wall hung a lush medieval tapestry depicting the moment in the Garden of Eden when Eve found herself on the receiving end of an offer *she* couldn't refuse, the mother of mankind rendered with an apple between her teeth and the lower end of the snake disappearing between her legs.

Ding. Dez heard the elevator chime, and soft footsteps padded into the apartment.

She was trapped.

She was dead.

Unless.

The tapestry hung to the floor, and there was a gap of about ten inches between it and the wall—room for the centuries-old fabric to breathe—so Dez slipped behind it, listening as the steps paced unnervingly close. But the tapestry smelled musty, and was tickling her nose. Any moment she would sneeze—

But then something clicked back under her hands, and the section of wall she leaned on silently slid slightly backwards. She pushed harder and the wall relented, swinging open without a sound, and Dez didn't stop to worry about what was behind that trick door before slipping inside and pushing it shut. She found herself in a hidden chamber, cozy but uncluttered, a Renaissance-style "closet" or "Retiring Room," meant for the sole use of the master of the house. The walls were lined in red flocked velvet, and it was exquisitely lit to highlight the paintings that lined the walls.

These were all portraits; the works spanned centuries, but they all contained the same subject. And unlike the more subtle likenesses in the rest of the apartment, the model for them had been rendered with unquestionable faithfulness, and there was no mistaking the features of Mr. Dark on every canvas. There he was in a smoky DaVinci, a mournful Raphael, a muscular Michelangelo. Manet painted him in a morning suit, in a medieval Van Eyck he'd been rendered with an audacious purple head wrap, and Jacques Louis David had depicted him in military uniform. There were couples portraits too, in which he'd posed with different women painted by different painters at different eras, standing behind them with his hands placed on their shoulders like a husband. And one piece was still to come; a prime space on the wall had been cleared for something largish, the empty spot already lit, pencil marks around where the missing piece would hang.

Another dirty wineglass and an office binder sat on the floor, plastic-sleeved pages in a pile collated beside it as if someone were swapping them out. Dez carefully leafed through them and saw that each sheet had a photograph of a painting and a list of previous owners and years owned: provenances, the paperwork of a careful collector. The headings contained the names of the subject or subjects:

Portrait of a Man with a Lavender Chaperon, 1431

The Marquis and Marquesa de Villeneuve, 1610.

The Earl & Countess Kingston-Upon-Hull, 1875.

Portrait of a Young Man (unnamed), 1509

Cupid on His Throne, 1610

Count Franz Lónyay and the Countess Zsofia on the occasion of their First Anniversary, 1730.

Lots of names, lots of titles, lots of women and a few men, but in every portrait, that same face and shimmering blond head. Hundreds of years were represented in those paintings, eons of Dark preying on the wealthy, marrying for money, and then letting his wives and lovers die from his amorous ministrations and leave him their fortunes. Dez marveled that such an ancient being could exist for so long, and so brazenly, without the Order catching up to him. But then the memory of any Order member was necessarily limited to a normal human life span, and Dark had centuries to learn to elude them.

She thought fast. That room held a lot of valuable artwork—Dark's most valuable—and it would be a tinderbox during a fire without a back exit. If the authorities or the Order came raiding, the place had to have an emergency exit.

Or perhaps, another trick door.

Dez slid her hands along the corners of the walls, feeling for hidden catches. The steps outside came closer, and she looked around frantically for somewhere to hide, but there was no furniture in that chamber except for one swiveling leather armchair that Dark probably sat in to confer with his collection. But if this was going to be her last day on earth, she didn't want to die surrounded by so many pairs of the same mocking golden eyes.

Then, as if in answer to a prayer she hadn't yet bothered with, her fingertips found a seam. A hidden panel in the back corner clicked open under the light pressure of her hand, revealing a cutout door spilling out to a narrow, fluorescent-lit stairway that led, she hoped, back down to the main floor. Slipping through it, she pulled the hidden door closed just as the secret door on the other side of the room swung open. Then, praying that none of the metal stairs squeaked, she fled downwards.

Seven stories of stairs ended at yet another hidden door, the seams barely visible in the low light. Dez pushed on it and stumbled out into a service hallway. Employees rushed by with dishes from the kitchen, stained pillows, and extension cords for whatever depraved electronics needed a few more inches, but nobody noticed Dez slip out the hidden door panel. She saw a red EXIT sign at the end of the hall: the service entrance. She hurried toward it, smoothing out her sticky dress and trying to look innocent, and the two bouncers guarding the back door never even looked at her as she pushed between them and stepped into a the crisp, exhaust-perfumed air of the club's back alley.

Chinatown
    Friday night

Teo was dead.

And according to the voicemail left on Giulio's phone by his cousin Benny, it wasn't a normal bullet that killed him, but a custom-made hollow-point round filled with an amalgam of silver powder and glue. The average werewolf could survive most normal gunshot wounds to any body part except the head, but that cruel little bullet hit Teo's hipbone and shattered, spraying silver dust into his organs, both shredding them and preventing healing. It had clearly been purpose-made by an expert to kill werewolves, and after several agonizing days, it did the job. Teo never woke up, and what had occurred in that alley was now a secret between Giulio and Vito alone.

Giulio sat in the bathroom of a boba cafe weeping so hard his stomach cramped, while his cell phone flashed silently with missed calls. *Teo shouldn't have even been there that night*—it was pure stupidity, always following Giulio uninvited, ever since they were kids. *And now Teo was dead, and that was punishment enough.* But nothing had happened to Vito, and that seemed unbearably unfair.

Vito reckoned he'd pulled one over on Giulio that night when he'd sent him out to pick up dinner and then sneaked out to go get a fix. He'd sworn that he was going clean, but Giulio knew better than to take an addict's word for anything, and so he followed him. And later— when Giulio walked in with dinner *a full hour and a half later*—Vito didn't even have the guile to ask, "What took you so long?" It was disappointing that Vito wasn't a better liar, if he was going to bother.

Giulio loved his cousin—everyone in the family did. Vito was so handsome and so charming and so much of everything that mattered. His streak of abashed self-indulgence had been more endearing than not before all this: a side effect of being his father's only son, and the baby in the family. The rules weren't the same for everyone—Giulio knew that all to well— but anyone could die equally easily, including Teo, that happy-go-lucky idiot who always made sure someone else got the last meatball on the plate.

So Giulio, with fresh venom in his heart, picked up his phone and dialed his Uncle Massimo's number, determined to make things right.

———

Dez headed for the subway, gulping the night air like black coffee and quavering at the thought that she'd just been in the home of someone old enough to remember the black plague. An oppressive sense of deep time came over her and she felt like a tiny raft adrift at sea. Most in the Order regarded individuals like Dark as more or less mythical, if they were aware of them at all, but certain factions deep within the organization made it their sole mission to follow traces of such people through the ever-dimming historical record, eliminating them when they possibly could. Such a being was the embodiment of evil for them, on par with the devil himself. Dez knew she should tell someone about him, but could hardly do so without explaining *how* she knew.

As she sobered up from the air in the club, she reflected that nobody she'd encountered that night even appealed to her, and some had frankly repelled her. But her body had gleefully imbibed them all, drawing in their putrid essences even as she gagged on their smells. And it wanted more, the traitor. She felt less urgently horny now, but still nauseated and weary and excited all at the same time, like a child after too much birthday party. It was more dangerous than she realized for her to go to that club, and not just because of Dark; the more time she spent there, the bigger the predatory part of her grew. Presented with such bounty, it threatened to overtake her. She should not go back there, not even to find Vito, whom she had almost forgotten about in her distress. And anyway, if Vito *was* a regular at the Second Circle, there should be no reason for him to pick up girls on the street.

And there was menace there, hovering in the sweet, sticky air. Dez recalled Dark's unforgiving attitude toward competition, and his acidic comment about not allowing freelancers. It could be no coincidence that the vape-loving succubus she'd met under the bridge was an ex-employee, and that first dead girl could easily have been one as well. Were an employee to leave the club, they would be nothing but a liability, and a business that relied on client blackmail might be unwilling let its former employees go their own way.

But, she realized, Dark might be loathe to ask any of his other more thick-armed employees to do the job—keeping that quiet in-house would be tricky. *We'll let him pay in-kind*, Dark had said of the deputy mayor, and Dez wondered if Vito, too, had been offered another way to pay his nightclub fees. Tearing up a few troublesome succubi who may or may not have already been acquainted with him would have been barely a night's work, and if Vito did prefer succubus sex, he'd be paying himself simply by doing the task required.

Win-win. For everyone but the dead girls.

Given all these distracting thoughts, Dez might have been forgiven for missing that someone was following her. But then, following people without being noticed was Rat's stock-in-trade. He first caught sight of the Order girl as she left the club, charging out the back door where he often loitered, his wiry body tucked into a corner, all the better to eavesdrop on the private conversations of other employees who used the alley to smoke. At first Rat registered her only as some anonymous clubbing beauty who'd had too much of what the Second Circle served up. It was only when she trotted away from the club without a coat that she caught his attention. The contours of her shape from behind looked familiar, but when she flicked her head around to glance behind her—furtively, Rat thought—he recognized her. She looked different in that whisper of a dress, with her hair down and all that smeared makeup, but Rat was good at remembering faces, and hers was memorable.

A Roach. Adrael's cadre of musclebound idiots were supposed to kick out any Order members, but Rat recalled then that he himself had forgotten to put her photo in the book of Order faces that they kept in the security room. He began to panic; he doubted any of those thickheads would even have recognized her in that getup as the straight-laced girl in those pictures, but Adrael would surely remember her, because Rat had been fool enough to point her out to him that day at the crime scene.

Thus her infiltration, if discovered, could be considered Rat's fault.

Stalking Order members was unwise unless one meant to kill them; the risk of being caught and dissolved in thoughtwater was too high. But Rat was good at following people who were good at not being followed; people didn't smell him in their vicinity the way they often instinctively smelled werewolves. New Yorkers were perpetually within a few feet of rats, so through sheer olfactory fatigue, no one noticed them anymore; a fact which applied to Rat as well. Humiliating though that was, it meant that Rat was able to move among people largely unobserved, and he wasn't about to let whatever mess this Order girl might make cost him his job.

Or, if it was bad enough, his skin.

————

Chinatown

Massimo Luppi stalked through the streets of downtown Manhattan, his collar turned up against the pissing rain. He usually had a posse all around him—thugs, bodyguards, relatives—but tonight he was out in the city alone for the first time in years. What he needed to do, he had to do without an audience.

He found the flophouse, the Pacifica, a fluorescent-lit establishment coated in cheap white tile like a third-world dentist's office, the air vibrating with an incessant low-fi buzz. The building looked too skinny to be a hotel, as if it had been hastily glued into place between two real buildings, and everything inside was thinner than normal—alright for the recent Chinese immigrants it catered to, but a tight squeeze for Massimo these days. He passed through the empty lobby with its fake marble counters and plastic plants, and stomped up the cramped stairs. The air in the stairwell smelled of bad breath and poverty, and as he climbed, the gun in his pocket dug into his thigh. He felt itchy and hot under his shirt as every hair on his body stood on end. *It* was under there waiting to emerge, but Massimo hadn't let it break through in a decade and didn't plan to do so here. Not in Chinatown like some mook. Not with what he had to do that night.

When he reached the door he sought, he knocked. And he waited. Somebody in socks tiptoed up to the door looked through the peep-hole. A long time passed, minutes, during which that person didn't move at all, but eventually the door opened and Massimo found himself facing his youngest child and only son. Vito looked strung-out, his hair unwashed, and he was half-transformed, but in a tired way, as if he'd done it so often recently his skin was getting stretched out. The look in his bloodshot eyes was that of a rabid dog that knows it's about to be put down.

Massimo stepped into the room and closed the door without saying a word. Vito turned around and sat on the bed facing the brick wall outside the room's sole window, his back slumped, half from the sagging mattress and half from shame, and waited for the bullet he deserved. But Vito was glad his father had come himself instead of sending his goons. Having faced his father in that moment of truth, he thought he could handle facing his God. Vito knew it wasn't personal. Everyone in the family lived under the same rules, and Massimo, as head of the family, had to set the standard. A king could pardon others, but he couldn't pardon himself, or his son, not without losing his integrity. And it wasn't the first time they'd made that choice in that branch of the family.

So Vito waited. And said a prayer, and waited some more. But all that happened was that his father sat down next to him on the bed, put his big arm around Vito's shoulders, and kissed him, for the first time in a long time, on the top of his greasy, matted head.

Chapter 12

Mooning Around

The Upper West Side
Saturday morning

Dez sat at her desk at home clicking listlessly through a cascade of website tabs on her laptop, looking up the few names she could remember from the paintings in Dark's penthouse. One "Marquesa of Altamira"—a woman Dez recalled as a pale face framed by a powdered wig—had suffered an untimely death from "consumption," and patchy 17th-century legal records noted the transfer of her estate to her husband, the then-marquis. But, combing through a particularly chatty family history compiled by a later Victorian descendant, Dez read that the siblings suspected the marquis of doing away with her and so prevented him from taking ownership. After that, he disappeared into the smoke of history, off to some other principality to pull the same trick on some other titled woman under yet another name. Dark's Bluebeard chamber was a gruesome testament to the many wives and lovers he'd consumed, his steady diet of sweet nothings reducing them to sagging corpses between linen bedsheets.

She closed the laptop with a thrill of triumph, peeled off her bathrobe and headed to the bathroom, sure that she'd find more on Dark in the Order archives now that she had some breadcrumbs to follow. But when she was showered and dressed, she searched the apartment for her coat for several minutes before she realized that she'd left it at the nightclub coat check.

Along with her phone. And her wallet.

Fuck.

She had promised herself that she'd never go back, but even if she was willing to lose a tailored coat she particularly liked, she couldn't just leave her phone and wallet there. The staff might not notice it immediately—some guests didn't leave the club until the early morning hours, and people forgot their belongings all the time. But after a day or two the coat check girls were sure to spot the missing numbered key, pry open the locker, and investigate the contents. No Order member's driver's license stated their real address, but Dez's did have her real name, which would let Dark know exactly whose phone that was. The phone itself was a throwaway burner, and Order members were trained to delete all texts and photos and voicemails regularly and never store phone numbers under names. Agents who lost electronic devices were told to inform the tech department of the loss, and steps would be taken to mitigate leaks. But Dez couldn't tell the Order she'd lost her phone at the *Second Circle*, and if anyone from the Order called *her* and got Dark on the line instead...

She had to get that phone back.

But the club didn't open until nine p.m., and Dez was loath to go in early and draw attention to herself. She would sneak in under cover of a crowd that night and retrieve her items from the coat check when the attendants were at their busiest, and then leave and never come back. In the meantime, she dared not go into the Order without a phone to leave at the door—suspicious in itself—and then be forced to wait all day for a call to come in that would hang her. She could only stay at home and wait, like a bat in a cave, for the sun to go down.

"Something wrong?"

Dez turned around to see the man in grey standing in her apartment, leaning nonchalantly on the window ledge. She wasn't entirely surprised to see him — it had been roughly a week, as he'd promised — but it was unnerving that she'd had no inkling he'd come in, and having his potent presence inflicted on her without warning filled her with irritation.

"Don't you knock?" she snapped.

"Never." He flashed her a cheeky sideways smile, but it went unreturned, and he found himself unable to draw on his usual buttery charm. During the five hours he'd spent in the car driving to and from Albany the previous night, the idea of her was a constant presence in his empty passenger's seat. He hadn't even bothered to stop by the club when he came back, driving directly to her apartment instead, as if compelled. Now that he was standing in front of her, the warm reality of her made his memory seem like an anemic shadow by comparison, as she stood there blinking at him like an owl from across the room.

He hadn't spoken to her in a week, but he *had* seen her, since she and her Order friend happened to pick his favorite spot in the Park to have lunch. Of course, what she did with herself—and with other men —was nothing to him, although it was awfully daring of her to flirt with one of her dangerously judgmental colleagues, given what she had to hide. The moonie investigator was admittedly a handsome man, in that rumpled way some women liked, but he was still just a mere mortal who had no clue what he was tapping pinkies with on that bench. A girl had a right to keep her hand in the game, he supposed, but it rankled that this creature he'd been regarding as his own personal secret was in reality a flesh-and-blood woman whom others might get to examine from closer up than he did.

When Adrael felt acquisitive, he generally cured it by indulging in the thing he wanted—eating the cake, so to speak—and after a few bites he was usually over it. It was a bit awkward that he was extorting her, but with Adrael, women usually got past such things without any coaxing. In her case, though, he was unsure if she even *liked* him. He could tell she liked the way he *looked*, from how her body responded to his presence; that was a fact of life, when you looked like him. But she also seemed to want to push him off the roof sometimes, and not in a "foreplay" sort of way.

"Those have really come into their own," Adrael observed, nodding at the peonies, fluffy as overturned can-can dancers, fanning their transgressive perfume into the air. A few openly displayed their strange alien hearts, in which six little buds peeked out like a clutch of carnivorous clitorises surrounded by tantalizing layers of soft pink petals.

"If you like that sort of thing," she shrugged heartlessly.

"How was your week?" he sighed, resorting to facile pleasantries. "Did you find Bigfoot?"

"No, just another dead nightcrawler. That girl from the alley. The one I tried to...save."

"Ah. I'm...sorry." He even managed to look almost sincere.

"We weren't exactly friends," Dez reminded him, with more vinegar than she intended. "It's just lucky that we found her before the police did."

"Lucky for who?"

"All of us," Dez replied.

"So you're putting that murder down to Vito, too?"

"In the absence of a better notion, yes. But I am alone in that assessment, unless you happen to agree."

"If he killed one, he probably killed the other," he allowed. "So do you have something for me?"

I sure do, big boy. Come and get it. Dez shook off the voice in her head, which sounded annoyingly like Cherry. She had no business getting wet over an extranatural criminal with the morals of a shark who would despise her if he knew the truth about what she was. She wondered if human women ever felt this compulsive and voracious and enraged all at once, like a hungry spring bear biting at a freshly fertile world.

"Here you go." Dez pulled a notepad out of her desk drawer and tossed it across the room at him. "This is what we have in the file, including every address for every member of the Luppi family. Home addresses, businesses, offices, restaurants. Everything."

Well, almost.

She had, of course, omitted Carmine, and had also made no mention of Vito's connection to that treacherous nightclub, purely to prevent that stupid man in grey from running in there, guns blazing, and getting his beautiful head blown off for his trouble. Dez couldn't bear the idea, for the same reason she hadn't tossed away his stupid peonies. And even if Vito *was* working for them, he clearly didn't *live* there, since Cherry said she hadn't seen him for weeks, and that notebook contained plenty of information to find him outside it, if this beast in grey put his rather broad back into it. Surely Vito would resurface when he felt safe, or run to a relative when he ran out of money, and every one of *them* was listed on that notepad, other than Carmine, who was Vito's least-likely option.

Adrael glanced through the notes; they were thorough, describing in detail the Luppi family structure, their famous crimes, and even the tea they drank to tamp down their condition. The address list ran on and on, spread over all five New York boroughs and even spilling into New Jersey. He'd be driving around for days, but he welcomed that task; it was a more useful version of the pointless pacing he'd been doing in his mind ever since meeting this irritating woman.

"This is a lot of information," he remarked. "Yet you people let them keep walking around."

"We're not the police. There's only so much we can do without tipping our hand."

"So it's only the weak that have anything to fear from you."

"Yes, but I'm sure you only pick fights with bigger boys," she sniped.

"If you see a boy bigger than me, feel free to point him in my direction," Adrael retorted.

Dez could think of several. Sizable though he was, he was still smaller than many of those meat-demons guarding the Second Circle. But she suspected this cocky man would consider that a challenge, even though those bruisers were unlikely to take anyone as pretty as him seriously.

"There, that wasn't so hard, was it?" he chirped, nodding approvingly at the notebook and tucking it in his pocket.

"You'd be surprised."

"Is your position there so very precarious? That goo on your fingers can't be all it takes to pass or everyone would do it, so they must trust you for some reason."

He must trust you. The thought of her on the bench with that man flared up in his mind again, making him feel unaccountably sweaty.

"Of course they do."

"Why?"

Dez blinked at him, but didn't have a ready lie, and Adrael twisted his lips in frustration. She seemed different today, even more guarded and nervy than before, and her evasiveness was maddening.

"Why do they trust you?" he repeated more intently.

"I—" Dez began, but no—that was surely too much to admit, particularly to *him.* "Because I am above reproach," she sniffed.

But Adrael was not feeling quite himself that day either, and as her eyes once again shifted away from his, something in him snapped. Before he realized what he was doing, he had moved across the room until he stood inches away from her, close enough to throttle her if he liked. She startled and backed away until her back hit the wall, but he stepped forward, placing his hand on the wall by her head and leaning on it like a high school bully.

"Why?" He repeated, and his voice became a throaty purr that vibrated through Dez's chest.

"I have the...required provenance," she ground out.

"Then what are you so afraid of?"

"Who says I'm afraid?" Her skin burned as if the molecules in the air were heated to a frenzy by his presence. The scent of him swamped her senses, and the urge to touch him was far more intense than anything she'd experienced at that nightclub. Images of his heavy, naked frame curving over her in the dark swamped her mind, and she could practically feel the rough weight of him along her limbs and the firm flesh of his neck and chest against her lips. The only thing keeping her from pulling him towards her and devouring him was knowing that as soon as she touched him he'd discover what she really was, and his ocean-blue eyes would go cold with disgust.

"I'm good at knowing when people are afraid," he said. "And you're trembling."

"You climb in my window anytime you want and threaten me, and you have the nerve to ask me why I'm afraid?" she shot back; she *was* trembling, but it wasn't out of fear.

Maybe he should just fuck her and get it out of the way. Adrael's heated mind conjured the image of her slipping out of all that black wool, her lithe body lying naked beneath him, her dark hair spilling across the pillow, her mischievous eyes gazing up at him with raw desire. The idea made him even twitchier than such thoughts normally did, and his body surprised him by going instantly, alarmingly hard.

"How do you get away with it?" he pressed. Not knowing had become unbearable, even though he couldn't think of a reason it should matter to him.

"I...I didn't join the Order the usual way," she confessed, once again finding herself miserably unable to lie to him. "My mother was already in the Order when I was born."

"And she just pretended you were human?"

Dez nodded tersely.

"But the Order must still have baptized you as a baby. Not in some church birdbath, but with the real thing." Holy water had always been a dividing line between the clean and the corrupt, from Hindus to Catholics, and the devoted still sprayed each other with droplets of it to make sure everyone present was "clean." Of course, the holy water that filled the fonts of the world's temples and churches was always just regular water; the Order made doubly sure of it, in fact, since they hardly needed priests inadvertently dissolving extrahuman babies while horrified godparents filmed on their phones. But a baptism for an Order member's baby would necessarily have been done with the genuine article.

"I gather that she somehow switched out my baptism water," she told him in a small voice, and then instantly regretted it; stated out loud it sounded shameful.

"How did she manage that?"

"She never told me and I never asked."

"Not asking seems rather out of character for you."

"Some things are better left untouched," she swallowed, even as she imagined stroking the hollow of his clavicle, the curve of his jaw, and the wave-like curl of his upper lip. He leaned even closer, telling himself it was to menace her and not because he was being drawn to her dewy skin like a magnet.

"So you went into the family business, just like Vito," he observed drily. "How—"

"Just find him so we can all feel better about ourselves," she sniped, flushing red. It was all Dez could do to stop herself from leaning forward and finding out what a man that beautiful tasted like, and the effort frayed her last nerve.

"No one who looks like you should have an issue with self esteem," he murmured tartly, meaning to sound caddish but managing only testy, and he realized he'd said more than he meant to.

She narrowed her eyes at him.

"Was that...a compliment?"

"Have you not heard one in a while?" He abruptly stepped several feet back, feeling off-kilter. "Anyway, thank you for the—um—assistance." He tapped the notepad in his pocket, his manner stiff. "I'll let you know if I find Vito so you can put little 'x's over his eyes in your file."

"Yes, do that."

"I should probably point out that you're not nearly as afraid of me as you should be," he said then, but to his infinite annoyance he sounded more petulant than threatening.

"Are you jealous that the Order is more frightening than you?" she scoffed.

Jealous. The very word hit Adrael like cold water. His agitated brain denied him an appropriate riposte, so he threw her a sarcastic smile that just felt like failure. Dez turned triumphantly away as he left hastily via the window, only to see those blasted peonies winking at her from across the room.

———

Rat remembered the first time he saw an Order member, watching through his childhood bedroom window the night they came for his neighbor. Mr. Strykowski was just an old crank in a bathrobe who shook his fist at the kids who picked his roses, but Rat knew even then that he and Mr. Strykowski had something in common. That "thing" made them different from normal people, and even as a ten-year-old, Rat understood the reason that the people in black came for Mr. Strykowski when, in a fit of senility, he lost control on some teenagers who were pissing on his lawn. Rat did not know the word "werewolf" then, but he realized that whatever he and his brother (and poor Mr. Strykowski) were was a problem, and that if those people in black found out that Rat and his brother existed, they'd start watching them too. The high-rolling immortals who rolled up to the Second Circle were usually too big to pick on, but it was people like Rat, or Mr. Strykowski, who they harassed with impunity, and the injustice of it ate at Rat's soul.

He sat outside the building on the Upper West Side all night, hidden behind a parked van, but now that morning had broken he'd soon have to explain his presence; no matter how invisible he believed he was, some old lady with binoculars would always spot a loiterer. He was on the point of leaving when he saw the Bentley pass the Order girl's building, turn a corner and park. Adrael came around that same corner moments later, jumped up two stories like it was nothing, grabbed the fire escape, and climbed into a window on the fourth floor, moving so quickly that Rat would have missed him had he blinked.

Rat's wiry body flooded with relief. *He must have gone up there to kill her.* Rat was impressed at Adrael's balls; killing Order members was a tricky business, no matter who you were. He must have recognized her at the club, and decided to take care of the issue before it matured into something worse. Rat sat back with grim satisfaction to wait for Adrael to reemerge, hopefully literally red-handed with her filthy Order blood, although Rat suspected that Adrael was likely more of a neck-breaker than a stabber where women were concerned.

Either way, Rat expected the whole thing to take no more than ten minutes. Or maybe fifteen.

After thirty minutes, Rat began to worry. Maybe Adrael was interrogating her; that might take a half-hour. Or even something more prurient, but Rat didn't get a rapey vibe from Adrael. Rape required a tacit admission that one *wanted* something, a human frailty that Adrael seemed to think himself completely above.

Eventually, the window slid open and Adrael slid out, dropping into the alley like a tomcat and slipping around the corner back to his car. Rat stared up at the window, imagining what the girl's corpse might look like crumpled on the floor, so it was rather a shock when her fingers split the slats of her Venetian blinds, briefly allowing him to see most of her unbroken face peeking out.

She was alive. And not only was she alive, she appeared to be perfectly fine as she sank back into the apartment with a flippant flick of the fingers that looked like nothing more dire than annoyance.

Adrael must have...what? Fucked her? He hardly thought Adrael was dog enough to cozy up to an Order member just because she happened to be nice-looking. But after seeing him climb in her window, she'd hardly be fooled into thinking he was human. He was a good-looking guy, yes, but an Order member wouldn't...

Would she?

Then Rat recalled that Adrael had been miles away on some errand of Lucius's last night, nowhere near the club. He wasn't back yet when Rat saw the girl leave out the back door; Rat knew because he received a text from him hours later, just before sunrise, asking where he was. Therefore Adrael could not have known the Order girl had been at the Second Circle at all, unless...

...unless Adrael *already* knew her, and was therefore *a collaborator.* A collaborator who was possibly selling out Dark, and the club, and thus, by extension, Rat himself.

But why would Adrael bother? Rat couldn't conceive of what the Order had to offer Adrael that he couldn't take for himself. In all the peppery conversations Rat had witnessed between Adrael and Dark, the subject of pay had never once come up. Rat suspected that Adrael didn't even particularly care about money, although he did like wearing those bougie watches and driving that ridiculous Bentley. But just because Rat couldn't *imagine* a reason for Adrael's betrayal didn't mean he didn't have one. Adrael was a close bastard, maybe even *intentionally* enigmatic, and Rat suspected he had all kinds of hidden agendas. And Rat, who was a native-born New Yorker and never learned to drive, reflected that if Adrael insisted on sneaking around on his boss, he really shouldn't do it in such a flashy car.

He did not relish the idea of crossing Adrael, but he saw no way around it. Any other corruption he might have countenanced—Rat was hardly a paragon of virtue—but dealing with the Order was a matter beyond conscience or morality. He had no idea what Lucius would do about the situation, but surely once those asshole bouncers discovered that Adrael was selling them out to the Order, they'd turn on him. Even Adrael couldn't take on that small army of thugs alone.

Rat was, however, not in the habit of meeting with Lucius on his own, so it was with trepidation that he tapped on the office door.

"Don't knock," one of the Boys called from the dance floor below, waving at him. "Just go in." So Rat did so, missing the suppressed smirks on several of the other Boys' faces as he stepped inside.

He found Lucius in the office sitting shirtless on the couch. A teenaged bike courier lay across his lap, his messenger bag splayed on the floor, and Lucius sipped a cocktail while lazily stroking the boy's raging red erection.

"What?" Lucius snapped at the sound of Rat's raspy cough. "Don't you knock?"

"I...they..." Rat began awkwardly.

Lucius bit his tongue and restrained himself to a growl, flicked the messenger boy on his turgid glans to tell him to get up, and the boy scampered out the door, pulling up his pants.

"The payment from Mr. Deloitte is in." Lucius tapped the forgotten bag with his toe, spilling plastic-wrapped stacks of hundred-dollar bills onto the carpet.

Rat cleared his throat again. He'd prepared his speech on the ride over, but Lucius's bad temper, gleaming eyes and flagrant beauty were jarring, particularly still burning with the flush of a heartless predator.

"So? What is it? Spit it out."

"There's...there's a couple of things you need to know," Rat stammered.

"Is it a 'good news/bad news' situation?"

"Um...I think they're both bad."

"Of course they are," Lucius sniffed.

Rat began by explaining what Giulio told him about the Order's supposed susceptibility to Luppi bribes.

"And you think he's telling the truth?" Lucius asked.

"I think he thinks it's true. Who knows what the deal is, really."

"Hmph." Lucius was disappointed in the Order. He'd spent much of his long life glancing over his shoulder for them, and while he privately suspected them of being corrupt in some undefined way, finding out that they were willing to sell out to a bunch of Guido gangsters for plain old money brought them down in his estimation. *A man is defined by the quality of his enemies*, a great man once said; Julius Caesar, maybe, or Oscar Wilde. Or Lex Luthor.

"And the other item?" Lucius asked, sucking his teeth.

"There was an Order member in the club last night."

"And?" Lucius hated the way Rat drew out a story. "That does happen. Was she not in the book?"

"She wasn't," said Rat, leaving out why. "But I've seen her before. And I saw her leave out the back door, so...maybe I tailed her."

"You what?"

"I...followed her. At a distance. She didn't see me."

"Was that wise?" growled Lucius. "We want them to go away, not provoke them."

"Still," Rat pressed on, "I saw where she lived."

"Was she an attractive Order member?" Lucius interrupted archly.

"If you like that sort of thing," Rat snuffled. "I was there this morning, you know. Just to look..."

"...I bet she *was*..." Lucius continued.

..."But then I saw the Bentley pull up outside, and figured the big man had it covered."

"The Bentley?" Lucius's gold eyes glittered.

"Yeah. You know. The blue Bentley. *His* car."

Lucius stared at Rat until Rat's crevices started to sweat.

"And?" Lucius prodded. "Is she a dead Order member now?"

"That's the thing," Rat squirmed. "She ain't."

Rat could not bring himself to elaborate, but he didn't have to—Lucius was fluent in the language of insinuation.

Lucius's face clouded over. *Impossible.* If he couldn't trust Adrael—if he couldn't *completely* trust Adrael—he might as well light up a cigar, ash onto the carpet, and burn the nightclub to the ground.

"This Order girl must be fascinating," said Lucius testily, "for *both* of you to pay attention. What does she look like?"

With shaking fingers, Rat extracted his camera from his backpack and scrolled through the photos of the crime scene to find a clear shot of the girl, and showed it to Lucius.

"Where...where did you take this photo?" Lucius's beautiful face betrayed nothing, but Rat noted that his fingers were clutching the arm of his chair like a talon.

"That crime scene the other day. The dead hooker. The Roaches always show up for a little fresh meat."

"And you forgot to put these photos in the book?"

Rat kicked himself for tripping over his own lie.

"Yeah," he admitted. "I did."

"I see." Lucius tried to collect himself, and almost managed it. "Maybe that's for the best. Send me these pictures and then delete them, and show them to no one. Don't mention this to anyone. *Anyone.* Do you understand?"

"Sure," Rat nodded, comprehending the delicate nature of the situation, if not Lucius's actual intentions. But Lucius, at least, had a fanatical aversion to the Order that Rat could appreciate, and Rat had no doubt at all of *his* sympathies.

"Oh, and Rat," Lucius added, as Rat turned to go, "Thank you for telling me." He flashed Rat a beatific smile so dazzling it made Rat's stomach flip.

"No problem." Rat then darted out the door as a wave of reflexive loyalty towards Lucius surged in his breast.

CHAPTER 13

———————

HOODWINKED

Little Italy

Red. Red, red, and more red. It was on the apartment's faded wallpaper of mawkish roses, on the lampshades that turned the light the color of cheap chianti, and in the mound of meat and tomato sauce running over twisted ribbons of pasta that Vito couldn't force himself to eat.

He felt it like rage, a full-body emotion in the form of a color. He hated to see it but when he closed his eyes he was left with only smells— the food in front of him smelled like his childhood, his grandmother's apartment smelled like saccharine perfume, and underneath it all was the smell of the brewing tea, acrid and vegetal, with notes of marijuana, iron, and sulphur; the scent he imagined wafted from underneath the door to Hell. But Hell was too good for Vito after what he'd done, and he could only be grateful that if he was there in his grandmother's apartment with a cup of the family tea in front of him, God had decided to give him one more chance.

His grandmother watched him from the corner of the kitchen, a former beauty wizened into a leather-tough strip of beef jerky in a crocheted cardigan who watched over the Luppi family from behind her son's broad shoulder. She raised her bushy grey eyebrows at Vito—the distinctive, upturned Luppi eyebrows she shared with both Vito and his father—and he acquiesced to her silent order by downing the tea in one burning swallow. This was one cup of many that he would drink during the coming days—the sensation of razors sliding down his throat a worthy penance for his sins—and he would suck down every one of them until red became just another color again. As the tea hit his stomach and radiated through his body, it turned his bones to lead and his mind to cotton, ratcheting down the dial on the intoxicating strength that constantly boiled under his skin. He began to feel faded, like an oft-washed t-shirt, and the part of him that was dangerously vital clawed for existence, even as the tea burned it away and left only a weakened husk. His reflexes were dulled, sounds muffled, smells muted. Teo once suggested that maybe that's what it felt like to be human. It was a sensation Vito hated, like his father hated it; like they all hated it. But it was necessary, and it was right, so Vito kept it down and hoped God was watching, and would forgive him his transgressions and let his cousin live.

———

Brooklyn

Carmine had settled into his La-Z-Boy with a dish of leftover baked ziti to spend the evening watching a *Gunsmoke* marathon when the doorbell rang. He ignored it, reluctant to haul his body out of the sweet spot in his chair, but it rang again, so he stomped to the door. By the time he yanked it open he was already in an old man's bad mood.

"Oh. It's you." Carmine recognized Hunter through the screen.

"Open the door," said Hunter, not so much commanding as

reminding Carmine not to have this discussion where someone could see them.

"Yeah, yeah," Carmine grumbled, letting him in and heading back towards the kitchen. He poured a vodka-and-ginger ale and added a squirt of the concentrated tincture his mother made from the family tea. Dealing with the Order frayed his nerves, and twice in a week was a bit much for him. "You people are killing me," Carmine said. "I got high blood pressure, I can't take all this harassment."

"I'm here to talk about your nephew Vito," said Hunter, confused, because he hadn't spoken to Carmine in over a year.

"Like I told that girl the other day, I got no idea where he is."

"Girl?"

"Maybe she forgot to take notes," Carmine scoffed. "I mean, she didn't write anything down. It's just old Carmine, so whatever, send an intern, right?"

Hunter very badly wanted to ask what this "intern" looked like, to confirm his gut-wrenching guess, but he didn't dare give away that anything untoward was going on.

"I have some follow-up questions," he said instead.

"Shoulda come yourself in the first place, 'cause here you are anyway. She was nice to look at though—I'm old but I ain't dead." Carmine winked in a way that made Hunter ill, but his suspicions were confirmed. "Hot blood runs in the family. Not for nothin' Vito owes that nightcrawler sex club five-hundred K. I got no idea what he does there for that much money, but I'm old-fashioned. I don't go in for that fifty-kinds-of-grey rubber-duck stuff."

Hunter followed Carmine's disjointed statement with the ease of a career detective. That explained why Desdemona had been looking at the Second Circle file. And if she'd found out about Carmine, she must have looked at the Luppi file in his office.

He hoped so, anyway—if she'd gotten that information any other way, that could be a bigger problem.

———

Adrael sat at the apex of the Brooklyn Bridge tower and watched the setting sun turn the edges of the Manhattan skyline orange, the buildings appearing to burn in the chilling air. On the street level it was already dark, the sun blocked by towering concrete. On the bridge the day was slightly longer, lasting until the sun dipped below the real horizon, pouring out red and purple and yellow and blue light all at once, as if the sky was trying to use up a day's worth of bright colors that the endlessly grey city had no use for. The East River dimmed to grey oil, stipples agitating on the surface as the water conversed with the scudding wind above it.

Adrael loved high places. As a child he would climb to the top of his father's castle tower, rising out of the highest point in the highest hill for miles. He'd spend hours up there sometimes, since the day he grew tall enough to see over the stone crenels, staring out at the undulating sea that stretched before him. The world had seemed enormous then, and as a boy he wanted to see every square inch of it. Now that he'd done so, he sometimes wished himself back in that turret again, with the solid feeling of "home" under his feet. These days, perched up there on a stone bridge tower with an infinity of air above his head was the only time he could truly breathe.

But mere fresh air was not enough to quell the tremor in his stomach that night, not with the inevitability of ugliness approaching like a train down a track, and Desdemona tied to the rails. He told himself there was no way to avoid it, but maybe there had been one moment, in that vacant building watching that crime scene, the first time saw her. He didn't have to follow her home. The decision to look into her was all business, or so he told himself at the time. But faced with the angrily setting sun, he had to admit that if some ex-priest in a stiff white collar had done all the same things she did, Adrael probably wouldn't have noticed.

He wondered if she thought he was stupid. He'd spent the day driving around the five boroughs after every address on her list, but after pulling up to his tenth house, a Brooklyn brownstone with bamboo window treatments and a Prius peppered with Rainbow-Pride bumper stickers, he'd given up even turning the engine off, much less getting out of the car. That was clearly *not* the home of an old-school Italian Mafia family, so he just crossed another line off that blasted piece of paper.

On which every single address was wrong.

She must have known he'd check—that was the point of the exercise —but if she wasn't lying, that meant that the Order file itself was wrong, which seemed unlikely, to that degree. Maybe she didn't want him to find Vito, but Adrael could think of no reason for that. Strictly speaking, he *should* go to her apartment and ask her why she'd deliberately misled him, but then she'd deny it, and he'd have to press the issue, and there were only so many ways to do that effectively.

He didn't have to go there that night, though. What was one more night, in the long chain of nights that preceded it and nights that would follow? A painful pressure was building in his head, but he ignored it. Maybe tomorrow he'd figure out some way to find Vito without reference to Desdemona, and then he could leave her alone forever. That thought did not please him either, but Adrael was used to choosing among an array of bad options, and that was the least evil he could imagine coming out of that situation.

CHAPTER 14

GOING TO THE DOGS

The Second Circle
Saturday Night

Dez slipped in late via the employee entrance, trying to disappear into the throng. The Second Circle was like a living thing on a Saturday night, the building's steel and concrete frame shuddering, the pumping bass forming rhythmic ripples in the drinks. It was a particularly energetic evening; a bacchanalian free-for-all of vodka shots slurped from high-heeled shoes, and the air tasted like ripe strawberries crushed between sweaty thighs. She wore a dress she'd purchased hastily that day, a cheap, stretchy black polyester rag that she intended to have on just long enough to get in and out of the club. The music was louder than last night, the dancing more fervent, but Dez was determined to ignore it all. She'd spent her whole life practicing the restraint she needed—all she had to do was keep her breaths shallow and her hands to herself.

Where was Dark? Was he in the office? The door was closed and the glass wall was a black mirror. The vampire coat check girl didn't seem to remember her, taking her key with a generic smile and sashaying back behind the curtain. She didn't come back for a several minutes, but Dez, mesmerized by the club atmosphere, barely noticed until she felt a heavy hand placed on her shoulder, and she looked up to see one of the bouncers staring down at her.

"Boss wants to see you," he said.

Dez entered the office like a prisoner stepping onto a gibbet, outwardly calm while making frantic deals with a god she didn't even believe in, wondering if there was a tank of sharks in her future. Dark was waiting for her, perched on his desk, tapping his fingers with coquettish impatience. Even in her distress, Dez marveled at him; it seemed unbelievable that this lithe, youthful man was possibly half a millennium old. A personage so ancient should have been dried out to a Nosferatu-like husk after all that time.

Another man sat in an office chair in the middle of the room, a burly Black man with a mane of manicured dreadlocks and arms covered in white ink tattoos. He was strapped into the chair by bungee cords, blindfolded, and part of his face that wasn't covered was ruggedly attractive. After her initial shock, Dez eventually recognized him as one of the werewolf bouncers from downstairs.

"You're late, Desirée," said Dark. "And it's only your second day."

"I'm sorry," Dez managed, trying to sound casual. "The trains..."

Lucius brushed past her excuse as if he hadn't heard it.

"Tardiness is an insult. It suggests that you don't value other people's time. We frown on tardiness here. It feels like...betrayal." He narrowed his eyes as he spoke, but then flashed Dez a smile so congenial she thought everything might be alright. "Ah, I'm sorry to be such a bear, it's just that we've been waiting for you. I prepared a little exercise." He nudged the man in the chair politely with his toe, swiveling him around. "Cherry tells me you're interested in moonies. That's pretty advanced stuff, isn't it, Jerome?" he asked the blindfolded man. Jerome grinned his assent and nodded; clearly he was not in that chair against his will.

"Oh, no..." Dez stammered. "I was just asking...I've never..."

"Don't go soft, darling," Dark chuckled pleasantly. "I can see why you might find the idea intriguing. Moonies have a lot to offer us; they're close to human, but they have so much more stamina. They're almost husband material, when looked at that way. But I'll bet *that's* occurred to you already."

Of course it had. If Dez was being honest, the idea crossed her mind several times since looking at that Luppi dossier, and it had even been hovering treacherously in the background of her consciousness when she was standing outside Vito Luppi's apartment.

How stupid she'd been just a few days ago.

"So let's see if you can handle him."

"What?"

"Go ahead," Dark prodded. "Have at it."

"Right here?" she stammered. Her pulse felt like the music downstairs—too fast and too loud.

"Desirée, usually our new hires *over*indulge, which is bad enough, but this anorexic behavior of yours is not serving my purposes at all. The difference between civilized people and animals is in the deliberate nature with which we consume our food. People use forks and knives and buy organic tenderloin *before* they get hungry. Animals wait for their urges to get the better of them and then just lunge at whatever happens to be nearby. You're too pretty to feed like a starving dog, so I think it's time for you to evolve."

Dez realized that Dark wasn't going to allow her to walk out of that room unless she did as he asked. Jerome waited patiently, a magnificent creature, all coiled muscle and animal heat, already sporting a full erection in his jeans. The bungee cords that held him to that chair were a fiction at best, but surely Dark wouldn't have him kill her right there, on his white rug.

"Why is he blindfolded?"

"Consider it training wheels. Eye contact makes the effect so much stronger, and I'd like to keep this carpet clean. Climb aboard," Lucius prodded.

It was hard to think—the hungry part of her taking over her brain was trying to quiet the part that feared that this was how she was going to die. But Dark's expression told her that "no thank you" was not an acceptable answer, so she slid tentatively onto Jerome's lap, straddling his legs and pressing her hands against his chest, which was hot against her palms. His jeans were tight against his bodybuilding-swollen thighs and a cloud of floral cologne wafted up from inside his shirt.

Then she felt Dark behind her, wrapping a blindfold around her eyes as well.

"To keep it fair," he said, his voice like a velvet bee in her ear.

Damned if she did, damned if she didn't. Her only chance was to take over the situation the only way she knew how, so she sank into a wild, anonymous kiss against Jerome's pillowy lips, his tongue fruity from mango-flavored vaping. He tasted different from a human, exuding a muskiness that spoke of primal moonlit nights and blood rites to hairy gods. A wave of raw heat surged through her body as she pulled his vitality out of him like the moon pulling on a tide.

Then, out of nowhere, her brain began to flood with images: torn flesh, hot blood spurting out of pulsing veins, joints cracking from the strain of bending the wrong way. She didn't feel the pain yet, but the thing within her kept drinking, and the more it pulled at Jerome, the more ravaging rage came with it. Now she felt the ripping skin, the twisted bones, and the whirlwind of violence flowing from his mind to hers. She tried to hold him at bay like she did with human men, but she couldn't stop consuming him and thus couldn't stop what he was doing either, and as the bungee cords around his straining arms began to fray, it became a race to see who would finish first.

Then the air snapped like a rubber band and Dez jerked back to consciousness. She ripped her blindfold off in a panic to discover that she was still in one piece. Jerome, meanwhile, was swiftly passing out underneath her as Lucius pulled a syringe out of his neck, and Dez jumped off his lap as he slumped over in the chair.

"Is he..." she gasped.

"It's just horse tranquilizer," Lucius informed her. "He'll be fine tomorrow. These idiots shoot this stuff up for fun in their downtime."

Dez sank onto the couch, overcome.

"I had to stop you, darling," said Dark. "You were about to kill him."

"*I* was about to—"

"Not on purpose, I know," he sighed. "But I think there's too much human in you. He can't stop himself, and then you can't stop yourself... it confuses the whole situation."

Dez objected to the idea that it was her humanity and not the rest of it that was the problem, but kept her mouth shut.

"So I'm afraid you won't do," continued Dark, shaking his pretty head. "We can't let you kill the clients."

Dez felt a surge of relief. She was only getting fired, not murdered.

"I understand," she nodded, trying not to sound overjoyed. She stood up to go, but then he added:

"And besides, I gather you have another job already. Isn't that right, Adrael?"

Lucius turned to look at someone behind him, and Dez then saw, standing against the wall in his usual stolid fashion...

...the man in grey.

His big arms were folded, and his kissable lips had hardened into a contemptuous line.

———

Lucius eyed Adrael carefully. He'd engineered this situation, drawing the two of them together to see the truth of their feelings laid bare by surprise. *And it was so illuminating.* Adrael's eyes revealed shock and disgust in equal measure; it was nothing good, but too much of a reaction for Lucius's liking. The girl's face wore a mixture of surprise, recognition, and shame, but not enough fear, and a bit too much shame. Whatever was between them, Lucius felt it like electricity in the air, and he knew he needed to get in between and break that connection.

Perhaps by breaking something else.

"You two have met, I believe," said Lucius.

"I ran into Miss Cross in an alley," Adrael replied. "She was working." That last comment had some venom behind it, which Lucius found reassuring.

"Well, lately she's been working here," Lucius informed him.

"That comes as rather a surprise."

Adrael had been preparing for an evening of skulking through Brooklyn's Italian restaurants for Luppi family members out on the town when he received a text from Lucius to come back to the office. At first he thought nothing of walking in to find Jerome strapped to a chair with a succubus on his lap; Lucius was endlessly creative and came up with new sex games every day to amuse himself. It was only when the blindfold came off the girl that Adrael realized what he'd been watching. And now he couldn't take his eyes from Dez, much as he wanted to. The cheap black lycra tube she wore outlined her figure unapologetically, giving him his first detailed view of the curves and hollows that her usual clothes only hinted at. He couldn't help but trace the lines of her elegant collarbones down to full, provocatively perky tits, take in her slender waist and its dramatic terminus in her curved hips, and continue on to a pair of creamy thighs made for gripping. But even as his body responded automatically to the sight of her, his brain was disgusted to see it presented in such a vulgar wrapping, and sitting, like a present, on the broad lap of his favorite lieutenant.

Lucius didn't think Adrael was capable of lying to him, but a lie of omission was still a lie, and it unsettled him deeply that Adrael hadn't bothered to mention this Order girl to him. She was obviously dangerous; even Lucius felt the tug of her bumbling, unconscious allure, but something about her seemed to push Adrael's buttons precisely. The man who supposedly couldn't feel did indeed seem to have feelings of some kind for *her*, so now Lucius just had to make sure those feelings were bad ones.

"Did you know she wasn't human?" Lucius asked.

"I divined that much, yes." A familiar pressure was building between Adrael's brows, and he tasted bile on the back of his tongue as he noticed that Dez's nipples had hardened to delicate peaks under the tight fabric, from either the air conditioning or arousal.

"I assume her name isn't really Desirée."

"No. It's Desdemona. Desdemona Cross."

"Ugh," Lucius huffed. "That sounds like a torture device." Lucius glared at her as if she had two heads and horns. "And...is she really in the Order?" Adrael nodded, and Lucius flashed pink with barely suppressed rage. "An Order member who isn't human," he ground out. "And you didn't think to mention it?"

"It never occurred to me she'd come here," said Adrael, his jaw tight. "It didn't seem relevant."

"But...but is that even possible?" Lucius sputtered. "If we can't even trust that they're human, then...*then* what?"

Then what, indeed? Adrael had to admit that Lucius was right to be so dismayed at the idea, since the Order's necessary human-ness was the only guarantee one could count on with them, and was also one of the principal reasons Lucius allowed no humans in his organization in *any* position.

"They don't know she's not fully human," Adrael informed him. "She's foxed them quite effectively in that regard."

"How? I mean, granted, half the staff here thought she was human at first...and even I briefly..." Lucius huffed, frustrated. "But I assume those people have *tests.*"

"Apparently it's...complicated."

"Did she fool you?"

"You'll have to be more specific," Adrael replied coldly. He couldn't help noticing the flash of triumph in Lucius's face, but though he did hate giving Lucius such satisfaction, he was too deeply dismayed to hide it. "I knew she wasn't human."

"But you somehow didn't realize out what *else* she is," Lucius assessed with a canny smirk.

"Somehow, no," Adrael admitted. "I did not." His blue eyes glittered like sunlight on seawater with some emotion Lucius couldn't place, until he realized, with a start, that it was *rage. Rage?* Adrael didn't feel rage. He got irked frequently, annoyed occasionally, and once in a while went so far as to be irritated, but the extreme side of his displeasure had always been limited to disdain. Lucius had never even seen him angry before.

Dez thought her heart might explode. She glanced frantically from one of them to the other as they discussed her as if she wasn't there, but there was nowhere to run and nothing to do but wait to see what was to be done with her.

"I believe Desdemona is here because of Mr. Luppi," Lucius said dramatically, as if dropping a bombshell.

"I know," Adrael assured him.

Lucius cocked his head at him, about to explode himself.

"You *know?*" he squeaked. "How can you—"

"Remember that dead girl downtown we told you about the other day?" Lucius nodded testily. "Well, the Order found another one. And as it turns out, they were both...like *you.*"

"Oh?" Lucius chewed on that for a moment. "That is...interesting." Dez noticed that he and Adrael exchanged a meaningful look at that, which only gave her terrible suspicions more weight. "And since both girls were savaged by moonies, Desdemona here believes that Mr. Luppi was the perpetrator," Adrael concluded. "Something to do with his car, I believe?"

"But how did she know to come *here?*" Lucius pressed.

Adrael could only shrug again, so they both looked at Dez for an answer.

"The girls were dead nightcrawlers," Dez fumbled for a believable semblance of the truth. "This club is the obvious place to start."

"Ah, but this isn't the only place in this town to get supernaturally sucked off," Lucius pointed out. "And no rational person would possibly connect my frankly *extremely* high-end nightclub with a couple of dead streetwalkers. In fact," he said, turning back to Adrael, "the only reason I can think of that she'd be *here*, pretending to take a job *here*, is if she wanted to get closer to *me*. And that, you thick Viking blockhead, is because Desdemona is...what's the phrase?... 'on the take' from the Luppi."

"Pardon me?" Adrael blinked at that.

"What?" Dez's jaw dropped.

"Oh, is that something you *didn't* know?" taunted Lucius.

"I don't think the Order...does that."

"We...we do not," Dez interjected.

"I didn't think the Order did a lot of things," Lucius shrugged. "Today has been quite the mind-fuck, as the kids say. But it's only explanation that makes sense to me. I think she's Massimo Luppi's personal Order pet, and he sent her here as an errand-girl to spy on me."

"That's ridiculous," Dez gasped. "That's not even believable."

"It's far more likely that she's here looking for Vito on the Order's behalf," Adrael scoffed. "What makes you think she's being *paid* by the *Luppi*?"

"Let's just say I had a hot tip."

Rat. It had to be. And however he found that out, the little shit wasn't usually wrong. Adrael considered the possibility. As implausible as it seemed, some things did line up. He stared at Dez afresh then, as if she were an optical illusion that became an entirely different picture when seen from a new angle.

"Oh, surely you don't believe that," she objected, meeting his eyes.

"Why were you stalking Vito that day I met you?" Adrael asked her.

"I—I told you," she stammered. "We had a dead body. Vito came up on a list of potential perpetrators."

"So did a lot of other people, according to you."

"But he was the only career criminal. And you recall, he did pick up another girl that night, and we found that same girl dead afterwards."

"I recall that you just happened to be in that alley next to his building when I showed up, and then when I almost had him in that other alley across the bridge, the whole thing just happened to go balls-up because of you," Adrael mused. "And that might be too many coincidences."

"But I looked up the Luppi file for you. I gave you what you wanted. All those addresses."

Adrael blinked at her, his expression grim.

"Those addresses were all bad," he said.

"What do you mean by *bad*?"

"I mean they're wrong. I know, I went to every single one, and no Luppi live at any of them. And I've been pondering all day how that could be...I could only assume you didn't want me to find him, but I couldn't think of a reason for that. Until now."

"Maybe I wrote them down wrong," Dez stammered. "Or maybe the Luppi...moved..."

"All of them?" Lucius sneered.

"I swear, I'm not here for *you*," Dez objected, her brain spinning, clutching for the threads of a functional lie. She wondered frantically if he knew she'd been upstairs in his penthouse, but as angry as he was at her already, she suspected if he knew *that*, she'd already be dead.

"I'm here because Vito owes you five hundred thousand dollars," she said, hoping a morsel of the truth would look like a meal, "and I assumed he'd be here finding a way to pay it back. Perhaps by killing those girls for you."

"What possible reason would I have for telling Vito Luppi to kill a bunch of street rags?" Lucius scoffed.

"Well, you told me how little you like competition—"

"Oh please, I did not invent prostitution, Desdemona. I merely perfected it. Anyone who wants to eat something they find on the street is perfectly welcome to do so."

"And the second dead girl told me she used to work here," said Dez.

Lucius raised a quizzical brow at Adrael.

"She looked familiar," Adrael shrugged. "I can't remember her name. She was always sucking on a vape pen."

"Oh, Lolli." Lucius waved dismissively. "I fired her for giving a client a heart attack. That girl had no self-control."

"You *knew* her?" Dez gaped at Adrael. "She didn't say…"

"There was a lot happening in that alley," Adrael said drily. "I doubt she bothered to look at *me.*"

"So it's not a problem for you to have ex-employees running around telling people the secrets they learn here?" Dez asked.

"The Girls don't care about anything their food is saying for longer than it takes to consume it," Lucius smirked. "People tell *me* their secrets, not them. And we fired Lolli…what…a year ago? We wouldn't wait until *now* to kill her."

"But how do you know Vito owes us money?" Adrael asked. "*We* know about it. *Vito* knows about it. His cousins know about it. But *you* shouldn't know about it, unless someone on the Luppi end told you."

"I—I found out myself."

"From whom?"

Dez, whose life was built on lying about how she knew things, was at a loss. Even after everything she'd done, she couldn't sell out Carmine to these people. Quixotic it was, but she clutched at her last fraying strand of integrity as if it might save her, and she kept her eyes on Adrael, begging him silently to intercede.

"Do you think *he's* going to help you?" Lucius snapped, and at that moment he looked his age, the thousand years of hostility flickering across his unlined face. "You may think your bouncing around has him addled like any other man, but trust me, darling, he's ignored better than you." He turned to Adrael, his face purple now, partially because he wasn't completely sure he was correct. "Show her what I mean," he ordered.

Something sank inside Adrael's chest. He knew this was coming, it was unavoidable, inevitable, fated. But it still felt like getting hit in the face with a brick.

"Don't make me repeat myself," Lucius snarled.

And then, between one blink and another, Adrael was standing right in front of Dez, holding her bare wrist in his stony grip. It was the first time he'd ever touched her, skin to skin, and it felt to her like fuel igniting, a thousand times more potent than any human, more potent even than Jerome, as if he was shooting electricity into her through her cells. Despite a spike of fear, the warm area between her legs began to ache with angry, bewildered need.

"What are you doing?" Dez's mouth went dry and she tried to pull her hand away, but while he wasn't holding her wrist tightly, exactly, there was no give to him, as if he were made of concrete.

"How did you know Vito came here?" Adrael asked. A tingle spread across his palm as her vile succubus skin nipped at his own, but it was accompanied with a kick in his gut, which he'd never experienced with one of her kind before. If she were a real girl, he might have called it chemistry, but given what she was, it had to be just another physical trick in her rotten arsenal, so he tried his best to ignore it.

Dez stared up into Adrael's eyes, but their expression was blank, as if someone in his brain had switched off the lights.

"You won't hurt me." Her voice sounded small, like a prayer. But he didn't let go, his eyes on her face. *Never look away*, his father told him. *If a man was going to do something terrible, he should have the balls to watch it happen.*

"Do it," Lucius growled. *Thumbs down from the Emperor.*

With a flick of his long fingers, Adrael snapped Dez's wrist. It was a gentle movement, as if he were crumpling a gum wrapper, but pain shot through her like lightning and she yelped in agony, sinking to her knees.

He then let go and stepped calmly back, like a waiter leaving a dish on a table.

"I'd like to say that hurt me more than it hurt you," Lucius informed her, "but I don't think that's true."

Dez crouched in a ball on the floor, clutching her wrist. It was her first broken bone and she wasn't prepared for the ribbons of pain shooting up her arm. Her brain exploded in white starbursts as her system fought for the numbness that should have come with a spike in adrenaline, but the pain sang fresh and sharp through her veins with every frantic beat of her heart.

"Do we have an understanding now, sweetheart?" Lucius sneered, crouching down to speak to her. "I hope so, because there are something like 300 bones in the human body, and I will have him shatter every single one if you keep playing stupid. You can tell me what I want to know with lots of broken bits, or you can tell me with just the one. Those are your options."

It was beginning to feel pointless to Dez to endure so much agony for some moonie whose only claim to virtue was that he'd sold out his family. It had made sense before, but now, with her body throbbing, she couldn't remember why.

"I'm not taking money from the Luppi," she gasped. "I was here about the dead girls. I was just putting the pieces together."

"Then how did you know about the debt?" Lucius pressed.

"Because Vito's uncle told me," Dez spat, her voice shaking.

"Vito's uncle?" Lucius scoffed.

"Carmine Luppi," Dez muttered through gritted teeth.

"There was no Carmine Luppi on that list," said Adrael.

"I left him off," Dez confessed dully, "because he's an Order informant."

The room stilled as the two men processed that surprising new tidbit, and waited for Dez to elaborate.

"Carmine is Massimo's older brother," Dez explained, spitting it out quickly so they'd stop making her speak. "He should have been head of the family, but he got into a fight decades ago and transformed in public, so they shunted him out to the suburbs. It's possible he... resented it."

"If Carmine knows about the debt, that means Massimo knows about the debt," said Adrael.

"Carmine didn't think he did," Dez ground out, determined to be accurate despite her agony. "And Carmine certainly didn't tell him."

"But then how does this family pariah know that if Massimo doesn't?" Lucius scoffed.

"I don't know," Dez hissed. "Ask him yourself. He lives at 2828 Avenue J in Brooklyn."

"And I'm supposed to believe *that* address is right?"

"I went there myself yesterday," she winced. "He was home."

Adrael watched her writhing on the floor, pain like needles singing in his head, flexing his thighs to stop himself from stepping forward to help her up. Lucius wanted her groveling, spilling her secrets, so there she would have to stay. But an uncharacteristic tautness on Adrael's face betrayed his rebellious thoughts to Lucius, who turned back to Dez with loathing. While Adrael's distaste for succubi was strong, all prejudices could be overcome in time, especially when incentivized by big eyes and bitable lips like hers. And while Lucius didn't care who Adrael slept with, he did not want him to develop any quandaries about his priorities.

"Well, I'm not sure there's much more we need from Miss whatever-her-name-is," Lucius said then, casting disdainful eyes at Dez on the floor.

"Cross," said Adrael.

"Ugh, that *name*. Awful."

"Do you want me to take her home?"

"No," Lucius replied smoothly. "I want you to kill her."

There was that brick again. Adrael should have known they'd inevitably get around to that, but it hit him no less hard when it came.

So this is how I die. Dez wasn't surprised, but she was struck with the unfairness of it. She'd given them what they wanted so there was no need to kill her, but there was no reason not to, either. The choices she'd made to get to this point ran through her mind in reverse, and she kicked herself for every single one. This might have been avoided if she'd learned the lesson she'd been force-fed as a child:

If you see something you want to touch...

Don't.

She looked up at Adrael, wondering what he would say.

"Okay," Adrael agreed.

"Okay?" Lucius scrutinized Adrael's face, but his superciliousness had slid back into place.

"Okay," Adrael repeated with a careless shrug. "If that's what you really want."

Damn him. Damn him to Hell. Lucius hated that tone of voice, that sentence construction, those words. *If that's what you really want.* Whenever Adrael said that it sounded like a threat, although Lucius could never have explained what, exactly, was being threatened.

"And why *wouldn't* I want that?" he asked wearily, knowing that Adrael was prepared to tell him.

"Well," Adrael folded his arms didactically, "Miss Cross is an enthusiastic liar...obviously...and she goes through some impressive contortions to keep the Order from finding out what *else* she is. But now that *we* know, we have her at our mercy. And if the Luppi have their own Order member on the payroll, whoever that is, then maybe we should have one too."

"What...*her*?" Lucius gaped.

"She is probably our best option, yes," Adrael replied drily.

"Yes, but as you said, she's a liar. She could be lying to you about all of it. She *should* be lying to you, in fact."

"I know what fear looks like."

Lucius chewed on this new suggestion, conflicted. The Order had bedeviled him in one form or another for his entire existence, and while he'd been coasting on a wave of blessed anonymity, he never really felt safe. Even daring to own that nightclub was risky. The Order got into everything like smoke, infiltrating his inner sanctums and leaving their filthy residue all over his life. Only after acquiring Adrael did he feel a little bit secure, and now this wretched interloper was on the verge of ruining it all.

"I just think we could find some use for her other than fertilizer," Adrael added. "And since she's one of—you—she won't be much use for that."

"Half," Lucius corrected him with a snarl. "She's only half one of us. The human part probably rots." It troubled him that Adrael seemed to be trying to convince him that the girl should be left dangerously alive rather than comfortably dead; everything coming out of Adrael's mouth *sounded* rational, but Lucius, who hadn't lived as long as he had by ignoring subtext, sensed something more primal underneath and didn't like it. But she'd already proved useful, and the idea of having one up on the Order for a change struck him as an opportunity that might be too good to resist.

And with Lucius, greed had the edge on caution every time.

He sneered down at Dez then, still full of hate but with a new acquisitive gleam in his eyes.

"I suppose I might be able to think of one or two other uses for you. Well, you wanted a side gig, darling, so now you work for *me*. And when I want something done, you do it. When I want to know something, you tell it to me. Anything I want to know, anytime I have the urge. Wherever, whenever, whatever, whoever. *For*ever." Dez, not in a position to bargain, didn't object, and a cruel smile spread across Lucius's face, all the more terrible because it was so beautiful. "You can start by bringing me a full report tomorrow of everything that's in your rotten files about me and my nightclub."

Dez nodded with a defeated wince.

"You know why you're so good at *pretending* to be human?" he asked her then with a nasty sneer. "It's because you pretend to *be* human. Even to yourself. And that, *Desdemona*, might be the single saddest thing I have ever witnessed." He flopped down onto the sofa as if to signal the game was over. "Now you'd better go to the infirmary so Adrael here can fix you. You'll heal faster than some human, and if that wrist sets wrong, he'll just have to break it all over again."

———

Rat stood on the catwalk above the seething dance floor and watched Lucius's office door. Seeing that girl so plausibly dressed as one of their own Girls made Rat squirm afresh. He'd always been aware that any human he met could potentially be in the Order, but the existence of this girl now forced him to take stock of everyone else he knew, wondering if any of them were Roaches in disguise. When Lucius told him what she *really* was, he hadn't wanted to believe it; the fact that Rat himself hadn't been able to recognize her true nature was unsettling enough, but the idea that there was such a thing as an Order member who wasn't fully human disturbed him to his core.

And Lucius gave her a job there, the prize idiot.

When Adrael showed up several minutes after the girl, Rat waited tenuously for the fireworks. Rat could think of no innocent reason that Adrael should have been in her apartment *not* hurting her, and he was betting that Lucius wouldn't be able to think of one either. Jerome was in that office with them, he knew, ostensibly acting as Lucius's auxiliary muscle since Adrael would doubtless be wrathful when confronted, and a fight between those two blockheads could bring that lofted office itself crashing down on to the dance floor crowd below.

But then minutes went by, then tens of minutes, and he heard no gunshots and saw no one thrown through the one-way mirror wall. *Maybe,* he conjectured, *Adrael was all bark and no bite.* Maybe he was crying. In Rat's experience, big men tended to cry when they were cornered. Not that Rat relished Adrael's downfall particularly—Adrael was more collegial to him than anyone else he'd ever worked with—but an Order informant was unworthy of pity.

Then, after an unsettlingly quiet hour, Lucius's office door opened and Adrael walked out with the Order girl in tow. She looked pale, clutching her arm to her chest, but she was still on her feet, without even a limp. Adrael's stony face was green, but he was still in one piece and walking under his own power, stalking toward the infirmary with the girl following behind him.

Adrael paused on the stairs and looked up at the catwalk, his vivid blue eyes instantly lighting on the very spot where Rat stood in the shadows. Rat realized then that Adrael had never truly looked at him before; he'd glanced at Rat sideways, observed him from afar, and cast his shiny eyes in Rat's direction, but had never graced him with such a direct, ice-cold stare. Panic rose in Rat's system, but he told himself it was just an artifact of his rodentine DNA, a vestige of a primordial past as a scurrying prey animal rather than a, perhaps, rational response to a very real predator. He ducked back into the dark and waited for Adrael and the girl to disappear behind the infirmary door. Only when it clicked shut did Rat slink off the catwalk and down to Lucius's office, where he found Lucius curled up on the couch, clutching a bottle of Cognac, a murderous look on his face.

"Boss?" Rat ventured timorously.

"Did you delete the photos of that Order girl yet?" Lucius grumbled.

"Yes," Rat assured him.

"Good. Say nothing about her being Order to the staff. Or anyone else."

" 'Course not. But..."

"But what?" Lucius cocked one golden eyebrow like a trigger.

"Why are they both still...walking around?"

"Well, the thing is," Lucius mused to the ceiling, processing the situation, "her bosses don't know what she is. They think she's a human, if you can believe that."

"I don't know if I do," Rat coughed, confused. "But then what's she doing getting a job here?"

"Moonlighting. Poking her nose where it doesn't belong."

"Suuuuuure," Rat hedged. "But then why…"

"Because the fact that she has something to hide from her employers, something we are aware of, makes her useful to us," Lucius explained with forced patience. "So I guess she's mine. Mine." He tried the word out in his mouth, seeing how it tasted. "And I'll squeeze her out like a rag before I'm done with her."

"Does Adrael know she's…like the Girls?" Adrael's loathing for succubi was well-known to everyone on staff.

"He does now," Lucius replied.

"All right," Rat coughed, his mind racing. After the look Adrael had just given him, he wondered if he should run out the door and jump on a plane to anywhere.

"Don't worry about Adrael," Lucius assured him, and once again, Rat had the eerie feeling that Lucius could look inside his head. "You work for *me,* not for him. You *both* work for *me.* Remember that."

"Ok, boss," said Rat, and he tried to believe it.

"Remember that," Lucius reiterated, swigging directly from the bottle.

———

The infirmary at the Second Circle was small but well-equipped, as the club could be a hazardous place to spend an evening. Dez sat on a sheet of cold sanitary paper on an examination table holding out her arm as Adrael tended to the wrist he'd broken. It was the last place she wanted to be, but Dez was nothing if not practical; for obvious reasons she couldn't go to a hospital, so she sat in sullen silence and stared at her lap as he gently manipulated her bones, feeling for the break, setting it flush. She gritted her teeth from the pain, but may as well have eaten a box of Tic Tacs as taken a bottle of painkillers. That was one of the downsides of not being human: one had to put up with one's physical discomfort.

At least, until Adrael touched her. To add insult to actual injury, the mere brush of his skin felt like some divine balm flowing into her wherever they connected. Neither of them wanted to acknowledge it, but her wrist almost stopped hurting as he wrapped the palms of his strong hands around it. Then he moved the joint experimentally, and the pain was back. Dez gasped and reflexively pulled her wrist away, but he held her fast and laid his other big palm flat on her thigh, pressing down as if soothing a lamb.

"Hold still. It should heal straight if you don't move it." Adrael knew exactly how much pain she was in; it took the force of a truck to break one of his bones, but he'd still snapped or cracked or fractured them all at some point. He continued to make subtle manipulations to her joint, pretending that touching her skin with his fingertips was not making his body feel like it was burning in slow coals, or that the soft give of her thigh under his hand wasn't sending fire through his limbs.

Dez seethed; he was behaving as if he'd spilled wine on her dress—no, as if he'd been bumped by someone else *resulting* in wine spilled on her dress. She hated herself for misreading him so badly, but she was always a fool for a pretty face, and he and Dark were equally pretty, and equally vile. *Did Dark have something on him? Blackmail? Extortion?* No, if it was something like that, there would have been a trace of guilt in his eyes, and there was none. *Was he a sociopath?* No, Dez had met one or two true sociopaths in her life, two-dimensional people who looked whole from one angle and flat from another. That didn't fit him either. He was the most solid person she'd ever met.

Solid, like a block of ice.

"What sort of name is 'Adrael'?" she muttered.

"An old one. Don't read too much into it."

"What will I find if I look it up?"

"I don't know." He methodically wound the bandage around the heel of her hand. "Have at it."

"I suppose you and Dark are...together?" Dez ventured sourly.

Adrael flicked his eyes up at her with a surge of hot contempt. *How could he have missed it?* She was one of *them,* a night-crawling, man-eating, stranger-fucking sex vampire. It was obvious now that all her charms were too beguiling to be natural; the elegant way her head arched on her neck, how she coyly tucked her hair behind one ear, the dance of her lashes as she glanced over his face; all of it was a ruse calculated to ensnare. Never mind that, since meeting her, something in him that was empty had felt unaccountably full.

Because now it was just full of acid.

"I just work for him," he replied stonily.

"Yes, I think I understand the business model."

"At this point, I'm quite sure you do."

"How did he find out we knew each other, if you didn't tell him?"

"Did you see the little Rat-man up on the catwalk?" Adrael asked, and Dez nodded; she'd spotted him watching them walk out of the office, his sharp eyes gleaming like black BBs, and Dez could tell he was a were-person, though not quite a werewolf. She had come across the term "were-rat" once or twice in the archives, and thought it fit. "Well, I didn't see him this morning outside your apartment when I came by for the addresses, but I suspect he was there," Adrael continued. "And he and I both watched you and your colleagues hovering around that crime scene the first time I..." *The first time I saw you* sounded absurdly sentimental, so he bit it down.

"So he knows who I work for?"

Adrael nodded somberly.

This was a mess. Dez was well and truly enmeshed with these monsters now, and while Adrael and Lucius were bad enough, the little Rat-man was an as-yet-unknown issue.

"Who else knows about me?"

"No one. We're not insane. The Boys downstairs would mutiny."

"And the were-rat won't tell them?"

"He will not." He sounded quite sure, so Dez had to take his word for it, though the magnitude of her compiled mistakes felt like glass in her gut.

"Do you really think I'd take money from the Luppi?" she asked then; of all the accusations leveled at her that day, that one rankled most.

"At this point I'd believe almost anything of you. And frankly, given all the...you must see why *you* might be inclined to..." Adrael floundered. The idea that her tendency toward subversive mendacity made her an obvious candidate for such corruption made sense in his head, but the reality didn't fit. The woman was an unapologetic liar, yes, but she also had a twisted, ironclad integrity that Adrael could not discount. "And if you're not, somebody else is," he concluded.

"That's ridiculous," she shook her head. "None of us would do that."

"None of you? Not one?" he cocked a skeptical brow.

"You don't understand," she replied with a proud little lift of her chin; a rather heroic show of poise, under the circumstances, Adrael thought.

"Then why were all those addresses wrong?"

For that, Dez had no good answer, although she supposed that the Order, like any other record-keeping institution, got bogged down in its own paperwork. And since the Luppi were such a low priority—model werewolves, in a way—those addresses probably hadn't been updated in years. Even Hunter had been surprised to see Vito's new apartment in the database.

"You really don't think Massimo knows about Vito's debt?" Adrael asked then.

"Carmine didn't think so."

"But how does *Carmine* know about it if Massimo doesn't?"

"I expect there's not a lot about the Luppi that Carmine doesn't know. He may be the family goat, but he seems to make it his business to pay attention. Vito's debt is for the usual services, I suppose?"

"We don't sell leather jackets here, so, yes. He was an enthusiast, let's put it that way."

"So when he couldn't afford the club rate anymore, he tried to get what he needed out on the street?" Dez felt around for the truth, but nothing had quite the grip she expected. "But those girls weren't as... skilled?"

"I'm sure you understand the parameters of that far better than I do," Adrael sniped, and Dez could only bite down her surge of shame.

"Then he'll just do it again and again until somebody stops him."

"If you care so much, then you should be glad you finally gave me some useful information," he retorted.

"Vito would never go to Carmine. And Carmine didn't know where he was when I spoke to him yesterday."

"Carmine told *you* he didn't know where he was. I suspect you asked more politely than we will."

"Well, if the Luppi are paying the Order off, then wouldn't Carmine be *more* likely to cooperate with me?" Dez shot back.

"That could just make him think you'd believe anything he told you. He might even think you were a bit...naive." Adrael snipped the bandage neatly as he'd done a thousand times before, for a thousand broken bones, only some of which had been of his doing.

Fair enough. "Naive" was not an unfair assessment, given the givens.

"Are you going to tell me you did this for my own good?" she asked, glancing at her wrist, sarcasm dripping like venom.

"No," he explained mechanically, clipping the bandage down. "I did it because I was told to."

"Yes. I know. I was there."

"I don't expect you to forgive me. I just want to be accurate."

Was that an apology? It sounded like one. A bad one.

"I can't give Dark what he wants," Dez dropped her voice to a desperate plea. "I can't betray my colleagues like that."

"You don't have a choice."

"Then you should have just killed me."

"That would have been easier." A ripple of temper broke through his hauteur. "You're rather a liability; I had to think on my feet to give him a reason to keep you alive. Next time, if you prefer, I won't bother."

She digested that like a piece of bad meat, her expression surly.

"How old is Dark?" she asked then, her relentless curiosity undaunted even by her pain. "You have me at your mercy now, you may as well tell me."

"What makes you think he's old?" The question was purely perfunctory, but Adrael wanted her to fight for every scrap of information she got from him.

"That's him in the center of that Bosch in the office, isn't it?"

He chuckled at that.

"I told him someone would notice eventually, although you're the first to mention it. But if I were you, I wouldn't mention it to him." He spoke flatly, without a trace of menace, less a threat than a simple warning. *Don't touch the hot stove. Don't grasp the live wire.*

Don't make me hurt you again.

"So you do anything he says," she said.

"Yes."

"Without question."

"More or less."

He appeared unbothered by having to repeat himself, like a computer with only one command.

"Why?"

"Because it's better than the alternative." But he was surprised at how regretful that sounded. He thought he was done with regret, and it was dismaying to discover otherwise.

"What's this better than?" Dez held up her bandaged wrist.

"Lots of things," he assured her.

They stared at each other like two boxers sizing each other up before a fight. Adrael's waist was only a breath away from her knees, and it occurred to him that if he leaned forward a bit, his face would hit hers, maybe lip to lip, mouth to mouth, tongue wrapping around tongue. Maybe a kiss was even enough to fix her wrist, given what she was.

The idea made him ill.

"I can imagine the things Dark has you do," she retorted.

"You're done," he informed her.

Her wrist was, he meant, so she slid off the table, and Adrael stepped aside to let her go.

"Don't forget these. Again." He picked up her coat, wallet, and phone from the table behind him and handed them to her. She took them in her good arm with as much dignity as she could manage.

"Why did he call you a Viking?" she queried.

"Because I'm violent and I steal things."

"Yes, well, I already knew you were a criminal. But I didn't take you for a pimp."

"Some things about you surprised me too," he replied.

She didn't respond to that, since one hand was holding her things and the other was bandaged, so she didn't have an available middle finger.

———

Adrael leaned on the exam table in the infirmary and waited for the wave of disgust to break. Once he took the measure of it he would know how many thousands of sit-ups and smacks with the heavy bag it would take to exorcise it. He could still feel the brittle shiver of Dez's bones snapping between his fingers; Adrael had never injured anyone by accident, but he frequently did so on purpose, and he'd known where the tensile point was, and where one micrometer more would make the bone crack. The look in her eyes when he did it was pure pain, which was a blessing. There was none of that cow-eyed betrayal, or plaintive beseeching or, much worse, forlorn forgiveness that one got from children or nuns. It hurt and she was mad and she hated him now and that was that. He couldn't have asked for better from a man.

"So those two dead girls were, in fact, *Girls*," Lucius mused, leaning on the infirmary doorjamb as Adrael methodically rewound a length of excess bandage.

"Seems that way," said Adrael.

"Well, at least now we know it's not Vito."

"We don't know that. He's still a moonie. You forget what that means sometimes, I think. "

"Think what you like. Not that you have any idea how we conduct our business upstairs. Whenever I try to tell you about it you get that glazed look in your eyes that tells me you're off somewhere in your mind, slaying peasants."

"I think Vito prefers take-out over fine dining these days."

"Just keep this quiet, please, and don't just blab it all to that rugby team you call a staff. Some of them have big mouths, and if the Girls upstairs hear about this they'll get paranoid. And then they'll be unbearable."

"Do you need anything else?" Adrael's tone was dangerously neutral as he tucked the butterfly clips back into their drawer with exaggerated precision. He was, Lucius realized, *pouting*. For Adrael, whom Lucius generally regarded as an amiable nihilist, pouting was unusual; men who cared about nothing didn't pout. This new mood was a sign of impending trouble, and Lucius wanted to nip it in the bud.

"Care to explain how you met the girl?" Lucius asked, despite the uncomfortable prickle on the back of his neck. In theory, Lucius could trust Adrael with his life (and had to do so) but while the only thing that stood between him and the howling wilderness was Adrael, the only thing standing between him and Adrael was also Adrael.

"I saw her at the crime scene for that first dead nightcrawler, with her colleagues," Adrael told him. Then I met her again stalking around outside Vito's apartment, and by the end of the evening she'd gotten me shot in the leg." He had to chuckle, if grimly, at how much sense that made when he said it out loud. "How did you find out that I knew her?"

"I have my ways."

Adrael once again felt the urge to crush something small, like a rodent skull.

"You had him follow me?"

"He was following *her*. *You* should consider a less conspicuous car."

Lucius chuckled then, no less grimly than Adrael. "You know, at first I thought you were just being vindictive when you insisted on hiring that fuzzy little shit."

"It was a mistake I'll deal with shortly," Adrael replied.

"Don't you dare. He's starting to grow on me. Like a lichen. Anyone that sneaky is worth whatever it is we pay him."

"I'm an excellent judge of talent."

"But you still had no idea what *she* was." Lucius gloated. "That *is* a surprise. She does pass awfully well though. She'd have been quite a unique offering for us."

"If someone was buying."

"You're obviously not the right market."

Adrael could only snort at that. Succubi were crazy about Adrael, his warmth, his energy, his quietly voracious libido that pulsed like a race-car engine. But as hard as the Girls went at him, he rebuffed them with an iciness that bordered on cruel. Lucius didn't take Adrael's bigotry personally, however; though he was himself a ravenous consumer, he wouldn't much care to be consumed.

"I knew she wasn't human. But she's a little more sly than she needs to be."

"I hope so, if she going to be useful to *us*," Lucius reminded him. The idea of having his own personal Order member was beginning to appeal to him. If she was afraid of her bosses finding out what she was, it incentivized her to make sure that they never got anywhere near Lucius so that he couldn't snitch on her. And if the Luppi could buy someone in the Order with money, he, Lucius, could certainly own a girl with blackmail like he did everyone else.

"If not, I suppose she's breakable," Adrael muttered.

"She's a big girl. She'll fix herself right up," Lucius replied coldly. "The usual way."

Lucius and Adrael stared at each other for a long, pregnant moment, but at the end of it, Adrael just inclined his head deferentially and said nothing else. *Fair enough, boss,* the nod said, and Lucius hoped it meant that they were more or less square. In the four years they'd worked together, that broken wrist was hardly the nastiest thing Lucius had ever had Adrael do. He'd get over it.

"I can't believe you told her your name, though," Lucius huffed.

"I didn't," Adrael replied curtly, stalking past Lucius and out of the infirmary. "*You* did."

———

Downtown

The air was damp with a light rain that couldn't decide whether to fall or just hover like a sooty vapor. Dez asked her cab to drop her off somewhere "with nightlife," so he took her to the West Village. New York had a thousand bars where a girl could give a fake name to a stranger, follow him to an apartment she would never see in daylight, and leave before the early morning coffee shops opened. One of them had to contain someone Dez could handle.

She checked her reflection in a darkened shop window but didn't like what she saw. The broken bone was healing by the minute and the healing felt just like the breaking, only slower and in reverse, and it was sapping her body's vitality. She was white as a vampire, her limbs dragging like lead, and with pain coursing through her body and rage shooting through her soul, she was not disposed to suffer another minute of agony for the sake of some man.

The street was peppered on both sides with lines of well-dressed people itching to pay too much for drinks, damage their eardrums, feel glamorous, and maybe get laid—and Dez scanned the various bars and lounges as if surveying a buffet. *Too goth...too punk...too eurotrash... .* She paused at the doorway of a retro-futuristic lounge with a preppy crowd at the door; Upper West Side trust-fund babies and midtown investment bankers mixing with Greenwich Village graphic designers and Ivy

League-educated boho artists. There had to be a burly CrossFit instructor or fireman in there, or maybe a New York Giant. Something emanating alpha-male heat and cocky masculinity. Something nutritious.

Like Adrael. His strange name sounded like a caress but likely meant something sinister, and while his smile was boyish, his sense of humor was a hundred years jaundiced. She burned with shame to have fleetingly indulged in the fantasy of him protecting her from Dark, from the Order, from New York, and from all the things that went bump in the night, wrapping her in his brawny arms and twining his big hands in her hair, pressing his forehead against hers and mingling their breath as his lips brushed her own in shivering anticipation.

Because now he could just go fuck himself.

Standing in one of the lines, Dez spotted a six-foot-two gym-built pretty boy with tawny-blond curls and a wholesome, Captain America countenance. He was too good-looking not to be an aspiring male model or an actor; and since he was queuing with the common folk, he was probably a waiter during the day. All her natural shyness had been burned away by rage and pain, and Dez was now operating on pure venom, which freed her inhibitions considerably. She locked eyes with him without preamble and her pupils dilated, constricting her brown irises down to razor-thin circles. He caught his breath, rapt, and his heart gave an extra hard push to pump blood through his veins and down to his awakening cock.

A few minutes later, he, his friends, and Dez were all through the bouncers and in the door. The club was flashy and sleek, with horizontal lines of lights striping the walls like the inside of a spaceship. The patrons spilled bespoke cocktails to throbbing music, white teeth flashing purple in the strobing blacklight as they laughed. Captain America and Dez hovered by the bar, and she silently waited as he took the edge off his inhibitions with a whiskey and Coke. She then leaned on the bar next to him and looked him directly in the eye as if they'd already met.

"What happened to your arm?" he asked.

"I fell."

"Oh, okay. You wanna dance?"

"No," she replied.

"Ok," he said, as if she'd agreed to something.

Emboldened by pain, she slipped two fingers into his waistband, his warm stomach pressing against the backs of her fingers, and pulled him willingly through the crowd toward the back of the club and then through the door that led to an emergency stairwell, illuminated only by a buzzing overhead light and a blaring red exit sign. They weren't quite alone; she heard another couple moaning on the stairs one flight up, but she pushed her prey under the stairs and out of sight.

There was no time for foreplay, but fast food was what Dez wanted —quick and dirty and cheap, best consumed in the dark and never spoken of again. He wanted to be in charge, so she let him, ignoring the searing agony in her wrist as his hands tugged urgently at her clothes, pushing the cheap Lycra dress up over her bra and yanking the fabric down to let her breasts bounce out. Her body locked into the alarming momentum of his ratcheting desire as the unholy part of her clicked in to everything in him that was wired to be male. He smelled like frat-boy cologne, all water notes and fresh greenery, the scent of vapid detachment. The scent was stronger behind his ears as she bit at the powerful muscles in his neck. She had no idea what he was like as a person, but as a raw animal, he was sublime, and she was glad he didn't say anything. There was a reason no one had invented the talking dildo, after all.

He slipped his cock out of his pants; he had a member like a hammer, girthy and long with an oversized knob, but as he plunged it towards her she deflected it between the warm flesh of her thighs. Her eyes were locked on his and he was too addled to notice the difference. It would have been nice to have taken him inside her, but Dark was right: Dez had poor control under the gun, her wrist throbbing in agony, her system starving, and she didn't trust herself not to kill him by accident if she enjoyed herself too much. Dez didn't care what fantasy women his brain might be evoking as he ground his body against her, thrusting forward like he was trying to get somewhere, biting at her lips and neck and nipples like a hungry animal. She didn't want *him* either, exactly, but she was drunk on his desire, and she gripped the soft mounds of his butt, pulling his hair, letting him devour her while she devoured him in turn. His skin felt like it was melding onto hers, the firm wall of his stomach with its trail of ruddy pubic hair slamming into her clitoris with a force that was rather too hard but still welcome. She closed her eyes and imagined that he was someone else, indulgently allowing the lines of a svelte, muscled body to flash through her brain, an other-worldly scent flushing into her nose like a memory on command.

Adrael. Her eyes shot open in horror. The thought of his disgust stomped out the flame of her arousal just as the man between her legs finished, spraying his warm jet on her thigh. Even so, a pulse of silvery heat radiated from between her legs up to her brain and back down her extremities; it was his orgasm, not hers, but she sensed it and it shocked new life into her cells.

He leaned on the wall and panted, and then pulled up his pants and staggered back into the club alone with a mixture of distress and bliss on his face. Once he'd left, Dez tugged the bandage off her wrist and wiggled her hand experimentally. The joint was fine now, just like new, so she wiped off her sticky leg with the bandage and tossed it into the trash, trying not to think of Adrael's sneer if he saw her feeding on some random man like late-night shawarma. She then pulled down her dress, tidied her hair, and walked out, feeling dirty and unsatisfied, but—for the moment—acceptably sated. The couple on the stairs kept at it, but from the sound of it, they didn't quite have the expert touch.

Part Four

Chasing Tail

CHAPTER 15

OLD DOGS, NEW TRICKS

Brooklyn
Sunday morning

Carmine squinted through his screen door, dismayed. No one had come to see him in months besides his mother—and his brother, Massimo, once, on Carmine's birthday—but just that week the Order had showed up twice out of the blue already, and now two new men were on his porch ringing his doorbell like Bible salesmen. He left the screen closed and had a look at them. He doubted they were selling anything; they'd rolled up in a Bentley and looked like a couple of GQ models, so he hoped they just had the wrong house.

"Who the fuck are you?" Carmine asked.

"Perhaps we should talk inside," the larger of the two men suggested, his blue eyes hard as diamonds.

"I ain't letting you in my goddamn house."

"If I wanted to kill you," said Adrael, "you'd already be dead. And if I change my mind, that screen door isn't going to stop me."

Inside the house, Lucius perched on the edge of the dining table, nudging aside several dusty boxes of coins with his elbow. Carmine stood at his kitchen counter, too uncomfortable to sit down. The GQ models looked a lot more dangerous up close. The buff blond guy seemed a little fruity, but the man standing behind him with the short dark hair and the Windex-blue eyes was another story. Carmine had been in the family business long enough to know a "fixer" when he saw one. And while the man had an annoyingly pretty face and looked like he spent too much time at the gym, something about him spoke of burning ashes on a barren wasteland, and Carmine thought it best not to become something he considered a problem.

"Whaddaya want?" Carmine asked cagily.

"Your nephew Vito owes me a great deal of money," Lucius informed him silkily. "He's been frequenting my establishment and has racked up a largish bill."

"You the guy owns that thump club downtown?"

Lucius sighed inwardly, but decided not to debate that description.

"I am he."

"I see. Well, you got the wrong Luppi brother, boys. I got no idea where Vito is, and I can't do nothin' about what he owes you. Unless you want some limited-edition silver dollars."

"I'll pass."

"Does your brother know about Vito's debt to us?" Adrael asked.

"Nah, I'd have heard. *That* would be a real family scandal," Carmine said. "This have somethin' to do with my other nephew gettin' ganked?"

"*Three* of your nephews used to come in quite frequently," said Lucius, "and to some degree they all got—"

"Not...no. *Ganked*. Killed. Somebody shot my nephew Teo and left him on his mother's porch, and now he's dead."

That Carmine didn't definitely know it was Adrael who shot Teo was interesting, since the man knew almost everything else. Adrael had waited all week for some retaliation from Massimo Luppi, but nothing occurred, no bullets, no bombs, no bodies, which had to mean that Massimo didn't know, either.

"Condolences," said Adrael. "Was that recent?" He tried to keep the ghoulishness out of his voice, but he was always curious to know how long his custom-made bullets took to do their work.

"Friday. Was that you boys too?"

"No, no," Adrael shook his head, a picture of detached sympathy.

"Teo didn't owe us a dime," Lucius added.

Carmine looked as if he didn't believe them, but he wisely left it there.

"So how you come yer askin' me about all this instead a' Massimo? What can I do about it? I can't pay you."

"We thought you might be more receptive," said Adrael. "Under the circumstances."

"Which are what?" Carmine had to ask.

"I want to know if your brother still has the pieces from the Alexandretti job," said Lucius.

Carmine let out a jaundiced chuckle with no mirth in it.

"Oh, yeah. Pretty sure he does."

"All of them?" Lucius pressed, gold eyes gleaming.

"Probably. After that ding-dong Giorgio Alexandretti told everybody he'd nail their skin to the wall if he found out they had his paintings, the buyers kinda dried up. But you know, I don't think Massimo cares. Our dearly departed grandfather planned that art heist as a fuck-you to Alexandretti 'cause Alexandretti was a douchebag carpetbagger buying up all the property in the village our family comes from. It was, you know, symbolic. Now it's a Luppi tradition. But to be honest, Massimo gives no shits about art. He's never even laid eyes on those Alexandretti paintings, they just sit in storage getting chewed by rats. I think he just likes knowing they're still in the family."

Lucius glanced at Adrael. To Carmine, both men looked disconcertingly pleased.

"Where *specifically* does he keep them?" Adrael asked.

"Man, this guy never misses leg day, huh?" Carmine snorted evasively, sizing Adrael up like a cattle dealer. "Looks like he's standing on a couple a' smoked hams."

"Mr. Luppi, where does your brother keep the art?" Lucius repeated.

"You're outta your minds, boys," Carmine shook his drooping head. "I know you can kill me if you feel like it, but if I sell out my brother, I'm dead anyway."

"Your nephew owes me a boatload of money, Mr. Luppi," Lucius replied, sucking his teeth. "I will be paid one way or the other, even if I have to kill enough of your family to make up the difference by selling your corpses for parts in Chinatown."

"You don't want to fuck with my family," Carmine shook his head.

"Is that a threat?" Adrael queried.

"Psh, you think they give a shit if you kill me?" Carmine scoffed. "That's just friendly advice, boys. You don't want a war with my brother. He'll take out three of your people for every one you get of ours."

"That's fine," Lucius shrugged. "None of my people are related to me, and I can always replace employees."

Carmine raised an eyebrow at Adrael, but Adrael only tilted his head in silent assent.

"If you give me the information I want, I'll consider it fair payment," said Lucius. "And if your brother is as indifferent to the pieces in question as you say he is, he'll never miss them. You have my word, and that of my gentle friend here, that it will never get back to *anyone* that we got this from you."

Carmine's eyes shifted from the blond *fanook* who seemed able to read his mind to the man who looked bored enough to shoot him for fun. He could lie to them, but he'd get an uglier repeat visit from them afterwards, with zero thank-yous from his brother for his loyalty. Or he could tell them the truth, and clear Vito's debt in a way that nobody else in the family would have had the stomach to do. And they were right; as little as Massimo cared about any of the family's stolen art, he'd never notice it was gone.

"You'll never be able to sell any of it," Carmine snorted.

"It's for private consumption," Lucius assured him. "I have a powder room I need to decorate."

"And then you and Vito will be totally square?"

"Equilateral. Trust me, I will be delighted never to have anything to do with your family again."

———

Brooklyn
Sunday

Massimo Luppi finished his phone call with his cousin Carlo and took his first real breath of the day. He'd been up since dawn, making dozens of such phone calls, because on Wednesday the family would descend upon his home for Teo's funeral, and there would have to be a brunch, and then the service itself, and then more food at Teo's mother's house... Pushing aside the reheated veal piccata that his wife had placed in front of him, he poured another glass of whiskey and called his mother, two things that had to be done in that order.

"How's my son?" he asked her without preamble.

"He's watching *The Price is Right*."

"Did Giulio come by?"

"Is Giulio somebody?"

"What, Ma?"

"You told me to not to let anybody in, and if somebody came by, you wanted me to tell you. If Giulio is somebody, I would've told you if Giulio came by, wouldn't I? So no, he didn't. Or I would've said so."

"Aright, Ma," Massimo rubbed his temples wearily. "Anyway, the funeral for Teo is on Wednesday."

"Wednesday? What kind of day is that for a funeral?"

"Ma, there's holy days this week when they can't do funerals, and Mona's gotta sort out the whole... I have a lot on my plate, Ma."

"A little too much lately. Just like your father. Always with the nose in the fridge."

"You think Vito'll be ok by Wednesday?" he asked, ignoring that.

"I wouldn't push my luck," she told him, lowering her voice. "The *bambino* needs at least two more weeks before you let the family see him."

"Ok, ok," Massimo sighed. "I'll say he's in Florida."

"What's he doing in Florida?"

"I'll figure it out, Ma."

"Sure, sure," she whined in a tone of voice that made Massimo cringe. "So," she added then, "is that Claudia coming?"

"Yes Leo's wife is coming, Ma, everybody's coming, and that means everybody from Jersey."

"Then I'm not going. Tell them I'm in Florida too."

Massimo hung up the phone and downed more whiskey, deciding it was for the best that Vito stayed put, all things considered. One less thing to worry about until this was all over.

"Massimo," his wife said from the doorway, her hand quivering on the doorknob the way it did when she was upset. "Massimo, *he's* here to see you."

It took Massimo a moment, but only a moment, to know who she meant. Mona was not easily unsettled, but there was one thing that reliably gave her fits.

"Tell him to come in," he said. "Then go upstairs or go shopping or something."

"But Massimo—"

"I'll be fine," he assured her. "I'm sorry, honey, you shouldn't ever have to talk to him."

Mona gave him a plaintive stare and then headed upstairs for her gun. She wouldn't leave her husband alone in the house with a *corvo sporco*, a filthy crow, as she always thought of those people in black. They could not be trusted, even though Massimo assured her their arrangement was a collegial one. Mona would have preferred the Feds; they at least had families to lean on if they proved treacherous. Those crows were like ghosts, nameless and untethered, and such people could never be trusted to keep their word. The man at the door, who Massimo had been dealing with for years, had never even told them his name.

————

The Order

Adrael. Azrael. Dez thumbed through a fat binder that hadn't been dusted in decades, looking for variations on the name for the hundredth time, in a section devoted to ancient files on demons with Biblical monikers. Such files were not considered urgent, since many of their subjects were probably mythical, but Dez thought it was the logical place to look. Because "Azrael" was the name for the archangel of death in Islam, in Judaism, and in the old Christian texts, popping up like a red thread woven through the warp and weft of recorded history, whispered in the darkest corners of the darkest places by people in their darkest moments. Those heavy tomes bound in crumbling leather were full of drawings of bat-winged creatures, grotesque demons with goats' feet, and black-cloaked reapers, and the specter of some mythical "Azrael" was present at every crusade, every battle, every crime ghetto; everywhere people died in droves.

She'd found plenty of references to the name "Adrael" (or *Adriel,* or *Adreal,* or even *Adrel)* among the more modern files too, but no matter the spelling, it was inevitably a reference to some ordinary supernatural pickpocket or thief, most of whom the Order had definitively dealt with, and none of whom answered the description. Whoever *this* Adrael was, the Order knew nothing about him. Still, maybe he was just one more Unnatural thug who went by a bad-boy street name. After all, the only person she had any proof of him hurting was herself.

She touched her wrist reflexively. The bone and skin and muscles were healed, but her nerves remembered the reverberations of the fracture shooting through her arm like ghostly electricity, reminders of her own carelessness. She peeled off her gloves and examined the index and middle fingers of her right hand, which had already healed from the thoughtwater she'd touched just an hour ago. Whatever she'd taken from Captain America at the bar had been potent. She wondered how he was doing; if he'd caught the flu, if his bones had become brittle, or if some burgeoning cancer cells, emboldened by his temporarily drained immune system, had taken root in some vital organ that would kill him in a decade. Maybe nothing would happen to him—the customers at the Second Circle seemed happy to keep going back. Although to be fair, the place had only been open for three years, so any long-term effects had yet to be determined.

She herself was glowing with health, shiny hair and dewy skin a guilty testament to her predations. She felt physically better than she had in months, and it made her sick to think that she had Dark to thank for that, especially as he found her so pathetic. It *was* pathetic to be solid enough to feel human but not human enough to stay that way without feeding on someone else, and even more pathetic to be in denial about it. She wondered how many people like her existed in a city that size. Sex demons were generally thought to be sterile, but the Order knew very little about them for certain. Plenty of cases existed of women *claiming* to have been impregnated by incubi, but that included those using supernatural ravishment as an excuse for infidelity, and those that had been impregnated by some other type of entity and didn't know the difference.

She wondered if pure sex demons like Dark were *born* at all. Dez had always been inclined to believe that they crystallized into existence around the nucleus of other people's desires, growing more and more "real" as they aged, evolving from clouds of formless consciousness to solidify into physical entities as they consumed the substance of their victims. But it was also plausible that such a creature could form in the belly of some hapless human woman and, in due course, be expelled into the world like a real baby. Dez suffered all the ignominies of flesh and blood, needing to eat, needing to drink, and even needing to sleep sometimes, but she wondered what life had been like for the boxes of dust in the archive that had lately been succubi. They had probably never been "told" what they were, and had simply followed their instincts from meal to meal like any other creature on Earth. Maybe if the girl in the red booty shorts had been sent to posh private schools to study comparative religion, she might *not* be dead today. The two modes of living were not mutually exclusive, as Dez herself could attest.

And that Adrael-person had no business sex-shaming her, since he was just muscle for the biggest pimp in town. She should have known that anyone that attractive had to have something significantly wrong with him. He'd almost convinced her he cared about her welfare, and she'd even bothered to worry about his, trying to "save" him from the nightclub that he himself ran. *She was such a ninnyhammer.* She burned with the shame of it; her lies had put her under the power of a demon, and everyone she worked with was compromised as a result.

She also felt bad about Carmine. Asking him about Vito would get Adrael and Dark nowhere; his pain would just be a waste of everybody's time. And in all the horror of the previous evening she'd even forgotten that she'd been accused of working for the Luppi, of all things. It wasn't out of the question that an Order member could be corrupt, but the Umbra served as such a threatening deterrent that most thought better of it. *Yet Adrael insisted those Luppi addresses were all wrong.* It was possible that Solomon's injunction to leave the Luppi alone had resulted in some shoddy record-keeping, but that would have meant a *few* were wrong, not all. *All* implied—

A tap on her door interrupted her train of thought.

"Yes?" she called, irritated.

The door nudged open and a timid teenager with a mangled eye pushing a mail cart peeked in to hand Dez a parcel covered in Dutch writing.

It was the Bosch file.

———

Little Italy

Antonella "Nana" Luppi stirred her tea as if it offended her, the spoon threatening to crack the porcelain. *Curse Claudia Luppi,* that bleach blonde Barbie doll. In Antonella's day, which was admittedly some time ago, they would have known what to call a woman like that, but these days she was considered marriage material. Though Antonella didn't know how that Claudia nursed her children with breasts made of plastic; that was a modern miracle Nana didn't want to understand.

A siren prompted her to glance out her window at the street, something she avoided doing more and more these days. She'd lived in that same apartment in Little Italy for the last seventy years, watching the buildings slowly grow up around her and the business signs go more and more foreign as Chinatown encroached on her block. She hated seeing those squinty-eyed strangers walking down her block—back in the day, they would have known better than to set their little warped feet in the Italian part of town. This wasn't her city anymore, or her neighborhood, but that was still her home, all expenses paid by Massimo without her having to think about it. And it would be so until she died, whenever that was; after all, her grandmother, also a *lupino,* had lived to a hundred and thirty-three.

Nana didn't want to go to Teo's funeral. She showed up for christenings and weddings, but the funerals of young people were too much for her. It was—as her late husband had repeatedly told her—necessary grist for the mill in their business, but when they died, it was a family trauma, a huge to-do. And it was a shame, with all those people coming in from out of town, that Mona never quite got the catering right.

But what did Nana know? She was still going strong though, these days she only needed half a cup of the tea once a month to keep her condition in check. It was worse for Vito; that's what Massimo got for marrying a first cousin. But it was easier to do so, in that family, so much less to explain. And though Mona was human, the Luppi blood was strong, and Vito was even worse off than his father had been at his age.

Vito had been sitting at Nana's kitchen table for days, pecking at her large-print crossword puzzles like a broken man, though today he'd graduated to watching television. Massimo hadn't gone into detail about what Vito had done, but Nana had pieced it together. The cousins came to her apartment three times a week like clockwork for refills on dried family tea and home-made pasta, and they yapped at each other constantly as if Nana wasn't there, so she knew exactly how much money Vito owed that *fanook* club owner, and why. She suspected the rest of the family didn't know, though, and she wasn't going to tell them, because then Massimo would have to punish Vito like her husband Cesare had punished Carmine all those years ago.

Carmine. He was Antonella's first born and forever her favorite son. Massimo, by contrast, was just like his father, and while she grudgingly admitted he would have been the right choice to be the family *capo* whether Carmine had his fall from grace or not, he didn't have to sequester Carmine out there in the suburbs like he didn't exist. Carmine was the only one who would listen to Nana talk, and she told him everything she thought and everything she heard the rest of the family discuss, even those naughty boys. Antonella abided by the family's code of silence, but Carmine, separated from the rest of the clan, was a safe well in which to pour her opinions.

She did not tell him that Vito was getting clean in her living room, however. Massimo's protection of his son was blisteringly hypocritical, given what Vito had done, but telling Carmine about it would just be pouring salt into a wound that had never even begun to heal. Her oldest baby hardly needed more fuel for the poisonous resentment he secretly nurtured.

The phone rang again. Her caller I.D., a modern knickknack that Nana did love, told her it was Massimo, again. She glanced at the clock —she had no sense of time anymore—but it had been only an hour since his last call.

"*Sì, signore,*" she singsonged flippantly into the phone. "What can I do for you now, eh?" She listened to what he was saying and noticed that he sounded jittery. "*Perché?*" she asked, wrinkling her already-wrinkled forehead, because what he was saying seemed unnecessary.

"Just do it, Ma," he insisted, "and don't tell anyone, *anyone,* that he's there."

Fine. Even though she'd given birth to Massimo and wiped his baby ass and force-fed him vegetables, he was the family *capo* now, and she would do as she was told. She made another cup of tea for Vito, giving him his usual dose of the heady herbal blend that kept the Luppi clan half-sane: damiana, wolfsbane, cannabis, turmeric, a pinch of foxglove. As the water cooled from boiling, she looked around to make sure Vito was in the other room, and then pulled a little brown bottle from the back of her tincture cupboard. It was unmarked, the liquid inside slightly oily, and she added two tiny drops to Vito's tea and gave the concoction a stir. She then went into the living room where Vito was curled up on the sofa watching the History Channel and placed the mug in front of him.

She returned to the kitchen to call Carmine to let him know when and where the funeral would be. Massimo always "forgot" to invite Carmine to things, but it was a family event, and Teo was Carmine's nephew too. They all had the same monster hidden inside them; Massimo, Nana, and that sad mess lying in her living room, who, she hoped, would eventually turn back into her precious grandson again, and they all had to stick together. If they didn't—as her late husband had often reminded her—the wolves would descend.

Interrogator: You met the devil.

Bosch: Yes.

Interrogator: He posed for a painting.

Bosch: Yes.

Interrogator: How did you meet him?

Bosch: Through friends.

Interrogator: What kind of friends do you have that know the devil?

Bosch: Rich ones.

The painter Hieronymus Bosch was known by the Order to be "bedeviled"; his sprawling canvases teeming with bizarre figures cavorting with nightmarish demons made it clear, even to a layman, that there was something troubling him. He was suspected of being cursed with "the sight," so the Order tested him for blood impurity, and then possession, but found evidence of neither. They settled on a diagnosis of "torment": an archaic Order catch-all term for a vague state of harassment by the invisible world that sometimes led to the kind of trauma that let a human see beyond the veil. The medieval version of the Order had interrogated him at length, in their typical fashion, and the result was a rambling, metaphor-laden transcript of the spewings of a frightened elderly madman, all laid out in a document that someone in the Amsterdam office had helpfully translated into English.

And there, at the bottom of the page, Dez found the tidbit she needed: at some point in his life, Bosch had completed a painting of Dante's nine circles of Hell on commission, with a portrait of the devil himself in the center.

A portrait drawn from life.

Interrogator: What did you call him, this Devil? What was his name?

Bosch: He called himself Lucius Tenebrus.

Interrogator: Light in the dark?

Bosch: Yes! Light-in-the-dark! The morning star! The prince of fire! Lucifer, bringer of light! Ha ha! He glows, you know, he glows like fire...

The interview devolved from there, the scribe indicating in the margins that Bosch broke down into a fit of incoherent laughing, and eventually the Order let the aged painter go home. It was quite the story, but there was no evidence that the painting he spoke of existed at all, no provenance for it, no list of owners, no photographs. There was only the painting itself, hanging in the subject's office in his own nightclub, but to see it the Order would have to get in. And even if that were possible, Dez couldn't let anyone know the painting was there without outing herself and all her own terrible secrets.

At the end of a long, frenzied afternoon in the archives, she laid her gloved hands reverently atop her newly compiled file like it was a talisman. Research had yielded hundreds of mentions of specific incubi, "vampires," and "demons" that she now recognized as Dark himself, scattered like dust throughout time under a thousand different names. Sometimes the reference was obvious, sometimes it was merely a suggestion; it didn't matter, she collected them all. She didn't know how old he was exactly, but he'd spent several centuries of life moving around to wherever existence was the most decadent at the time: medieval Turkey, the court of the Sun King, 1920s Paris—marrying frequently for money and killing for the same. There were some sketchy indications that even dated him back to the Roman Empire, although that seemed impossible. Latinized names had been a popular affectation in Europe during the Middle Ages, and the idea that he was even *that* old was already dizzying.

And if the Order saw the rest of that troubling art collection, it would be lights out for Mr. Dark. He must have spent years compiling his hoard, obsessively searching for the pieces, stealing them if necessary. A smart man would have destroyed them, but Dez suspected that for him, it would be like destroying his own soul, if he even possessed one. *Lucius Tenebrus. Could that be his real name?* Surely he wasn't so stupid. Surely he'd never tell some mad painter who he truly was; no one could be that much of an idiot and stay alive for so long. Then again, if there was one thing she now understood about Mr. Dark and his penthouse full of priceless selfies, it was that vanity was just one of many vices he considered a virtue. But if she held her nerve, she might be able to use it to extricate herself from Dark—or rather, *Lucius Tenebrus*—and his machinations for good.

INTERLUDE

INCUBUS

Rome
31 B.C.

Rome had an Emperor. There had never been an emperor before, but there was one now, and that was something to celebrate. The whores' quarters at the House of the Golden Salamander swirled with silks and linens and perfumes as the most desirable women in the city prepared to celebrate their new ruler by engaging in their own joyous form of commerce, painting their sinuous bodies with gold, and braiding strands of gold chain into their silky tresses. Elaborate jewelry dangled from their ears, wrists, and nipples, slapping their oiled skin as they moved. The festivities across the city would be epic in scale, and the Domina did not intend to be outdone by her competitors.

The Golden Salamander was not the most expensive—or most exclusive—brothel in Rome, but it was the most decadent, and senators, social climbers, and attractive trash mingled fluids gleefully together in its bacchanalian salons. The Domina had her lovely girls and boys resting up for weeks, bathing in tubs of goat milk to soften their skin, under strict dietary restrictions to make sure every part of them smelled fresh. Meanwhile, she stockpiled cartloads of exotic fruits, slabs of the finest meats, and vats of the best wine for what promised to be the party of the millennium.

The orgy lasted three days. Half of it was unforgettable and the other half everyone was too drunk to remember, but on the morning of the fourth day, after the last guest stumbled home, the prostitutes woke up and groggily shuffled to the central fountain to wash the night's sticky residues off of and out of their weary bodies. And there, splashing around blissfully in the sun-warmed shallow water, was a baby.

He was so radiant that the women who found him dropped to their knees at his feet. His wee head was already covered with silky blond curls, and his buttery skin sparkled in the early morning sunlight. But his eyes, a rich gold, were the most arresting thing about him, and tiny as he was, he already perceived the world around him with preternatural canniness. None of the girls would confess to having birthed him. Perhaps whoever did so had no memory of it, or perhaps he'd materialized out of the slurry of fecundity and fertile juices swirling in the fountain's lukewarm water. No one knew. No one cared.

It was year 723, *ab urbe condita*, and people didn't try to tell themselves that a child like that was human. The women bundled him up in gold silk and nursed him by turns, considering it their sacred duty. They discovered that sucking on their breasts was enough to sustain the infant, though they weren't pregnant and no milk flowed. His divine lips on their nipples threw them into unheard-of ecstasies of matronly affection, leaving them as spent as they were after their most vigorous clients. They named the boy Lucius Tenebrus, or "Light-in-the-Dark," because he seemed to glow, especially at night when he was the most active.

Within weeks, the baby was a toddler, crawling around and making word-like sounds with his rosy mouth. Months later, he was a sturdy child playing musical instruments to delight his myriad mothers, speaking with the vocabulary and erudition of a well-educated adult.

Within the year he grew into a coltish teenager, and then a strapping youth. The morning of his first birthday found Lucius a fully grown man with a blond beard, the body of a statue, the face of an Adonis, the mind of a senator, and the cock of a horse. As he grew, the women of the brothel continued to feed him in the same manner they employed when he was an infant. There were a few important additions to the fare, but the basic method remained the same. He needed, and wanted, nothing else.

CHAPTER 16

SEEING RED

Little Italy
   Sunday afternoon

Vito woke up with a head full of mush. The evening news was on TV and it was dark outside, but he remembered falling asleep to the morning show. He must have slept the day away. For Vito, who had barely slept at all the previous week, that was…interesting.

But though his head was splitting, the world was painfully clear. He sensed everything: the rough lint on the sofa cushions, the oil coating his tongue, the lines his jeans had etched into his thighs from lying on them for so long. He stared into the empty teacup on the coffee table, now bone dry, a residue coating the bottom in sickly green.

"You awake, mi amore?" his grandmother called from the kitchen. He peeked over the back of the sofa—her back was to him, frail in a faded flannel nightdress, and she was already making him another cup of tea. She turned to see if he was conscious, but he ducked his head down. When he peeked back up, he saw her reach into the back of the spice cupboard where she kept her tinctures and pull out an old brown bottle he'd never seen before. She dropped some of whatever it was into his new cup of tea, and then padded into the living room where she found Vito lying down with his eyes closed.

"*Vabbé*," she shrugged, plunking the cup onto the table. He would drink it when he woke up and then fall back asleep for the rest of the night and into the next day. The couch would mold to the shape of his recumbent body if this went on, but she'd just have Massimo buy her a new one, finally. Contemplating the merits of velvet verses leather, she trundled off to the bathroom, and thus didn't see Vito pick up the mug she'd just delivered and pour the contents into her spider plant.

———

The Second Circle
     Sunday afternoon

Adrael laid out his equipment for the evening in a concrete-walled back room adjacent to the Second Circle, a spartan chamber devoid of soft leather furniture and sex swings, and fitted out instead with cold metal tables and wall racks that held guns rather than whips. In front of him sat an array of firearms fitted with silencers, along with wireless walkie-talkies and a row of combat knives. He didn't bother with night-vision goggles—he and the Boys could see perfectly well in the dark—but he did lay out two boxes of the same custom bullets that he'd used to shoot at the Luppi cousins in the alley.

He hoped he wouldn't need bullets that night, however. The point of this operation was to get in, take the one item Lucius wanted, and leave without being noticed. The operation would therefore be a lean one, and Adrael would have preferred to go alone. But the item they were stealing would be unwieldy and would be hard to find once inside the warehouse, so he'd tapped his two most reliable Boys to go with him: LeShawn, a vampire, which Adrael generally preferred as a lookout, and Jerome. Both of them possessed the extra ounce of discretion that their compatriots lacked, and could therefore be trusted not to say anything to anyone about what they were doing that night, although Adrael never told them the details. If all went well, no one other than Adrael, Rat, and Lucius would know what deed, specifically, had been done.

Well...and Carmine. But he was unlikely to talk about it.

Adrael, LeShawn, and Jerome methodically prepped the guns, checking that they were clean and loading the ammunition. Pushing bullets into magazines with a flick of the thumb was so automatic for Adrael that it usually served as a form of meditation. But maybe it was something about the curve of the grip, or the gamey scent of the gun oil, or even the act of shoving a bullet into a slot that abruptly summoned images of Desdemona. His gut lurched at the thought of her, as if something he'd eaten earlier that day had decided to come back to life and kick its way out. The image of her sliding across Jerome's lap made him clench his jaw with disgust. He worked in a sex demon brothel, he of all people should have known...

"Hey boss," Jerome hedged then, "what's up with that new girl? She get fired or what?" Jerome had been unconscious on the floor in Lucius's office during most of Dez's ordeal, so he missed all the subsequent drama.

"Don't know," Adrael replied, his eyes on his bullets. "Why? Do you like her?"

"She's interesting," said Jerome with a sheepish grin. "Different. But she won't last ten minutes in here."

"That was my feeling as well," Adrael said curtly, and Jerome added nothing else, though he and LeShawn glanced at each other behind Adrael's back. In their experience of their enigmatic leader, he was usually more amiable than not, facing even the most devilish problems with a snarky, detached amusement that bordered on psychopathic. This tight-jawed testiness was new and unsettling, and they preferred to stay out of its way.

Another magazine loaded. Adrael pushed it aside with the others, annoyed with himself. He'd never had a problem with Jerome before—he'd rather liked him, to the extent that Adrael liked any of the career criminals who worked for him. Jerome was reliable, always in the right place at the right time with the right attitude, and normally Adrael was happy to see him in his peripheral vision. But Adrael found his hands flexing a bit too hard around the gun grips, and he imagined what Jerome's head would look like splattered against the concrete floor. He banished the thought immediately, however—the world was full of beautiful women, but good help was hard to find.

Speaking of which.

The door clicked open and Rat strode through the door without knocking, but at the sight of Adrael standing in front of a table covered in weapons, his ears visibly twitched.

"Yes?" said Adrael, looking up at him with a combat knife in his hand. Adrael's expression was perfectly bland, but Rat sensed a vibration in the long fingers wrapped around the hilt.

"Nuthin'," Rat muttered. "Wrong room." He started to back out, but before he could pull the door shut again, he heard Adrael clear his throat.

"Since you're here..." Adrael began, and then waited for Rat to come all the way into the room to hear the rest of whatever he had to say.

"Yeah?" Rat swallowed, as the door clicked shut behind him.

"Could you do something for me?" Adrael asked, his voice echoing in the hollow room.

" 'Course."

"Would you give this back to Lester?" Adrael held the knife in the air, dangling it by its handle between two fingers like bait. "I found mine."

Rat approached the table uneasily, refusing to acknowledge the teasing expression on Jerome and LeShawn's faces, his nose twitching at the scent of gunpowder and testosterone. The closer Rat came, the brighter Adrael's eyes gleamed. Rat reached out his delicate hand to take the knife, trying not to shake, fully expecting Adrael to slice his fingers off but unable to think of an alternative to complying.

But Adrael simply flipped the knife around a the last minute and placed the hilt in Rat's palm with exaggerated delicacy.

"Thank you," Adrael smiled tightly, then looked back down at his weapons, dismissing him, and Rat tried not to scamper as he rushed out of the room.

"Hey boss," another Boy said, popping his head in before the door shut all the way.

"Yes?"

"Did you fire that new girl? Desirée?"

Adrael sighed; the Boys were incorrigible gossips.

"Why do you ask?"

" 'Cause...she back."

———

On Sunday nights the Second Circle was closed. The cleaning crew spent the evening chiseling sticky residue off all the surfaces and waving blacklight wands over the floors and furniture, making sure to remove all the bodily fluids. Vampire bar backs lazily prepped their stations, pouring water into phallus-shaped ice molds and polishing martini glasses. Upstairs, sheets were being changed and minibars replenished, and ideally someone would remember to swap out the batteries in the vibrators.

Dez came in through the employee entrance, ignoring the raised eyebrows. The Boys didn't move to stop her, but they'd all seen her stalk into the infirmary the night before with Adrael, cradling her arm like a wounded bird, so they were a tad surprised to see her back there, unsure what her connection to the club was at that point.

"Girl, didn't nobody tell you? We closed Sundays," said Martavius, the white-eyed neckbiter bouncer guarding the employee entrance with a gun holstered under each armpit.

"I'm here to see your boss," Dez told him.

"Which boss?"

"Mr. Dark," she clarified.

"Boss, the...the new girl's here to see you," Martavius announced into a walkie-talkie.

"Send her up."

She walked into the office to find Lucius wrapped in a champagne silk bathrobe, the sheen of the fabric dull compared to the dewy vibrance of his skin as he sipped Cognac out of a coupé glass. He flashed Dez a smile as she came in—an acid smile, yes, but still radiant. He seemed to be in a notably good mood, for which someone was probably paying in blood. His line of computer monitors had been swiveled around to face into the office, and Dez realized then that every inch of the nightclub was under constant surveillance, including the elevator, and that she'd truly been an ass for thinking she was getting away with anything on that property.

However, watching Dark vigilantly and noting only mild irritation and a bit of contempt, she began to suspect that he was somehow unaware that she'd been in the penthouse. Surely if he knew, he would have killed her the night before, and certainly not let her go home to the Order if even the possibility existed that she'd feel guilty and out him. Maybe, she realized, no one watched the cameras all night except Dark —that would make sense, given his controlling tendencies—and when she'd been up there, he'd been first in some private room with the Deputy Mayor, and then had come up to the penthouse later, missing her entrance entirely. And given his apparent dislike of boring tasks, it was likely he only bothered to watch old footage if there was an incident, or if someone needed to have a salacious clip sent to them as an inducement to pay up.

But it didn't matter anymore, because she was about to tell him everything.

"Hello, lover," Lucius purred, swishing the liquor in his glass for effect. She did not look like the same girl whose arm Adrael had broken the day before, miserable and pale with pain. She seemed downright cocky, in fact, her cheeks glowing from whatever deliciously sordid thing she'd done to heal her wrist. "You look radiant today," he pointed out cruelly. "Doesn't she, Adrael?"

Adrael had followed Dez into the office, but she didn't realize he was there until Lucius addressed him.

"Hello," she said, without bothering to look at him.

Adrael's head hurt. A tiny mote of pain, like a jab from an insect, was swiftly growing into a throb. Even with only a few moments to steel himself for the encounter, Adrael had been sure that he was prepared to see her. But her face was glowing with the pink hue of a woman who had been recently fucked, and something inside him snarled.

Lucius, watching them carefully, was not appeased; in his experience, hostility was often a type of foreplay.

"So, tell us," Lucius said, waving Dez down to the sofa, "what your people know about us."

Dez sat, which helped to hide the fact that she was shaking with nerves, propped up by the warmth of sadistic enjoyment surging in her breast knowing that she was about to dismay both of those complacent peacocks so thoroughly.

"Well," she began, sliding into the pedantic cadence she used with undergrads, "we are more or less aware of the particular nature of this establishment. But I'm sure you already know why we have to leave you alone."

"Yes, I went to a lot of trouble to make sure of it."

"And there's not much about 'Mr. Dark' anywhere. My supervisor thinks you're a vampire and my colleague thinks you're a powerless frontman for an illegal corporation. Either way, you're not particularly interesting to them. And *you*—" she slanted a glance at Adrael, "may as well not exist at all."

"That's excellent news," Lucius grinned. "You were right, Adrael, she is useful. I'm so glad we didn't shove her in the incinerator." But to Adrael, Dez looked suspiciously canny, like she had something in her metaphorical back pocket, and he hoped it did not mean that he would have to hurt her again.

"We do, however," Dez added then, "have several mentions in our older records of a *Lucius Tenebrus.*"

For a moment, no one spoke. Dez could have sworn the air conditioner paused to listen.

Inside, however, Lucius was silently screaming.

How? How how how how how… His eyes slid over to Adrael—*had he betrayed him?*

But Adrael was unquestionably dismayed, staring at Dez with the look he reserved for imminent explosions. *He didn't want to kill her.* He let the thought escape the black box in his mind before he could stop it, and the pressure behind his eyes intensified as he realized that Lucius was about to order him to flay her skin off and mount it above that stupid rug.

"I'm sorry, where did you hear that name?" Lucius choked.

Dez pointed smugly at the painting behind his head.

"I didn't hear it anywhere. I read it. That painting is a *genuine* Bosch, if I'm not mistaken. And while we do not have a file on you, we do have a file on Bosch, in which he mentioned that very painting during an interrogation. He also mentioned *who* he made the painting for *by name.*" Dez related the facts with ostentatious placidity, though her heart was racing and she was sure they could hear it. "And once I figured out your real name, I found quite a lot about you in the archives, peppered all over the place, spanning…oh, gosh…centuries. I suppose nobody has bothered to connect it all until now, at least not in the New York office. It took a lot of reading, which most of them don't… But frankly, I'm surprised how often you used your real name. Although 'Dark' isn't a terribly obscure cypher for 'Tenebrus' is it? It's almost as if you *wanted* to be found."

The sweetest sound to anyone's ears is the sound of one's own name.

Lucius had used thousands of aliases over the centuries, but he never really felt like himself unless someone was moaning his name—his musical, poetic name—into his ear. What he resented most about the Order, really, was that they'd stolen his identity from him; by rights his name should have been chiseled in stone on marble monuments, throngs of virgins offered up as willing sacrifices to him as a golden god of love. But that dour cult of death in black ruined it for everyone, and now Lucius, an immortal as radiant as a slice of sunshine, was forced to hide in the shadows. Of course, telling people his name was an indulgence, and a dangerous one, but Lucius was indulgence personified, and he could rarely help divulging it as a secret to his favorite lovers, especially those who engaged in the intimate act of rendering his image, unable to bear the idea that they would adore him, paint him, or sculpt him without knowing who he really was.

"Nobody bothers to learn Latin anymore," Lucius snarled quietly. "Except people like you."

"Well, the Order has a long memory, Mr. Dark. We may necessarily be only human—"

"Who's 'we'?" Lucius interrupted. "You aren't—"

"—but we have a dedicated division whose mandate it is to track down individuals who think they can outrun us purely by outliving us," continued Dez grimly. "In fact, those individuals are a top priority for the Order, and if they were to find out that this nightclub is owned by someone who is at least five hundred years old..." she shrugged, and let the implications of that sit in the room with them for a long, silent moment.

"If." Lucius bit on the word as he locked his eyes on her, fully appreciating the implication.

"Does anyone besides the three of us have any idea how old you are?" she asked.

"You mean those meatheads downstairs? How stupid do I look?"

Dez thought it best to treat that question as rhetorical.

"You know, you can't prove anything," Lucius continued, his voice dangerously calm. "Nobody knows what this painting looks like. It's never been photographed, it has no provenance, and if asked, I can say it's a fake."

"We're the Order, not the police," said Dez. "Nobody has to *prove* anything to anyone. The file I've already compiled is enough to pique their interest, and all they have to be is interested. The division I mentioned has rather different priorities than we do at the local level. They won't bother to raid your nightclub or harass your employees, they'll just come directly for *you*. And then you'll have to run, again. And of course, to be safe, you'll have to burn your precious Bosch. As well as the rest of what you've got upstairs." Dez dropped that bombshell with painstaking placidity, and thoroughly enjoyed the color Lucius face began to turn. "Collecting all that art with your face in it is a smart thing to do, in theory, to keep anyone else from seeing it," she added, twisting the knife, "but it becomes rather a liability if you aren't willing to destroy it."

She'd been upstairs. Lucius's Cognac-flavored blood boiled over.

"Do something," he snarled, turning to Adrael, his eyes aflame. "Do something now. Something bloody."

But:

"I suspect Miss Cross isn't stupid enough to walk in here and tell us all this without expecting to walk out again," Adrael assessed archly. "Is that right?" He kept his expression neutral, but a subversive smile threatened to bubble up at the sight of Lucius's apoplexy.

"How could you let this happen?" Lucius spat, seething with impotent rage.

"I'm not the one who gave her a job here," Adrael reminded him drily.

"You know, that trick lift isn't as clever as you think it is," said Dez. "You might consider using a keycard or something."

"He loses keycards," Adrael shrugged. "He flings his clothes around all day and everything just falls out of his pockets."

"Fingerprint sensors, perhaps?"

"He doesn't have fingerprints," Adrael shook his head, a gleam of true amusement in his eyes. "The retina scanners don't work on him either. There is a state-of-the-art alarm system up there, with motion sensors and lasers and everything, but it's disarmed once you punch in the key code. How did you sort that out, if you don't mind me asking?"

"I'm very clever as well," Dez replied. "And you—" she glanced at Lucius, "should wash your hands more often. Glitter is tenacious."

Adrael's smile emerged fully, and Lucius looked murderous, which amused him still more.

"I also suspect most of those security cameras only feed into this office," Dez continued. "And when I peeked in on your penthouse, neither of you were in here watching, correct?"

"Blackmail is only really effective if it's a secret," Adrael replied. "Many of the downstairs cameras feed into the security room downstairs, but anything above floor three—and that includes the elevator— was deemed too sensitive for general surveillance." He glanced archly at Lucius, indicating that it was he who had done the deeming.

"And you haven't watched the elevator tape from Friday night?"

"It's been a busy couple of days," Adrael shrugged again, still casually, though he was beginning to feel annoyed now at that obvious failure of his supposedly airtight protocols. Lucius's complicated combination of paranoia and laziness had, it seemed, proven as problematic as Adrael had always known it would, but Adrael now had to allow that a certain complacency regarding his own terrifying prowess had, perhaps, lulled him into a false sense of security. That bothered him enormously; the sin of hubris was something he understood intimately, and had long thought himself above. "I should tell you that if you'd entered in the wrong code twice that panel would have exploded in your face."

"But I didn't, did I?" she retorted coolly.

"What. Do. You. Want?" Lucius ground out. He was afraid that if he moved he wouldn't be able to stop himself from ripping Dez's throat out, but he managed to squeak out the question.

"The file I put together on you is currently sitting in the bottom of a drawer in my desk in my office at headquarters," Dez told him. "Normally, no one goes in my office but me, but if I don't show up for work for a while—say, because I'm *dead*—someone else will inherit my office, and all my work, and they'll find that file sooner or later. And then, Mr. Dark, you'll have bigger Order members than me to worry about. So you must understand that whatever arrangement you *thought* we had is now over." She smiled then, and to Adrael, it looked unsettlingly like Lucius's own expression when he had someone under his foot.

Lucius stared at Dez with an ugly glare like the wrong side of a mirror. He didn't want to look at Adrael, which would make him even more angry, or look out at the club he loved, or at the Bosch that had betrayed him. Instead he kept his eyes on his beautiful, human-scented tormentor, and silently swore that he'd have her head on a plate one day.

"If your people come for me I will get away," he told her, his voice shimmering like an oil slick. "I always do. But before I go, please understand that I will let them know everything I know about *you*."

"Of course you will. And since *I* don't want my bosses to find out about *me*, and *you* don't want my bosses to find out about *you*, I think we'd both sleep better if we just left each other alone from now on, don't you think?"

"I don't sleep," said Lucius with a sneer. "I'll bet you don't either."

Adrael flicked his blue eyes from one sex demon to the other, a laugh now threatening to ripple out of him. He would never have thought Dez had this much salt in her, and inconvenient as this whole situation now was, he couldn't help but be impressed. And, unbelievably, she looked like she had something *more* to say.

"Oh, did you by chance find Vito Luppi?" Dez then asked airily, as if the question were merely academic.

Lucius and Adrael glanced at each other, and Adrael shrugged one big shoulder.

"Did you visit Carmine Luppi?" she persisted.

Again, Adrael shrugged enigmatically, revealing nothing.

"Did you hurt him?"

"We didn't touch the old bastard," Lucius spat. "He was very help-ful. We *can* be civilized, when people cooperate."

"Did you make some sort of deal with Carmine to cover Vito's bill?"

"More or less," said Adrael.

"Are you now accepting collectible coins as payment?"

"Carmine has some other resources available to him," said Lucius.

"So...you no longer care about finding Vito at all?" Dez was genuinely dismayed. "But if he's murdering succubi, I'd...I'd think that would be alarming to you, considering your operation here."

"Please. We are more than capable of keeping our employees safe," scoffed Lucius. "And most of the Girls never even bother to leave the building. So if you people run across him, feel free to kill him. We don't need him anymore."

"But you do think he killed those street girls?"

"Vito did have strong needs," Lucius shrugged. "Maybe more than your average moonie. Personally, I think it's all that Catholic repression, the way that family tamps down their natural urges. Not that you'd know anything about that, would you, Desdemona?" He looked directly into her eyes and Dez felt violated, as if she'd caught him reading her diary. "All that pressure builds up and has to come out somewhere. We were happy to serve as his release valve, but that kind of service doesn't come cheap. I wouldn't be surprised if he tried to get the knockoff version at a discount."

"But, I suppose, those girls couldn't control him."

Lucius's eyes slid over to Adrael, his expression unreadable.

"You get what you pay for," he replied.

Dez narrowed her eyes at both of them; she should have known better than to expect any fellow-feeling from Lucius, since he thought he was a different breed of nightcrawler from those he employed, and Adrael could hardly be expected to care, since he despised the species entirely.

"But..." Lucius then added, cocking his head like a meerkat.

"But?"

"But let's just say that I think what you're suggesting is...out of character."

"It's out of character for a moonie to kill a prostitute?" Dez raised an eyebrow. "I thought that was...."

"No, of course, you're right," Lucius shook his head dismissively, but a crafty smile in his eyes told Dez she was being played with. "And it's not that I don't *care*. It's just that it's no longer my problem. You people are more than equipped to put down a rabid dog like Vito, and I'd be happy enough to hear he finally had to pay for something."

"But...but if it's not Vito Luppi doing the killing, who should we be looking for?"

"Try Jack the Ripper," offered Lucius. "Now, as nice as it's been visiting with you, Desdemona, we have other things to do, so get the fuck off my property."

Dez glanced at Adrael for a comment, but he said nothing, so she got up and went to the door, casting one last significant glance at the Bosch as she went.

"You know, according to the file, Bosch thought you were the devil himself," she said to Lucius.

"Do you really believe that?" Lucius sounded pleased.

"I doubt the devil needs a bodyguard, Mr. Dark," Dez replied coldly.

"Just call me Lucius," he spat back. "I prefer it."

"Obviously."

She stalked down the catwalk stairs in silence. The bouncers glanced up curiously as she passed, but looked down again when they saw Adrael following her. Dez didn't acknowledge him, a jolt of fear spiking in her gut. His tread behind her should have been heavy, but was silent and barely caused a shudder in the tensile metal, as if he was a massive cat stalking on soft paws. She reached the employee exit in a hurry and pushed on the bar to open the door, but he reached out his arm and held it shut.

"That was..." he cocked his head and looked for the right word, "unexpected."

"I thought it unwise to call ahead."

"If you're smart you'll never come back here."

"I don't intend to," she assured him.

"Funny as it was," he added with a wicked little smirk.

"I'm glad you find this all so amusing," hedged Dez, unsure how to parse that reaction; Adrael seemed to constantly vacillate between severity and barely hidden amusement. "Does Lucius really think it's out of character for Vito to have killed those girls?" she asked then.

"Lucius has his opinions," Adrael allowed.

"You think otherwise?"

"I spend more time with moonies than he does. And when Vito came here, he wasn't angry at us. Now he is. Anger can change a man's behavior."

Too true. Of Vito and, probably, Adrael himself; a reality that Dez would do well to remember.

Adrael smiled then and abruptly released the bar, allowing the door to swing open. Dez stumbled through it into the alley behind the club, and turned to glare at him, indignant.

"And you're going to let him get away with it?"

"We are not responsible for every moonie in the city, Desdemona," Adrael reminded her. "That is the purview of you people, I believe."

"And suppose those girls are the *last* people in the world you'd bother to care about," she muttered as the door began to slide shut.

"Were both of them wearing red?" he asked, pausing it with his foot.

Were they? Dez sifted through her mental images of the bodies, and realized that among all that rusty-colored blood there *had* been shreds of bright red clothes left on both of them.

"Yes, come to think of it, they were."

"Then it's too bad all those Luppi addresses you gave me are wrong."

"How did you know they were both wearing red?" she demanded.

But Adrael just smiled at her enigmatically again, letting go of the door and allowing a giant block of steel only slightly less cold and hard than himself click shut between them.

———

Bushwick, Brooklyn
Sunday night

Giulio rolled over in the hotel bed and rested his head on the freckled butt-cheeks of the ginger construction worker, who was snoozing, tuckered out from his recent exertions on Giulio's butt's behalf. But Giulio was wide awake. Sleep, lately, eluded him.

He wondered if Vito was in the ground. He'd had no choice but to tattle on him; the cousins were all used to covering for one other's peccadilloes, but each of them had a line they never crossed. Back when Giulio was just a pimply teenager, his uncle had caught him fumbling with a school friend in the back of his car, and Giulio expected a beating, but Massimo simply told him that he didn't care what he did in private as long as nobody in the family had to hear about it. Giulio took the warning to heart and never let his sexual orientation become a topic for discussion. Perhaps his mother would eventually stop dropping hints about him getting married, but it was unimportant to Giulio to be accepted for "who he was," like it said on those faggy rainbow posters he hated. All he wanted was to be allowed to keep his personal life personal, and to retain the things that mattered to him: status, position, bags of cash, free time. He didn't want trouble and he never made trouble, and if he did, his uncle Massimo would murder him and that was that.

But Vito got away with things that Giulio would never have dreamed of, like "borrowing" Massimo's Mercedes and driving it into a fire hydrant, or fooling around with his uncle Nico's much-younger girlfriend. Fast cars, fast women, and fast getaways were Vito's repertoire, and his father always let him off with an indulgent wink. But this time was different. Vito broke the cardinal rule of the family: he lost control of their "condition," and Uncle Carmine had been stripped of his primogeniture and banished to the suburbs for the same. Vito had been compromised by a pimp, and as a result had almost betrayed his own father. And while Giulio could have forgiven him any of that, Teo *died* for Vito's sins, and that was something Giulio could not live with. Somebody had to speak for Teo, although Giulio was turning his heart inside out like a dirty sock over the idea that maybe a part of him also found it satisfying to finally get Vito in trouble.

Now maybe Vito was dead, or worse. Massimo wouldn't have wanted to hurt his beloved only son, and it would have broken his heart to do so, but he was the *capo* and would have to be fair, both to keep the family honor intact and, frankly, to keep his own skin on his body. The Luppi did not tolerate weakness in that regard, and there was always somebody ready to drag down the guy at the top of the pile.

The phone rang then, and Giulio answered it, even though talking to his uncle Massimo when he was in bed with a man made him squirm.

"Yep?" Giulio tried to sound innocently casual but felt like he failed.

"G, I need you to do something for me," said Massimo.

"Yep," Giulio agreed, because "no" wasn't an option. Giulio had been avoiding his family all week, but if Massimo had told anyone about what the nephews did, there would have been no avoiding anyone, so Massimo had clearly protected him.

"I need you to check on my son."

"Check on Vito?" Giulio repeated, not sure he understood. "What... uh..." *Holy Christ, was he holding him in some warehouse? Or locked in a box, or limbless in the trunk of a car?*

"He's at Nana's," Massimo told him.

"Nana's?"

"Yeah."

"Oh. Okay." Giulio started to flush, and a familiar prickling tickled under the skin on the backs of his hands. "How's...uh...how's he doing?"

"That's what I want you to tell me," Massimo barked, exasperated. "The family's coming in for the funeral, and I got a lot going on over here and can't get over there tonight. *Capice?*"

"Uh-huh." Giulio struggled to understand, wondering if his uncle was speaking in code.

"Look, Nana's not as young as she used to be. She does alright, but she misses things sometimes. So I need you to go over there tomorrow and make sure Vito's sticking with the program. She's got him on the tea, he's cleaning up, this'll all be fine in a couple weeks. I'm taking care of it. Just keep your mouth shut, which I know you can do, and it'll be like you boys didn't do nothing at all."

"Alright, Uncle," sighed Giulio, finally understanding. "I'll go over there now."

"And Vito don't know that Teo's dead, so don't talk about it. It'll just set him off. I'll tell him later. You got it?"

"Yep," said Giulio, and hung up.

"You going someplace?" the ginger asked groggily, his mouth full of pillow.

"Nah," Giulio told him. And then he picked up his cell phone and called a number he hadn't dialed in days, because he'd been afraid of how it would feel to hear it ring endlessly into infinity with no one there to pick up.

But after only two rings, Vito answered.

"Hey." Vito's voice sounded strained, tired maybe, but more like his old self, confirming that he hadn't been punished at all; Massimo had simply tucked him away at their grandmother's apartment in Little Italy to dry out and wait for daddy to fix everything. "That you, G?" Vito prodded hopefully on the other end of the line.

Giulio opened his mouth to say something, but the ceiling was spinning, and he was itching all over. Everything he wanted to say scrambled in his mind as the world went red.

"Teo's dead," he spat, and then hung up and crushed his phone in his swiftly hardening palm.

———

Little Italy

Red. Everything was red again, all at once. Vito held his phone up to his ear, listening to the silence in which Giulio's words repeated like an echo.

Teo's dead.

His heart pulsed in his ears, and the room snapped into vivid relief. *Red roses on the wallpaper, red embroidery on the tablecloth, red pen on the unfinished crossword puzzle*—it was as if he'd been blind to the color for days, and was just now able to see it again. It started to drizzle outside; hesitant droplets hit the windowpanes, and a traffic light outside flashed "STOP" and turned them the color of blood.

Teo's dead. It's your fault. Giulio hadn't said as much, but Vito recognized that tone of voice, the one Giulio used when Vito went too far and Giulio was tired of him. His cup of tea had gone cold and he could have sworn it was hot when he answered the phone. The apartment seemed too small and he couldn't breathe, his lungs filling with the acrid smell of sulphur and melted cheese instead of oxygen. He needed a walk, some fresh air.

His grandmother shuffled into the kitchen in her prehistoric slipper-socks, intent on making another cup of the cranberry tea she drank gallons of every night. She put the kettle on to boil and shuffled back to the bedroom, leaving her cup on the counter next to the stove. Moments later, Vito was standing over her teacup, reaching for the brown bottle in the back of the cabinet, and he squirted a dose of whatever was inside it onto the damp, bleaching teabag that she would reuse several more times that evening. He then lay back down on the couch and pretended to sleep as she came back into the kitchen, poured hot water over that very teabag, and took it back to her bedroom. Ten minutes later, her ancient nasal passages were gently humming as she snored, and Vito pulled on his leather jacket and slipped out into the night.

His head was clearer than it had been in months, unencumbered by the effects of that damned tea, or by guilt, or by any desire to conform to the societal constrictions that he was done bothering with. His shirt collar grew tight, his eyes pulsing in their sockets as the change began. It forced its way through what was left of the noxious herbs, their effect burned away by his growing rage. Modern society was run by duplicitous, lipstick-wearing sheep, making rules designed to protect themselves from a world full of sharp teeth. But it was the role of the soft things in nature to be fodder for its apex predators, and Vito would no longer obey rules put in place by sheep when he himself was a wolf. His attempt to behave himself had ultimately ended up costing Teo his life, and he wasn't interested in being a good boy anymore.

He found what he was looking for without having to try: a flash of bright red against pert flesh, a head of curly hair dyed strawberry, and dark lashes coated in mascara. *Hey, honey—do you want some company?* They found a secluded corner behind some construction fencing and it was over in minutes. The girl's blood was in Vito's mouth and nose and eyes, his claws tearing through her flesh. Everything was good about this, the deliciously chewy give as hair was ripped out of a scalp, the dead weight of bones and muscle lying in his arms like so much barbecue; even the smell of shit and piss as her bowels released the pungent tang of exotic seasoning. He could smell nature in it, and rightness, and when he ejaculated into the cavity he'd dug into her womb with his teeth, he felt like there was nothing more to wish for in the world.

Eventually the girl became nothing but bleeding limbs loosely connected by congealing tissue, so Vito lifted up the manhole they'd been standing on, shoved her inside, pulled his sweatshirt and jacket back over his blood-spattered body, and ducked into the shadows to trot home before anyone saw him.

CHAPTER 17

———————

BAD MOON RISING

Little Italy
Monday morning

Little Italy smelled like baking bread. The scent wafting out of the neighborhood's ovens lured morning commuters out of their weekend stupors, promising a warm handful of pastry as compensation for returning to the workday grind. The sun had barely turned the edges of the buildings pink, but already a few early risers were emerging—city workers, retail workers, restaurant workers, and yawning dog walkers taking their fur babies out before they'd even brushed their teeth.

A chubby bleached blonde in a black velour tracksuit trailed a fluffy pomshitz at the end of a leash, languidly sipping a coffee while the dog examined every post and hydrant. Then, abruptly, the dog stopped in its tracks next to a sheet of construction scaffolding, snuffling as it worried at the bottom seam of the barrier. Peering through the mesh wall, the blonde noticed what looked like a mound of flesh and some fingers in a pool of blood beside a manhole in the blacktop behind the netting.

But instead of inspecting the site, the woman kept walking and the well-trained dog walked with her, because too many people were milling around on the street for her to jump the fence and have a look inside. The woman instead texted her location back to Order headquarters, and a subterranean retrieval team was dispatched to approach the manhole from underneath and retrieve whatever horrors lay within. The dog, proud of a job well done, walked on with its tail swishing with a self-congratulatory wag, unaware of the nature of the sad, crumpled horror it had found.

————

Back at the Order
Late Monday morning

The girl's lipstick-red jumper was too skimpy for fall. The girl was also too skimpy, all elbows and knees, underfed either because of poverty or for beauty, with the same result. Dead, she crumpled up like a puppet, which made it easy for her killer to fold her in half and stuff her down a manhole. Now she lay on the gurney scrunched up in the position in which the Recovery Team found her, her head almost bitten off at the neck under her jaw. Her intestines had been yanked down and out through her vagina, where they protruded like some eldrich tentacular afterbirth, puncture holes had been gouged on either side of her chest as if the killer used her ribcage as a handhold for his claws, and her lips been chewed off down to the teeth by an overly vigorous kiss.

Dez heard about the new body from Reilly in the hallway, so she followed him to the morgue, where Solomon, Hunter, Beatrix, and Dr. Boiko were already assembled, their heads bent curiously over the gurney while Brother Justin hovered uncomfortably by the door several feet away. They were all perturbed, whispering fervently as they shook their heads over the corpse.

"Another one?" Dez asked quietly.

"Well...sort of," Hunter coughed, as Dr. Boiko procured a drop of thoughtwater from the vial. She plopped the liquid on the back of the girl's limp hand and they all waited for the inevitable hissing as it ate through her flesh, revealing her as other-than-human.

And they waited.

And waited.

But it didn't happen.

Dr. Boiko tried again, with two drops this time, on a the other hand, but the water just beaded off the girl's cooled flesh.

"As I said before," Dr. Boiko intoned patiently, "no effect."

"Are we sure of this water?" Solomon asked.

"I'll check it," she shrugged, with the pleasant officiousness of one who is humoring a colleague. Dez fought the reflex to tuck her own gloved hands away as Dr. Boiko brought out a clear plastic perforated box containing a creature that looked like a rat with a jarringly human face and hand-shaped paws. Dr. Boiko slid the lid open and the rat-creature whimpered and crammed itself against the opposite side of the box. Undaunted, Dr. Boiko plopped a single drop of the same water on the rat-creature's thigh, and they all heard it hiss as it ate through its flesh like acid, the rat choking out a squeal of agony that sounded like the word, "no."

"As you see," Dr. Boiko concluded, dropping the plastic lid back over the whimpering animal, "it works. Which means..." she raised her eyebrows at Hunter.

"Which means this dead girl's a human," Hunter concluded grimly.

He let that fact sit among them like a bad smell. *This dead girl was human.* Which made her a real victim and not just some extranatural debris.

But why, Dez wondered, *would Vito start killing humans, if he was angry at sex demons?*

"Maybe our guy couldn't tell what she was," Reilly offered. "Maybe even *they* can't tell sometimes."

"I would think he'd be more likely to mistake a succubus for a human than the other way around," said Beatrix drily, "unless this girl was so intoxicating he thought she couldn't be a mere mortal."

The girl was not unattractive, but not remarkable, so none of them thought it likely.

"They found her in the middle of Little Italy," said Reilly. "One of the Night Watch guys says he recognizes this girl from the neighborhood hitting on tourists out for late-night cannoli."

"Was she in another dumpster?" asked Dez, noticing the film of grime on the girl's body.

"Shoved down a manhole. We only found her because he left so much of her on the ground outside it."

"So he bothered to hide this body instead of just tossing her away?"

"Kind of," Hunter hedged. "He didn't hide her very *well*. The kill site was right next to the manhole, and we had a hell of a time cleaning it up before the construction crew showed up."

"Maybe he hid her because she's human and he didn't expect her to dissolve like the others," Reilly suggested.

"He made a real mess this time," Hunter added. "We had to hose everything down into the manhole and then break some pipes in the building to flood the bottom floor a little so no one would notice. Took forever."

"If he keeps escalating this, we're going to lose control of the situation," Justin fretted. "Another body like this in the city morgue will be a front-page headline."

"Also..." Dez hemmed, "I notice she's wearing red. Just like the other two girls." She cocked her head thoughtfully, as if that observation had just then occurred to her.

"I noticed that too," Dr. Boiko nodded. "Twice could have been a coincidence. Three times seems like a pattern."

"He's selecting them by *color*?" Solomon raised his brows.

"Red has a similar effect on bulls," Dr. Boiko reminded him.

"What about the list Miss Cross compiled?" Solomon glanced at Dez.

"They've all been cleared," shrugged Hunter. "Except the Luppi kid. We haven't been able to find him."

"Not an unusual situation with mobsters," Solomon averred. "Hardly suggestive. The Luppi are organized criminals, and the killings in these cases are the opposite of organized."

"Hey..." Reilly offered then, reading from the notes he'd brought from the Situation Room but hadn't yet perused. "Says here that same Night Watchman saw *this* girl walking last night with a young dark-haired guy in a black leather moto jacket,"

"Black moto jacket?" Dez blurted out. "Like...Vito Luppi's black leather moto jacket?"

They all turned to look at her.

"How do you know what jackets Vito Luppi wears?" Solomon's glacial inquisitor's voice rang off the morgue's empty steel gurneys. Dez's stomach dropped—a prey animal's response to seeing the shadow of a hawk. But her brain shuddered back to life in time to save her.

"He was wearing a jacket like that in a photo in the Luppi file. You showed it to me," she reminded Hunter. "Remember?"

Hunter stared at her for what felt like an eternity.

"That's right," he nodded. "I did."

"And is she correct?" Justin piped up from the doorway. "Does the Luppi boy have a jacket like that?"

"In the photos he does," Hunter nodded wearily.

"Alright, enough," Justin's voice snapped like a whip cracking, surprising them all. "Miss Cross, I see why you might be uncomfortable leaving that thread loose, in a case like this. I certainly am." He flashed Solomon an eloquent glance. "Out of an abundance of caution, Father, I'd appreciate it if you'd interrogate the Luppi boy. I understand the reasoning behind leaving that family alone, but we cannot let this continue. These crimes are too obvious. And regardless, if we allow them to think they can get around us by being difficult, they will *all* begin to use that as a strategy, so we will undermine our own cause."

"You're right," Solomon grumbled. "This does cross the line, as you say. But this has to be handled with delicacy. This is a difficult situation, and it's not fair to put that burden on you, Alan. You have a heavy caseload as it is. I'll take over management of this matter."

And Hunter, after a long pause during which Dez wondered if he might object, simply nodded.

"I'll get you the file," he said.

"Find Vito Luppi and pick him up," Brother Justin added. "If the family makes trouble for us, we'll just have to make trouble for them."

———

Solomon and Justin stalked down the hall in silence, saying nothing until they reached Justin's office and closed the door.

"Is this how it's going to be?" Solomon scowled. "Kowtowing to a teenager because of who her mother is?"

"She's not a teenager." Justin pushed a file around his desk with an officious shrug. "Miss Cross is a Ph.D. candidate."

"She's here to keep tabs on us."

"Not as far as I'm concerned," Justin hissed, his temper sparking again. "I was presented with her as a candidate for Brother Pascal's replacement. She has an ideal background, and came highly recommended. There was no reason to say no."

"Except..." Solomon's brows lowered.

"Frankly, Desmond, if we lose control of this situation, Izumi Cross won't need her daughter to tell her so; she'll see it in the news like everyone else. And if that happens, we have to be able to say we left no stone unturned. One might suggest Miss Cross was watching out for us by helping us to that conclusion."

"I don't like it," Solomon grumbled. "Her presence alone feels like a threat."

"It is a threat, abstractly," Justin sighed. "I tell myself we have nothing to hide, but no matter how pristine our operations, *those people* never come in without taking some heads, if only to remind us that they can. We have to make sure they have no reason to do so. And it may very well *be* the Luppi boy doing these murders."

"It's unlikely that after all this time—"

"No matter how rationally a werewolf may behave, at the end of the day, he's still a monster."

"Do you know how many human lives we've saved by encouraging those monsters to toe the line?" Solomon spat. "We can't get them all. All we can do is encourage them to behave as much like humans as possible and make them believe *that's* what's keeping us from their door. Others will get the message and behave accordingly."

"You may believe this philosophy, but perhaps it's slipped Vito Luppi's mind," Justin replied tartly. "And even if it's *not* him doing this, *someone* is, and if you cannot catch the maniac before he kills again, we must make it clear we did everything we could, barring nothing. *Nothing.* I understand the logic you apply to those gangsters, Desmond. I don't want to have to expend resources fighting with them either. But the Umbra may not agree that you have things sufficiently under control to allow that degree of latitude. Izumi Cross is known for her willingness to lose *fifty* human lives to get at just *one* demon. And if the Luppi boy is the one causing all this mayhem, by your own logic, they'll have broken faith with this detente of yours, and you'll need to take the Luppi to task for it. So we may as well throw our weight around if only to remind everyone—including ourselves—that we can."

"Yes, I understand that. But don't get too comfortable around that Cross girl. There's something fishy about this situation. There's no reason in the world that Izumi Cross's daughter should hide herself away in the research department."

"Perhaps she just likes books more than you do," Justin offered.

———

Dez, Hunter, and Beatrix stood in silence in the morgue as Dr. Boiko wheeled the body away to cold storage, staring at one other as if they had all been chastised like children, even though they had essentially gotten their way.

"It's for the best, Alan," said Beatrix. "Solomon let this mess escalate, and now he'll have to deal with it, and it will be squarely on his plate if he can't. I think Miss Cross did you a favor." She beamed at Dez, her smile saccharine, her eyes sharp. "And it's lucky you pay such close attention to clothing, Desdemona."

Dez smiled blandly at her and then turned to Dr. Boiko as she returned from the body fridge.

"What will you do with the girl...afterwards? If you can't find out her name."

"Oh, we know her name, she had an I.D." said Dr. Boiko offhandedly, pointing at the battered red polyester bag that had been tossed into the sewer with the body. It sat on a cart nearby, along with the girl's clothes, which had been sliced into a pile of wrinkled lycra stained brown with blood, occasional patches of its original tomato-red color peeping through. But the perfunctory way she said it told Dez everything she needed to know. The Order would not contact the next of kin or bother to give the girl a headstone, or even an urn with her name on it. A body found by the police was a problem to be solved, but a missing prostitute was just a statistic. It was far more suited to the Order's ultimate purpose that this body disappear like the other two. But a human body would not obligingly dissolve in a few days, so it would have to be helped along by the Order's incinerator, and whatever was left would be swept up into a tiny box and stored in the vault, just like the remains of the succubi. And at that point, Dez reflected, there wasn't much difference between them after all.

"I don't know why he'd start with nightcrawlers and move into humans," Hunter sighed, rubbing the back of his neck wearily.

"This isn't the first time that's happened," Beatrix replied grimly. "Let's not forget the Ripper case."

"The Ripper case?" Dez blinked at her.

"An oldie but a goodie. And very on-topic, I'd say. It perfectly illustrates why those creatures are a cancer on society."

"Nightcrawlers or hookers?" Hunter remarked.

"Please, Alan."

"Do *we* have a file on the Ripper case?" Dez blinked.

"We certainly do," Beatrix nodded with kittenish satisfaction. "It's right there in the archives."

"Ugh, all this nightcrawler stuff is too esoteric for me," sighed Hunter. "Give me a nice, solid moonie any day. At least I know what I'm looking at."

Dez was beginning to agree with him. But at least now the Order was going to put their considerable might behind apprehending Vito, so hopefully there would be no more dead girls. In true Order fashion, they'd show up at the Luppi homes in the middle of the night and—

Oh God. The addresses.

She followed Hunter out of the morgue and sidled up to him as he walked to his office.

"May I speak with you?" she whispered, her voice barely audible in the empty hallway.

His eyes told her to follow him, so she did, both of them walking as if nothing was wrong, until they reached his office and he closed the door.

"Yes?" he leaned on his desk and flashed her a wolfish smile. He obviously had the wrong idea about what she wanted to speak about, and Dez was genuinely sorry to disappoint him.

"The addresses in the Luppi file are all wrong."

"What?" he blinked at her.

"Check them," she repeated miserably. There are no Luppi family members living at any of the addresses you have listed. Perhaps you haven't had time to update them in years, I don't know. But when Solomon begins tracking down Vito, he'll figure it out quite quickly, I think."

Hunter looked at Dez, then at the file, and then at Dez again, his mind churning.

"Did you come in here and take the file?" he asked.

"Well, I didn't *take* it anywhere," she sighed. "But I did read through it. Nobody was interested in going after Vito Luppi and that seemed *off* to me."

"And how do you know the addresses are wrong?"

"I went there," she lied.

"You went to *all* of them?" He raised his eyebrows. "You physically went to all these places? Even the ones in Jersey?"

"I went to a few," she amended with manufactured petulance, trying to sound as if she'd been exaggerating instead of outright lying. "But the ones I visited were all wrong."

Hunter sighed and slumped on his desk, looking defeated.

"That fucking file," he groaned. "We aren't supposed to bother them, and they never make the kind of trouble we care about, so I just... didn't keep up with it. There's always a fresh case to deal with instead."

Since she was confessing, Dez thought it best to confess everything she wanted to right now, before she forgot what she was supposed to lie about.

"Also...I went to see Carmine Luppi," she said, crossing her arms against her chest like a sorry child. She waited for him to ask "why" or "how could you" or even "how dare you" but what he finally said, when he spoke, was:

"And what did he tell you?"

"He told me that his nephew Vito has been spending a lot of money on succubus prostitutes." She fudged the information in a way that would, if checked, seem like a plausible enough interpretation. "Which is another reason why Vito is worth questioning about these bodies."

"Yeah, he told me the same thing. Right after he told me you came to ask him about it."

Dez blinked at him, unsure she'd heard him correctly.

"Right after..."

"I know you went to see Carmine. I went to see him for the same reason you did. And he mentioned that someone else, my—ahem—*assistant,* already asked him all the same questions."

"Oh," Dez said quietly, unsure what to do next. He didn't seem angry, but she wasn't sure what *else* he was.

"I wondered if you were gonna tell me you went there."

"I intended to. Eventually."

"Uh huh." They stood in silence like a couple of cats who'd just broken a priceless vase.

"What are you doing to do now?" Dez asked.

"Nothing."

"Do you think Solomon will talk to Carmine?"

"Solomon never talks to our Unnatural sources if he doesn't have to. Makes him feel sticky. If anything, he'll tell *me* to go talk to Carmine. Which, obviously, I already did. I'll just change the date I went to see him in the file, and I won't mention *you* at all."

Dez exhaled the breath she'd been holding. "Thank you," she managed.

"What about that address for Vito in the database?" he continued. "Was that one right?"

"Oh, that was…" but then, just in time, Dez realized what she would give away with that statement. "I have no idea," she amended. "I stopped by, but there's no way to know if he lives in that building, since I didn't see him. You said you went there, did you see him?"

"Nah," Hunter shook his head as he raked his fingers through his hair. "But I guess that's our best lead, so I'll have to tell Solomon to start there." He rubbed his face wearily, looking ill.

"I'm sorry," she said, and this time she meant it. "I just—"

"Couldn't let it go? I know the feeling." Hunter took one of her gloved hands, giving it a squeeze. "You're so much trouble," he told her, but he said it fondly, and he kept hold of her hand. "Do you really think it's Vito?" He was clearly asking more than one question, as his eyes flitted from her face to her neck and back again.

"Don't you?"

"Yeah," he nodded. "I do. And if so, you might've saved some poor hooker's life. And I know I might suffer for it, but damn...I'd pay to see that look on Solomon's face again. The balls on you, Cross." He smiled again, a little wider.

"It's really the thought of my mother that scares them." Dez's heart fluttered as his eyes kept finding hers. He was so solid, and so human, and so kind, and she wanted to fall into him like a warm bed.

"I hear getting an Umbra audit is like getting a colonoscopy with a chainsaw," he said. "Nobody wants to tempt fate. I don't blame Justin for wanting to have all his bases covered. I wouldn't pull that card too often though. Solomon'll find a way to make you regret it."

"Not with you to cover for me, surely."

"Anytime," he breathed. "Even if you are a sneaky little liar."

"Even if—" Dez began, but then his burly arms pulled her close, and his lips were on hers.

No. Her body crackled instantly to life, and though she willed it to stop, it and her mind were not on speaking terms. Her clothes saved most of Hunter from her touch, but his warmth rushed into her from his lips and the rough stubble of his chin pressing against her cheek. He uttered a low moan of need and grew hard against her thigh as the rebellious region between her legs bloomed like a dewy flower.

The sharp tone of Beatrix's voice just outside the door hit Dez's ear like birdshot, followed by a lower rumble that was probably Reilly responding. Hunter gaped as if he'd surprised even himself, a hectic look in his eyes. Dez stepped back and collected her limbs, waiting for him to say something, even if it was to raise the alarm. *That was so stupid, stupid, stupid. Could he tell what she was?*

But he just flashed her a guilty smile like a naughty teenage boy.

"Thanks for...uh...coming clean. About everything." His eyes scanned up and down her body, thinking about something other than the Luppi.

"Yes, well, I should...be going...now," she said inanely.

"Yeah," he nodded, dazed. "You should."

"Alright."

"So do that."

"I will."

She smoothed her dress, steadied her breath, and then opened the door and stepped out of the office, hoping that both their faces were composed enough for an audience. Beatrix was in fact standing right outside Hunter's door, but Dez ignored her searching eyes as she walked away.

Now she'd done it. Dez recognized that gaping, hungry look on Hunter's face—she'd seen it in all her former lovers. He would want more, if for no other reason than because she was...what she was. And she wouldn't be able to resist, because she was what she was, and unless she somehow found a way to master that "restraint" about which Beatrix was so skeptical, the two of them would ride that speeding train around every bend in the track until they lost control and plunged into the abyss.

With that cheering thought, she slipped into the archive to find out what it was exactly about Jack the Ripper that Beatrix thought would be so goddamn enlightening.

CHAPTER 18

NON CHIEDO LA LUNA

Brooklyn
Monday night, 11 p.m.

In theory, robbing people who couldn't call the police was a piece of cake.

The warehouse was a shabby concrete rectangle on a rundown block by the wharf, encircled by chainlink fence topped with barbed wire and surrounded by old car parts. No one would have any reason to guess that the crumbling building contained millions of dollars worth of stolen goods and invaluable works of art. There were no guards, which made sense; nothing said "rob me" to thieves or "investigate me" to cops like round-the-clock armed muscle at a grimy industrial warehouse. Disabling the alarm was relatively easy—Adrael had never met a security system he couldn't ravage in under ten minutes. He tapped on the microphone of his wireless headset to let LeShawn and Jerome know to start counting the time, and slipped alone through the warehouse door.

It was pitch black inside, with no windows to let in the moonlight, but Adrael didn't need a flashlight to get around. The topography of the warehouse unfurled before him according to a map created by the forces of heat and proprioception acting on the surface of his skin, the tiny hairs in his ears, even the film across his eyeballs. He scanned the snarled mess of boxes, crates, and treasures half-draped in dusty white cotton sheets, and picked his way silently along the floor. The place was packed with contraband; cases of high-end sardines shared space with cases of brand-new iPads and pallets of guns, and in the close air he smelled dust, must, rust, old canvas, wood, and tobacco, and even an acrid hint of cocaine emanating from some false-bottomed crate.

Unfortunately, there was a lot of art in there—far more than he'd anticipated. Everywhere were sculptures, triptychs, tapestries, and rows and rows of paintings leaning against each other, uncatalogued and unseen. There was even a largish marble fountain that had been lifted out of a piazza, topped with a looming, muscular, marble angel, sword in hand: Michael, that most sanctimonious of seraphim, keeping watch over the Luppi's ill-gotten hoard.

And inconveniently, what Adrael was looking for had been rendered in two dimensions, which made things more difficult. He could see the shapes of the physical objects around him, but to look at paintings, he needed at least a bit of light. He pulled a penlight out of his pocket and pointed it at the canvases, tugging gently at the shrouds draped over the accordioned rows of once-vibrant works that had become nothing but flat, fading corpses in a dusty mausoleum with no one to look at them. They were all of them precious, all of them museum-quality treasures. But Lucius was interested in only one piece out of the lot; a piece that, to Lucius, was worth all the considerable trouble of ensnaring Vito Luppi as a client in the first place.

Bang.

Adrael dipped down to tug a sheet caught on a loose nail, and suddenly there was a bullet hole right through the forehead of the wooden baby Jesus statue in front of him, where his own head had been only seconds ago. Then *bang*—another bullet, so he dropped to the floor. The bullets had come from different directions, and judging by the sound of the reports, from different guns. He was surrounded.

He tapped twice on his headset for LeShawn and Jerome, but got no response, so he assessed that he might be on his own against an unknown number of Luppi goons. He hadn't sensed them when he came in, so they must have been waiting at a distance outside, which suggested they knew he was coming.

Fucking Carmine. The old dog sold them out.

He crawled along the floor as bullets whizzed over his head, blowing holes in boxes and crates. He placed his hand down on something wet and wondered briefly if it was blood, but his nose told him it was extra-virgin olive oil spurting from a newly shattered case of bottles.

His attackers smelled like moonies, so they could doubtless see in the dark as well as he could, but in that maze they were befuddled, spooking and calling out *"I see him!"* when they'd just caught sight of one another. As the operation was already a mess, Adrael decided a few dead Luppi guys wouldn't make much difference, so he pulled a pistol out of his thigh holster and crab crawled across the floor until he reached the nearest pair of legs, flipped over onto his back, and shot once upwards at the young man standing above him. The bullet went through the man's chin and exited the top of his head, spraying blood at the ceiling.

"Over there! Benny! Oh shit!" the others raised a cry and rushed over, impeded by crates and statues and falling paintings. One man slipped on the olive oil, and Adrael was swiftly on top of him, stabbing him in the eye sockets with a combat knife, and the olive oil mixed with the blood, creating a scent reminiscent of raw beef *carpaccio*. Adrael rolled over a crate that smelled like it was full of leather and crouched behind it, waiting for the next man to approach, who he pulled to the floor by his legs and slashed once across his throat, leaving him to bleed out into the crate. That left a door clear, so Adrael slipped through it into the night, leaving the rest of the Luppi to die some other time.

———

Dez found the archive's copy of the Jack the Ripper file sharing a shelf with the likes of Victorian-era killers H.H. Holmes (suspected of having some occult shape-shifting ability, unconfirmed) and Sweeney Todd (who was not entirely fictional, as it turned out). The file was a dusty brick of paper yellowing at the edges, and she cradled it on one arm, poring through drawings from the crime scenes, phrenological head measurements of suspects, and detailed maps of the Whitechapel slum where he'd done his killing. The Ripper case was a classic, but was so enshrouded in pop culture and ubiquitous myth that most Order members were unaware that they'd been the ones to catch him.

The man in question was, however, not a werewolf, but a human—specifically, a strapping sailor with the lyrical name of Shane McShane, who initially came to the Order's attention because he believed that he was killing vampires.

He was incorrect, of course. All his victims were humans.

All but one.

Dez was shocked to read that his first kill was, in fact, a succubus. Her name was Fairy Fay, and she preyed on the Whitechapel district just as enthusiastically as McShane himself did later. McShane, Dez saw from a photograph in the file, was a handsome, lusty specimen of manhood, and he became a favorite of Fairy Fay. But when he realized what she was doing to him, he reacted badly. McShane didn't know what a succubus was, but he was an avid reader of Penny Dreadfuls and thus had an idea of what a *vampire* was. Perhaps his madness interfered with her ability to control him, since he managed to stab her through the heart with a stake, as the literature said to do. Fairy Fay's body was inconveniently found by the police, but the gothic impalement aspect of the crime got the Order's attention. By the time they managed to abscond with the corpse, it was already dissolving; not into powdery crystals like a dead vampire, but into the flesh matrix they had learned to identify with sex demons. No one in the Order mourned a dead nightcrawler, so they tossed what was left in a jar that still sat somewhere in the depths of the London Order's vault, and if Shane McShane had stopped there, that would have been the end of it. But he didn't.

And the rest of the victims were humans.

While the current incarnation of the Order did not bother with human crime, their Victorian forbears had a wider, more moralistic mandate, and in their view, McShane's initial corruption by a night-demon made his subsequent deeds their purview. And he was happy to tell the Order why he did it when they interrogated him. *He was doing God's work,* he said, taking it upon himself to do away with all of Whitechapel's vampires, which to him meant any woman whose business it was to seduce. He no longer saw the difference. *Those she-devils,* he declared, *had to be expunged.*

Dez closed the file, feeling sick. So Beatrix had a point—sex demons did get innocent people killed, even ones they didn't know. And "*anger can change a man's behavior,*" as Adrael had said. Being preyed on by sex demons could make a man angry at women in general; the corruption they created eroded sanity, driving people to homicidal madness, getting innocent women burned at the stake, ruining lives.

But...how did Adrael know about the red clothes? Yes, he'd seen the first body at the crime scene, but not the second, and certainly not the third. Surely only the killer, (and the Order) would know the girls all wore red.

A dreadful suspicion whispered through her mind. Too often anything that looked like werewolf violence got diagnosed as werewolf violence by the Order, whether it was or not, but perhaps they ought to be seeking a different kind of monster. *Azrael, the angel of death.* Adopted moniker or not, it was an apt one. Breaking Dez's wrist had taken just a snap of strong fingers, so it would take no effort for him to rip a succubi to shreds and toss the body into a bin like discarded trash. Lucius had seemed skeptical of Vito's guilt, and perhaps he knew his business. And Adrael had scoffed, exactly what a guilty man would do. He hadn't been at all concerned for that girl in Vito's car, and Dez now wondered if that was: 1.) because he knew Vito wouldn't kill her, 2.) because he knew Vito *would* kill her and he didn't care, or 3.) because he himself would take care of the job later either way? Werewolf violence could be faked if one knew what one was doing, just like the Order did to that to that poor Jane Doe in the morgue. Surely Adrael was equally capable of such ghoulish artistry, and he knew where to find that succubus with the e-cig as easily as Dez or Vito did. True, the violent enthusiasm involved in the murders seemed a tad off brand for him, but his hatred for sex demons was undeniable. She wondered if that only applied to the females, or if it included Dark as well. Maybe being around sex demons all day—and having to work for one—was beginning to grate on him.

Maybe he'd even wanted to do that to Dez herself.

But then why would he tell her about the color? Perhaps he was playing with her, or perhaps he wanted her to know; McShane had been rather proud of his work too.

Still, even if Dez could believe Adrael was murdering the sex demons he loathed, she couldn't see him killing a *human* woman for no reason. While Adrael had confused Dez for human at first, he was unlikely to make that mistake in reverse.

And, to her eye, that newest crime scene did not look like the work of the same killer. The two nightcrawlers had been ripped apart like dog toys and tossed in the trash. The damage had the flavor of contempt to it, which made sense for Adrael. But the damage pattern on this new human corpse had a more baldly sexual flavor, as if the poor girl had been fucked to death by a harvesting combine. And this time the killer had tried to hide the body, something a man who still had either a soupçon of shame or at least a fear of discovery would do. The presence of the color red in this instance might be a coincidence, and perhaps, not even a very profound one. Red was the de facto heraldic color of wanton sex, favored among ladies of the night. And this latest dead girl was a winter, complexion-wise, so red would have suited her.

CHAPTER 19

RED-HANDED

Brooklyn
Tuesday morning

Massimo reclined in his chair, sipped a tart espresso pulled from the thousand-dollar machine Mona had insisted on buying, and closed his eyes as he listened to his nephew Angelo explain to him on the phone what had happened at his warehouse. *Sorry Uncle, the man got away. Sorry Uncle, Fatso Ricky is dead. And Benny the Biter. And Lorenzo. The doer, whoever he was, didn't take anything, but guns went off and things maybe got hit, or torn up, or bled on.*

It's alright, Massimo told him. *It's alright.*

He opened his dog-green eyes, the whites rheumy from drinking and sleeplessness, and glared at the painting his wife had propped up on the mantlepiece, one of several that he'd pulled from the warehouse right after Vito told him about the deal he'd made with Dark. Vito swore he hadn't told Dark where Alexandretti's paintings were kept, but Dark had a reputation for having an uncanny ability to get what he wanted, so Massimo had been waiting for him to try to steal the art ever since. Now he'd done so, and despite all his precautions, Massimo had lost three men and thousands of dollars in destroyed merchandise and artwork, and Angelo could not be more sorry.

But this was all fine with Massimo. The dead men were a shame; two were made guys, but not relatives, as the Luppi selectively recruited other werewolves into their ranks to fill out the numbers. Lorenzo Two-Bones was a second cousin though, which would tweak some family noses, but that was the cost of doing business, in their business. And Dark, with his act of predictable venality, had given Massimo exactly what he wanted—a plausible excuse to start a fight. This was a far simpler story to tell the rest of the family: Dark wanted the paintings, Massimo had the paintings, Dark tried to steal the paintings. It required no reference to Vito or any disclosure of Vito's sins. And so Massimo let Angelo off the hook with the gentlest of chastisements for what, to Angelo, seemed to be a giant fuck-up, cementing Angelo's lifelong loyalty into the bargain.

For Massimo, considering the circumstances, the whole thing was a win-win.

Ironically, had Dark's guys tried to steal the artwork at any other time, Massimo would never have noticed. He had no love for art, and neither did his father, nor his father before him. But for the Luppi it was a rite of passage to steal expensive pieces from local big cheeses—a fuck-you to the establishment and a dog whistle to the lower orders in a way that no mere murder or act of vandalism could be. Art was the world's most pointless thing, sitting at the top of the pinnacle of the hierarchy of needs, and so to declare themselves the lords of the upside-down, art was what the Luppi had to take.

Massimo instinctively knew that the painting on the mantle was *the* painting that Dark had really craved. The others, though priceless, were forgettable, but this canvas looked down at Massimo with eyes that shone as if a soul was trapped inside. It depicted a nubile young man dressed as Bacchus, the figure rendered in sharp Renaissance *chiaroscuro* wearing a crown of grape leaves and not much else, lounging on a marble fountain with a suggestive leer that made Massimo uncomfortable turning his back to it. Massimo didn't see the appeal, but then, he wasn't a *fanook* like Dark supposedly was. He wondered if he'd ever meet the man in person, or if he'd have to settle for killing all his guys and running him out of town. Either option was fine. Dark's timing could have been better, though; Massimo should have been getting a good night's sleep to fortify him against his family. But revenge, when one was in the business of revenge, could not wait. And maybe a little blood on the dance floor would remind the more antsy members of the clan why he, Massimo, was still the alpha of that pack.

He decided he felt good enough to tolerate hearing his mother's voice, even at that early hour of the day.

"Hello?" she croaked into the phone.

"Good morning, Ma," he said brightly.

"Who is this?"

"You know who it is, Ma," Massimo sighed. "How's my boy?"

"He's aright. Sleeping. But I keep him like this too long, might make him a little, you know. Mushy-headed. Like your cousin Mario."

"It's just this week, 'til after the funeral, and after everyone goes home."

"Oh, mi amore, about that..."

Massimo zoned out for ten minutes while his mother complained about Mona's taste in casseroles, and only tuned back in when she mentioned Carmine's name.

"You what, Ma?" he said, not sure he'd heard her correctly. *Hoping he hadn't.*

"I invited Carmine to the funeral," she repeated.

"Why, Ma?" Massimo moaned, sinking into his chair.

"Because he's your brother and he's family," she snapped. "And you can't pretend he doesn't exist."

Massimo rubbed his forehead as she scolded him. With his entire family descending for Teo's funeral, he was deeply ashamed that he'd needed to order his mother to incapacitate his only son until he could determine if his Order visitor had been right about Vito being...well, surely the term "serial killer" had been hyperbole. Vito had confessed everything; he told Massimo about the nightclub, and the debt, and his addiction to the things those filthy unnatural whores did to him, but the kid never said anything about killing anyone, particularly not a couple of sex-demon hookers. Still, Massimo gave the man an extra stack of cash in his monthly payment as insurance against the Order "figuring it out." But those hounds could not be kept at bay forever, so Massimo would have to sort Vito out soon. A shrink, rehab, an exorcist, whatever; it made his head hurt to think about it. The last thing he needed that week was to have to babysit Carmine in public.

———

The Order

Dez flipped pensively through the file in front of her, containing everything she'd been able to find about Lucius thus far. It was unwise to keep taking it out of its hiding place when her office had no lock, but she felt compelled to keep touching it, woozily marveling at the realization that Lucius could plausibly have witnessed any historical event she'd ever read about. The file was collated in chronological order, from notations in the margins of illuminated manuscripts to Post-its scrawled with the names of the ex-wives from the paintings she'd seen in his penthouse, and flipping through it she could trace him across time and space. She had spent hours already guessing where he might have been living during, say, Prohibition or the Salem witch trials or the reign of the Sun King, chasing him through history, combing through the archives for whispers of him in the margins of other cases.

And looking for some point where he might have crossed paths with someone named Adrael.

Of course, if she was lucky, she'd never see Adrael and his treacherously beautiful face again. She couldn't get the image of him ripping up those nightcrawler girls out of her head. She wondered if he'd do it again, or if he'd gotten it out of his system. She also wondered the same about Vito, but if he left any *more* bodies Solomon would now have to go after him, which would remove one rabid dog from the streets, at least.

Even if countless more still roamed free.

With a feeling of vengeful satisfaction, she shoved the file into the very bottom of the bottom-most drawer on her desk, under an already swollen stack of files yellowing with neglect.

"Hey Cross..." Dez shoved the drawer closed just as her door nudged open and Reilly peeked his head in.

"Knock, please," she coughed.

"Oh, sorry," he hemmed. "Hunter told me to tell you...they got him last night."

The werewolf sat drooling on the metal stool in the interrogation room, a chthonic chamber carved out of the city's unforgiving stone bedrock, its walls spiky with well-oiled instruments of torture, some out of the dark ages, some ornately Victorian, some ominously modern. The werewolf, whose name was Norman Patrick Pryor, was strung up like a marionette, attached to the walls, ceiling, and floor by several steel chains ending in manacles around his wrists and ankles. His overgrown eyebrows met in the middle of his forehead and a curly beard took over the lower half of his face like kudzu vine. He hovered between human and half-turned, his features an agony of unnatural angles, a blue vein on his temple threatening to pop. Luckier werewolves were able to manage their transformations, even learning to control them, but for many, like Mr. Pryor, it was painful. Coarse hair pushed mercilessly through the skin, creating raw, bleeding rashes, talons extruded roughly from behind nails, and his teeth shoved their way out of splitting gums. The process often made them insane, temporarily or permanently, and they'd lose time and wake up surrounded by blood and police, naked in the woods, or in a cell.

Solomon and Justin were already in the observation chamber when Dez came in, along with two armed guards and a recordist to document the proceedings. The observation chamber was separated from Mr. Pryor by one-way glass, as the Order did not like to let its captives know what Order member's faces looked like, in case they had to let them go. But the "technicians" were in the room with Mr. Pryor: a pair of men in long black rubber gloves and black rubber aprons with black calabashes over their heads. A third unmasked man sat with them: a trim Asian named Ling who had previously been a professional psychologist and CIA interrogator, and whose job it was to talk to the deranged.

Drool spilled through Mr. Pryor's pointy teeth and pooled onto the floor as his woozy head drooped over his chest. Interrogation subjects were often plied with chemical cocktails of benzodiazepine, scopolamine, or barbiturates to make them more lucid, or more docile, or more inclined to talk—whatever the situation warranted.

"You may have given him too much," Justin muttered to Solomon.

"It is hardly an exact science," Solomon muttered back.

Hunter leaned against the back wall behind them, his eyes tired. His sweat smelled like whiskey, but he flashed a weary half-smile at Dez as she picked up Mr. Pryor's brand-new file, which stated that he was a vagrant who migrated daily between the Battery and Port Authority. He'd been caught by Hunter's team under the Manhattan Bridge clutching the fresh remains of a skinny brunette, her blood still seeping between his teeth, her cheap red windbreaker, depressingly thin for the cold weather, lying crushed beneath her mangled body.

"This man is homeless?" Dez asked.

"He sleeps at Port Authority. Near where that first girl got picked up."

"So he doesn't possess a silver Porsche."

"It seems the car was a red herring, Miss Cross," said Solomon, overhearing her. "Eyewitness testimony is notoriously unreliable, but even if there *was* a car, most likely the first victim finished her business with the driver and then ran into Mr. Pryor afterwards. But the car was a reasonable place to begin, with nothing else to go on," he allowed with ponderous magnanimity. "This is a methodical process. Somebody has to go down all those rabbit holes. That's the purpose of the research department."

"And the moto jacket?" she pressed.

"I gather it's a popular style at the moment," said Solomon witheringly.

Dez looked from the file to the wretched werewolf behind the glass, trying to sort doubt from disbelief. Maybe this wretched man did kill all those girls. After all, she'd never *seen* Vito actually kill anyone. Perhaps the whole thing was a series of coincidences. Millions of people lived in Manhattan, so there were probably many dark-haired men in moto jackets looking for dates on its streets on any given night.

Through the glass, Ling signaled that his questions were at an end, as the two technicians injected something into the werewolf's neck that made him slump down into the chair.

"I'm satisfied," Solomon said. "Mr. Pryor will remain our guest until the formalities can be completed."

"And then what?" Dez whispered to Hunter.

"And then Mr. Pryor checks out," Solomon answered for him.

The file in Dez's hands was relatively slim, but contained all the sad little details of Pryor's sad little life. He was 48 years old according to his driver's license, with an estranged sister in Denver and a police rap sheet for petty theft. And, like too many broken men who found themselves lost in the streets, he was a combat veteran. His service record was tacked into the back of the file, and it stated that he'd been honorably discharged from the army, though it contained no particular heroics. Werewolves often excelled in the military, but while Mr. Pryor been an ideal physical specimen as a younger man, his application to Special Forces had been denied due to...

Due to...

Dez threw a glance at Hunter and inclined her head towards the door.

Come with me.

He caught the glance, but didn't move towards her, nodding his head instead.

Go ahead. I'll follow you.

———

Fifteen minutes, depending on your perspective, is either a snap of the fingers or an eternity. For Dez, waiting in her office for the tap on her door, it felt like forever. A few seconds past forever, the door opened and closed, and she and Hunter found themselves alone together.

They kissed in a blind frenzy, his hands coiling in her dark hair as he tried to press all of his body against her.

"I thought about you all night," he growled. "All night under that bridge, picking up that lunatic, dealing with that poor dead girl, it sounds awful, I'm sorry...but...all I could think about was you."

"What did you think about doing?" she murmured when she meant to say *"no, stop, save yourself."*

"Everything," he said, his hands sliding around her waist and under her breasts.

"Not here," she whispered.

"You're right," he panted. "We should go back to my place. Or your place."

This felt nothing like Dez's encounter with that anonymous boner Irish-Green; her own desire for that man had been practically absent in the awkwardness of the encounter. That absence had saved him; she'd taken only what she needed and he'd been able to walk out more or less unscathed. But her body surged like a wave toward Hunter, and it was that desire, on her part, that was always the problem.

"I...I should go," he whispered, pulling awkwardly away when she didn't say anything.

"Wait." She slipped her hand off his shoulder but held his arm. "I didn't ask you here for this. I mean...I just...there's something else."

"What?"

Dez, addled by her own need and the hungry gleam in Hunter's eyes, struggled to remember.

Mr. Pryor...

"The...that moonie you arrested," she said, clutching for a thread in the labyrinth of her mind. "Something is off about him."

"Off?" He cocked his head at her, trying to understand what she meant, his faculties deranged by the stiffening rock in his pants.

"It's all just...a bit too convenient."

"Trust me, if you'd been at that mess under the bridge last night, you wouldn't say—"

"Did he confess?" she prodded.

"Not yet," Hunter chuckled darkly. "Give the drugs some time to work."

"I think he might be a diversion to take our attention off Vito." Dez knew even as she said it that it sounded insane.

"We caught him in the act, Cross. He had her blood in his teeth."

"Just like any moonie killing any girl would. It happens all the time in this city, as you keep reminding me. But that doesn't mean *this* man killed any of those other girls. Who saw him first? A Night Watchman?"

"Another homeless addict saw him and ran out into the street screaming about the bogeyman. Night Watch saw *that* guy and then alerted us, and obviously we were out there anyway.

"Who is 'we'?"

"Me, a couple of Enforcers, and two of my team."

"Who on your team?"

"I..." Hunter shook his head and when he spoke, it was clear he was humoring her. "Well, the two Enforcers, and Andrews, and Reilly."

"Apprehending a werewolf in the middle of an attack is a little chaotic, I imagine."

"To say the least."

"So any one of them could have dropped that flimsy red jacket at the scene at any time."

"Dropped? You mean...on purpose?"

She nodded.

"Cross, no," he scoffed, "there's no way—"

"If she wasn't wearing that red jacket would you still have connected this to the other killings?"

"I might have, yes, all things considered," Hunter replied drolly.

"Are you sure?"

"Okay, maybe I'd have to think about it twice. I guess. But Solomon is sure this is the guy, and I don't have any reason to doubt it."

"No? Did you read Mr. Pryor's file?"

"Yeah, of course."

"*All* of it?"

"Shit, Cross, I didn't look at his high school transcript or anything. Reilly only put that file together an hour ago, none of had time to read—"

"You might want to have a look at his army record first," Dez told him. "Which states that a young Mr. Pryor was denied his application to Special Forces because he failed the vision test. He's completely *red-green colorblind.*" Dez watched Hunter's face as that fact sank in, his flushed face going pale. "And it seems unlikely," she continued, "that a man who cannot see the color red would pick his victims that way, doesn't it?"

Hunter sat down on his desk, his face pale.

"Did you actually see the girl wearing the jacket?" she asked.

"It was on the ground," he sighed. "I...I guess I didn't. And... I didn't even see it on the ground, someone just handed it to me and told me where they found it."

"Who?"

"If I remembered, I'd tell you. We only had about five minutes to tear him off the girl and take off with him and the body."

"I think Mr. Pryor came along just in time for someone to pin all the deaths on him. Whether that jacket was planted or not, it is clear that all those incorrect Luppi addresses aren't just *old.* Surely some of them would still be correct, in that case, surely not *everyone* would have moved house. Someone *changed them.*"

"Why would anyone do that?" Hunter blinked.

"I know it sounds ridiculous," said Dez, "but it's possible that *somebody* in our office is being incentivized to keep us out of the Luppi's business."

"*Incentivized?* You mean paid off?"

"Maybe," Dez hedged, unable to say *how* she knew.

"Well, if that's true, then the most likely suspect is *me.*"

"It's *anyone,*" Dez insisted. "We don't have door locks. Even I managed to slip in here and read that entire file when you were gone."

"You don't...you don't think it's...Reilly?" Hunter looked sick.

"Well, I don't know who dropped that jacket, if anyone even did, but I do know that Reilly doesn't have the authority to consistently order you to leave the Luppi alone."

"Oh Cross, you can't mean..."

"*He* could have changed all those addresses in the file years ago." She dropped her voice instinctively, though they were alone. "And while his reasoning only makes sense up to a point, if he thinks Vito killed those first three girls—" *or any of them at all,* she added silently— "he must realize that Vito will kill another one eventually if he isn't stopped."

"But if Sol—if *he's* taking money from the Luppi—which I can't believe I'm even saying out loud—he'd be stupid to let that happen. The man is pigheaded, but I don't think he's dirty."

"I think he would have rejected my transfer if he could," Dez told him. "He's cagey about me working here because of who my mother is."

"I can hardly blame him there," he chuckled, "but you are the smartest person in the building. You might also be crazy, but the two aren't mutually exclusive, I guess." He sighed miserably. "Alright. Let me see what I can find out. Quietly. Don't do anything. *Anything.* We'll talk about this later. I repeat, don't do *anything.* If you're wrong, and I really hope you're wrong, you'll end up—just don't. Please. For me." Then he surprised her by wrapping his arms around her and pulling her close for one more long, agonizing kiss that tasted like man and musk and a trace of Glenlivet. "It sucks that you're this smart," he murmured. "Stupid people are happier."

"Please be careful," Dez begged. "You don't want to be on the receiving end of whatever occurs if this all becomes...obvious."

"Let's hope it doesn't. What a fucking mess that would be. No offense, Cross, but I have no desire to ever meet your mother."

Then with one more lingering, knee-buckling kiss, he let her go and slipped out of the room.

<h1 style="text-align:center">Chapter 20</h1>

<h1 style="text-align:center">The Wolf At The Door</h1>

Tuesday, twilight

It would be terribly convenient if the murderer of all those girls turned out to be the wretched Mr. Pryor, but Dez couldn't square it in her mind. Still, if the killer—whoever it was—intended to strike again, there was nothing more she could do about it.

However, if Solomon was taking money from the Luppi to bury their file, that was a crime in itself, and a far more nefarious one, by Order standards, than mere murder. Back at her apartment, Dez compulsively combed through the internet for any details on Luppi misdeeds that the Order had either ignored or failed to list. The various three-letter agencies fingered them for robbery, extortion, racketeering, black markets, smuggling...so many criminal codes broken, so much money moved around...the dryness of it all calmed the insistent thoughts of Hunter's body that sizzled through her mind every few minutes.

But one item in the Luppi rap sheet caught her attention, banishing even the soft pressure of Hunter's kisses to the back of her mind.

Because having spent so much time contemplating Lucius's painting collection, she thought it interesting that Luppi also had a propensity for stealing art.

Interesting, and probably not coincidental.

The Order had made a note of this tendency, but since it did not involve bloodshed, it had been consigned to the "et cetera" section of the Luppi file and never elaborated on. The FBI database documented the family's activities in more granular detail, including the notorious robbery of a playboy hotelier named Giorgio Alexandretti. Vito's grandfather Cesare had broken into Alexandretti's Sardinian palazzo, lifting the paintings from under the noses of his armed guards. Alexandretti had unwisely sworn that anyone who tried to buy any of them would pay twice, once in money, and once in flesh, so unsurprisingly the canvases were never seen again. He had, however, provided Interpol with descriptions, provenances, and photographs of all the missing works, which were in full Kodachrome color, vintage in hue but still crystal-clear. Ten pieces had been taken: five priceless but uninteresting 17th-century Italian masters, a smallish Goya study, something Dutch with fruit in it, a savage Artemisia Gentileschi, a subdued and lovely Monet...

And then Dez clicked on the last image and saw, once again, Lucius's face.

The painter was Michelangelo Merisi, better known as Caravaggio, Italy's most troubled bad-boy genius of the Renaissance; a master of both dramatic *chiaroscuro* and dramatic feuds, variously rumored to have died of a fever, in a bar fight, or at the hands of the Knights of Malta. And while any Caravaggio would have been the jewel of a private collection, Dez knew that Dark would have found this particular canvas irresistible, as it contained his favorite subject: himself. In the painting he was nude, a grown-up iteration of Caravaggio's erotic boy-Bacchi, draped on the edge of a fountain, his blond head ringed by a crown of grape leaves. His impressive flaccid cock had been rendered in vivid detail between his thighs, and he dangled a cup of wine between two fingers in a louche gesture with which Dez was now familiar. No coy adolescent Pan, this god of excess was a fully mature man, more predator than prey, his honey-colored eyes staring directly at the viewer, a sly smile eternally poised to spread across his sensual lips. And, looking at the orgy of naked revelers lying either exhausted or dead at his painted feet, Dez had to allow that it was an uncanny likeness.

But now that Caravaggio—the very *existence* of it, in fact—was potentially an enormous problem for Lucius.

And thus, unfortunately, also for her.

————

The Second Circle
Tuesday night

"You're sure it wasn't Carmine?" Lucius sulked on his couch and glared out at his darkened nightclub, which that evening was being stalked by armed muscle instead of dancers, while the softer staff were all sequestered in their rooms upstairs.

"Yes," Adrael nodded. "I made sure." Carmine had woken up that morning to find Adrael sitting at the foot of his bed, and Adrael didn't even have to touch him to know that his stammered protestations of innocence were sincere. But now Adrael was down two of his best men. He found LeShawn dead near the warehouse with his throat slit down to his spine, his adamantine vampire body already dissolving into dust.

Jerome and the Escalade hadn't returned at all.

"Maybe Vito went home and confessed everything," Adrael ventured.

"If he had," Lucius grumbled, "this place would be in flames."

"Boss," Martavius squawked over Adrael's walkie-talkie, "you might wanna come down here."

"Why?"

"*She's* back. Again."

Lucius startled as he saw Desdemona in the monitor standing outside the employee entrance, her arms crossed impatiently.

"What is she doing here? Did you call her?"

No, Adrael hadn't called her. He'd intended to never see her again if he could help it, as the sight of her made his blood boil in a way he didn't enjoy.

"She says it's important," Martavius added. "But they all say that, I guess."

"Send her up," Adrael replied.

"Hello," said Dez, marching into the office a few minutes later with all the brass she possessed. But faced with Adrael's fierce blue eyes, she quailed. Instead of his usual grey, he was dressed in a skin-tight black shirt of tactical material that was too slick to grab onto, black combat pants with pistols strapped to each thigh, and two more guns dangling in a torso holster. He looked ready for a fight, or a world war, but was no less beautiful for it, the lethal quality of his body on full display like a three-dimensional silhouette.

"What do you want?" Lucius prodded. "Spit it out or get your muddy boots off my fucking rug."

"I just wanted to find out..." Dez began with a deep breath, "if this whole mess is really just over a *painting*." The two men blinked at her with bald dismay.

"Sorry, what—" Lucius choked.

"A painting," Dez repeated tartly. "Specifically, a lost Caravaggio."

"And how do you..." But then Lucius had to laugh, the way hyenas laugh before biting into carrion. "How do you know that, honeybun?"

"If I know that, that means it's knowable," said Dez, trying to stop staring at Adrael. "But I'd venture to guess that Vito didn't just *happen* to show up at your club one night, and just *happen* to overspend his bill for months, and then just *happen* to offer to pay you with a painting that just *happens* to have your face on it."

"Just tell her," Adrael sighed. "She'll figure it out anyway."

Lucius was, for a moment, unable to simultaneously speak and suppress the urge to throttle her. When he'd mastered the latter, he gamely gave the former a try.

"We went after his cousin to begin with, the gay one," Lucius ground out, "but Vito turned out to have the more interesting problem."

Invited to the club for a night of comped debauchery, each of the Luppi boys had taken up Lucius on his offer of a free "consultation," but Giulio proved to be inconveniently romantic and disgusted by the idea of sex-for-hire, so aside from the usual problems of being gay in a Catholic family, he had few useful buttons to push. Teo was a giggling idiot whose lack of shame about his childish love of oversized breasts made him useless for Lucius's purposes.

But Vito's little garden of private neuroses turned out to be fertile soil for what Lucius wanted to plant.

"What was the problem?" asked Dez. "His need to tear women apart?"

"More or less," Lucius shrugged. "That's not unusual for a were-wolf, obviously, but Vito had quite a lot of shame about it. And shame is always something I can work with. So when I discovered that Vito was having trouble with 'little Vito'..." He smiled and glanced suggestively down at the mound in his pants. "He's a young man and there was nothing physically wrong with him. So the problem"—he tapped his golden head—"was all up here."

That problem, it turned out, was a girl. Not even a girlfriend, just a girl that Vito met in a bar one night and with whom he lost control. The girl was mostly fine afterwards, and since he paid her well to keep her mouth shut, only his two cousins knew the incident happened at all. But still, it haunted him, ruining his sex life and his sleep for months until Lucius stepped in with his "solution."

"Most moonies don't genuinely want to kill you," continued Lucius. "They just get a little overexcited sometimes. And frankly, I think that's how it started with Vito. But the way his family is, he was so ashamed, he was afraid to fuck *anybody* after that, in case he lost control again. So I gave him a guarantee: he could do what he wanted to do—what he *needed* to do—and nobody would die, and nobody would find out."

"And...what was that?" Dez asked, not sure she wanted to hear the details.

"Oh, in the end it was so unoriginal," Lucius scoffed. "He just wanted to relive the experience with that girl over and over. And over. And over. Frankly, what the man really needed was a therapist. But a therapist won't suck your cock. Not these days." He smiled cannily. "And I do so love shame. That's the stuff real sexual obsessions are made of."

"You were enabling him," Dez frowned, twisting her lips like a schoolmarm.

"I think of it as a public service," Lucius retorted. "There are some terrible people who crave terrible things, and if they don't have a safe way to play them out, they inflict it on society. Here, we take one for the team, for a modest fee."

"So you made him addicted to your 'public services' and then cut him off, and told him that instead of paying you with money he didn't have, he could give you the Caravaggio, correct?"

"More or less." Lucius sucked his teeth.

"Which, I surmise, he did not want to do."

"More or less."

"You do realize that's a bit like letting a rabid dog loose on a playground."

"Oh, well, in theory," Lucius rolled his eyes. "Still, I'm pretty sure he didn't kill those two dead succubi you keep going on about."

Dez's eyes flicked to Adrael, but if he was stirred, he didn't show it.

"Why not?" she asked.

"Because Vito wasn't capable of it," Lucius grinned. "We just made him *think* he was."

"Pardon?" Dez blinked.

"In Vito's case we perhaps exaggerated how much effort it took to manage him," Lucius smiled like an unrepentant child. "Actually he was easy to control. Once a Girl clicked into his mind, he was like pudding. Even *you* could have managed him on a good day."

Dez could have sworn Adrael flinched at that, but perhaps it was her imagination.

"But...but Cherry said..." Dez floundered.

"Most of those cats downstairs aren't any smarter than they need to be," Lucius scoffed. "They all like to brag, and they *love* to gossip, so I just paid the two Girls he always worked with a little extra to spread around the rumor that he was a 'big, tough psychopath,' and 'impossible to control,' so they did. And the others ate it up. Everybody loves a good scandal."

"But...why bother making him believe he was more dangerous than he was?"

"So he'd think he *had* to keep coming in here and paying our astronomical fees. Obviously."

"I...see." Dez chewed on that cynical statement like it was vile nugget. "Very creative."

"That," Lucius blinked beatifically, "is because I'm an artist."

In truth, it would have been easy for Lucius to help Vito overcome his fear and even the need to kill, allowing him to regain his ability to enjoy sex without panic by training him to control himself. Such things were doable with succubi as a proxy. But Lucius was a drug dealer, not a doctor, and in the case of Vito, his agenda required ever-increasing repeat business. So he told the Girls to ratchet up Vito's dependence on them for his elusive release, making him addicted and also ashamed of that addiction in a terrible self-perpetuating cycle that, conveniently, could be billable.

"What would he be like with a human girl?" Dez queried.

"Oh, a human girl, he would have easily torn to shreds," Lucius chuckled. "His whole problem was that he couldn't figure out how to control himself with a human like your average moonie learns to do. For Vito, the tap was either all the way off or all the way on."

"Well, we found a third dead girl yesterday," Dez said, "and this time, she *was* human. "

A sour smile spread across Lucius's pretty mouth, and he got up and poured himself a drink before he spoke again.

"Now *that one* could very well be our boy." He played with his glass snifter as if watching the scene in its rounded reflection.

"But we *saw* Vito with a succubus," Dez protested, already disagreeing with herself in her confusion. "If that works so well for him, why switch to humans?"

"Why *wouldn't* he?" Lucius shrugged, amused at her obvious frustration. "You're missing the point, Desdemona. Nobody really wants to fuck a *nightcrawler*."

At that, Dez was *sure* Adrael flinched, though he said nothing and kept his gaze steadily on some neutral spot just above her head.

"Then...then why do they come here?" she sniffed.

"We're a reasonable stand-in for what—or who—they really want," said Lucius. "And we even *mostly* make them think they're getting it." He seemed unbothered by what that assessment said about himself. "But only mostly. The only thing stopping Vito from touching human women was his so-called 'sense of decency,' but maybe he's finally over it. As hard as we try here, I'm told there's no substitute for the real thing."

"So then who killed those two succubi?" She glanced at Adrael again, but he didn't flinch at all.

"Someone else that you people have failed to catch," Lucius shrugged.

"Was this new girl also wearing red?" Adrael asked, finally deigning to speak.

"She was," Dez nodded. "Was that...just a lucky guess, on your part?"

Their eyes met then across the room, neither able to read other's cold, level stare.

"Oh, were the two succubi also wearing red?" Lucius asked. "That's odd." He turned to Adrael. "Now I get why you were so...But I'm sure it's a coincidence. We are talking about prostitutes, and red is, you know, kind of a slutty color."

"Why is that odd?" Dez pressed. "What's a coincidence?"

"Because red is Vito's very favorite color," Lucius informed her, oozing with insinuation. "His *very very* favorite."

"But...you *both* know about the red clothes?"

"Of course we both know, who do you think told *him*?" Lucius pointed his head at Adrael and grinned as the implications of Dez's reaction dawned on him. "Oh lord, did you think that he was..." He laughed then, with a tinge of genuine amusement that made him look insufferably charming. "See," Lucius said to Adrael, "I told you if you didn't drop that accent someone would eventually confuse you with Jack the Ripper."

Dez's head was beginning to buzz with confusion. She felt relieved, which was, she knew, inappropriate, since Adrael had doubtless killed *someone* recently, and planned to do so again soon, judging by his attire. And she wasn't sure if Adrael had intentionally led her to think he'd killed those girls to amuse himself, or if she'd come to that conclusion on her own, but his contemptuously raised eyebrow suggested the latter.

"Not that our man here is above it, of course," Lucius added, turning back to Dez. "He's not above *anything*, really. But Adrael doesn't kill anyone I don't tell him to kill."

"Funny, I was told the same thing about Vito Luppi and his father," Dez huffed, cognitive dissonance making her churlish. "The question is whether you or Massimo has the more obedient dog."

Lucius cracked a terrible smile at that, with a thousand years of vicious mirth behind it.

"With dogs, it's all down to the training. Take Vito, for instance. He didn't really remember that first girl who kicked off his problem. He couldn't even picture her face. But he did remember her red dress. Memory is funny that way, and the color became...significant. And a little reproduced verisimilitude is helpful when you're dealing with memories."

"It's also possible we encouraged that color to become *more* significant than it was to begin with," Adrael added then, and Dez was impressed at how haughty he managed to sound despite his complicity.

"For the sake of efficiency," Lucius agreed. "After a couple of weeks, all it took to get him into a frenzy was the color itself, which saved us a lot of time." Lucius turned to Adrael with an unrepentant smile. "You're always telling me to conserve resources."

"I suggested you turn off the lights when you leave a room," Adrael muttered. "That's not quite..."

"The red clothes were already a trigger," Lucius continued, ignoring him. "We just made it more forceful. And automatic. Like Pavlov did with *his* pets."

"You created his kink?" Dez gaped.

"All kinks are created," Lucius explained sententiously. "No one is born getting turned on by colors, or shoes, or English nannies. Sometimes one develops preferences from, oh, sitting on washing machines maybe, or having a pretty sister...anything that excites you can start to push those buttons." He leered at Dez as if he knew exactly what pushed *her* buttons, and Dez swallowed, quite sure that he did. "But a real artist can engineer a whole garden of arousal by choosing what to plant and when to water it," he continued. "I think of it as 'educating the consumer.' "

"So you're suggesting there are *two* unrelated moonie maniacs running around Manhattan killing working girls in red at the same time?" Dez shook her head. "Vito and...someone else? That seems highly unlikely."

"I've heard of weirder things in this town," Lucius retorted.

Dez glanced at Adrael for input, and was glad to see him shake his head.

"Adrael thinks I overestimate my understanding of my clientele," Lucius smirked.

"I think you overestimate your understanding of moonies," Adrael replied. "And underestimate other things."

He threw a glance at Lucius so patronizing that Dez wondered, for a moment, which of them was truly in charge.

"Either way, if Vito hadn't been such a little welsher, this all would have been fine," Lucius replied, glaring sourly back at him. "We agreed that his father would never miss that painting; that classless fuck has never even bothered to look at it. But I guess his daddy scares Vito more than we do." He glared at Adrael, considering that, at least, to be his fault.

"So...what deal did you make with Carmine?" Dez queried.

"Carmine told us the address of the warehouse where the family stores the artwork, in exchange for which we cancelled Vito's debt," said Adrael. "And we agreed to never interact with the Luppi family again."

"And so you went there this evening and stole the painting. I assume. Hence the kit." She flicked her eyes cannily over Adrael's gear.

"We were...interrupted," Adrael admitted with a tiny grimace.

"Aha. Bad luck. But academically, what were you planning to do with Vito once he gave you the painting?" she asked. "Cure him somehow?"

"Oh I don't know, who cares?" Lucius pouted, curling up on his couch like a child. "It makes no difference. Now that he's started killing human hookers, he'll just keep doing it until you people catch him, no matter how hard you apparently try not to. And then—" Lucius made a finger gun and mimed shooting a marble satyr by the door. "Problem solved."

"Eventually, yes," Dez allowed testily. "But let me tell you something, Lucius. Werewolves are difficult to kill—you know that, that's why you have so many of them guarding your doors. Now, if the Order doesn't get a good interrogation in before an execution, they always feel a bit cheated, so they will try to bring him in alive, which they will likely do, because moonies often live through whatever methods we use to catch them, no matter how violent. And then we'll torture him, of course. Then he'll tell us about you, and what he's been up to over here…"

"Well, surely you people already know that much about us…"

"…and eventually he'll tell us *exactly* what it is that you wanted from him in exchange. And *that* odd fact, sir, is bound to catch someone's attention."

"But Vito has no idea which painting I wanted. He's never seen any of them. Those goddamned Luppi barbarians leave them sitting in some warehouse rotting away, improperly cared for." Lucius scowled as if that might be the worst crime of all. "I told him I wanted *all* the Alexandretti paintings, and just needed to know where his father kept them."

"But you understand that it would be a problem for you if the Order were to figure out that the painting you were really after was a six-hundred-year-old portrait of *yourself*."

"Obviously, yes. But since no one's even seen the thing since Massimo's father stole it back in the fifties, I don't…"

Dez pulled a folded piece of paper from her coat pocket and held it up for him: a printed color photo of the Caravaggio, in all its glory.

Lucius's face went white.

"Where did you—how—"

"The internet. Alexandretti was the legal owner, so there are insurance photographs on record with Interpol, which, unfortunately for you, has digitized many of its old art-theft files. And if the Order does catch Vito, and he tells my employers what you *specifically* asked him for, someone will get curious about what that Alexandretti art looks like, look it up at Interpol just like I did, and see the painting, just like I did."

"Alright, well…" Lucius bit his lip nervously, "they still don't know what I look like."

"No, but if Vito blabs to us about how 'Mr. Dark at the Second Circle' so very skillfully entrapped him in order to get his hands on a few paintings, you *will* become interesting to them. And then they will have to send someone to stalk you with a camera until they finally get a face to put to a name. Which means that if you don't want the Order to realize that the face in that painting is *yours,* you won't be able to set foot outside your nightclub until...well, until the Order loses interest. Which I suspect will be decades rather than months. But you've been around for a while, so you'll appreciate that."

Lucius took the photo from her and gazed at it. It was centuries since he'd seen that painting, but he'd never forgotten how beautiful it was. That passionate lunatic Caravaggio captured his essence with every brushstroke, caressing him with his eyes in a way that Lucius could still feel across his skin. Theoretically, Lucius could have made Massimo Luppi an offer; Lucius was unbothered by Alexandretti's threat, and the painting was destined for a spot in Lucius's private viewing chamber. But he suspected that Massimo would never have sold it to him, and all asking would have achieved would have been be to let him know who to come after when Lucius had Adrael steal it.

"So we need to keep the Order from ever having a reason to look at that painting," Adrael surmised.

"Right," she said.

"By finding Vito *before* he can tell them what we asked him for."

"Right again." *And killing him,* she added silently, though the only thing that kept her from saying so out loud was the hypocritical pretense that if she didn't, she wasn't complicit.

"Are your people out looking for him yet?" Adrael asked.

"No. They've pinned this whole mess on someone else. But they'll realize their mistake when Vito kills another girl, which will be soon. He could be killing someone right now. By the time the sun comes up there could be another body stuffed in a sewer drain for us to find, and then they'll have to reconsider." She looked pained, as if she were personally responsible—which, of course, she was. Perhaps being a pedantic stickler for the truth was an indulgence that she, as a habitual and necessary liar, could not afford.

Adrael's walkie squawked, startling them all. He raised a finger to ask Dez to hold that thought, and answered it.

"Yes?"

"Boss?" It was Mateo, one of the vampire Boys. "I think Jerome's back."

Adrael turned to the monitors on Lucius's desk; specifically, the camera in the parking garage.

The Escalade had returned.

The garage door opened on its own—all the company cars had a remote opener clipped to the visor—and the the Boys in the garage, including Mateo, pointed their guns at the SUV as it rolled slowly inside.

"Who's driving the car?" Adrael asked into the walkie.

"Jerome," Mateo told him, as the SUV continued to move towards them. But instead of stopping where it normally would, it drifted inexorably forward until it hit the wall with a fender-crunching *bonk*.

"Mateo," said Adrael, "get out of there."

"He's fine," said Mateo, cautiously approaching the car. Through the windshield he saw Jerome with his eyes wide open, sitting in the driver's seat. But Jerome wasn't moving, so Mateo tapped on the driver's side window with the muzzle of his gun.

"Hey, J," he called through the glass. "What the fuck?"

There was no response from Jerome.

Adrael rushed out the office door and down the catwalk stairs, across the dance floor, and down the fire stairs in less than a minute, but not fast enough to keep Mateo from pulling the car door open to find Jerome dead in the driver's seat, his eyes superglued open, his hands tied to the steering wheel. The wheel itself was tied to the parking brake handle to keep it steering straight, and the the stick shift was sitting in neutral.

"Holy sh—" Mateo started to say, but then the Escalade blew up.

Adrael was about to run into the garage when the emergency door flew into him, slamming him against the back wall. Coughing, he hauled himself to his feet and stumbled through the smoke. The Escalade was on fire, the garage was full of dust and strewn with rubble and bits of car. And the Boys who had been the garage were now in pieces on the floor, so the men running in brandishing machine guns thus had to belong to the Luppi.

Adrael tugged a pistol out of his thigh holster and shot blindly into the smoke, running backwards into the club. Shots rang out on the dance floor, hitting parquet and wood and steel and flesh as the Luppi rushed the building through the garage entrance, firing as they came, hitting three of the Boys and one overeager neckbiter bar back who had insisted on coming in to clean the keg lines. *One, two, three...*Adrael crouched behind the half-open door and counted seven Luppi in the ballroom now, as the rest of the Boys rushed in from all sides to fire back. He saw a few that looked like Luppi family members; they had obviously stopped taking their tea for at least a day, since one did not bring a man to a dogfight, but were still only half-turned. The rest, though, were also werewolves, and were hired guns and thus had no such restraints in their system.

Adrael watched everything unfurl as if in slow motion, assessing the Luppi's tactics. The bomb was meant to gouge a hole in the Second Circle's defenses and give the Luppi a point of entry, as well as take out several guards at once. By shooting up the main floor, they were drawing more of Adrael's men into the middle of the club, leaving the perimeter weakened for more Luppi to break down the outside doors.

But the real target was, of course, up those catwalk stairs, in the office, probably shitting himself on his white fur carpet.

———

Dez wondered if Adrael was dead. She saw the garage explode in the monitor, but a piece of shrapnel then obliterated the camera. She and Lucius dropped instantly to the floor, only cautiously raising their heads a few moments later to peek through the two-way glass as the Luppi shot up the nightclub.

The Luppi had the drop on the Boys and came in shooting. The Boys writhed in their own transformations as they shot back, the stretchy shirts they all wore expanding as their muscles grew with alarming speed, and though most of them had learned to control the process, it still slowed them down. The vampires in the group had a slight advantage; less breakable and not dealing with the throes of physical change, they held the Luppi at bay with their guns while their colleagues collected themselves.

A heavy foot kicked open the office door and a werewolf brandishing a shotgun marched through it. He fired at the desk, shattering the monitors.

"Come on out, Dark," he taunted, "my uncle wants to talk to you."

Bang. Lucius fired at him from the floor with the revolver he kept strapped to the underside of his desk, but he missed and hit the wall.

Bang. The attacker fired again and blew the hand off a two-thousand-year-old marble satyr, exploding it to dust.

"Come out or I hit the bullseye on your dartboard there," the intruder snarled, firing again and leaving a gouge in the wall an inch to the right of the Bosch.

"Not the painting!" Lucius snarled, turning purple. He slid the gun across the floor towards the attacker's boots and crawled out from behind the sofa.

"The girl too."

Dez stood up on shaky legs, her hands on her head.

"Leave her alone," said Lucius. "She's just my masseuse. She has nothing to do with this."

At first Dez was touched—*was he protecting her?*—but no, Lucius expected to get out of this alive, and she'd made it a problem for him if she didn't survive too. Leverage, it turned out, was as good as kindness. Better, if she was being honest.

"Just stop destroying my club," Lucius scowled.

"It's gonna be my uncle's club soon." Their attacker motioned them toward the door with the business end of his gun. "And he's probably gonna renovate. This place is a little fruity for him."

Dez and Lucius slunk down the metal stairs in a crouch into the maelstrom of bullets and harder-than-normal bodies smashing into furniture. Dez had no idea how fragile Lucius's body was, but if one of those bullets hit *her* she'd probably die.

"Hurry up," the Luppi goon barked at them, poking Lucius's head with his gun to direct him to the outside door, and Dez realized that they were heading for some Luppi vehicle to be taken to some other location where things would only become worse for them.

Then she heard a choking noise behind her, and Dez turned to see Adrael's arm wrapped around the Luppi goon's throat. The goon still managed to pull the trigger, but Adrael yanked the gun upwards, blasting a hole in the disco ball above them, and then, with cold efficiency, he stabbed the man several times in the spine with a knife, dropped him on the floor, pulled a pistol out of his thigh holster, and shot him once in the head.

He then did a quick assessment. *Dez was fine. Lucius was fine. The disco ball was toast.*

"Get down," Adrael ordered, and Lucius and Dez flattened themselves on the dance floor and crawled behind a heavy sofa. Adrael positioned himself between them and the rest of the room like a weapon-studded bulwark, his body locking into its familiar cadence, limbs finding their natural arcs, bullets finding their mark as he fired. Two Luppi henchmen hurled themselves bodily at him but he was ready with his knife, cutting one man's head open from crown to chin, and with his next movement slashing the other man's throat. He did not exactly enjoy causing pain, but he did appreciate a thing done efficiently, and a surge of electricity lit up every cell, synapse, and vein as his body slipped into the patterns etched into it by centuries of muscle memory. Adrael had fought in more wars than his employees had teeth, and he was, truthfully, most at home in a bloody melee, where he knew what to do without having to think. It wasn't that he didn't feel the pain from the blows and slashes and bullet wounds he received—he did, even more than a human—but it all blended together in an ecstasy of breaking bones, slashing throats, and gouged eyes. He had no idea where Lucius was now, and was losing track of where he himself was, and why he was there, and of anything besides the glorious feeling of knives on flesh and triggers shuddering beneath fingers. His thoughts flattened against the sides of his skull like passengers in a tilt-a-whirl, until he couldn't distinguish the heady joy of his unfettered energy from the sting of his own lacerated flesh.

Dez winced as blood, sweat, and plaster sprayed at her from all directions. Howls shuddered through the dance floor like horrible music, and shockwaves of emotion sizzled through the beams of the floor, reverberating through her sensitive body while the furniture exploded into splinters as bodies flew against chairs and tables. The air was furry with cotton and feathers from torn upholstery, and everything smelled like blood and excrement and adrenaline as werewolves and vampires died all around her. They moved far faster than humans, but Adrael was just as strong, if not stronger. And while violence emanated from the werewolves like a snarling instinct, Adrael's demeanor was more measured, like dancer whose every movement drew blood. If the spectacle hadn't been so gruesome, Dez might have suspected he was enjoying his frenzied ballet of blood and flesh. He fought like a ruffian tearing the world limb from limb in a back alley, grabbing at clothes, slamming heads into furniture, ripping off body parts, pulling out extra guns from everywhere and yanking knives from secret pockets. He seemed most dextrous with the knives, plunging them into eyes and spines and throats with unsentimental precision, like a gardener trimming an unruly hedge.

But Adrael was not invincible, and he finally missed a step and took a slash across his ribs, as a bullet grazed his shoulder and a pair of hands like rocks smacked his head into a pillar. Pain shot through him, exploding in his mind like fireworks. Someone kicked his legs out from under him and he landed on the floor with a *thwack*.

He lay on the floor for a long moment, staring inanely up at the half-shattered disco ball. Maybe this time there would be too many men and too many bullets, and the frightening power that surged through him would finally swallow itself up in the violence he'd created. If he just lay there one microsecond too long, someone would surely land on him with a machete or a machine gun and finally put him out of his—

Then he turned his head, and when he did, he saw not Lucius but a woman in black, her body curled up against a shredded red leather sofa, gloved hands clutching her head, staring out at the whirlwind with terror. She was crumpled up on the floor just like she had been the other night, when Adrael had...he swiped the memory away. But for some reason, the way her body startled painfully with every loud bang struck him as more unbearable than the hail of shrapnel that was zinging into his flesh from all directions. And then her brown eyes met his, silently begging him to get up.

He snapped abruptly back to clarity, the spinning room screeching to a halt. Once again he could see everything around him happening as if in slow motion. A werewolf launched at him, slathering teeth aimed to rip out his jugular. But with a spasm of pain, Adrael arched his back and popped up onto his feet. He pulled up his elbow and the werewolf smacked into it with the upper part of his mouth, slashing Adrael's arm to the bone but breaking his own jaw in the process, and then Adrael grabbed him by the head and flung him against a pillar, cracking his spine.

Massimo had sent an army, and the Boys were disadvantaged by surprise. But Adrael trained them to fight almost every day in the cavernous gym he'd built in the warehouse next door to the club. He preferred to hire veterans and career mercenaries when he could, so many of the Boys had seen combat before, and in the end their enthusiasm for violence proved up to the task. They eventually got their feet under them and took control of the situation, barricading themselves behind the bar and firing into the approaching Luppi with destructive glee as their compatriots dove into the armory in the back room and tossed fresh weapons at them through the door. The remaining Luppi goons, none of them Luppi relatives, decided that dying wasn't worth what they were getting paid, so they ran out of the ravaged building and into their vehicles to speed off into the night.

Lucius and Dez emerged from behind the sofa, gaping at the damage. The fighting had gouged craters in the floors and riddled the walls with bullets, and the contents of the main bar had become a river of glass shards and alcohol ribboning across the dance floor, pooling around the bodies of the dead. Rat, too, emerged from behind the bar, tugging his jacket into place as if he'd done something other than crouch in a corner. Adrael glanced at him with distaste; he'd halfway hoped Rat had been killed in the crossfire, but vermin always survived an apocalypse.

"Guess we shoulda seen this coming," said Rat, stepping over the head of a coworker he'd particularly disliked.

Adrael surveyed the carnage like a panting bull lording over a pile of gored toreadors, lakes of perspiration spreading out from his armpits and lower back, sweat coating his skin.

He strode unconcernedly through the broken glass and pools of blood toward Dez.

"Are you alright?" he asked her, scanning her for broken bits and finding nothing obvious.

"Are *you* alright?" She was woozy, possibly from terror, and possibly from the divine scent of adrenaline and testosterone roiling from Adrael's body.

"Never better," he assured her with a princely nod and what looked like a glow of post-coital satisfaction on his face.

"What are you going to do about all the dead people?" she asked, watching the Boys hurriedly drag corpses toward the basement as sirens wailed in the distance.

"The police know better than to see anything inconvenient," shrugged Adrael, "And we have an incinerator for the bodies." One of the Boys tossed him a roll of bandage, and he began wrapping his bleeding arm. Now that the adrenaline was subsiding, he was beginning to feel the bruises, lacerations, cuts, shrapnel wounds, and bullet burns. He sometimes regretted his enthusiasm when forced to take stock of what he'd done to himself, but he always healed so fast he never had time to really learn his lesson.

"Hey boss, what do we tell the cops about the garage?" one of the Boys called to Adrael.

"Tell them a gas line blew up, and that we'll be filing a claim with the city." He nodded for Dez to follow him up the stairs to Lucius's office to get out of the way of the arriving firemen.

The office was inanely serene after all that carnage. Adrael peered at the bullet holes in the walls near the painting like an artist examining another's work. Dez sank into one of the sofas, her head in her hands.

"You should go home," Adrael told her, crouching down in front of her, ignoring the blood from his elbow dripping onto the white fur rug.

"I'm fine. Nothing hit me."

"Already a hardened veteran of the wars." The corner of his mouth threatened to smile as he he reached out and took her hands to show her they were shaking.

Even through her leather gloves, his touch sent a spark through her body that startled her in her chair.

"If I didn't know better," she said pettishly, "I'd say you were having fun down there."

"I enjoy my work. Sometimes."

Adrael didn't know why he was continuing to hold her hands; he'd initially just intended to prove to her that she was trembling, but the tremor subsided and he didn't let go of them. This was the fourth time he'd touched her; the first was the spasm of rough contact when he yanked her into his car in that alley, the second was when he'd broken her wrist, and the third was when he'd patched her up. The problem was not that he couldn't remember if there were more little moments he was forgetting about, or whether it counted as a touch if it wasn't skin-on-skin.

The problem was that he was counting at all.

"Will they come back?" she asked.

"Not tonight." He meant to sound terse, but it came out as a low, chesty murmur, like he was sharing a secret.

"Those barbarian motherfuckers!" Lucius shoved through his broken office door like a petulant rhino, slamming what was left of it, with Rat trailing him like a nervous duckling on a string. Lucius was red in the face, unhinged. Adrael abruptly dropped Dez's hands and stood up, snapping back to supercilious.

"Is *she* in one piece?" Lucius asked.

"I think so." Adrael took Dez's hand again to pull her to her feet. *Was that number five? Six?* He plucked a white upholstery feather off her shoulder with theatrical delicacy. *Let's call that seven.* "She's just a little dusty."

"Well, obviously Vito went home and told his father everything," Lucius fumed. "You were right about that."

"And you were right about the club being in flames," Adrael quipped blithely, as smoke and firemen spilled into the dance floor from the ravaged garage.

Lucius glared at him, livid; as was often true with Adrael, a little frenzied violence had improved his mood considerably.

"There's no way Massimo would come at us like this if he thought we could get to Vito," Lucius pointed out. "The little shit is probably stashed away at home, which will make it *impossible* for us to get our hands on him."

"It will make it more difficult for the Order too," said Adrael.

"Still, I'd prefer if we had him tied up in our basement, as we're now at war with them and have *no* other leverage."

"But if Massimo has Vito on ice, how is he running around killing prozzies?" Rat piped up.

Adrael thought for a moment about that, and about everything he knew about the Luppi, and about families, and about fathers.

"I think...I think Massimo doesn't have him staying at his house," said Adrael. "Massimo's the family *capo,* and in that family, this matter with Vito would have to stay a secret from the others. So he'd put him someplace more private to recover."

"And maybe Vito's just...not staying put," Rat surmised.

"So where is this 'someplace else'?" Lucius stormed. "He could be *anywhere—*"

"He's in Little Italy," said Dez.

All three of them turned to her, eyebrows raised.

"How do you know that?" Lucius blinked.

"I was about to explain before, but..." Dez gestured at the mess outside the glass. "In our Luppi file, it says that the family used to own several apartment buildings in the vicinity of Little Italy—or what was then Little Italy, I suppose, I gather that area's rather changed since... anyhow, they bought those buildings in the twenties, and there's no evidence they ever sold them, so they're probably still collecting the considerably higher rents to this day. And the building where we found Vito the first time was in..." Dez struggled for the neighborhood.

"Nolita," Adrael supplied.

"Right. Which means 'North of Little Italy' I believe? I very much doubt Vito bothers to pay rent, so that was probably one of Massimo's buildings as well."

"But Vito didn't go back there," Adrael assured her.

"No," she explained, as if the two of them were slowish children, "but he might now be staying in another one."

"If he's hiding out in Little Italy, why would he kill a girl right in his own neighborhood?" asked Rat. "Why not drive to the Bronx or somethin'?"

"Because his father probably took away his car and his money," said Adrael. "To keep him from doing that very thing."

"The fact that she was killed in Little Italy is exactly why I think he's there," Dez insisted. "I've been to all three crime scenes now; the first two girls were picked up under overpasses near the river on opposite sides of the city and left in dumpsters just blocks away from where he met them. Those are lonely, dark places with no foot traffic at night. But on the way here, I stopped by the block of Little Italy where that human girl was found. It's right in the middle of the neighborhood." Dez had, in fact, stood in front of that plastic-sheeted construction site for many minutes, staring into the grimy alcove where the girl had been ravaged, right between an Italian bakery and a Chinese pharmacy; hardly the ideal place to fuck and then kill someone, but certainly the most expedient choice for several blocks. And as she stood there trying to imagine the "how" of it all, she couldn't shake the feeling that Vito Luppi was somewhere nearby, a strange, prickly feeling that was equal parts smell and vibration. At the time she hadn't yet worked out the "why," but now that she knew the whole story, it all made sense. "When we saw Vito pick up that girl under the bridge, he was in his car, and he was looking for a particular kind of girl," she continued. "But if he's not limiting himself to nightcrawlers anymore, then he can hunt anywhere he wants to, *as long as he can walk there.* Because, of course, he couldn't take a subway or a cab back home covered in blood after a kill, looking like a *werewolf.* He'd have to walk, and he wouldn't want to have to walk too far. And someone is probably *trying* to keep an eye on him, wherever he's staying, so he probably can't leave the place for very long either."

"So he's hunting in his own neighborhood out of necessity." Adrael nodded, both impressed and annoyed that he hadn't come to that conclusion himself.

"How often was he coming in here before?" Dez asked.

"Practically every night," said Lucius. "He couldn't get enough."

"Then he'll kill again sooner rather than later. Little Italy isn't that big, just a few blocks really, and there can't be very many areas with bodegas that serve French fries." She raised her eyebrows at Adrael. "Surely you and your team of frightening men can watch those corners for Vito to show up."

"You can walk all of Little Italy *and* Chinatown in an hour," Rat averred.

"Slightly longer in hooker heels, perhaps." Lucius said, as he sidled over to a shelf on the wall of his office, pressed a hidden latch, and the wall panel slid open, revealing a built-in hidden closet, out of which he pulled a shiny red garment on a hanger.

"What are you doing?" Adrael asked, his deep voice growling with leonine warning. But Lucius, unperturbed, unfolded the garment, revealing a short hooded raincoat made of see-through red plastic. It was the kind of jacket purchased for pennies off the internet and modeled by Chinese preteens, cheap and sexy and designed to fall apart.

"Is that..." Dez stared.

"It's Vito's favorite," Lucius smiled nastily. "His taste is a bit bridge-and-tunnel, unfortunately. But if he's out hunting tomorrow night, we can lure him in with it. Or rather, *you* can."

"Me?" Dez's eyebrows shot up. "You want *me* to put that thing on?"

"Why do we need to lure him?" Adrael asked. "He'll find a date, we'll follow him to wherever he takes her, and—"

"And he'll put up a fight and you'll have to kill him and that will do us no good at all," said Lucius. "Because we need him alive now, as leverage to keep the Luppi from destroying more of our property, as I said already."

"You mean...to trade for the painting," Adrael surmised.

"I consider that our property at this point," Lucius sniffed. "We've certainly worked for it."

"And what if his date screams?" Rat piped up. "The Girls obviously don't, that's part of the deal. But a human hooker might scream once he starts in on her. And that'll just bring out the Roaches."

"Then use one of the Girls," Adrael shook his head stonily. "A professional."

"He's not interested in sex demons anymore," Lucius reminded him. "He's got a taste for women. *Human* women. Or something that passes for human." He blinked at Dez nastily. "He'll be out looking for another piece of *human* flesh to chew on tomorrow evening, and we won't get anywhere fishing with the wrong bait."

"But he's seen her before," objected Adrael.

"He saw her for a few minutes in the dark," Lucius scoffed. "He definitely won't recognize her out of her usual Order Barbie outfit. You know as well as I do, that in the right clothes, she becomes an entirely different girl."

"It's too dangerous," Adrael insisted, ignoring Lucius's efficient jabs. "It would be rather a *shame*, Lucius, if she died." He ground that last out with a significant stare, reminding Lucius of their stake in Dez's continued existence.

"Don't try to manage me," Lucius shot back. "If Vito kills another girl and the Order gets to him before we do, we'll be facing the very same problem."

"Then you'll have to make sure he doesn't kill me," said Dez.

They all looked at her with surprise, belatedly remembering that she was capable of having an opinion on the matter.

"You don't have to do this," Adrael told her.

"Yes, I do," she nodded morosely. "Because let's say you watch Vito pick up some girl on the corner and take her to some construction site. You'll just let him kill her before you apprehend him, correct? Because he'll be easier to manage afterwards? You almost did that with the girl in the car the other night."

Adrael shrugged slightly in assent.

"Or let's say you *do* save her from him," Dez continued. "What then? You'll just kill her yourself to tie up all the loose ends. And even if you do let her go, she'll either tell someone what happened and end up institutionalized for her trouble, or bottle it up and let the nightmares turn her into a pill-popper maybe, or an alcoholic. The minute she sees Vito change, or sees you appear out of nowhere and pick him up with one hand, or sees you both fighting with magic chainsaws and regrowing limbs, her life is over. If enough people tell her she's crazy, she'll eventually believe it herself. That's how it almost always goes with humans who have these encounters. And that," said Dez, looking directly at Adrael, "is really why I joined the Order."

"You don't have to try to save everyone."

"I'm not equipped to save *anyone* most of the time. But if I do this, I can save *one* girl, whoever she would have been."

And if I don't do it, I'll have to live with knowing I chose not to, she added silently. Dez did not want to have to look at another mangled body she could have prevented; or worse, obsessively track the girl's life as it deteriorated year by year, knowing she herself had allowed her to be used as bait and treated as disposable.

"See, she's up for it," Lucius smiled, as if he'd bothered to ask her. "Besides, she's not going to be in any danger. *You* will be right behind her, big boy."

"She didn't do much of a job passing as a pro in here," said Adrael.

"All she has to do is walk around," Rat offered helpfully.

"I'm pretty sure she can walk around," Lucius averred. "And in the right dress, any woman can plausibly be mistaken for a hooker."

True enough, Dez thought sourly, and while playing prostitute in the nightclub had been difficult enough, the idea of walking the streets of New York dressed as a common streetwalker was both terrifying and humiliating. But two girls were dead because she'd said nothing, so this was the least she could do. Still, she wondered if she'd have been quite as willing to go the extra mile if it weren't ultimately her own neck on the line if the Order captured Vito first.

She suspected not.

All the more reason to do it.

Adrael ran his tongue angrily over his teeth, but didn't argue further. She was correct—the girl had to be plausibly human, and the operation would be far cleaner with Dez as the bait. Besides, Adrael reflected tartly, he wasn't worth much if he couldn't protect her from one goddamn deranged werewolf from twenty feet away.

"Well, I'm sure no matter how many other ladies are out there, you'll get his attention," Adrael muttered. Dez was unsure if that was a compliment or a dig—his neutral tone betrayed nothing.

"As long as she looks the part," Lucius added, handing her the raincoat. It squeaked when it moved, like a garbage bag, and smelled like bleach and petroleum with a fleeting trace of blood, semen, and adrenaline in the seams; remnants of the last time it was used. "Pull whatever else she needs out of wardrobe, and then take her home. I'm sure some of those Italian assholes are still outside watching, and we don't want them snatching her as she walks out the door. That would really put a damper on the evening."

Little Italy

Vito peeked through the cracked door of his grandmother's bedroom. The dusty chamber was bathed in a hellish red light that blared through the window from the electric sign of the mediocre pasta joint downstairs, the calligraphic "PAULIE'S" rendered in tomato-colored neon, making him twitch.

The mound on the bed didn't move. He'd added drops from the brown bottle to her cup again that night, just as he'd done the night before. After the dose he'd given her, he figured she'd sleep until the next day at least. So Vito pulled on the leather jacket he'd spent all day cleaning of blood, and stepped into the bathroom to tame his black curls to best advantage before he headed out into the street in search of what he needed.

It was thus a shock when he walked out of the bathroom and saw his grandmother standing in the kitchen in a faded red flannel nightgown, waiting for him.

"Where you going, Vito?" Her voice was creaky, as usual, but her tone was sharp, her watery eyes gleaming. They were his father's eyes, hovering below the bushy family brows, the pupils dark as onyx.

"I...I'm just going for a walk, Nana. I need some air."

But Antonella Luppi had raised boys, so she knew when they were lying. If he was awake, he hadn't drunk his tea. And she'd been watching him drink his tea all day, or rather, watching him put an empty cup to his lips and pretending to drink, just as she'd been doing herself, which told her all she needed to know. She slowly raised one of her gnarled fingers to point at him and began mumbling something in Italian. The light from the sign outside the window spilled through the doorway into the hall, painting one side of her in its vivid crimson cast, rendering the other half a dark, twisted shadow.

The sight set Vito's head buzzing. He caught sight of his reflection in the darkened, red-tinted window behind her—he was turning already, his body swelling into his clothes to the fullest capacity of seam and thread, giving him a bulky, over-built hunch. He startled in shock; it had been years since he'd seen himself doing this—not since he was a teenager and would sit in his bedroom alone and watch it happen, with horror and morbid fascination, behind a locked door.

Meanwhile, his grandmother kept muttering, but he didn't understand her. He'd never learned more than ten or so words in Italian, most of them dirty, and what she was saying didn't even sound like proper Italian. The words were staccato, maybe an old country curse, the consonants hitting his hypersensitive ears like marbles on glass, and all he could see was that fucking red nightgown rendered even redder by the light from outside.

And then she reached for the phone, and Vito couldn't take it anymore.

———

The Bentley, luckily, had been parked on the street instead of in the garage, so it remained whole. The rain started as Dez and Adrael climbed inside, a metallic-scented pissing that evaporated before hitting the pavement but managed to coat the car's windows with a sheen of slime. A steady stream of yellow cabs flowed up and down the avenue, mirroring the rivers of human urine flowing through the sewers below; just another vein of the city's false gold.

Dez clutched the ugly red raincoat on her lap and stared sideways at Adrael as he drove, willing her body not to react to his proximity, though his presence always made her bones feel like they were melting.

"You're still bleeding," she said, nodding at his arm.

"I'm always bleeding." He negotiated the car through the police cars and firemen and news vans milling around the wrecked nightclub. "Occupational hazard."

"So I see."

"I'm glad you caught that issue with the painting," he said testily. "That could have become...inconvenient. But if you have more bad news, tell me first. Lucius is about to lose his sense of humor."

"I wasn't aware he had one."

"He only had me break *one* of your wrists before, so he must."

"Next time it'll be my kneecaps, I suppose."

"That is an option," Adrael shot back. "There's no reason he can't hurt you anytime he likes."

"No reason he can't have *you* hurt me, you mean."

Adrael exhaled once, like an angry bull.

"Just...no more lies," he huffed. "They serve neither of us at this point."

"Does that go both ways?"

He huffed again, but didn't reply. He was pondering something, but Dez was too tired to try to guess what. The night's horrors had kicked the vinegar out of her, and, annoyingly, as her body grew weary, her rebellious hands ached to stroke his bare forearm as it stretched out to nudge the steering wheel. But she had no business wanting to touch him, no matter how beautiful he was. This man was not her friend; more like a reluctant colleague at a job neither of them wanted her to be doing. There was no reason to believe that he was interested in her in any other way, despite all his blasted hand-holding.

"Did you really think *I* killed those girls?" Adrael asked.

"It was a reasonable hypothesis given my imperfect information. The Ripper comparison wasn't off the mark."

"Oh, there were lots of men murdering women in Whitechapel in the late '80s," Adrael shrugged. "The 1880's, I mean. And the press did rather make it worse with those blasted letters. But your people caught the worst of them...McShane, I think it was."

"What?" Dez blinked at him. "How do you know that?"

"Everybody knew that. Occasionally you people can be useful. The man was a menace."

" 'Everybody knew that?' When did they know that?"

"Back then."

"How old are you?"

"Too old and not old enough," Adrael replied maddeningly.

"I don't know why I even bothered asking," Dez huffed.

But while Dez had already suspected something of the kind, confirmation that Adrael was at least over a hundred years old was disorienting, imbuing every word he said with a tinge of the arcane, despite how contemporary he seemed.

"Were you up all night reading your little Order file on the Ripper case?" he asked.

"It seemed pertinent when Vito switched to humans."

"Why's that?"

"Because McShane's first victim was also a succubus," she told him, her chin tilted in triumph. "I see you didn't know *that.*"

"Really?"

She nodded. "He was insane by the time we apprehended him. You should have read his interrogation." She sighed bitterly. "And *she* made him that way." She stared moodily out the window, frowning either at the grubby night or at her own reflection.

"Perhaps, but he also had syphilis," said Adrael. "Which makes people go barmy too."

"You didn't *know* Jack the Ripper?" Dez gaped.

"No, but I was acquainted with his doctor."

He paused for effect. Dez, nonplussed, rolled her fingers at him to go on.

"I was living in London at the time," he continued obligingly. "I was in my usual pub one night, and this doctor chap came in bragging that one of his patients had been interviewed by the police in the Whitechapel Killings. It was all anyone could talk about at the time, so people kept buying him rounds, and he got so drunk he forgot he wasn't supposed to tell everyone the man's name. 'Shane McShane' is a hard one to forget. Sounds like something out of a Penny Dreadful. The police never bothered with McShane again, but later I heard the Order caught him."

"And this doctor said he had syphilis?"

"He told us he'd been treating McShane for the pox with mercury. Either or both of which were bound to turn the man into a nutter."

"But what Fairy Fay—the succubus—did to him could only have made his condition worse."

"Yes, but she didn't give him the syphilis in the first place, did she? *That* he must have gotten from a human."

"That's true."

Adrael noticed that she brightened at the thought, which made him feel oddly warm.

"That's one thing you can say about the Second Circle," he added pleasantly. "At least we won't give you V-D."

"I'm sorry about the nightclub," Dez sighed.

"It's just concrete and plaster. Nothing piles of money can't fix."

"But some of the art upstairs got damaged. Those things are priceless."

"If they're priceless it's only because so many of them are stolen," he smirked. "And without provenance, we can't exactly get a fair valuation."

"I'm sure Lucius is upset."

"Oh absolutely." Adrael smiled as if genuinely tickled at the idea.

"Is this all a joke to you?"

"Everything is a joke. Some are just funnier than others."

"I don't understand you," Dez sighed, frustrated. "You spend all your time doing...business...for Lucius...but I don't think you care about any of it. I'd say it's about the money, but I don't think you care about that either. I also don't think you need Lucius to make money. Frankly, I think you make it possible for Lucius to make money." He let another smile slip at that; a more cunning one. "Why do you do it? I'd think this would all be beneath you."

"You may have too high an opinion of me."

"I'd think *you'd* think it would be beneath you. Does he have something on you? Some blackmail? Or are you paying off a debt too?"

"I don't owe Lucius anything."

"I don't think you even like him," she insisted, as the car pulled up to the curb outside her apartment.

He cocked his head to one side in his quizzical way, as if he'd never pondered the question before.

"He's alright sometimes," he decided, and Dez suspected that was the highest praise this cynical man ever dished out to anyone. "Anyway, tomorrow night, sundown, be at the corner of Hester and Elizabeth... that's in Little Italy, obviously. Don't look for me. I'll be there. Just walk around, like Rat suggested, until you and Vito find each other. If he finds someone else first, make him change his mind. I think you'll be able to do that." Adrael cleared his throat as if he'd said more than he meant to, but continued, "Let him to take you to wherever he wants to go—an alley or a construction site—and I'll take over from there."

"It's a date," she nodded grimly, and Adrael nodded back like a man staring at a gallows.

"You're not a fan of this plan?" she ventured.

"This is that night in the alley all over again," he huffed.

"And bait is better when it's sacrificial."

"Yes, it is," he snapped. "This is exactly the sort of thing that goes wrong when you try to complicate it with sentiment. You never use the *actual* diamonds in a sting."

"Diamonds? That's kind. It almost sounds as if you care."

"You've made your well-being Lucius's problem, which makes it my problem," he replied coldly. "That was clever of you, by the way. Now, no matter how much you irritate him, he can't make me kill you."

"They don't call me a genius for nothing," she spat back. "And it's rather fatuous of you to be concerned when you're the one most likely to attack me in the middle of the night."

"*Attack* you?" his jaw dropped. "Why would I ever...for *what?*" He threw the question at her like a slap.

"You're the one who brought me flowers," she heckled suggestively. "And only one person in this city has actually harmed me, and it was *you*. Not the Order, not any of those Luppi thugs...*you.*"

"Lucius," he corrected her stonily.

"That wasn't Lucius's hand snapping my wrist. All he did was stamp his feet and you obeyed. Like a dog."

He clenched his jaw, his nostrils flaring as the part of his mind that got angry woke up from its long slumber, sending a spike of acid through his blood. *Why on earth was he mad?* he wondered. What she was saying was true. Maybe it was the way her eyes flashed at him with contempt so potent he could taste it, bilious and sour. He caught himself flexing his hands on the steering wheel, every sinew in his body tight as a rubber band about to snap.

"I..." But the words wouldn't come. The haughty tilt of her chin made him forget what he'd meant to say.

"Though I suppose you wouldn't really attack me," she continued. "You'd just unenthusiastically snap my neck and I'd never see it coming."

"That is more accurate, yes. If I was going to Romeo my way into a bedroom to ravish someone it wouldn't be a..." He had just enough self-control to stop there.

"Charming."

"And in that...situation...who would really be doing the attacking?" he added, helplessly aware that he was being churlish. "Frankly," he continued, his tongue running away from him, "you might consider how unwise it is to fish in your own pond. *I* shouldn't have to point out to *you* that the last person you should be sharing sausage with in the park is one of your colleagues."

"Sharing sausage." Her face went red. "I see. You really do have nothing better to do than follow me around."

"Trust me, it's the last thing I'd like to be doing," he retorted hotly. He opened his mouth to point out he'd only seen her with Hunter by accident, but he stopped himself—somehow, in that argument, the admission felt like weakness. "But now I have to keep you from dying, which you make difficult to do when you play with dynamite. So have some bloody self-control."

Dez opened her mouth to say something else, but a shame-flavored lump rose in her throat.

"Hester and Elizabeth," he repeated, trying to sound polite and managing only priggish.

"Fine." Dez opened the door and stepped out of the car. He reached over her seat to pull the passenger door closed, but she paused in the doorway, one more thing to say. "At least I have the option of controlling myself," she said icily, "and don't let someone else do it for me." She slammed the door then, and he pulled the car away and sped off into the street.

She was still seething as she unlocked her apartment door and, as usual, was greeted by those blasted peonies. But she noticed with nasty satisfaction that they were finally beginning to wilt, their silky petals drooping like faded spinsters, so with a feeling of vindictiveness the poor flowers did not deserve, she plucked them out of the vase, stuck their blooms down the garbage disposal, and flicked on the switch. It roared to life with a cruel metal hum, and her hand vibrated in sympathy as the gears ground the blossoms to a floral pulp, the coral petals briefly turning the water in the drain the vivid red of cartoon blood before swirling down into the sewer.

PART FIVE

IN THE HOOD

CHAPTER 21

―――――

HOMO HOMINI LUPUS

Brooklyn
Wednesday morning
9:30 a.m.

The suit still fit.

Carmine tugged on the jacket hem and looked at himself in the mirror from behind, making sure nothing was pulling where it shouldn't. The suit was appropriately black, for a funeral. It was the most recent one he'd purchased and that was seven years ago, a bespoke 100-percent Italian wool number made by an Italian tailor, because it was important, when you were somebody, to bring your people up with you. Loyalty ran both up and down the mountain, as his father used to say. Carmine had been dreading putting it on, sure he wouldn't be able to get into the pants, but while they *were* a little tight around the waistband, they fit. He could even comfortably sit down, a realization that made the drizzly September world feel like spring.

Despite the occasion.

It was important to look good when one was representing the

family. Mafia funerals were like awards ceremonies, everyone dressed to the nines for a built-in audience. The inevitable press, undercover cops, and Feds would snap photos for their files, and he didn't want to look like a schlub for posterity. Plus there was the family to impress, most of whom Carmine hadn't seen in years, not since Teo's father's funeral, which was the last time he had put on that suit—or any suit at all.

His phone rang. Caller ID said it was his brother Massimo, and Carmine felt a bit high answering the phone while wearing a suit that made him look like a man who might plausibly be in charge of something.

"Well, shit," Carmine said into the phone, giddily jocular.

"Hello, Carmine," Massimo replied. "How the hell you doin'?"

"Alright, alright, you know. Pretty quiet out here." It had been months since he'd heard from Massimo—not since Carmine's birthday dinner last June, when Massimo had eventually shown up during dessert. "Hey, Momo, I wanted to do something for Ella, you know, whatever she needs, to help her out. 'Cause she ain't got nobody now."

"Ella's alright," Massimo told him. "We're taking care of her. Ella don't need to worry about nothing."

"Sure, sure. Course you are. Aright. So waddaya want? You need me to bring anything today? Or later, to the thing...I can pick up somethin' sweet at Angelino's..."

"Yeah, Carmine, about that."

"What?" Carmine's face fell.

"Thing is, Carmine." For a long moment Massimo said nothing else, and Carmine's blood began to boil. Typical; his brother always dragged out whatever shitty thing he wanted to say so that Carmine would guess out loud what it was and spare him having to say it.

"Spit it out, Momo," Carmine said instead.

"I think it would be better..." Massimo began, pausing again, but Carmine refused to take the bait, forcing Massimo to speak for himself: "I think maybe you should give the funeral a miss."

Carmine, his heart on the floor, still declined to reply.

"Carmine, everybody's gonna be there. Everybody," Massimo whined. "You understand that? Big Tony, Uncle Tommaso, you know how Tommaso feels about..." He sighed. "They aren't expecting to see you, Carmine. You know how they get."

"Uh huh." Carmine flashed back to every time his father had this same talk with him. His father had been more direct than Massimo, but that somehow felt less insulting. And Carmine had never loved his father, not the way he loved his baby brother, who he'd carried around everywhere like a backpack when they were kids.

"We just want to get through this," said Massimo. *We.* Carmine wondered if "we" in this case included him. It usually did not. "Look, Carmine, if it was up to me..."

"Well, you're the *capo,* it is up to you," Carmine reminded him. "But sure, sure, tell yourself whatever you want. Because you saying it makes it true, right?"

And then he hung up, because Massimo had nothing left to say to him that he wanted to hear.

*If it was up to me...*But everything *was* up to Massimo. Carmine looked in the mirror again and saw a sad middle-aged man standing in his faded bachelor's bedroom in his socks and a tightish suit. *His family.* They were nothing but skin pulled over the monsters they harbored within, just like he was, and the rest of their act was nothing but leather and cash. Carmine hadn't been invited to the dinner when Massimo had been declared *capo,* and he'd even gotten the side-eye from his relatives at his own father's funeral, although Carmine's sin was twenty years in the past by then. They thought they'd gotten rid of him, hiding him out in the suburbs like a mistake, and he'd acquiesced for the good of the family, although a few too many drinks and one unfortunately public fight somehow equalled forty years of shame. It seemed, to Carmine, too high a price to pay.

So when the Order came to harass him, he turned snitch for—he firmly believed—the good of the family. Letting the Order see the way they valued self-control and kept their urges to a minimum might convince them that the Luppi were worth leaving alone. And it had worked for years. But nobody would have thanked Carmine if they'd found out about it. *Thank you for your sacrifice, Carmine. Thank you for your love, Carmine.* Thank you for working for us all from the rafters when you couldn't even get a ticket to the show. That's all it would have taken, a simple thank you, ripped from the mouth of his bratty little brother who he'd had to protect from their own father until Cesare decided the lisp Massimo couldn't shake until puberty didn't automatically make him gay. Because protection was what being *capo* was all about, and that's what Carmine had been doing all along.

But now, Carmine thought, swigging vodka directly from the bottle, maybe just fuck it all.

———

Carmine was an asshole. He could have been big about the whole thing and offered not to come to the funeral. Then Massimo could have said *"you understand"* and Carmine would have said *"sure sure no problem"* and it all could have been a pleasant lie that would have tasted so much better than the shit sandwich they'd both had to chew on because Carmine insisted on "having the conversation."

Massimo rubbed his forehead and sipped his tea in his undershirt, listening to voices bouncing off the walls in the kitchen outside his office. Mona's soft contralto was a soothing counterbalance to his sister Leona's soprano shrillness. Then he heard the baritone rumblings of his uncle Tommaso, and his half-brother Carlo "Cappuccino" Luppi, answered by something else from Mona. Bless Mona, who wrangled his family like a master wolf tamer, a bulwark between him and their squabbling. But it was Massimo who had to deal with his mother, because he would never put that chore on his beloved wife. And his mother was definitely going to call and give him an earful after Carmine tattled to her about the conversation she should have had with him in the first place.

Meanwhile, last night's operation had been a debacle, but ultimately Dark's nightclub was in tatters, and a bunch of his guys were in the ground. A bunch of Massimo's men were dead too, and the ones who survived told him that Dark's bodyguard had mowed through the rest of them like a lawn. One guy swore he was a neckbiter, but another swore he bled; a third even insisted he could turn invisible, though Massimo thought that unlikely. Either way, this was shaping up to be an expensive fight, though it had gone over well with the family that Massimo had won the first round.

Round two would have to wait until after the funeral that afternoon. Massimo's freshly pressed black suit was hanging on the closet door, his shoes were shined, his rings were polished. Mona would be elegant in chic black silk. But his beautiful son would not be there, the family pride and the family future, and with his relatives teeming outside the door, that bothered him. Vito's two older sisters were there, and Massimo could hear their boisterous cublets running back and forth upstairs as their mothers tried to get them bathed. Vito was Massimo's only boy. Two stillborns preceded him and two miscarriages followed him; childbearing problems were not unusual in werewolf families. But Vito was better than ten other boys would have been, no matter what that creature at that nightclub had turned him into.

Massimo glared at the portrait on the mantle with virulent hate. The subject's curved lips now appeared to be laughing at him, so he grabbed the letter opener off his desk, stood on a chair, and wiped the smirk off the Bacchus's offensively pretty face.

———

The Order
2 p.m.

The explosion at the Second Circle Nightclub was front-page news. Luckily, the media bought Adrael's story about a gas line explosion, and there was no mention of a gang war. If anyone heard the gunshots or heads going through walls, they weren't talking, so the newspapers and websites filled their columns with outraged paragraphs excoriating the "city's crumbling infrastructure" and quotes from neighboring business owners fretting about safety. Even the Order was not immune to manufactured panic; Dez heard Justin whispering to Solomon about having the gas lines adjacent to headquarters checked for leaks.

She'd spent the day fetching and replacing files at random, refreshing cups of coffee she didn't want, and stepping in and out of the bathroom just to have an excuse to eavesdrop for theories that might stray too close to the mark. The Order received all the city's newspapers, and Dez read every page and clicked through every website, scouring the stories for mentions of the club's proprietor. Perhaps Lucius was paying off the city's metro editors, because not only was his name absent, not one reporter even speculated on the "club owner's" reaction. It was just a lot of hand-wringing about lax building codes, rerouted traffic, and the occasional gossipy nugget about how lavish the club's interior would be once it was repaired.

Hunter's team pored over the nightclub explosion like it was the latest celebrity breakup, and Dez lingered nearby, watching the array of TVs that they used for monitoring the news, all tuned to different channels with different news anchors chewing endlessly over the same situation. She saw Beatrix talking to Hunter, and drifted close enough to listen.

"Gas line," Beatrix scoffed. "Oh please. We have two murdered nightcrawlers in a week, and then a notorious nightcrawler den blows up? Don't try to sell me that gas line stuff. This smells to me like retaliation."

"For what?" Hunter asked.

"How would I know that?" Beatrix shrugged primly. "But I'll tell you something else—" and here, Beatrix dropped her voice further, "I'm not convinced that Pryor person you arrested the other night killed those two succubi. Oh, I'm sure he killed both the humans, as you said... I mean, you caught him red-handed with one of them. But I've seen a lot of victims, and to me, the damage done to those two *creatures* didn't look like they were done by the same hand as the one that killed the girls."

"Two werewolf killers murdering girls in red at the same time? That seems...I dunno." Hunter noticed Dez standing behind him, and flicked her a canny glance.

"Coincidences exist, Alan. And it's not that far-fetched," Beatrix shook her head. "This is a sick city, and a sick society in general. And maybe whoever *really* killed those two creatures had something to do with this so-called 'gas explosion.' "

Dez's blood chilled; Beatrix was far sharper than was convenient.

"Don't worry," said Reilly, leaning on the doorway next to Dez. "This place'll flood or collapse before it explodes from some bullshit gas line." He spoke offhandedly, trying to be comforting. But seeing him reminded Dez of something that had been nagging at her since discovering the Luppi addresses were fake.

"Reilly," she whispered, "that address you put into the database for Vito Luppi...where did you get it?"

"What? I don't remember...oh wait, yeah I do. The dumbass used his credit card to order take-out online and he put in his home address for delivery. Those guys are usually not that stupid, but I guess we've been leaving them alone so long they've gotten careless. Hunter was pretty pissed at me yesterday for forgetting to tell him, though." He sighed. "We never surveil those Goodfellas, but Hunter's a real stickler for details."

"Someone has to be.'

"Hey, I'm the one who found the address."

"He'd be lost without you," Dez assured him.

"You think Kragin's right about Pryor? About him not being the only killer?" Reilly dropped his voice to the barest whisper.

"I think she just likes to have something to talk to Hunter about."

"Heh." Reilly smiled. "You know, I think you are as smart as everyone says."

"Let's hope so," Dez replied.

————

The Second Circle
2 p.m.

The nightclub's resurrection had begun. An army of cleaners were clearing away the debris and broken concrete chunks on the club's main floor, and luckily the explosion and its attendant fire and water damage had been largely contained in the garage. Not for nothing had Lucius insisted on reinforcing the building's frame like a nuclear bunker during initial construction three years ago; it was, Lucius reflected sourly, a triumph of the value of paranoia, if nothing else.

Now, instead of disco balls and lights, the club shimmered under oceans of plastic sheeting lit by the unromantic glare of halogen work lights. Lucius watched a beefy laborer in a hard hat crouch over a floor seam, checking for cracks. The man radiated virility, his square muscles sealed in with a layer of healthy fat, like a gladiator. Lucius flashed back to his days of sneaking into the *ludi gladiatorum* and feasting on the nervous new recruits. Overcome with nostalgia, he made a mental note to find the man at quitting time and discover what—besides heavy lifting—made him sweat.

Adrael sat behind him at the desk, tinkering with the brand-new bank of computer monitors he'd spent the morning installing on Lucius's bullet-riddled desk, patiently reconnecting them to the security cameras that remained intact. Lucius had called in some favors with his clients in city government, so a heavy police presence had been sent to guard the property day and night until the work was done. The dead bodies of the werewolf Boys had been sent to an understanding mortician, all expenses paid. Two of the dead Boys had been vampires whose bodies were now lying in state in the club basement, and in a day or so when they crumbled to dust, their clothes and jewelry would be boxed up and either sent to their loved ones or destroyed. The Luppi bodies had gone straight into the incinerator.

Rat walked into the office wearily, shaking his head.

"The bad news is there's a lotta Luppis left. We'll have to go at 'em one by one, and they're spread all over the place, Manhattan, Brooklyn, the Bronx...it's gonna be a bloodbath. Even if you make Carmine tell you where they all live—and I assume yer gonna have to pull out his fingernails for that—you torch one house, some other cousins'll be here the next minute blowing up the VIP room. We don't got the numbers to go at 'em all at once, especially not now half our moonies are dead. We'll kill some of theirs, they'll kill some of ours, and it'll come down to whoever's the last one standing."

Lucius had lived through the Middle Ages and was familiar with melee warfare. Standing on a hill holding up a severed head surrounded by legions of his own dead men in the smoldering remains of his kingdom would be a hollow victory indeed.

"What's the good news?" Lucius asked.

"Some of them live in Jersey, so at least they'll have to take the tunnels to come at us," said Rat.

Adrael's phone buzzed in his pocket, but when he checked the caller ID, he raised a confused eyebrow.

"It's Carmine," said Adrael with bald surprise. He had been planning to call on Carmine himself that evening, to either wrangle or strangle his family's home addresses out of him, but he hardly expected Carmine to contact him first.

"Give it to me," said Lucius, reaching for the phone and putting it on speaker.

"Hey boys," Carmine singsonged into the phone. Adrael thought Carmine's voice was suspiciously jovial; maybe even a bit drunk. "How's it going?"

"Oh, you know," Lucius sighed drily, looking down at his decimated dance floor. "The usual."

"Yeah? Bet you get up to all kindsa *fanook* orgies an' shit down there, amirite? Alrighty. Aaaaalrighty." (*Yes, Adrael decided, drunk.*) "You boys got plans tonight?"

"A little housecleaning," said Lucius. "We're a tad upside-down over here. Your brother's friends made a bit of a mess."

"Aaaaaah, yeah, I toldja that'd happen. I toldja. I had nothin' to do with it though. No hard feelings on my end. I was just calling to see if you boys wanted to go to a funeral this fine evening."

"A funeral." Lucius looked at Adrael, who could only shrug. "Whose funeral?"

"My nephew Teo. You boys shot him, I think, so it might be nice, you go and pay your respects. Everybody's gonna be there: my brother, my uncles, everybody. The whole clan."

"Where and when?" Adrael asked. He comprehended Carmine's oblique point immediately, though Lucius, his brow wrinkling, still hadn't caught on.

"The funeral's at St. Pat's at five this afternoon. It'll be a shit show though, right in the city, you can give that a miss. Feds everywhere, and just try parking, fuggetaboutit. But then the whole family, the whooooooole family—except me—go to my niece Ella's place in Great Neck for the reception. Teo was her boy. Everybody'll be there. Including my brother. And my nephew Vito, who I know you're dying to see. So if you wanted to talk to them about your business it might be a good time. 17 Ravine Drive. The white house with the bay windows and a hedge. You'll find it." A noise over the phone sounded like ice tinkling in a glass. "Oh and boys, it's a funeral. Wear black."

Then he hung up, and the room went quiet.

"It's a trap," said Lucius, and Rat nodded his agreement.

"Maybe." But Adrael didn't seem convinced as he swiveled thoughtfully in Lucius's captain's chair, biting the inside of his cheek.

"Yes it is," Lucius scoffed. "We show up together like a bunch of buffoons and they take us all out at once."

"They must think we're idiots," Rat shook his head.

"Maybe," Adrael murmured again.

"If not, Carmine Luppi just gave us his whole family on a silver platter," said Rat. "Which is ridiculous. Unless he's—you know—the 'special scissors' brother, that don't make sense."

"You don't think it's a trap?" Lucius asked Adrael.

"I think there are...other possibilities," Adrael replied. To him, the hectic note in Carmine's voice was revealing; Adrael's senses had, over the centuries, become finely tuned to the piquant flavor of a person ordering revenge.

"Yeah, ok, maybe he wants us to take out his brother for him," Rat conjectured, lips twisted. "That's an angle. But even if he'd give us Massimo, we're not going in for just Massimo. He's gotta understand that. When we're done, there won't be no family to head."

"He said he wasn't going to the funeral. And I think that's because he wasn't invited."

"That's assuming a lot," Lucius scoffed.

"I've only met the man twice. So I can't say for certain. But maybe Carmine is tired of being...surplus to requirements."

"I don't understand what you're saying," said Lucius.

"That's because you never had a family."

Lucius rolled his eyes, but a sudden stillness in Rat's face told Adrael that *he,* at least, understood.

"Maybe you got a point," Rat conceded.

"Well," Lucius smirked, "I'm certainly glad I *didn't* have one, then."

"So...what're we gonna do about this?" asked Rat.

"We're going to New Jersey," said Adrael. "And we will take care of business. All our business. Including Vito Luppi."

Which would make Desdemona's involvement blessedly unnecessary.

"And if you're wrong?" Lucius fretted.

"Fire me," Adrael replied.

Lucius glared at him, unamused.

"If we do this, no half-measures, you understand?"

Adrael replied with only a blink. He *did* understand, but he wanted to make Lucius spell it out.

"You take them all out," Lucius clarified. "All of them. Even the ones wearing both kinds of diapers. I don't want any little wolf cubs coming back for revenge ten years from now, so don't even contemplate getting sentimental."

"As you wish," said Adrael with a dismissively regal nod. Adrael did not subscribe to the idea that one should preemptively slay one's future enemies—the concept was depressingly Sisyphean—but Lucius was a paranoid creature and Adrael expected nothing less. Still, as always, he wanted to be clear as to who was really making the call.

He then reached for his phone and began to tap out a message.

"Who are you texting?" Lucius asked. Normally Lucius paid no attention to what Adrael was doing with this phone, but something about Adrael's eagerness to get to his device put him on alert.

"I'm letting Miss Cross know that our wolf hunt tonight is off."

"Don't do that," Lucius told him.

"Why not?" Adrael blinked.

"Because she's going to ask you *why* it's off," Lucius replied. "And if you don't tell her, she might use whatever freaky Order voodoo she has and figure it out. And she's going to have *objections,* especially about the *children.* Women are always going on about *children,* as if they aren't just little problems that inevitably grow up and become bigger problems. No long-term planning, with women. I don't want that saboteur throwing a wrench into things at the last minute because of her bourgeois scruples. She'll figure out the plan is off when you don't show up." He smiled at Adrael like a satisfied cat. "Vito won't be there, so she'll be fine. It's good for a pretty girl to get stood up once in a while."

———

Little Italy
3 p.m.

Vito had been sitting on the kitchen floor all night and day listening to the traffic ratchet up and down with rush hour, the morning lull, the lunchtime scramble, and the quiet before rush hour again, like the tide coming in and out. The pool of blood he sat in was sticky now, and none of it was his. In the afternoon half-light it looked brown, and the part of him that still understood things knew that he should start cleaning it up before night arrived with its blaring lights through the window that turned it *that color* again.

He was hungry, but his grandmother probably wasn't going to cook, so he'd have to take a shower and get take-out. An hour later the floor was reasonably clean, and he was clean too, his face shaved, his chest and wrists smelling of *Cool Water*. He walked out the door and headed to the Italian dive bar a block away, where he would maybe sit for an hour or two, have some fried mozzarella, and try to get a little bit of air.

Little Italy
  3:45 p.m.

Forgiveness is a gift, not a chore. That's what Father Almaviva told Giulio when he was a child, and that's what he'd told him the previous afternoon, when Giulio sat in the confessional and asked his pastor what to do when he was so sick with anger he could barely function. "Confession" for Giulio required the omission of certain important details, but Father Almaviva, cursed with what he called "a bit of the moon" in his own blood, was understanding about the Luppi's unique concerns. The broad circumstances—that Vito got away with things he should have been punished for, and that Giulio couldn't get over it—those Giulio openly divulged.

And in the gentlest possible way, Father Almaviva explained that his anger came from envy. Envy that Vito was the golden child, never punished for anything, envy that he was the hand-picked scion of the family, and envy that no matter how loyal Giulio was, Massimo would always look at him with an asterisk. Envy that Vito still had a father, when both Giulio and Teo's fathers had been sacrificed on the altar of the family business. And envy, Father Almaviva reminded Giulio, was a heavy stone to carry, and it was up to Giulio to exercise his option to put it down and move on.

The envy thing hit home and Giulio was ashamed of how much it had satisfied him to tell Vito about Teo's death. It had been sadistic really, because as self-indulgent as Vito was, he was full of love for his family, and for his cousins most of all. That love was so potent that it kept Giulio loyal to him even after years of aggravation. There was something magical about having someone as beautiful as Vito love you, like a gift from the gods, a rare and precious prize beside which all other concerns paled. It was, Giulio thought, why people fell over themselves when celebrities were just a little bit nice to them.

So hearing about Teo definitely hurt Vito to his core, and as naughty as Vito could be, he had the decency to feel guilty in equal measure. Giulio decided to see his cousin one last time before he left that rotten city for good. He didn't know where to go, but he had plenty of cash and had already packed his bags. Surely he'd be able to find someplace where every view didn't remind him of things he didn't want to think about.

But when he got to Nana's apartment, no one answered the door. So, as he'd done so many other times when his grandmother was out, he pulled out his wallet and used a credit card to shimmy it open.

CHAPTER 22

DARK SIDE OF THE MOON

St. Patrick's Basilica
Wednesday
6:45 p.m.

The church doors opened and people in black spilled out onto the steps. The men were stoic in their tailored suits, and the women chic in their lace veils—red lips dialed up to a hundred, hankies at their waterlines to keep their mascara from escaping. Mothers gripped the hands of children with chins dipped down in a show of grief they were too young to feel for an older cousin they had barely known. The handbags were designer, paid for by ill-gotten gains, but luxurious all the same, and the countenances of the Luppi men were dapper and bluff-browed, making a case for themselves in society. Style, it seemed, made up for a multitude of sins.

Giulio stood across the street and watched members of his family hugging one other and shaking hands with the priest like at a wedding, except with more crying and no rice. He couldn't bring himself to go inside and listen to the Latin liturgy for his friend and playmate, whose death was more or less an accident but felt so much like fate. So he just hid himself and watched as his family piled into cars and headed to Teo's mother's house in Great Neck where they could grieve in private, away from the prying eyes of the cops and the Order and whoever else cared to watch the city's most notorious wolves howl for one of their own. Vito wasn't there, of course, and neither was their grandmother Nana. *Very much of course.* Massimo knew better than to show weakness in front of the family, so Vito would have been told to stay home that day, and that's what he'd done, more or less.

More or less.

Carmine was also conspicuously absent, but that made a sad sort of sense too. Giulio didn't know Carmine well; he was an old man who smelled like booze and made sexist jokes that were too dated to be funny. But Giulio understood what it was like to be on the periphery of that family, to be a less-than, and he'd always nurtured a secret, unspoken sympathy for the uncle he barely knew. So he decided to let Carmine be the first to know something for once. He pulled out his phone, looked up the number he'd stored for emergencies but never called before, and told Carmine what had been done to his mother, and by whom.

And then Giulio made one more phone call, to that asshole Rat. Because while Giulio hated those Second Circle thugs with a soul-incinerating passion, he knew that they, at least, could be relied on to do what needed to be done.

————

Great Neck
8 p.m.

Rat needed to pee, but he wouldn't say so. He refused even to move, because the bulletproof vest and flack jacket he wore squeaked whenever he shifted his position. Three vampires were packed into that brand-new black Escalade with him, armed with a small arsenal of guns and clips loaded with hundreds of the silver-filled hollow-point rounds that he figured Adrael crafted by hand in his spare time. And in a car full of vampires, who didn't even need to breathe, every sound Rat made seemed painfully loud, and the last thing he wanted to be doing around those assholes was squeaking.

Adrael had brought *only* the vampires that night; too many of the werewolf boys were dead or injured, and their scent would warn the Luppi of their presence. Neckbiters smelled metallic up close, if they smelled like anything, and there was no reason not to use them since the operation was nocturnal. The other car was parked near the big brick townhouse where the Luppi were having their family event behind high privacy hedges; a car filled with more guns and more vampires, none of whom ever needed to pee.

Rat wouldn't handle any of those guns, of course; he'd never shot a weapon in his life. Normally he wouldn't have been at such an operation, but Lucius had taken him aside privately when Adrael was downstairs with the Boys loading the vehicles, informing him that he, Rat, was Lucius's extra eyes and ears from then on. He was there only to observe, and to make sure that what Lucius asked for was completed in its entirety. Not that Lucius was worried; Adrael could be relied upon to complete a job. But just in case something got muffed again, he wanted to know first.

And if it does? Rat asked. *What do I do about it?*

Not a thing, Lucius assured him. *You just tell me what you see. That's all I'll ever ask you to do.* Lucius assured him also that he had nothing to fear if he was truly working in Lucius's interests. But given that Adrael might not be too fond of Rat anymore, the smart thing to do might be to quit and flee to Australia. The outrageous salary they paid—and in cash, no less—was too good to pass up, though, and Rat truly loved his job, with its disregard for the rules of a society that he never much cared for, its intimate access to the city's one percent, and its endlessly interesting problems. So in the way of rodents, Rat thought he could find a way to live alongside—and perhaps outsmart—one of the world's foremost super-predators. After all, the dinosaurs were long gone, but the rats remained.

Around sunset, the family cars gradually pulled into the driveway and vomited out Luppis from every door. Rat counted at least forty individuals already, the men all armed, while additional hired guards stalked the periphery. He shrank down in his seat reflexively, his head dipping ignominiously into the collar of his flak jacket, and glanced down at his phone to mark the time.

He had, the phone informed him, one missed call, and one voicemail.

From Giulio Luppi.

Forgetting pee, and forgetting silence, he picked up the phone, held it to his ear, and played the message:

"Vito's holed up at my grandma's place. 130 Mulberry, Apartment 310."

That was the entire message, without greeting or preamble, and Giulio's voice sounded like he'd been crying. Rat hit redial, but Giulio's phone flipped directly to voicemail. Rat checked the timestamp; Giulio had left that message almost two hours ago. Surely Vito had since joined the rest of the family to mourn his dead cousin in the privacy of a family home.

But if not, it would have to wait, because just then, the Boys' phones simultaneously lit up with a text from Adrael.

It was go time.

Little Italy
   8 p.m.

The city was grey with the ashes of a dying sunset, but one by one its artificial lights came into their own, casting green, blue, orange, and yellow beams like party gels across the splotchy sidewalk, shining luridly through the red plastic hood Dez wore. She stood on the corner of Hester and Elizabeth in a swath of garish light from a Chinese supermarket. At night all the shops were shut, their gates rolled down like closed eyes, making the buildings look like they were sleeping. Only the supermarket and the bodega were open on that block, but there was still a vigorous trade happening on the corner. Ladies of the night drifted back and forth along the shuttered storefronts, some of them more subtly attired in tight jeans and crop tops, and others, like Dez, baldly on display.

The cheap red lycra dress clung to her every curve and undulation, and her feet teetered perilously in red vinyl boots that reached up to her bare thighs. The clear red raincoat she wore squeaked when she moved, and she felt like a piece of overripe fruit waiting to be squished into the concrete. There was nothing beautiful about the aesthetic; she was just an advertisement for sex without the euphemism of dinner and a movie.

It was intermittently drizzly, the sky upset but not quite ready to cry, so Dez flipped the see-through hood up over her hair against the ambivalent rain. Ripe updrafts luffed through the sewer grates, sending heated whorls of filthy undercity air up her skirt. It was too cold for what she was wearing, and she shivered. She should have worn a dress with sleeves, but she hadn't considered comfort when selecting a garment meant to function as a sausage casing. She tried to think like a cop, keeping her wits about her and her eye on the mission, but her pulse quickened every time a girl stepped up to greet a male forearm leaning out of a car window. Dez's brain wanted no part of it, but the hungry thing inside her woke up like a dog sniffing the air at fresh garbage. She blamed Adrael for revving up her engine. She resisted the urge to look around for him, since she'd never see him anyway. But she didn't see any of the other Boys either, though some of them were supposed to be out there, too. She shuddered to think how many other killers like them were lurking undetected in that city; or even creatures like that were-rat, who repelled her more than any vampire or garbage-entity.

Unfortunately, Dez was not the only girl out there in red that night; there was a bleached blonde in a red plaid polyester dress, an older MILF in a red satin jumpsuit, and a too-young Korean in a red miniskirt. Dez had spent much of her life trying to disappear into the shadows, so she had no idea what to do to stand out. Hopefully the plastic jacket, gleaming with tiny water droplets like fake jewels, would do the trick. She only needed one specific person to notice her. Vito Luppi's cherubic visage was imprinted in her mind after two weeks of straining for a glimpse of him in every dark corner, and she trembled not only from the cold and the dread over the deadly choreography to come, but in anticipation of meeting the the man she'd been chasing since she got to New York.

Meanwhile the sunset, as a parting shot, cast a vivid aura around the edges of the lowest buildings, outlining them in bright blood-red.

Brooklyn
8 p.m.

Carmine was in his yard, drunk to the gills. He was partially transformed, sitting in his plastic lawn chair wearing nothing but a faded bathrobe, growing sad as it dawned upon him that if everyone in the family was dead, there would be no one left to call and tell him so. Because his mother was dead too; that's what Giulio told him, and he told him how, and he told him who did it. And Carmine was relieved. Because in the cathartic rage of selling his family out to Dark, Carmine forgot to consider his mother. He knew she wasn't going to the funeral, but he hadn't considered that it would break her heart when she heard that all the children she'd pushed out of her body had been cut to pieces. The loss of all the nieces and nephews and cousins infinite times removed that she loved to gossip and complain about would kill her. When the red mist descended, all Carmine saw in his mind was his family sitting around a dinner table, each with Massimo's face where their own should be. His mother disappeared from his mental view completely until Giulio's call, and Carmine felt ashamed, both for forgetting about her, and for being glad Vito killed her before she discovered what Carmine had done.

Vito was a monster, of course, and had to be stopped. But Dark's freaky bodyguard was hopefully occupied in Great Neck burning out what was left of the Luppi clan, so Carmine called his other ace in the hole to deal with his nephew. It was fitting that the Order would take Vito down, considering all the carnage that Vito had supposedly committed over the past two weeks. Maybe the Order should have taken care of the family a long time ago. Carmine knew that everyone in the Order believed that the only good werewolf was a dead werewolf. His Order handler, a man who never even told him his name, doubtless felt that way too, as much as he pretended to be such a reasonable guy. So when Carmine got off the phone with Giulio he downed another drink and called the affable, sandy-haired bastard—a man whose name Carmine still didn't know—to tell him where his fucking nephew was. And the man answered, and listened, and understood, and promised to do what needed to be done.

When Carmine finished with his calls, he peeled off the suit that was beginning to burst at the seams as his body expanded in a way it hadn't done in decades, threw on a bathrobe because he felt ridiculous being naked in his own backyard, and went outside to transform under the moon like his ancestors. His lawn was littered with crunchy leaves, the first soldiers to die at the front of summer's oncoming war with winter. Winter inevitably won; summer had to let go of everything it had accomplished, let it all turn to shriveled brown dust, and bury the remains under a grayish-white ash of snow. Dust to dust, as the padre said at Carmine's father's funeral.

He had no idea how long he'd been out there; under the sensations of the "change," time tended to go fuzzy. But at some point, he heard a noise behind him that sounded like a *click*. He turned to see a man standing on his deck, outlined by the yellow light of the kitchen. He squinted, letting his eyes adjust, and realized it was his Order contact. His first thought was that the man had misinterpreted what Carmine said, and showed up at Carmine's house instead of Nana's. Carmine's second thought might have been something along the lines of, *what are you pulling out of your coat*, but it never formed, because the man fired a gun fitted with a silencer at Carmine's forehead, and Carmine died pretty much instantly.

Hunter then stood over the body and looked at his work. Clean, efficient, quick. It would come off like a mob hit, and no one would think twice about it. There were plenty of reasons why the Luppi family would want to get rid of Carmine.

———

Great Neck
   8:15 p.m.

Massimo reflected that his mother had been right about the casseroles. Mona hated having casseroles at any event that called for real silverware, but she'd ordered a few from Matteucci's anyway, and people brought still more, and they were getting eaten, scraped down to the bottoms of the foil pans, as if the spongy texture of baked ziti could absorb grief.

The sprawling suburban mansion looked bigger than usual when filled with family; fifty-ish relatives, the whole clan, speaking in hushed tones while the children played upstairs. Giulio's ten-year-old sister, Tamarind, was being good as gold of course, sitting downstairs with the grown-ups in her green party dress, delivering cocktails and wine to her aunties and uncles without even taking a sip first. She was a good kid, Tamarind, and deserved better than to be named after something her parents ate on vacation in Thailand, but Massimo's sister Leona was the artistic one in the family. At least she had dutifully given her older daughter, Talia, and her son, Giulio, normal names to please her father. Massimo could not conceive of how Giulio would have turned out if he'd been called Merlin like Leona wanted.

Ella was a wreck, sitting on the porch sobbing into the bosom of her sister. Her son Teo's death had been folded neatly into the overall narrative about Massimo's art theft beef with Dark, the timeline of which Massimo was content to leave fuzzy. Leona, meanwhile, gave up calling her son Giulio's phone. *"He's upset,"* she explained to Massimo. *"He loved Teo. You know that. And,"* she reminded him, *"Vito's not here either."* Massimo had told everyone that Vito was in Florida on business and was too distraught to come back for the funeral, and because Giulio's absence lent credence to the story, he left it alone.

Uncle Tommaso disapproved of the boys' absence, but was grumpier than normal; maybe because his much-younger wife, Claudia, who antagonized Massimo's mother by merely existing, was looking faded these days, with grey roots showing under the blond and a bit more weight to the silicone double Ds they'd all seen so much of at their wedding years ago. Whatever the reason, Massimo was avoiding Tommaso because he kept trying to ask uncomfortably specific questions about Mr. Dark—like what nightclub he owned, and what he'd been trying to steal, and where Vito and Giulio were if not paying their respects to their cousin. When Cesare died and the time came to choose a new *capo*, Massimo knew he'd weighed the pros and cons of having him killed and taking the title for himself. Tommaso still sniped about Massimo behind his back, and if too many more Luppi guys died in this war with Dark, he was going to start making a fuss with the rest of the family.

Something definitive would have to be done about Dark soon.

"Ey," someone said, tinking a spoon against a glass. "Ey. Shaddap, everybody." It was uncle Florio, ninety-eight years old and sharp as ever, which wasn't saying much, though he was the most lovable member of the family, with his oversized old man's ears and lispy tongue. "We gotta drink to the young." He raised his glass of red wine up towards the stairway platform, where dark-browed children's faces peeked through the bannister posts; and towards the kitchen, where two of the teenaged boy-cousins were practicing being men by sipping half-glasses of beer a few feet away from their mothers; and to Tamarind, who blushed and hid her face in her very-pregnant older sister Talia's shoulder. "We gotta drink to the young because we need 'em. We need 'em to fight for us, we need 'em to live for us, and sometimes, to die for us." His voice caught, but he held in his tears. "Teo was young, and he died young, and there ain't no sacrifice anyone can make that's bigger than that. So we gotta drink to that, and to Teo, and to the future of this family that he died to protect. *Salute.*"

Salute. It was a pretty set of platitudes, but coming out of Florio it sounded sincere, and it squeezed out plenty of tears as everyone raised their glasses, too distracted by grief to notice the faint—but alarming—sounds coming from outside.

———

The perimeter guards went down relatively easily—they were all hired Luppi guns, and all werewolves, but the rising half-moon made many of them distracted, pulling at their shirt collars and sweating. Adrael and his seven vampire Boys took one each, jumping out of the surrounding hedges to garrote them or shooting them with silenced pistols.

Then, stepping over their bodies, Adrael and the Boys stormed the house. They began with smoke bombs, tossing them through windows with only the jangle of smashing glass as warning. In the foggy chaos, they attacked from all sides, climbing through the windows and kicking in the front and back doors. Everyone started screaming and reaching for guns tucked away in calf holsters or handbags, but the Luppi were tipsy and slow and surprised compared to the neckbiters, who moved their stone-strong bodies like lightning. *Zip. Zip. Zip.* The kills were all at close range and the Boys' guns were fitted with suppressors, so they plugged away dispassionately at the Luppi family like they were zapping bugs. The Luppi began to transform, but too slowly, their normal reactions dulled by their faithful intake of the family tea. They got off a few shots; Tommaso, scrappy till the end, managed to empty the clip of his revolver before one of the Boys sliced his head halfway off with a knife that had been sticking out of the baked ham on the buffet table.

Adrael slipped through the carnage with cold efficiency, shooting, looking, shooting, looking, over and over as he stalked through the house. Luppi family members ran at him but he dodged them easily, someone fired at him but they missed. His clip emptied, so he slid in another and continued without missing a step. Compared to that fiasco at the club, this was workmanlike, systematic, rote. He didn't need to think or feel or even try, his bullets finding their targets as if it were all just a video game he'd played a thousand times before. He sensed someone behind him and turned to see Ella Luppi lunging for him with a knife in her hand, her soft face haggard and veiny mid-transformation. He calmly sidestepped the knife, caught her wrist in one hand, dragged her down to the floor and shot her in the back of the head, where she fell next to her dead niece Talia and whatever Talia had been growing in her belly.

"Clear," he heard from upstairs, as one of the Boys finished killing everyone in the master bedroom. "Clear" came from the porch. "Clear" came from the den, and the basement, and the study. He didn't hear it from the kitchen though, so he went in and saw one of his Boys dead on the floor, his head ripped almost from his neck by Massimo Luppi.

Massimo stood over the dead vampire, panting, blood and saliva dripping down his newly elongated fangs. He blinked impassively at Adrael and at Adrael's gun, which was pointed at his head.

"You Dark's fixer?" Massimo asked, his voice a weary growl.

"Nice to meet you," said Adrael.

"You don't look like I thought you'd look."

"People tell me that all the time."

Massimo sighed and leaned wearily against the kitchen counter, shifting uncomfortably in his clothes. He was still dignified as a transforming werewolf, his heavy brows growing more rakish, his expression appealingly predatory. But apart from his teeth he was handicapped, his thickening limbs trapped in his suit jacket binding him like an overstuffed sausage.

"You know, I'm beginning to wonder if any of this was necessary," said Massimo finally.

"It's a little late for that."

"You coulda just asked for that fuckin' painting."

"Would you have sold it to us?"

"I guess you'll never know." Massimo threw him a contemptuous sneer.

"If only I had a penny," Adrael sighed philosophically, "for all the things I'll never know."

"Mm-hmm." Massimo regarded him coldly for a moment. "So you're a genuine psychopath, yeah?"

Adrael had to smile.

"Wouldn't I have to be?"

"Just don't kill the kids," Massimo said with the last of his dignity. "Please."

"My employer considers them 'future Luppi soldiers,' so I'm afraid I have no choice," Adrael replied.

"I hope what Dark's paying you is worth your eternal soul."

"He doesn't pay me at all," Adrael told him.

Massimo blinked at him, but decided it wasn't worth exploring what was meant by that. He had other, more intriguing, final questions to ask.

"I'm curious," Massimo said, his quasi-canine eyes gleaming, "what the fuck are you, exactly? You cut through my guys like butter, but you don't look like no neckbiter to me."

"I guess you'll never know."

"Heh." Massimo shook his head, quite sure now that there, in his final moments, he had actually met the Devil, and was about to pay roundly for his myriad sins.

"Any last requests?" Adrael queried politely.

"Aim straight," Massimo replied, regal to the last.

So Adrael did, firing just once, and Massimo Luppi fell backwards onto his sister's kitchen floor with a bullet hole in his broad forehead, his swollen arms sticking out at his sides in his tight suit jacket like a child in a snowsuit, the back of his head finding its final resting place in a dropped plate of half-eaten eggplant roulade.

8:55 p.m.

Rat stepped into the house through the broken French doors, counting the bodies and marking off the names in his list. They were all there…Tommaso "Big Tuna" Luppi, Benny Blinders, Mikey Bullet…the Boys had murdered them all. Rat had to squint to recognize some of them, half-turned as they were, but the whole family was there, gathered to share grief, baked pasta and, now, a death date on their collective tombstone.

When he went upstairs, he saw the children. There would be no new generation of Luppi to rise up and avenge their dead fathers. Adrael was as thorough as Lucius could have hoped: each had a single bullet to the head, dead before their eyes closed all the way. Downstairs, one little girl in a green dress sat on the sofa, staring unblinkingly up at the ceiling with her dinner on a plate on her lap.

"That was...quick." Rat found Adrael in the bedroom, looking disturbingly calm and casual despite the splattered blood all over his clothes. "Very thorough," Rat added, with what he hoped was a collegial nod.

"I do as I'm told," Adrael replied blandly. Tonight was a task for him like any other, to be completed without emotion and without thought, because those were factors that belonged to men with choices. He had no choice and so felt nothing about any of it, not even the things that he had been raised to understand were the acts of cowards and villains. He shot the children himself, one bullet each. He always performed those tasks personally. Otherwise one of his guys would have had to do it, and if a man thought the idea distasteful Adrael would gain nothing from *making* him do it, and if he was overly willing, it seemed unseemly to let him. And this was hardly the worst thing Adrael had done in his long life; frankly, it barely rated on the scale. The Order would have done the same, children included. But for reasons Adrael wasn't up to parsing, he was glad that Desdemona had not been there to watch him do it.

"Real...uh...professional job," Rat said uneasily.

Adrael was annoyed to have his atrocities appreciated by Rat; it made him feel sordid in a way that stepping in the leaking brains of a ten-year-old no longer could. But he sensed a tremor of suppressed dismay in Rat's pale face at the sight of all those dead children lined up like paper dolls against the wall, and recalled then his first time witnessing such horrors as a participant. The frozen, grey faces of those first dead villagers still showed up in his dreams, even if the thousands more that followed did not. He felt an unwonted stab of pity for the wretched little man, who may have signed up for more than he bargained for with this job.

"Better us than *them*," Adrael purred in the soothing voice he used to help people rationalize the violence he performed on their behalf.

"You can imagine what the Order would do with a bunch of orphaned werewolves."

"They'd just kill 'em too, I guess," Rat allowed.

"Eventually. When they were done running tests and poking them full of holes."

"True," Rat agreed, and then he felt almost as if the Order *had* done this, and not the people he worked with. He and Lucius and Adrael were hardly a dream team, but, he had to admit, it was still the best employment situation he'd ever had. There was an unforgiving logic to the business they were in, and he was just glad that it didn't fall to him to do the dirty work. It was clear to him now that Adrael was far more than Lucius's snarky bodyguard and/or lover, and Rat was even beginning to doubt the latter, given how Adrael gazed at that Order bitch when he thought no one was looking.

"Sorry boss, Vito's not here," said one of the Boys, popping his head into the room. "I think he got away."

"Or...maybe he was never here," Rat said then, pulling out his phone. He brought up the message from Giulio and played it for them over the speakerphone.

Adrael blanched.

"When did you get that?"

"6:45. I was in the car with the guys, so it was on silent and I didn't see it for a while. And then it was go-time, so..."

But before he could finish his thought, Adrael was down the stairs, finished with Rat, and with the Luppi, and with everything that wasn't getting to Manhattan.

"Keys!" he called to one of the Boys.

Someone tossed him the keys to one of the Escalades and Adrael was gone, sprinting across the lawn to the shadowy side-lane where they'd parked. He left the Boys, competent criminals all, under the management of Rat to finish their business while he tried to get to Little Italy without getting stopped for speeding.

C H A P T E R 23

———

T H R O W N T O T H E W O L V E S

Little Italy
  9:30 p.m.

Dez was cold and her feet were in agony. She had been outside a half-hour already, pacing up and down the street in heels that felt like chopsticks strapped on with piano wire, while Adrael was probably crouching somewhere in combat boots and a jacket.

Next time he could wear the dress.

She had already turned down several "dates," which would begin to look suspicious if anyone was paying attention. Most of the business on that corner was from cars, and she saw no men on foot circling the area. Adrael had picked that corner at random, but it was just one of many neighborhood drains around which the local working girls swirled. Vito could be anywhere within blocks, hovering around a different clump of easy women. So Dez took a painful, mincing two-block walk to another spot, casting her eyes around for any Order members who might be surveilling the ladies of the night. The idea that any of those bodega owners or homeless vagrants—or even the prostitutes themselves—

might secretly be her colleagues was chilling. She was, however, reasonably confident that her costume of paradoxical exposure would shield her; in that trashy getup no one would recognize her in a million years.

Dez had to admit what a gamble this all was. If she didn't manage to land directly in Vito's line of sight, he'd just pick up another girl. She caught the corner girls giving her the stink-eye as a newcomer, so she stepped away from them and stooped down to check her lipstick in the side mirror of a parked car to give herself something to do, feeling slatternly as she did so, her back arched like a cat rubbing against a pair of legs. The scent of frying potatoes swirled through the air, along with the smell of cheap body cream, trash from a nearby dumpster, and...

And werewolf. Dez's body realized he was there before her mind did. Seconds after her nose registered the flare of heat and the whisper of musk, she spotted him standing under a construction awning just a few feet away. His pretty face was half in shadow, a hoodie pulled over his head, his infamous black moto jacket wrapped around his body. He was staring at her, and she didn't have to fake a blush. Vito then inclined his head at her in a surprisingly polite way, beckoning her over, and she approached him with a brash toss of her hair that hopefully made her look game.

Vito was sexy in his photos and continued to be sexy up close and in person, especially in more human form. But the photos failed to capture the softness in his expression, the heavy stubble on his heroic jaw contrasting with the childlike dew in big brown eyes under long, flirtatious lashes.

"You busy?" he asked. His voice was gentle and his manner sweetly abashed, even shy. He was devastating, this young man, triggering a woman's maternal and carnal instincts all at once. The sleeping beast within her gave a twitch and her blood began to course, her heart to pound, and her pussy to bloom.

"I have time," she said.

"Nice jacket." He stared at the red plastic, his eyes glassy, tiny beads of sweat clinging to his temples. "Did you buy that around here?"

"Online. Why, do you want one?" It came out saucy, and she was amazed that she had sufficient salt to put on that persona. But she felt very unlike herself in those clothes and makeup; her own voice sounded smokier than normal, her body obligingly moving the way a woman who dressed that way would move.

"Maybe. My mom says red's my color," he chuckled, the hectic gleam in his eyes dissipating as he registered that as funny. "Maybe we can swap."

"I'll throw in the boots," Dez quipped, leaning into her role. *This was so easy*. But of course acting came readily to her; acting was just an advanced form of lying, which she did every day.

"You wanna hang out?" he asked then.

"Ok," Dez shrugged.

"My place is around the corner," he told her.

My place?

Dez thought he'd lead her to a construction alcove or alley—*why did he kill that girl in the street if he had a nearby apartment?* This was a new wrinkle, but it was too late to worry about it. Adrael would sort it out shortly, likely down the barrel of a gun. They walked the two long avenue blocks to an unremarkable former tenement-turned-condo building, and she followed him up the stairs to the third floor. She did wonder how the hell Adrael would know which apartment to go to, but he'd figured out which apartment was *hers* without being told, and had gotten in despite it being on the fourth floor.

She didn't know if he'd done it quickly, though.

"You're pretty." Vito smiled as if he couldn't stop. "Wow." He sounded like a teenager on a first date, not a monster who frequented the city's most jaded professional prostitutes as part of a regular routine. "I haven't seen you before. In the neighborhood, I mean."

"I'm new in town."

"You do look familiar though," he said, squinting at her.

"I think I just have one of those faces."

"Nah," he chuckled. "You do not."

As the apartment door opened, she was hit with a wall of smells, all of them bad. *Old perfume. Old Italian food. Musty bathroom. Air freshener. Marijuana. Dirty dish sponge. Old kitchen pipes. Blood.* And coating it all like bad breath, the smell of recent death.

Then the door clicked shut behind her, and Vito locked it and flicked on the kitchen light.

Anytime now, Adrael.

"Do you want a drink?" Vito asked.

"Sure," she said, trying not to breathe. The house was an old woman's nest, neat but worn and faintly grubby. The kitchen table was covered with a red-and-white checked Italian-restaurant tablecloth and several half-finished Times crossword puzzles. The sink was full of dirty teacups. On the walls were macrame doilies and watercolors of big-eyed cartoon children holding lambs. Catholic paraphernalia was everywhere: garish ceramic Jesus plates on the walls, a rosary draped over the television, and statues of the Virgin Mary tucked away on the shelves. Indoor planters and pots overflowed with gnarled herbs—Dez recognized cannabis and oregano, but the others were a mystery.

She glanced out the window at a brick wall that was jumping distance away. The apartment faced an alley, and Dez told herself that Adrael was already scaling the wall, alerted to which apartment she was in by which window had just lit up. She grew emboldened knowing he must be there, though she did wonder what he was waiting for now that they had Vito trapped in a snare he'd willingly walked into.

Vito, meanwhile, produced a dusty bottle of Chianti.

"Hope you like red," he said.

Dez thought she was meant to go into the bedroom, given the situation. Vito didn't stop her as she wandered through the apartment, peeking into the bathroom with its rose-printed shower curtain and counter covered in ancient beauty products. The bedroom was down the hall with its door ajar, but the smell of death was much stronger there. Every instinct told her not to go inside but she could not bear to live with the mystery of a locked box or an X on a map. Or a cracked door.

Adrael will be here in a second. It will be fine.

So she nudged the door open. The bedroom was half-dark, lit only by a bedside lamp and a cross-shaped nightlight on the floor. But someone was in bed, their head resting on a lace-edged pillow. Dez opened her mouth to apologize, unsure if the person—an old lady, judging by the white swirls of hair—was asleep. But the sleeper lay motionless, and while the breath of the elderly is shallow, the smell in the room told Dez that she would not mind the intrusion. Holding her breath, Dez reached for the coverlet and pulled it gently back.

And there, tucked in for the night, was Nana Luppi. She'd been savaged, her head twisted the wrong way around, her wattled throat ripped to strings and crusted with drying blood. The sheets beneath her were soaked to brown-red, her wizened body shredded like old chicken into a mess of veins, bones, and flaps of mottled skin. And there wasn't quite enough of her there—chunks were missing from what would normally have been the meatiest parts of her, and where her organs should have been was a gaping, empty hole.

"Wine?"

Dez whirled around to see Vito, a glass of Chianti in each hand, staring at her in her red coat as he started to transform.

———

The Manhattan Bridge
   9:30 p.m.

It was raining again. The air had been pregnant with moisture all evening, and the water finally broke. Rain splattered on the Escalade's windshield, dirty torrents of water from the putrid rivers that surrounded the island. Adrael wished for a smaller car as he maneuvered the SUV through the angry traffic. New York drivers became worse in the rain, throwing on their brakes as they turned on their wipers, cutting each other out of lanes. He called Dez for the hundredth time and sent ribbons of texts as he drove, but they went unanswered. He knew it was possible that Vito wasn't out hunting that night, and that Dez was, at worst, standing outside getting slightly damp. It was even possible that the Order had gotten to Vito first, which would not be ideal, but preferable to the bloody alternative that Adrael could not stop imagining. Or perhaps Vito had found some other girl in a red outfit to mangle, which meant that Adrael could just go to the address Giulio had given Rat, wait for Vito to come back, and then neatly strangle him, since they didn't need him alive anymore.

Red. The maddening color flashed before his eyes as a sea of bright red brake lights flashed on for an accident ahead.

———

"Would you like some *vino?*" Vito repeated calmly, as if unaware of the dead woman rotting in the bed, his hand swelling around the glass of syrupy red liquid.

Dez, no trained psychologist, still recognized a psychotic break when she saw one.

"Okay," said Dez carefully, reaching out to accept the glass. But Vito held onto it, as if reconsidering, and his face turned grey.

"I'm—I'm sorry," he faltered, his features surging from human to grotesquely canine and back, as if his body couldn't decide whether to change or not. Along with her horror, Dez felt his tortured misery quivering through her own body, making her stomach churn and her heart drop. Vito had been weaponized, years of repression stoked to a frenzy by the city's most heartless predator, and the imprint his hidden addiction left on his face as it clawed its way out of him was familiar from her own mirror.

"It's alright," she said then. "I understand."

"You don't," he whimpered.

"I do. I know it's hard to stop, even if you hate yourself. I know what it's like to have that *thing* inside you telling you want to do."

"You do?" he blinked, struggling to understand. Dez then took a conciliatory step toward him, which was unfortunate, because her body had been blocking the shaft of red light spilling from the gap in the side of the shuttered window blinds. As she moved, a red beam shot into the apartment and hit the shiny plastic of her coat, making it gleam like fresh blood. And as the color hit Vito's eye, his instincts responded to his months of training. He jolted as if tapped by a cattle prod, and his eyes took on the hooded gaze of a horny man. A glance at his crotch showed he was already bursting at the seams, his cock fighting his thigh for space in his pants.

Dez silently begged Adrael to show up. Surely he was hidden in that apartment somewhere, ready to prevent her from being torn apart.

"Vito, please," she stammered, "Just—"

"How do you know my name?" His voice was wet with an animal's snarl.

Whoops. Dez had spent so much time thinking about Vito over the past two weeks that she'd forgotten that, to him, she was a complete stranger.

"Lucky guess?" she offered lamely. She backed away but he grabbed her wrist, and when he did, they both felt the electric tingle of her succubus skin nipping at his.

"You're one of *them.*" Vito hurled the wine glass against the wall and lunged at her, knocking her onto the bed. They landed on top of his dead grandmother with a sickening crunch, her brittle bones crumpling.

Alright Adrael, Dez pleaded silently. *Now would be brilliant.* She thrashed in Vito's grip, but the slick soles of her cheap boots could get no purchase on the threadbare carpet and the two of them slid to the floor together in a pile of elbows and stiletto heels. She tried to crawl toward the door, but he held her legs and flipped her onto her back, pinning her arms above her head. Vito was heavy and his thighs crushed hers together like a clamp as he sat on her, reached up her skirt, ripped her flimsy red panties off, and then pulled at the zipper of his jeans.

"I know what Dark did to you," she gasped. "I know you didn't want to kill those girls, I know—"

"You don't know anything," he snarled. "You're all the same. Human or...not..." —he seemed unable to decide which she was, exactly —"you're all the same, you stupid bitches. You turn me into this and make me think it's *my* fault. You blame us for what you make us do and we're the ones who feel bad about it. But I got news for you, gorgeous: I ain't interested in feeling bad anymore."

Vito's eyes had frenzied gleam to them, the gently bashful young man totally superseded by whatever beast lived inside him. Bloody saliva dripped onto Dez's neck as he lowered his grotesque face to hers and licked her from nipple to jaw, and she knew, instinctively, that he was about to bite into her, so she caught his eyes with hers and held them.

Her pupils dilated in a flash as the beast within her woke up and began to take over.

Vito felt the familiar magnetic shiver wash over him, as if his brain was on the receiving end of a vacuum cleaner. He'd experienced it a hundred times before; he'd even sought it out and paid the world's highest price for it. But he didn't like it anymore, not now that he knew the feverish one-way release of taking a woman without giving up anything in return. He tried to shake it off, but his conscious mind was a jumble, unable to get a grip on a raging body driven mad by the color she had stretched all over her nubile body.

Dez tumbled into narcotic cloudiness as Vito's desire locked into her brain. Her mind's eye saw flashes of red: blood, clothing, red every-where in the rapacious impulse of a wolf tearing into a freshly killed deer. It almost overwhelmed her with its violence and promise of pain, but she pushed back, her mind shutting out the fangs, the bestial features, and the talons as she drew his savagely violent life out of his body and into hers. She had never experienced such abandon—*well, almost never*—and sank into the ecstasy of drinking him dry. His cock was leaping out of his pants, so he freed it and pointed it towards the target, but he was so woozy that he kept missing the mark. Dez knew she was already pulling too much out of him, even killing him, but she relished the delicious burning on bottoms of her feet as he held onto her for support instead of control. A tenuous balloon in her head popped, and she and the creature inside her merged into one entity, simultaneously ecstatic and vengeful, enraged and aroused, and without meaning to do it, she shifted her feet and pushed Vito all the way inside her. He moaned in what sounded like agony as the walls of her pussy gripped him the way he'd been gripping her wrists. He couldn't help but thrust, and even as she watched him ravaging her in his mind, she was the one ravaging *him*. And if she let him continue, she knew she would drain the life out of him and not have to feel guilty if he died.

A high-pitched zipping noise erupted above them; it sounded as if it were coming from far away. She then startled and bit down a scream as blood dripped onto her shoulder, trickling out of the fresh holes in both of Vito Luppi's temples. His gyrations became spasms as the full weight of his body collapsed onto her, and she kicked her way out from under him, his cock sliding out of her. He'd been shot through the side of the head.

And a man in silhouette stood above them, pointing a gun fitted with a long suppressor.

"I'm sorry, V," the figure said sorrowfully. "It's the end of the road."

The figure with the gun stepped into the garish light coming through the window, and Dez saw his face. She didn't recognize him at first, but the brows and snarling canine teeth betrayed him as another Luppi. He was only half-turned; the family tea still coursed through his body, slowing down the transformation, and he remained human enough for her to make out his features. *She'd seen him before, she knew she had...in those photos in the file...*

He turned Vito's body over tenderly, like a lover or a brother, and brushed the hair out of Vito's glassy, expressionless eyes, his thumb rolling softly over the bullet hole as if caressing it, tears rolling down his swelling cheeks.

"I'm so sorry," he whispered, and it sounded like a growl in his werewolf chest. "It's over now. And...Nana..." He reached up and squeezed the dead woman's hand. He then turned to look at Dez with hate in his bloodshot eyes.

"Did Dark send you?" He picked her up by the hair and pressed her against the wall so he could stare into her face. "Yeah, you're one a' his. I can see it."

"I don't know what you mean," she squeaked; a lie too flaccid to be entertained.

"And you call us monsters. Look what you did to him." He grabbed Dez by the jaw and turned her head to look at Vito's body. "He was beautiful, and you people wrecked him. And for what? For some trash out of my uncle's warehouse?"

Giulio Luppi. Dez's brain found the name and paired it with one of the photos from the file.

"Did Dark send you?" he repeated when she continued to say nothing, and his tone suggested it was the last time he was willing to ask without drawing blood.

"Yes," she said, deciding that he wouldn't buy "no." "He sent me to...to..."*wherethefuckwasAdrael* "He sent me to...find...he just wanted to...Vito killed so many girls. Two of...of *us*...and then a human..."

"He killed a human woman?" Giulio sighed, shaking his head, while continuing to hold Dez against the wall like a trapped insect. "Oh V, what did they do to you..." He choked down a sob, his voice fraying with sorrow. "He wasn't like that," Giulio spat at her. "He'd never hurt a woman—a real woman I mean. Not before he set foot in that club."

"I know that," affirmed Dez, hoping she might be able to agree Giulio into reason. "I know, what was done to him was criminal."

"Criminal," Giulio huffed, an ugly sneer creeping across his lips. "But you're never *punished for it,* are you? You jerks do whatever you want and nobody's the wiser. No one makes you take fucking tea to keep your urges down. You take whatever you want and leave the rest to figure itself out."

"I think Vito got confused," Dez explained desperately. "I think he was crazy at the end, when he killed—" Dez looked at the crumpled figure in the bed in horror—"I...I think after he killed those two succubus girls, he couldn't tell the difference anymore and..."

"Vito didn't kill those cheap little nightcrawlers," Giulio scoffed, his voice gravelly with hate. "He should have. That would have been only fair, considering they took his money *and* then took...I mean they got paid twice, right? That's no way to do business. But you saw how easy it was for you to control him just now. He was helpless. Always helpless." Giulio spat as he spoke. "He was wrecking his life like a goddamn addict. Then Vito couldn't go back to the club no more 'cause Dark tried to call in his tab by making him sell out his own family, so he swore he'd stop. But you know how it is with addicts; he just went out to find it on the street. I followed him so many times, and had to watch him crawl around like a junkie looking for a fix, and after he got it he'd get weak as a goddamn kitten. It was fucking *heartbreaking.*" Giulio glared at Dez as if she were personally responsible. "You assholes are no better than fucking drug dealers; I mean, hell, you can buy rotten pussy on the same corners you buy meth, it's all the same. It was criminal, just like you said, and I couldn't—" he choked on his own rage. "We all bought that shit Dark was selling us that Vito was 'too much to handle' and 'needed premium services' and all that, and it wasn't...even...fucking... *true.*" With each word, he shook Dez for emphasis, smacking her head against the back wall. "So... *I made it true.*"

"What?" Dez gasped. "*You* killed them?"

"Oh please, is it really even killing, when you're all just parasites?" Giulio snarled. "If you get fucking tapeworm you pop a pill and the damn thing dies and comes out your ass. Killing you girls is no different. You nightcrawlers are trash, and all I was doing was cleaning up after V, like I did our whole damn lives. I couldn't let those little monsters keep walking around like they had any right to exist. It's not like they were people." He snorted with infinite contempt. "If V killed some real girl afterwards...well, that's Dark's fault too. My cousin wasn't a violent guy. Not like...well...me." He tightened his grip even further, like a spasm, and Dez began to choke. "That first nightcrawler girl in Nolita fucking *laughed*, you know that? After he left, I watched her walk back to her damn corner laughing at him like he was some pathetic mook. But my cousin wasn't pathetic. He was just...fucking...*sensitive*. So I gouged that laugh off her stupid fucking face. And then I took the rest of her face off too, and I did the same to that bitch under the bridge, and I'm gonna do the same to you right now."

Dez pushed against his body with her own, but he was like a wall of granite. Giulio was wearing gloves, so he wasn't touching her skin, but Dez used the last of her panic-strength to wrench one of her hands free and grab his arm. When her fingers touched the flesh on his bare wrist, she felt the tingling, and she knew he did too, because he startled and his eyes went wide. She tried to lock into his head the way she'd done with Vito as he stared into her eyes, and waited for the wave of images as he began to see in her what he was looking for.

But a few seconds passed, and then some more, and it didn't happen.

And then Giulio Luppi smiled.

"It won't work, honey. Didn't work for those other two bitches either. 'Cause, see, thing is...I ain't into girls."

And with that, he raised his hand to rip out one of her eyes.

Zip.

Another buzzy sound whizzed by Dez's head, and Giulio dropped like a stone. She fell hard onto her gawky shoes, barely escaping a sprain as she crumpled to the floor next to Giulio, who was now dying on top of Vito with a bullet hole in *his* temple.

His head had been only inches from her own, so whoever fired was a hell of a shot. Bleary-eyed from choking, she looked up and saw who it was.

"Cross?" Hunter gaped.

Dez scrambled to her feet, pulling her dress down. Her mouth dropped open, but she was entirely at a loss about what to say to him. He obviously hadn't come there on purpose to save her; the look on his face was pure surprise.

It was all over. She could think of no way to explain this that made any sense, other than the truth.

"I..." she tried, wiping blood off her face. She couldn't find the words that would consign her to the fate she'd spent her whole life dreading. Hunter would have to tell Solomon, of course. This was too big of a secret for him to keep, even if he wanted to, which after viewing this distasteful tableau, was unlikely.

"It's not..." Dez tried again, but it died in her mouth. She had no words to mitigate this, no explanation that would suffice, no plea that would make it better. All that was left for her was to confess, which would feel wonderful, really, and let the cresting tsunami of dread finally drown her like the rat she was. "I can explain," she choked.

"I'll bet." The whites of his eyes reflected the red light from the window, making them look like he'd been weeping. That stuffy room reeked of death, and blood was flowing out of Vito's and Giulio's heads and soaking into the old carpet. "Nice outfit," he remarked. "Kinda off-brand for you, but..."

"You don't have to tell anyone about this," she managed, her voice small. "You can let me walk out the door and you'll never see me again."

"You mean nobody knows you're here?" Hunter cocked his head in genuine surprise. "What're you, freelancing? Did you go after this boy yourself?"

Wait, what? Dez paused, confused. *What did he think was going on here?*

Hunter turned Vito over with his foot, the dead man's twitching cock pointing at the ceiling.

"Nothing you won't do for the job, huh?" he scoffed, one eyebrow raised. "Jesus. Jesus, nothing you won't do, including...wow." Dez backed against the wall as she saw a new kind of disdain in

Hunter's eyes. "I knew what you were the whole time," he told her then.

It was Dez's turn to stare at him in bald surprise.

"You did?" was all she could cough up.

"Yeah," Hunter nodded sagely. "I knew there was no way you were really just some bookworm. No one who looks like you even needs to learn to read. You're really a bit 'much' for the research department, frankly. What are you, special cases? Level A? Or are you in the Umbra like your mother? God, I know you people are determined, but this is another level."

Wait. He thought she was Umbra? Somehow he'd misinterpreted the scene in front of him and had drawn precisely the wrong conclusion, and Dez wondered if perhaps the storied intelligence of the average Order Investigator had been a bit exaggerated.

"Seems like you got yourself in trouble, though." He glanced contemptuously down at the two former Luppi soldiers. "These boys are pretty hard to handle."

"Yes, he was...a lot." Dez eyed Hunter carefully, wondering if she'd pulled a get-out-of-death-free card. *Was this something she could get away with?* "I should say thank you for getting here when you did," she continued, riffing, "It was...um..." *Wait, why was he here?* Dez was too frazzled to quite trust her faculties, but she couldn't find a logical thread that explained his presence. "How did you even know to come here? This address wasn't in the file."

"Carmine called me and told me get over here. Said Vito was out of control. That he'd lost it." He shook his head. "Goddamn, these people are more trouble than they're worth. If he'd told me about all this...But maybe he didn't know. He didn't even know about my deal with Massimo. And Massimo didn't know about Carmine snitching to us. Not a lotta family communication going on there."

"Your deal with Massimo?" Dez repeated, dumbly.

No.

No, not Hunter. It couldn't be.

"Ten grand a month," Hunter shook his head ruefully. "They gave me ten grand a month, and we stayed out of their hair. Seemed reasonable to me. Solomon was adamant about not bothering them—'Too much trouble for us,' he said—so all I had to do was sit on my hands. But Massimo didn't know that, so I let him go on thinking it was *me* keeping the Order away in exchange for a little extra cash." Hunter chuckled at that. "Easiest money I ever made."

"*You* fudged all the addresses in the file," she gasped.

"I know you thought it was Solomon," he chuckled grimly. "But it doesn't matter—if you told anybody that, and they looked into it, they'd figure out who really did it pretty quick. And I'd be, you know. Fucked.'

"But why would Solomon protect the Luppi like that?"

"He doesn't see it as 'protection.' I had this argument with him over and over...and over," Hunter scoffed. "I thought it was pretty demented when I first joined up. I'd been a cop for almost twenty years, so letting a bunch of moonie psychopaths like that get a free pass because they're killing people the 'normal' way, instead of with their teeth, never jived with me. I mean, Cross, you're sane, I think. Maybe the sanest person I've ever met. Does it bother you that we watch people kill each other and do nothing about it because regular people killing regular people is considered 'natural?' "

"Maybe," she hedged, having recently pondered that very question.

"This one time, a couple of years ago, we had this rush of bodies showing up in south Queens," he said, ranting now, because he hadn't ever been able to tell this to anyone, and was finding it an enormous—if bittersweet—relief to confess. "Young guys, junkies, nobody you'd miss, all of 'em raped and slashed to death and left in trash bags. We kept finding those bodies, over and over, cops found a few, we found a few more. But the murders weren't 'extrahuman,' it was just some normal everyday Joe serial killer cutting people up every time the Giants played an away game. And you know what we did about it?"

Dez had a guess, but she let him continue.

"Nothing. We did nothing. We even had a pretty good idea who the doer was, but Solomon made us leave the bodies where we found them and let the 'official authorities sort it out.' But what got me, Cross, was that he said stuff like that was *useful*. Because a maniac killer out there in the wild makes people even less likely to believe in things like vampires." He shook his head again, as he'd been doing all night. "That really got to me. I mean, ok, at first I was on board with all this. I thought my life was ruined that night in that alley when that kid ripped into me and I was dumb enough to tell people what I'd seen—they took my badge away and locked me up. Solomon and Justin visited me in the institution and gave me a choice. Join up, they said, or stay there, as if that's a real choice. And I get why we don't want people to know about this stuff, and I've seen enough of the fallout of what happens when people try and live forever..." he frowned, disgusted. "I'd rather rot in the ground than rot on my feet. But all that Order shit about the one true universal God and the eternal fight against Satan and all his infected supernatural minions, that's all lunatic cult bullshit. If there is a God, Cross, he sure as shit don't care about any of us, so I don't see why we shouldn't return the favor. Or why we shouldn't do for ourselves."

Hunter was, in truth, thoroughly tired of the Order. He didn't buy into the program anymore, and maybe never fully had. Yes, he'd initially been grateful for the affirmation that he wasn't crazy, and that he was still a great cop and didn't belong in a padded cell. But the organization's black-and-white worldview about what was good and what was evil, meaning what was "natural" and what was "more-than," had always seemed wrongheaded to him. If the man in the alley that attacked him had been a human drug addict instead of a frenzied werewolf and had done the damage with a knife instead of claws, the outcome for Hunter's guts would have been the same. And he felt less comfortable with the fully-human hoodlums he saw walking around Bedford-Sty than he did with a relatively civilized werewolf like Massimo Luppi.

"So you're...on the take from the Luppi," Dez said, if only to make the situation crystal-clear for herself.

"On the take," he chuckled. "What cop show did you hear that on?"

"Is that the wrong term?"

"Nah. Just sounds ridiculous when you say it."

At first the money was just insurance, because Hunter ran through all his savings when he lost his job. The Order had faked his death to get him out of the hospital, making him entirely reliant on them; they paid his rent, his living expenses, his medical bills, everything, like the Catholic Church did for its monks. And as with monks, the free cash portion of his salary was far from lavish, because Order members were expected to live for the mission. But Hunter didn't want to live for the mission anymore. He wanted a houseboat in Antigua. In theory he could have faked a mental breakdown and tried to retire, even if they let him keep breathing instead of killing him, as they sometimes secretly did to those who left the fold. The pension they'd offer would hardly pay for the cushy retirement he wanted, full of sunshine and Hawaiian shirts and coconuts with straws. The monthly packets of unmarked bills he got from the Luppi for doing nothing seemed like a no-brainer. All he had to do was fake his own death on the Order end, since in the regular world he was legally dead already, and he had a box of fake passports and all the savvy he needed to survive until he died of old age with a cigar in his mouth and a Panama hat on his head. So, to that end, if Solomon didn't care about how the Luppi made their money, Hunter decided that maybe he didn't need to either.

"Since we never went after them, I figured nobody'd dig into the file enough to notice the addresses," Hunter sighed, his voice weary and sad. "I changed them in case an overeager puppy like Reilly got a hair up his ass to look them up for some stupid reason. Massimo didn't like to be surprised."

"Except Carmine's. That address was right."

"He was a source, so I had to register him in the ledger. I couldn't fuck with that. We send someone to drive by *those* people's houses once a week to make sure they're still alive."

Dez shivered, realizing how lucky she was not to have been seen that day in Brooklyn. She stared at Hunter, wondering where they stood now, and what he was planning to do. Because, despite all his verbal diarrhea and cathartic confessions, he was still pointing his gun at her.

"We both know what happens next, Cross," said Hunter miserably. "It's nothing personal. You're a lying sack of shit, but I'm a lying sack of shit too, so neither of us has that new car smell anymore." Genuine regret fought with disgust as he stared at her, and despite the gun pointed at her stomach, Dez felt a pang as she remembered those few stolen moments with him among the dusty files. "Was any of it real?" he asked her, his jaw clenching and his eyes going glossy with threatened tears. "You and me, I mean. It felt so...Jesus...But were you just...playing me?"

"It was all real," she replied quietly. "I didn't know any of this about you until now."

"Good," he said almost spitefully. "I'd hate to think I was that fucking deluded." His eyes ran over her body, a flash of old desire mixed with new revulsion in their alcohol-reddened depths.

"You can walk out the door right now," Dez pleaded. "I won't stop you. I won't tell anyone you were here. You can just disappear. Empty that gun and keep the bullets if you want, and hand it to me, and I'll say I shot Giulio. There's no reason for anyone to think otherwise."

"God, that would be great," said Hunter. "I mean, I think we understand each other a little, you and me." He flashed her a ghost of the smile she previously thought so charming. "But I'm not a kid, I know that only goes so far. I can't take the chance."

"What...what about that poor veteran you arrested?" If she was about to die, she wanted to at least put that question to bed.

Hunter sighed, a ragged sigh that smelled like the vodka he'd downed at Carmine's house before heading into Manhattan.

"I got lucky with Pryor. The girl he killed was wearing the wrong colors but I slipped that red jacket in myself. I had to—Solomon's got such a bug up his ass about who your mother is, I knew he'd start digging into that Luppi file if I didn't give him a good reason not to."

"As an ex-cop, you should be above planting evidence, I would have thought."

"Don't bust my balls, Cross," Hunter scoffed. "People like you and your mother do the same to the humans that get caught in your crossfire every day. The cause is worth more than a few lives, amirite?"

Dez didn't bother to argue, because as she glanced down with grim irony at the two dead men at her feet, she noticed a triangle of black plastic peeking out from under Giulio's body: the butt of his gun.

"Don't do it, Cross," warned Hunter. "Fucking don't."

"Are you going to shoot me, too? Just one more dead girl on the ledger?"

He sighed heavily again, the sadness and rage in his face hardening into a mask of determined misery.

"Solomon needs to think Giulio shot Vito and you, and that I then killed Giulio, which won't fly if I shoot you with *my* gun. That would put a big hole in that story. So you're gonna back up a few feet, and I'm gonna pick up Giulio's gun, and then you're gonna let me shoot you with it, because if you do, I promise I'll shoot you in the head and it'll be painless. But if you don't, I'll have to shoot you in the gut with *my* gun. Then I'll have to dig my goddamn bullet out and hide the mess by making it look like Vito or Giulio did to you what they did to those other girls. And I don't want to do that to you, Cross, I really fucking don't." His face was taut with misery, his voice cracking. "Please, just do it my way. You'll be a hero. A martyr, even. And I know that matters to you people."

Dez was hardly going to let him shoot her in the head like a slaughterhouse cow. If she dropped to the floor and grabbed the gun, Hunter would shoot her in the stomach, but she had no way of knowing what a body like hers could live through. Maybe she could survive it. If she managed to end up with Giulio's gun in her hand, she could shoot him back. She was fuzzy on how to toggle the safety, but children shot each other accidentally all the time, surely she could manage it on purpose. It was not an appealing plan, but although Dez had contemplated death as an alternative to her problems more times than she could count, confronted with the reality of it, she decided that she was going to go down swinging.

"It's such a goddamn shame," said Hunter. "You're so..." He brushed away whatever poetic thing he was going to say with a grimace.

"Fat lot of good it does me," Dez retorted.

Dez flicked her eyes down at Giulio's gun again, and Hunter's finger quivered on his trigger. But just as Dez was about to dive to the floor and seal her fate—*right* before—Hunter's face took on a funny expression that wavered between agony and surprise. Red blossomed outwards from a spot on his chest where the long metal tip of a blade was sticking out of his heart, and he fell forward onto the floor.

Adrael emerged out of the shadows behind Hunter like a ghost. He was wearing tactical gear again, guns and knives strapped to his thighs, his hands encased in tight leather gloves. His face was flushed with adrenaline and Dez guessed that the wet-looking splatters on his black clothing were sprays of someone else's blood.

"That took you long enough."

"You passed the time," Adrael replied tartly.

"How long have you been here?"

"You two were talking. I didn't want to interrupt."

"I think you were late."

"I had some other business," he told her.

Dez couldn't fathom what could be more pressing than saving her —and thus also Lucius's—life, but she was too horrified by what she'd just gone through to get into it.

"Then how did you even find me here?"

"I didn't, exactly," he said, nudging Vito's body idly with his foot. "Giulio called Rat earlier to tell him where Vito was, but I didn't find that out until after we..." He didn't say what they'd been doing, but Dez knew she'd hear about it later, probably at work, over another body on a gurney. "I suspected Giulio meant to lure me here to kill Vito, and when I arrived, Giulio would jump out of the shadows and kill me instead. So

I came to take care of both of them at the same time. Oh, and save your life, of course. But there was traffic on the bridge so it took longer than I would have preferred."

They stood in awkward silence, him splattered with the blood of the family he'd butchered on demand, her with thighs dripping with secretions and her latest sex partner lying dead on the floor. Neither mentioned it as they looked into each other's eyes, searching for judgement and unsure how to read what they found instead.

"Alright, let's sort this mess out," Adrael sighed as he crouched down to examine the bodies. "You killed Vito, I assume, with your... ahem. Giulio then tried to kill you, but your friend here showed up and shot him instead. And then *your friend* was going to shoot *you*, thus completing the round robin."

"I didn't kill Vito. I..." she didn't feel up to describing what happened next, so she skipped it. "Giulio came in and shot him."

"Really?" Adrael bit the inside of his cheek thoughtfully.

"I think he was putting Vito out of his misery. He had other plans for me."

"Those two dead succubi," Adrael realized, nodding thoughtfully. "Giulio killed them, didn't he?"

"He followed Vito when he went to do his usual business with them, and then dealt with them in his own way after Vito dropped them off."

"Lucius will enjoy being right about that," Adrael observed caustically. "He so prides himself on his understanding of his clientele." He stared down into Giulio's face, half-turned and still grimacing, his bulging eyes open and staring at nothing. "And I suppose that Giulio would have been difficult for those Girls to handle, since he didn't—"

"Since he didn't like women," Dez finished drily. "Yes, I too ran into a problem with a 'lack of verisimilitude,' as Lucius would say."

Adrael imagined the scene he'd missed with distaste. Dez met his stare, challenging him to remark on it. So purely to annoy her, he did not.

"I'm sorry about your friend," he said instead. He'd arrived in time to hear most of Hunter's interaction with Dez, staying silent and allowing them to talk to get an idea of the true nature of their relationship. In any other man Adrael might have called that behavior "jealousy," but he was sure he wasn't capable of that particular emotion anymore. And now that he and his knife had transformed Hunter into a hundred and sixty-something pounds of cooling meat, the question was irrelevant.

"I suppose he wasn't really my friend," Dez swallowed. Luckily Hunter had fallen forward onto the floor into a slowly-spreading pool of his own heart's blood, so she couldn't see the amiably dapper face she'd so recently kissed.

"I don't think he really *wanted* to kill you," Adrael offered.

"But he still would have. So what's the difference?"

A trace of something disarmingly human glimmered in Adrael's eyes as he flashed her a rueful smile.

"You should go home. You look like you're about to collapse. I'll deal with all this."

As usual, Dez couldn't tell if he was being concerned or critical, but she was too tired to argue.

"Bugger, this dress is half ripped open," Dez sighed, tugging the tattered lycra around her.

"That's probably for the best," Adrael replied, wrinkling his nose. "It makes you look like a hotdog."

He took off his black leather military jacket and emptied the pockets, extracting several loaded gun magazines, two knives, a nasty little karambit, a smoke grenade, and various other lethal-looking items Dez didn't recognize. He stuffed them haphazardly into the cargo pockets of his military pants, smiling sheepishly to apologize for how long it was taking, and handed it to her. She peeled off the red plastic raincoat and let it fall to the floor, draping his jacket over her shoulders. It enveloped her like a stiff black cocoon, warm on the inside and smelling deliciously of his divine body, but also of adrenaline, blood, and gunpowder—all of which were, she realized, part of his personal perfume.

"What are you going to do now?" she asked.

"To sew this up for the Order I have to make it look like they all killed each other." He surveyed the bodies like a pile of laundry that needed folding. "I think we have to arrange this backwards. Hunter should have shot Giulio first, since his bullet is in Giulio's head. In that scenario, Vito would then have attacked Hunter with the knife, killed him, and then...finally shot himself in the head from grief with Giulio's gun? Does that make sense?"

"As much as anything else," Dez nodded wearily. "The Order will talk themselves into it."

Adrael plucked Giulio's gun off the floor and placed it in Vito's outstretched hand, pressing Vito's fingerprints all over the butt and trigger as Dez carefully tugged up Vito's pants. As a finishing touch, he pulled the gun from Hunter's hand and kicked it across the floor, sliding it under the dresser as if scoring an air hockey goal.

"That'll give your people something to find," Adrael smiled. "People are more likely to believe a story if they have to work for it."

He and Dez surveyed their work together, checking their logic like a pair of chess players.

"I think that should do it," Dez nodded. "Except..." She sighed, depressed at what she had to say next. "They'll have trouble believing that a crazed moonie like Vito would watch Hunter kill his cousin and then just stab him once from behind. It will make them suspicious. It just isn't...werewolfy enough. Unfortunately."

"I suppose that means I have to give your friend here the moonie treatment." Adrael pulled his knife out of Hunter's back and kneeled down to flip the ex-policeman over. "Alright. Don't worry—I know how to make it look good. But I don't think you want to stay and watch. It could get..." He grimaced at her eloquently.

"Gooey?"

Dez looked down at the three bodies, two of the men pooling blood from their heads, the third from his heart. As terrible as she felt, there was no reason for her to punish herself further by watching the *coup de grace*. Adrael was more than capable of handling that without assistance. So, with as much dignity as she could muster, she picked her panties and raincoat off the floor, pulled her vinyl boots up over her knees, and stalked toward the door. Her legs shook underneath her, but she felt numb everywhere else. Once she got home she could collapse, cry, perhaps have a nervous breakdown in the shower.

As she walked out the door, she glanced back at Adrael crouching down over the bodies, his head cocked sideways like an artist arranging a tableau. He was a monster, this man, a killer-for-hire who had just arrived like a tardy date, fresh from murdering whoever's wet blood she could smell on the jacket he'd given her. No real-life Jack the Ripper could boast such a finely honed gift for violence or such a corroded set of morals. So it was strange that he was also the only person in that city she didn't have to lie to, and thus the only person she could call for help. That made him, if not quite her friend, at least her ally. And as his blue eyes gleamed steadfastly back at her, Dez supposed that, as allies went, she could do worse.

When Dez left, Adrael turned back to the bodies at his feet. He lifted Hunter up by the lapels to stare into his face, still ruggedly handsome in death; a face that Adrael had been imagining smashing with a rock for days. As he stared into Hunter's blank eyes, he almost smiled.

But instead, he breathed a weary sigh that tasted like equal parts shame, pity, and sympathy for the man, none of which were the right sauce for the meal he'd been contemplating. So he set Hunter gently back down on the floor and stepped back to consider how best to approach the squalid task before him, his lips twisted in thought, a bloody knife drooping in one leather-gloved hand.

EPILOGUE

GOODNIGHT MOON

The Second Circle

Thursday evening

The club would be open by Christmas. The contractors had so promised, and the increasingly useful Mr. Maitlin prodded along permits for improvements that would otherwise have taken far longer, and even allowed the employees to remain in residence upstairs and continue to see private clients, which at least kept the books balanced. Lucius should have been delighted, except that an hour ago, he opened a cardboard-wrapped package that had arrived the previous afternoon, via courier—a package that, in all the excitement, had been placed in a back room by the bouncers and briefly forgotten.

It was the Caravaggio.

It was a big canvas, the figure rendered life-size, so Lucius sat on the plastic-sheeted floor of his office and stared across the carpet at the painting as if he and it were having a meeting, tears of rage streaming down his golden cheeks. It was destroyed. The frame was intact, and much of the actual canvas remained, but where there had once been a rapturously faithful representation of Lucius's personal beauty, there was now only carnage. The graceful lines that had once described his limbs had been repeatedly slashed, the figures at the Baccus's feet rubbed with what smelled like nail polish remover into a mush of muddy color, and the spot where Lucius's face had once been now sported cigar burns smeared with fecal matter that flaked off onto the white carpet. Lucius wondered sourly if that was Massimo's own shit or if he'd borrowed some from a pet.

"The restorers are coming tomorrow to see if there's anything they can do about that," said Adrael, striding into the office with a piece of paper in his hand. "I got you this in the meantime." He propped a fresh printout of the painting from Interpol's database on the desk, making sure to arrange it where Lucius could see it from the floor.

Lucius was unsure if that was meant to be helpful or sadistic. From Adrael, probably both.

"I am not optimistic," he grumbled.

"That's the spirit," Adrael smiled. He tossed Lucius another of his subversively deferential nods, and then walked out of the office and down the catwalk stairs, through the contractors and power washing mist and flurries of dust and ash, and out into the chilly autumn evening in time to catch the burnt end of a sunset blaring a last hurrah over the oily river. Dusk would be crisp and clear, and Adrael decided to watch it from the bridge, where he could get a god's eye view of the millions of people who lived in that city, and console himself that he probably wouldn't be made to kill at least ninety-eight percent of them.

––––––––

Hunter was a hero and a martyr. Brother Justin noted as much in his personnel file as he packaged it up for archiving. *Why* Hunter had decided to take on Vito and Giulio Luppi alone in that apartment was a mystery, especially on the same night that Carmine Luppi was shot in the head in his home in Brooklyn, and the rest of the Luppi family were slaughtered at a house in Great Neck. There was no indication that the family's killers were anything other than human, as almost all the deaths were shootings, but all the bullets had been specially adulterated to kill werewolves in much the same way the Order did theirs, and that was troubling. If there was a turf war going on with some mysterious rival Mafia group that understood the special nature of the Luppi, Hunter hadn't noted it in the file, and now he was dead, so nobody could ask him about it.

They did need to replace Hunter though, and Justin had a stack of candidate dossiers on his desk. In the meantime, they would sew up the remains of the Luppi family empire, since no next of kin were left take care of the details. Even the family attorney was an uncle, his body found in the house with the rest. The children were moonies, too, so Justin was not officially supposed to care about their deaths, but he was secretly relieved that the bodies had all been burned along with the house, so he did not not have to roll their sad little corpses into the Order's incinerators.

"Here's the rest of the Luppi file, Brother," said Dez, popping in the door. "I updated everyone to deceased and closed their files in the database."

"Thank you, Miss Cross, that's very helpful."

"It's the least I could do." Best to let that file die along with the actual Luppi. Every name was crossed out now, including the children, and Dez knew who was responsible for that. It was their blood she'd smelled on Adrael's clothes when he showed up at Nana Luppi's. The memory of it made her ill when she saw the photos of the house as the Order found it, especially the photos of the children, each with a single gunshot wound in the forehead. Not that the Order would have been any kinder; orphaned werewolf children were considered useful as subjects of experimentation and study. At least this way the Luppi children died quickly, and there was something grimly efficient about the scene that told her that whoever pulled the trigger had done so without enthusiasm. It was the Order who subsequently set the Luppi house on fire, leaving an unsolvable puzzle for the New York Major Crimes Division and the FBI; and it was the Luppi themselves who had carved out a family business that required that they blow up someone else's night-club every once in a while to make a point. There were no saints in that situation, only demons dressed in black or grey.

"May I ask you, Miss Cross..." Brother Justin hedged, "you'd been working with Hunter...what do you think he was doing in that apartment?"

Dez paused, searching for something that felt like the truth but was lie enough to say out loud.

"I think he just couldn't leave it alone," she replied.

"Yes," Justin nodded sadly. "That was always an issue with him."

For Dez, it had been a long day of answering questions and remembering lies, and it was oddly draining to watch her colleagues spin their wheels in dismay over questions that she alone could answer. The door to the anthrochimera war room was shut, but she could hear weeping within from Hunter's team, and despite everything, she couldn't help feeling a wave of grief for him as well.

She found Beatrix leaning in the doorway of Hunter's office alone, staring in with red eyes.

"Why was he there?" she asked.

Dez wasn't sure if she was seeking information, or just asking the universe in general for a reckoning.

"I don't know," Dez lied. "I don't think we'll ever know."

"Never say never," Beatrix replied, and Dez noticed she had a file clutched in one hand that looked alarmingly like it had "Second Circle" on the tab.

Outside, the air pressure was low, threatening a flurry of early snow. Wind whipped around the buildings, kicking up dirty leaves and candy wrappers around Dez's boots. The street was quiet at that time of night, and almost deserted, but when she looked up she saw a man she recognized walking towards her.

It was Irish-Green. Dez pulled her eyes down and avoided his face as he approached, and he strode by her without a glimmer of recognition. Dez was used to that, and it suited her purpose whether she liked it or not, so she ignored him and kept walking the other way, the air rudely cold against her cheeks.

But then, then, as she neared her building, she felt a flare of heat spark behind her—and then it was gone. She pushed on through the chill, watching for traffic, holding her breath.

Waiting to feel that spark behind her again.

ACKNOWLEDGMENTS

A million thank yous to Kristina Melcher and Daniel Kosharek; Ellen Kleiner of Blessingway Authors' Services for all her invaluable advice about publishing; Ellen Lefkowitz for all her invaluable advice about life; Chris Conner, Jason Strykowski, Russel Antonio, and Kenneth Huynh for answering all my NYC questions; all my patient beta readers; Carlyle Eubank for his excellent suggestions; and Caitlin Eubank, for—among everything else—being the reader of my dreams.

About the Author

Tantri Wija was born in Bali, Indonesia to a Balinese shadow puppeteer and a musician/US consular agent, later moving to Santa Fe, New Mexico as a child. She studied international relations at Wesleyan University and Boston University before moving back to New Mexico, where she attended film school and wrote about food for the Santa Fe New Mexican newspaper while making several short films. She then moved to Seattle and is currently a regular travel/lifestyle writer for The Seattle Times, and authored a cookbook called "500 Indonesian Meals" for Bright Press. See: Succubus is her first novel.